Thicker Than Water

Thicker Than Water

Kendra Norman-Bellamy
Maxine Billings
Linda Hudson-Smith

BET☆ BOOKS

BET Publications, LLC
http://www.bet.com

NEW SPIRIT BOOKS are published by

BET Publications, LLC
c/o BET BOOKS
One BET Plaza
1900 W Place NE
Washington, DC 20018-1211

All Kensington Titles, Imprints, and Distributed Lines are available at special quantity discounts for bulk purchases for sales promotions, premiums, fund-raising, and educational or institutional use. Special book excerpts or customized printings can also be created to fit specific needs. For details, write or phone the office of the Kensington Special Sales Manager: Special Sales Department, Kensington Publishing Corp., 850 Third Avenue, New York, NY 10022, Phone: 1-800-221-2647.

ISBN 1-58314-646-6

First Printing: October 2005
10 9 8 7 6 5 4 3 2 1

Printed in the United States of America

CONTENTS

A Gracious Thanksgiving

Kendra Norman-Bellamy

1

Bridge Over Troubled Waters

"A bushel of wheat and a bushel of rye; who ain't hid, holla 'I.' Twenty nickels makes a dollar! I ain't hear nobody holla. You ain't hid, better run; 'cause ready or not, here I come!"

From the backseat of the yellow car marked "Southside Cab and Limo," Shandi watched the little girl turn from the tree she'd had her face pressed against and dash between two of the shabby apartments in search of her playmates. Watching the neighborhood children play was one of only a few things she would miss about living in Chicago.

The cab driver pulled away and Shandi glanced back at the door that once secured the front entrance of her housing unit. The pink eviction notice became only a colorful dot in the distance as they drove out of the poorly built complex and onto the streets.

In the heart of Interstate 90's rush-hour traffic, the drive to Chicago O'Hare Airport was almost agonizing. Though there were only a few days left of summer, it was an unseasonable eighty-five degrees outside and the opened windows provided no comfort with the slow-moving caravan of cars that was backed up on the highway. The cab driver, a man in his late fifties, offered no cordial conversation and neither did Shandi. The popular R&B oldies that streamed from the car's speakers were all that kept the ride from being totally boring.

Looking out the right-hand window, Shandi could see a familiar graveyard in the distance as they passed. She had visited the same cemetery two times in two years to bury her parents. The man she knew as her father had gone from being a cocaine user as a teenager to being a crack dealer as an adult. Dealing on the side and not reporting the monies to his boss was what got him killed. Her mom was a user too, and with her husband and supplier gone, she had no easy way of getting the drugs her body craved. Unable to ignore the commands in her head, she jumped from the Michigan Avenue Bridge into the Chicago River. Her body was found three days later. They were both in their early fifties when they died. It seems like they would have known better, but they didn't.

At curbside, the driver assisted Shandi with unloading her heavy rolling suitcase from the trunk of the car and disappeared as soon as she paid him his fare. She thumbed through the remaining cash she'd saved for the past three months while waiting tables. Shandi had planned well her departure from Chicago. She knew that she wouldn't be evicted until she was three months behind, so she kept all of her tip money and pretended not to have enough to pay her rent whenever the manager came to collect. His continual "one more week" threats fell on deaf ears. Her parents rarely, if ever, paid the rent on time, so Shandi knew the procedure well. With her savings, she was able to purchase a one-way airline ticket to Atlanta, Georgia, and the cab fare to get her to and from the airport. If she'd calculated it correctly, she had enough extra money to afford at least two weeks in one of the efficiency hotels there while she got her life together.

Shandi realized that she was taking a chance, but she had nowhere else to turn. For years, she'd hated the woman who gave her up for adoption. If it wasn't for her, maybe Shandi would have had at least a shot at a normal life; but because of this woman, whom she only knew as Peaches, Shandi had endured an abused and abandoned life that she felt could only be compared to hell.

She understood how the State of Georgia had allowed her adoptive parents to take custody of her. They weren't always drug users and dealers. Shandi remembered happier times when she was much younger—like the little girl who was counting at the tree. But those days were long gone by the time she reached her teenaged years. By then, her family had made Chicago their home and somehow things spiraled downward quickly. Her father's inability to find adequate work and her mother's unwillingness to work outside of the home combined for a lethal mixture, ultimately destroying their lives and the life of their daughter. Drug trafficking seemed like an easy solution, but the price Shandi's family paid was immeasurable.

Because she remembered once having a happy home in the suburbs of Atlanta, she didn't fault the State. However, Shandi never would have been in the care of the State nor legally given to Felix and Justine Manning had it not been for Peaches, her birth mother, who made a living doing stripteases for drunken truckers and anyone else willing to pay the money to watch her bare all. She learned of her birth mother's profession from Justine. During the times when Shandi would try and reason with her adoptive mother about her habit, Justine would lash out at her and dangle the alternative in her face.

"What? You think you can do better?" Justine would say while fidgeting from a much-needed fix. "You ain't no better than me and if you cared anything about me, you'd help me get what I need. I know you got some money somewhere 'round here. This is the thanks I get for all I done for you? If it wasn't for me and your daddy you'd be still bouncing 'round in some foster home. Ain't nobody else want you, so you better thank your lucky stars that we was good enough to get you. I might ain't got what other folks got, but at least I ain't laid up in the back room of no strip joint letting every Tom, Dick, and Harry get with me like that nasty momma who had you. I bet she don't even know which one of them no good men was your pappy. So, don't be looking down your nose at me and trying to act like you all that, 'cause I know the stuff you came from."

Shandi's tears would mean nothing to Justine. On days when Justine couldn't get the drugs she craved, her verbal abuse was relentless.

Finally surviving the airport security lines and the endless waiting, Shandi boarded the airplane, sat back in her window seat, and tried to relax. This was no time for harboring feelings against the woman who gave her away. After all, Peaches was the sole reason that Shandi was making this journey to a place she hadn't been to since she was a fifth grader. It was time to try and find a way to forgive and forget because now, more than ever, she needed her mother.

2

I Sing Because I'm Happy

Over the past two years, Mount Sinai Community Church had gone through a drastic transformation from the inside out. The old, bare wooden pews that had been in place since the church was built in the early seventies had been removed and replaced by comfortable padded benches. Red bricks now hid the ugly blocks that the structure had originally been built with. From the ceiling, modern chandeliers hung where old screw-in light fixtures had been. And the vacancy left in the pulpit by eighty-two-year-old Rev. Jacob Battles was now filled by a twenty-five-year-old energetic man, who had become a spiritual magnet used to draw the young and old alike to the sanctuary that had at one time been almost empty.

Finishing his silent prayer, Pastor DeShawn Griffin Jr., affectionately called DJ, got up from a kneeling position and looked at his reflection in the full-length mirror on his office wall. The robe, which his congregation had purchased as a gift celebrating his second year as their leader, fit perfectly. Over the speakers, he could hear the choir being summoned for a selection. DJ knew that that was his cue. The sermon always followed the choir.

The side door of his office opened to a short hallway that led directly to the pulpit. As the choir sang, he made his entrance and shook hands with other ministers while on the way to his chair. Immediately upon taking his seat, he looked at the front row and returned the smile given to him by the most wonderful woman in the world. Pregnancy had only made Traci more beautiful and DJ could hardly wait for the birth of their first child. God had been good to him.

By the time the choir finished the high-spirited song, the pastor almost felt no need for his sermon. Mother Milsap's wig was already crooked from her convulsion-like movements as she worked two ushers at the same time. Sister Shirley danced across the carpeted floor with one shoe on and one shoe off, not worried that her big toe stuck out through the hole in her stockings. Even Deacon Harris, who generally slept through the sermon regardless of how lively it was, got his shout in.

On Sunday mornings like this, DJ was tempted to give the benediction and just let the members go home, but every time he thought of doing so, the words of the late Rev. Battles would ring in his ear: "Don't nothing take the place of the Word of God, young man," the dying preacher told him as he lay in the ICU at Grady Hospital. "I don't care what else has gone on in the service, there's still always somebody in the midst that need to know what the Lord got to say."

Rev. Battles was an unfaltering believer that no message given by God went out without reaching its intended target. Under his headship, there had been times when very few or none at all had shown up for services. Even that didn't stop him from sharing God's Word. It was no uncommon sight to see the old man standing at the roadside near the church, preaching as though he had a listening audience. Some viewed him as extreme, but his tactic to reach souls never failed. Although he may have started out preaching into the air, by the time he was finished, he always had a small crowd. To Rev. Battles, even if he touched only one heart, it was worth it.

DJ was honored when the ailing preacher chose him to carry on when he knew God was calling him home. Accepting Christ as a young teenager, DJ had received his ministerial license through Rev. Battles when he was a sophomore at Clark Atlanta University. Two years later, shortly after DJ graduated, Rev. Battles suffered a stroke from which he never recovered. He was surprised when he was told by the board that the seasoned minister had fingered him as the most qualified to fill his shoes. True, there was only one other minister in the church at the time besides him, but DJ was sure that the older, more experienced preacher would be preferred. If not, he assumed that a new one from the outside would be courted to pastor the dwindling congregation.

It took a few weeks for the set-in-their-ways members to accept DJ, but he quickly proved himself and God's calling on his life. Within months, several of the college students and recent graduates who had known him at Clark Atlanta had joined the church. They were followed by people in the neighborhood who were drawn by curiosity after seeing the near-empty church parking lot become more and more congested with each passing Sunday. The membership grew by leaps and bounds, and by the end of the first year, they'd raised enough money to begin major renovations.

In the two years since DJ had taken the lead, Mount Sinai had grown from a group of less than twenty, mostly elderly members, to a flock of over two hundred people of vastly different backgrounds. Some of them were icons in the community and some were what society might consider rejects. Pastor DeShawn Griffin Jr. had a way of making them all feel at home in his sanctuary. The choir used to consist of seven men and women who chanted old, lifeless hymns. It now had grown to a chorale of twenty-five talented voices who sang a variety of songs that stirred the congregation almost every week.

The ministerial staff had grown as well, and DJ tried to be fair in giving them all a chance to speak on a regular basis. Most often they spoke during weekly Bible Study services, but occasionally he would surprise one of them by asking him or her to speak on a Sunday morning. Though the members preferred DJ, they were gracious in lending their hearts and ears to the other ministers as well.

When he finally took the stand for the sermon of the day, DJ was brief, but the words he used to expand on Acts 10:34–35 seemed to be just what his audience needed. Like sponges, they soaked up words that told them that God was impartial and He had no favorites among His children. Citing examples within his own congregation, DJ reminded them of how good God had been to them and how He had provided their needs despite social status or income level. By the time he closed his Bible and returned to his seat, even some of the ushers needed to be ushered and Mother Gertrude Milsap lay on one side of the pew while her store-bought hair, which could hold on no longer, had been given to one of her grandsons for safekeeping.

As on every Sunday following the dismissal, several of the attendees crowded the area surrounding the pulpit for an opportunity to greet their pastor. With the expanding membership, the process seemed to take longer each week; but DJ didn't mind. He loved the members of Mount Sinai just as much as they loved him.

After several minutes of hugs and handshakes, he ducked into his office to change from his ministerial garb that was moist with perspiration into a dry set of clothing. As soon as DJ finished and was preparing to slip on his shoes, a familiar tap on his door caught his attention.

"Coming in," Alice Griffin announced as she entered. "DJ, you sure did preach today, baby. Every time you take the stand, I can just see how God is using you more and more every week."

"Thanks, Mama."

DJ accepted the kiss on his cheek, and then sat down to tie his shoes. His mother sat in the vacant seat beside him and watched as though he might need help in getting the minor task completed.

"Did Dad leave you behind again today?" DJ asked with a laugh as he sat up in the chair. "You need to ride home with me and Traci?"

"I wish DeShawn *would* leave me," she said, tilting her head to the side for dramatic effect. "I told him I'd be out in a minute. It ain't like he got nothing to do but go home and watch some ole game or sumin'," she said.

DJ laughed at his mother's facial expression. She and his father had been married for forty years, and he admired the two of them for the love they'd showered him with all of his life and the sacrifices they'd made to ensure him the best of everything.

"What I came in here for is to tell you that we had a visitor today that wants to talk to you," Alice said as she handed him the visitor's card that had been completed.

"Today?" DJ asked. "Is she waiting right now?"

Alice nodded. "Uh huh. Traci was just keeping her company out in the sanctuary until I checked with you to see if you had the time to see her this afternoon."

Counseling sessions weren't common for DJ. In the short while that he'd been pastor of Mount Sinai, he could count on one hand the number of people who'd needed one-on-one time with him. He discovered early on that his youth worked against him when it came to counseling. The older members didn't see him as experienced enough to give them sound advice and the younger members didn't consider him old enough to respect in the capacity of a counselor. After all, many of the church's younger members were older than DJ.

To compensate for the limitations they'd mentally put on him, DJ set in place seven ministries within the church that specialized in addressing most of the basic needs of the growing membership.

There were the Couples Ministry, the Singles Ministry, the Divorced Ministry, the Youth Ministry, the New Converts Ministry, the Homeless Ministry, and the Prison Ministry. Each group was assigned a leader and met monthly for prayer, teaching, and chat sessions. Periodically, DJ attended these meetings to give his input and to offer members more scriptural insight. Though it was still a means of counseling, most members didn't view it as such and were always willing to accept DJ's instruction. Rarely did anyone ever need to see him outside of these settings.

"Well, I guess if she says she wants to see me today, then it's best I go ahead and meet with her," DJ said as he studied the note on the card. "I hate to keep Traci waiting, though. I know she's tired."

"Oh baby, don't you worry none about Traci. Me and your daddy will make sure that she gets home if she don't want to wait."

"Thanks, Mama. Of course, all of that hinges on the hopes that Dad hasn't already left you."

Alice peered at him over her glasses as she opened the door to leave. She didn't say a word, but her eyes gave him a nonverbal warning that caused DJ to burst into laughter. He hoped for the sake of his father's peace of mind that he hadn't decided to leave without her.

Gathering the scattered clothes he'd just changed from, DJ placed them in a duffle bag in the closet to clear the space needed for his waiting guest. His office was small but comfortable. The oak desk that sat in the middle of the floor was spacious and aside from family pictures that sat in one corner, it was void of clutter. A small bookshelf stood against the wall beside the desk. On it were mostly ministerial books that he used when he studied for his weekly sermons. A Crystal Springs watercooler stood near the side exit that led straight to the outside of the church, and on the wall was a framed photo he'd taken with the late Rev. Jacob Battles.

"Come in." DJ answered the knock on his door and stood from his desk to greet his visitor.

"Hi."

The woman spoke in a soft tone of voice, almost as if she was afraid, as she approached him and received his outstretched hand. She smiled, but her eyes were sad and the forced grin was too weak to last. Her skin was chestnut in color and the sleeveless dress she wore showed off good muscle tone in her arms. Soft auburn hair hung just above her shoulders and was curled neatly in a bob style. For a woman, she was tall, nearly standing eye to eye with DJ's five foot ten inch frame.

"I'm Shandi Manning," she said, only briefly looking up at him before turning her eyes down to the desk. "Thank you for seeing me today."

"I'm Pastor Griffin," DJ said as he motioned for her to take the seat across from his desk. "You're quite welcome. Thank you for gracing us with your presence in today's service. I trust you enjoyed it."

Shandi nodded and said, "I did. I've never been to one quite like it."

"Wonderful. I hope it won't be your last time coming. What can I do for you this afternoon?"

She folded her hands in her lap and looked around the office. Though she tried to mask it, DJ could see the tears that Shandi fought to suppress. One escaped the forming pool and made a single wet trail down the side of her cheek. Opening his drawer, DJ pulled out a box of tissue and placed it on the desk in front of her.

"I'm sorry," she whispered.

"No need," he assured her. "Take all the time necessary and when you're ready, I'm listening."

Several moments passed as they sat in silence. Each time Shandi attempted to begin speaking new tears would surface. Finally, unable to continue fighting them with heavy sighs and deep swallows, she buried her face in the tissues in her hand and allowed her tears to flow freely.

Without interrupting her, DJ watched. The last time a female broke down to this magnitude in his office was last year, when a fifteen-year-old came to him looking for direction on how to tell her mother that she'd become pregnant. Oddly enough, back then, although DJ felt her pain and fear, the teenager's tears didn't tug profusely at his heart. For some reason, Shandi's did. Without even knowing the reason for her sadness, DJ felt the strange urge to cry with her. Instead, he got up from his desk and walked to the dispenser to get her a cup of water. With his back still turned to her, he dabbed at the corners of his eyes to erase his emotions, and then walked back toward the desk, placing the cup beside the box of tissues.

"Thank you," she said upon calming.

A few more moments passed while she drank the water and wiped away the final evidence of her outburst. When she was finally ready to speak, she told him of her parents' death and her subsequent eviction.

"I came here with a plan," she told him, "but things didn't work out like I thought they would. My money is almost all gone now and I'm looking for a job, but haven't found one yet. The people at the hotel told me that you might have a vacancy in your women's shelter and I wanted to know if I could maybe stay for a few days until I get on my feet."

Shandi's voice broke as she finished her sentence. DJ knew that it was hurting her to ask for help. Her newest tears almost seemed to be ones of shame and disgrace that her life had come to this. It was obvious that for her, this was rock bottom.

The shelter that Mount Sinai had opened just a few months ago wasn't just for women, as Shandi had indicated. It was a privately owned and operated homeless shelter that was built solely for the use of church members who had fallen on hard times. The facility consisted of mostly children and females, some of whom had found temporary refuge there after ending abusive relationships; but there were a few males there too. Most of them were men who had been brought to Christ during the Prison Ministry's visit to local jails. Once they were released, if they had nowhere to go, the shelter provided a home until they could get their lives back on a positive track. Though they'd not had any problems from the former inmates, for insurance and safety purposes security guards were always on duty at the center to be sure everything ran smoothly.

"I'm sure we can help you, Shandi," DJ said, overriding the membership rule and hoping that they hadn't reached capacity at the twenty-five-bed center that was already in the process of being expanded to accommodate twenty-five more. "Are you without a place to stay right now?"

Shaking her head, Shandi wiped another tear. "I have one more prepaid night of stay at the hotel and then I have to leave."

Scribbling a name and number on the back of one of his business cards, DJ handed it to her and told her to call the leader of the Homeless Ministry if she needed a ride from the hotel to the shelter. She took the card from him and thanked him before leaving him alone with his thoughts.

DJ couldn't help but wonder what could have happened to such a kind, beautiful woman to put her in a place of desperation. She couldn't be much older than he—maybe even younger. He'd heard the story of the loss of her parents, but he knew that there was more. Whatever the reasons that placed her there, DJ knew he had to do all he could to help her recover and regain her self-respect.

3

I Won't Complain

Shandi sat with her back against the headboard of her bed and read the last chapter of a romance novel she'd begun reading on the plane ride from Chicago. Books were sometimes her escape from the real world. Reading about the happiness of others, however unrealistic it might seem, gave her hope for a brighter future.

The space she and her assigned roommate shared at Sinai House was small, but it had everything she needed to be comfortable. The bed seemed tiny in comparison to the full mattress she'd enjoyed at the hotel, and there was very little peace and quiet due to the fact that some adult or their poorly trained children were always moving about just outside her bedroom door. Right now, she could hear the clanging of pots and pans coming from the kitchen down the hall. It was nearing dinnertime and the cooks, made up mostly of ex-cons who had picked up the trade in prison, were hard at work earning their keep.

Inwardly, Shandi had vowed that she'd never, ever wait tables again. Since the age of seventeen, it was all she'd ever done, but she thought she could find better work in the city that was dubbed "the new black mecca." But even Atlanta could offer only so much to a woman who'd dropped out of high school in the eleventh grade. It was another pitfall in her life for which Shandi blamed Peaches. Whenever she found the woman who gave birth to her, Shandi had a lot to get off of her chest.

She wished she could have one of those happy reunions that she'd seen recently on an episode of *Montel* in which a mother, after three years of searching, had finally found the daughter she'd given up for adoption eighteen years earlier. But Shandi knew that wouldn't be her story. Peaches probably hadn't thought about her once since leaving her at the hospital for someone else to have to care for, let alone looked for her.

After several days of job searching, the only employment Shandi could find was as a waitress at a nearby Chili's Restaurant. It was on the public transportation line, so she could get there and back on MARTA every day. The environment seemed like a nice one and her manager told her that the people who frequented the eatery were predominately good tippers, but it still wasn't first on her list of desired jobs. As a matter of fact, it was last. Her first day of work would be in a few days, and although it was a job she already knew she'd hate, Shandi needed to make money somehow and move out of this shelter and into a place of her own.

"Girl, you still reading that book?"

The door swung open and in walked Velma Hayes. Not having her own room was one of the reasons Shandi longed to be free of the church's facility, but beggars couldn't be choosers.

Velma was a forty-something-year-old woman who had been in the shelter for six months. On Shandi's first day there, Velma informed her that she had a wonderful, rich son somewhere in Texas who was going to come to Atlanta and take her back to live with him. But somehow Shandi didn't believe her. It seemed too far-fetched that she'd have a wealthy son who would allow her to remain in a homeless shelter all of these months.

"That book must be mighty good," Velma added. "You done had your nose in it all month long."

In reality, Shandi had just picked up the book for the first time today, since putting it down when she got off the plane. And, she'd only been in the shelter for three days, so Velma hadn't even known her for a month. Shandi had become accustomed to the half-baked things that Velma said, but that didn't lessen the annoyance.

"It's a good book," she said, not challenging the older woman. "I'll be done with it before the night is over. You can read it, if you want."

"Oh, I ain't got time for reading. I'll be out of here by tomorrow," Velma announced, flashing a smile that showed every discolored tooth in her mouth. It was the third time in three days she'd . made the proclamation. "Yep, Junior is gonna be here bright and early to pick me up. Then you can have this room all to yourself."

Yeah, and I'm Oprah Winfrey, Shandi thought. *You're nuttier than a fruitcake.*

"I'm shore gonna miss this place, though," Velma said as she stood at the foot of her bed and turned in a complete circle to get a full view of the room. "It's gonna be hard saying good-bye to all of this here."

"All of *what*?" Shandi laid the novel to one side and turned to face her roommate. "You act like this is some Buckhead mansion or something. This is a *homeless* shelter, Velma. If I had a rich family member who was coming to pick me up tomorrow, I would have had my stuff packed two weeks ago. When they got here, they wouldn't even have to get out the car to come and get me. Heck, they wouldn't even have to *stop* the car. If they just slowed down a little bit and opened the door, I'd jump in and we could keep on rolling. You think I'd miss staying here and being reminded every day that I'm a charity case?

"I don't have nobody to depend on and I don't have nobody to come here to pick me up, but you know what? I wouldn't wait around for them if I did," Shandi said as she leaned forward. "I'm getting out of this place if it's the last thing I do. I'm gonna save up enough money on this new job so that I can move into my own apartment and have my own kitchen, my own bathroom, and my own bedroom where I can read without being interrupted."

Tears burned in Shandi's eyes as she returned to her initial position with her back against the headboard of the twin bed. In hindsight, maybe moving here and looking for her trifling birth mother had been a mistake. Peaches hadn't wanted her as a child, so what was the purpose of hoping she'd be interested in starting a relationship with her now? Though Shandi had grown up in a house with two adults, she felt as though she'd never really had true parents. In reality, she'd raised herself. She didn't have anybody to help her then and she didn't need anybody to help her now—not her parents, not Peaches, and not this shelter or the rules that came along with staying here.

"Chile, you shore is an ungrateful lil sumthin', ain't you?" Velma said.

"Excuse me?" Shandi was aggravated enough already. She had had about all she could take of the idiotic woman who now stood in judgment of her.

"Yeah, I said it," Velma said, raising her voice and stretching her eyes to let Shandi know that she wasn't at all intimidated by her aggressive attitude. "Preacher Griffin and these folks up in here ain't been nothing but nice to me for the two years this place been open."

"It's only been open for seven months," Shandi corrected her.

"*Whatevah,*" Velma said with a smack of her lips. "I might ain't got the dates right, but I know I was one of the first ones to move in here and these people been seeing about me every since. Yeah, I been having to share a kitchen and a bathroom and a bedroom with everybody else, but at least I had one to share. If it wasn't for them opening these doors to me, I would've had to eat, sleep *and* go to the bathroom outdoors. So, you think I'm gonna complain about having to share? Not me, honey. Sharing a little bit of something is a heck of a lot better than having a whole lot of nothing all to yourself."

"Yeah? Well, where's *Junior*?" Shandi challenged. "You ought not to have a whole lot of nothing when you've got somebody like him. What kind of son would let his mama stay in a place like this? You got a son about as much as I got a Mercedes."

Velma's breaths came quick and her eyes filled with a mixture of hurt and anger. With slow, almost threatening steps, she approached. In height, Velma didn't even come as far up as Shandi's shoulders, but her arm erased the difference as she swung as hard as she could and slapped Shandi's face with the back of her hand. The force drew a puppy-type yelp from Shandi and nearly knocked her onto her bed.

"Don't you *never* say another word about my boy, you hear me?" Tears were in Velma's eyes as she spoke. "Don't you *never*!"

Stunned and remaining silent, Shandi sat on the bed, holding her stinging face. Taking her eyes away from Velma's, she stared at the hem of her blue denim skirt until she heard the bedroom door close. The last time she'd been slapped with such vigor, it was by her adoptive mother. This time, though, Shandi felt as though she may have deserved it.

It was six o'clock before she saw Velma again, but she made no attempt to approach her. Shandi actually heard her before locating her in the crowd that had assembled for dinner. As soon as everyone was gathered into the dining area and the grace had been said, Velma began talking. Others were carrying on conversations as well, but as usual, Velma's voice seemed to carry and stand out above the rest. While going through the line preparing her plate, she laughed with the servers about it being their last night having to feed her. Shandi shook her head, feeling sorry for this woman who lived in a make-believe world. She had just reached the spread of food when she heard her name called.

"Hi, Miss Shandi."

When Shandi looked up, she saw a mysterious, handsome face smiling at her. The man was broad shouldered, well built and at least six feet tall. He wore his hair in neat corn roll braids, a small sparkling earring in one ear, and sported a tattoo of some type of knife on his left bicep. Shandi looked him over for any signs of familiarity but found none.

"Do I know you?"

"I should be so lucky," he responded.

One of the few good words of advice that her father had given her was to never talk to strangers, but this man's smile almost rapt Shandi.

"Then how do you know me?" she asked as he placed a heaping mound of mashed potatoes on her plate.

"A man's got a way of finding out the things he wants to know."

Wanting to talk to him more, but realizing that hungry people were waiting in the line behind her, Shandi moved on without responding further. She found a table near the corner and sat. Other than Velma, she'd not gotten to know any of the other victims of misfortune who lived in the shelter.

The food was delicious. As Shandi ate, she scanned the room and tried to figure out what everybody else's story was. She'd seen some of the faces surrounding her in church four days ago. Some of them had been the same ones clapping, singing, and dancing during the service. What they were happy about, she didn't know. Having no home to call your own was certainly no reason for celebration.

"Hi."

With her thought process broken, Shandi turned to see the guy from the food line just as he was taking a seat in the empty chair beside her. Now, getting an up-close view of his entire tall, brawny physique, she assumed that he was probably one of the church's security guards who also helped with the Homeless Ministry.

"I'm Avery Bevels." He introduced himself without offering his hand, realizing that she was in the process of eating. "I guess I need to explain what I said earlier."

"Only if you want to," Shandi responded, pretending not to be interested.

"I saw you when you checked in on Tuesday," Avery said. "When nobody was watching I looked at the sign-in sheet and saw where you'd written your name. I've never known a 'Shandi' before, but it's pretty. Fits you perfectly," he added.

The stinging from its meeting with Velma's hand had subsided, but a different kind of heated feeling came over her face, and Shandi could only hope that she wasn't blushing like a sixteen-year-old who'd never been complimented before.

"So what do you do here?" She quickly changed the subject as she bit into her dinner roll.

"Isn't it obvious?" Avery laughed. "I help in the kitchen."

"I don't mean *here*. I mean at the church. Do you work in security? I saw some of the guys working the parking lot last Sunday. Do you do that?"

"Not hardly. Those guys are packing, legally, of course. By law, I can't touch a gun for the next five years unless I want to risk going back to jail."

The tea that Shandi was in the middle of swallowing went down the wrong pipe, and she began coughing in an attempt to clear her windpipe and catch her breath. Those sitting nearby rushed to her aid and joined together in patting her back and shoulders. Velma grabbed the plate she'd been eating from off of the table and used it to fan her roommate, not even bothering to empty the contents out first. Scraps of food, grease, and gravy sprayed across the room, causing adults and children alike to duck for safety.

By the time the ordeal was over, it looked like a minor food fight had taken place, and her back was stinging from the pounding it had taken, but Shandi was finally able to breathe. She drank the water someone had provided and thanked those who had probably done more damage than good in their attempts to help her. As they slowly dispersed, Shandi wiped the water from her eyes that had blurred her vision during the choking spell and looked to her left. Avery had gone and once again, she sat alone.

4

Revolution

The rain was pouring and DJ sat in his vehicle waiting for it to let up a bit. He'd chosen the wrong day to forget to put his umbrella in his truck. A half hour ago without warning, the skies had just seemed to open up. It almost seemed meaningless now for him to wait it out, since his clothes were already soaked from the drenching he'd gotten running from the gift shop his parents owned to his truck just before heading home. From DJ's parking space to the front door of his house was only about fifty feet, but one soaking was quite enough. He was thankful for the leather that kept the water from transferring from his clothes into the fiber of his seats.

As he sat and contemplated whether or not the rainfall had slacked off enough to make a run for it, DJ saw the front door to his house open. A few seconds later, Traci emerged holding a large umbrella over her head.

"Aren't you sweet," DJ spoke out loud.

He couldn't help but laugh and shake his head as he watched her come to rescue him from the elements that held him hostage in his truck. He didn't intend for her to come for him, but DJ was glad that she had. Climbing from the truck and huddling under the covering with her, the two of them made it back to the house and removed their shoes at the door.

"Thank you, love," DJ said, being careful not to get too close while he kissed her lips before placing the umbrella in the ceramic stand at the door.

"You're welcome; but looks like the damage has already been done." Traci looked at his clothes that were so wet that they clung to his body.

"Something smells good in here," DJ said, turning his nose towards the kitchen.

"Yeah, well you'll never know what it is until you get out of those wet clothes."

"I think they're glued to my skin." DJ laughed as he started walking towards their bedroom. "But with the reward being food, I'll see what I can do."

"Need some help?"

"Oooh," he called over his shoulder, "I like that incentive even better."

"Never mind," she laughed.

DJ tiptoed over the carpeting in their bedroom and headed directly for the safety of the ceramic tile that covered the bathroom floor. Piece by piece, he peeled away the layers of clothing that were still dripping of excess water. Generally on Saturdays, he took advantage of the opportunity to rest for the busy day ahead. Today, he'd spent most of the morning at the church studying for tomorrow's sermon, and then he made an unusual stop by the church's shelter to visit the residents.

Deep inside, DJ knew that he'd gone there mainly to check on Shandi. Since her impromptu meeting with him a week ago, he'd not been able to shake her from his spirit. At the shelter they spoke over cups of tea, and he noted her lack of enthusiasm as she told him of her new job. Before leaving, he had prayer with her, and Shandi promised that she'd be in worship services on Sunday.

DJ turned on the shower radio and stepped inside the stall. The hot water immediately lessened the chill that the combination of air-conditioning and rainwater had caused, but did nothing to rid DJ's mind of the thoughts of the newest resident of Sinai House. By the time he'd dressed and returned to the kitchen, Traci had finished cooking and was setting the plates on the table in preparation for dinner. She turned around and smiled as she saw him approaching.

"Now I can get a real hug," DJ said, wrapping his arms around her waist and pressing his body into hers.

When he released her and attempted to step away, Traci pulled him back to her and found his lips with hers, delivering a deep, lingering kiss before letting go.

"I missed you today," she whispered.

Still catching his breath DJ replied, "Apparently."

Once seated at the table they held hands and graced the food before passing the dishes back and forth, filling their plates with a meal of baked pork chops, brown rice, corn, and candied yams while catching up with how one another had spent their day. DJ laughed while Traci told him how she'd spent most of her morning scolding Taylor for sitting on her bladder and constantly sending her to the bathroom.

Taylor was the name they'd both decided upon for their unborn child immediately upon finding out that Traci was carrying a girl. Taylor was both Traci's maiden name and DJ's mother's maiden name. The families were not related, but the irony was too fascinating to pass up. This way, the name would remain in the family and both DJ and Traci hoped that somehow, their daughter would continue the tradition they'd started by passing it along to one of her children, perhaps as a middle name.

DJ hadn't noticed that the lighthearted chatter between them had died down as he continued telling her of his day. He seemed to lose Traci somewhere in between speaking of his visit to Sinai House and the subsequent visit to his parents' business to see if they could possibly use an extra employee to help around the store.

"What is it about this girl that has you so involved in her life, DJ?"

"What?" He had been in the middle of a sentence when Traci interrupted him, catching him off guard.

"I'm listening to you tell me about your day and it seems that aside from your time studying at church, you spent the rest of your day either *with* this girl or doing something *for* her. Why?"

"She's homeless, Traci," DJ tried explaining. "She just lost both her parents tragically and she's trying to find employment to get back on her feet. I was trying to help out."

"Didn't you just say a few minutes ago that she told you she'd found work? Why are you trying to get your parents to hire her? She has a job now."

"But it's not what she wants. Shandi has worked tables her whole life and she wants a change. She just took the job because it's all she could find."

"And? Everybody in that shelter has a story to tell, DJ. At least she was able to find a job and in a short amount of time. There are people there who have been searching for employment for weeks—

even months—and haven't found any. You're not running all over town in the rain to try and assist them."

"Okay, baby, calm down," DJ said, placing his hand on top of hers. "You're getting all upset for nothing. I can't believe you're re-acting like this."

"And I can't believe you're acting like I'm overreacting." Traci slid her chair back from the table and carried her half-eaten meal to the sink, dumping it over into the garbage disposal.

"Traci . . ."

She turned from the sink to face him. "What if I took to some good-looking man at the shelter, DJ? How would you feel about that? What if there was this one guy there that I talked about all the time and then started doing things just for him? Wouldn't that bother you?"

"I don't talk about her all the time."

"Yes, you do, DJ! Every day this week I've heard something about that girl. It's been 'Shandi this' or 'Shandi that.' Sunday, you talked about your meeting with her. Monday, you talked about hop-ing the shelter had room for her. Tuesday, you talked about making certain that the Homeless Ministry had gotten to the hotel in time to pick her up. Wednesday, you called the shelter to be sure she had gotten registered and settled in. Thursday . . ."

DJ held up a hand to stop her. "Okay, you've made your point. But don't I follow up with all the new residents there?"

"Not to this degree, DJ. Saturday has always been our day, but I knew you needed your reference library while you studied, so I didn't try and sway you to study here at home. I had no idea that the rea-son I hadn't seen you all day was because you were having lunch with and seeking better employment for Shandi."

"Traci, that's not fair. We weren't having lunch together. We were just talking over tea."

"You just don't get it, do you?" Traci said with a deep sigh. "It doesn't matter to me if you were eating lunch, drinking tea, or cleaning toilets. The point is you chose to be doing that over being here. I don't know what this is that you have for this girl, DJ, but it's not normal and it sure ain't cute. So, maybe I should give you some time to figure out what it is and which one of us it is that you want to be with."

"Which one of you it is I want to, *what*? What's that supposed to mean?" DJ asked as he watched his wife walk towards the back of the house. "Traci."

The sound of their bedroom door closing was the only response his call received. Not long ago, he had bragged to his father of how he and Traci had not had a major argument in the two-and-a-half years they'd been married. DeShawn Sr. had advised him to be prepared.

"Just as sure as you born and as sure as you gonna have to die, the day is coming, son," his father had told him.

He was right.

5

How Great Thou Art

Training, for Shandi, was the worst part of being a waitress. Although the people at Chili's were friendly and she knew the procedure was standard, she couldn't help but feel a bit offended. She had years of experience at taking food orders and bussing tables. At the job she'd held for the past five years in Chicago, she was next in line for floor manager. To be treated like a beginner along with the other new hires felt almost insulting.

Shandi caught on fast and had memorized the menu items within the first three days. Patrons at the restaurant were impressed that she didn't need to write down orders to remember them and were amazed that she was constantly being shadowed by another "more experienced" waiter as though she didn't know what she was doing. It took her a few days to learn the restaurant's computer system so that she could quickly put in the orders, but by the end of her first week, she'd gotten that down pat as well.

Living at the shelter still depressed her, but Shandi had become more accustomed to the environment and had set a daily schedule for herself so that she could stay on task and not dwell on her predicament. In the mornings, she would get up at six o'clock so that she could work out in the shelter's gym before getting prepared for work. At the end of her hour as she prepared to leave, she'd generally see Avery coming in with a few of his friends for their daily session. They'd exchanged glances on several occasions, but he'd not approached her since the day of her choking. Shandi wanted to apologize for her reaction to his response, but she hadn't yet determined how to do it without sounding as foolish as she felt.

By seven-thirty, she had completed her shower and was preparing for work. Getting dressed never took long. She had pressed her uniform the night before, so it was just a matter of putting it on. Most days, Shandi pulled her hair back into a ponytail and wore very little makeup aside from face powder and lipstick. The MARTA stop was at the corner just across the street from the shelter, so getting to work in a timely manner wasn't an issue.

Every day, at the end of her shift, she counted her tips and mentally calculated how long it would take for her to save enough to move out on her own. The church didn't charge a fee for the residents who lived there, but they asked that each employed person be kind enough to tithe, or give ten percent of whatever salary they made to the ministry to help defray the expenses of keeping the doors of the shelter open.

Shandi made a decent amount of money during her first week of work, but counting out ten percent for the church hadn't been factored into the equation. She needed every dollar she made in order to get out on her own so that she could begin seriously searching for her mother.

According to what time her shift ended, some days Shandi would bring home a takeout dish from Chili's. She loved their hot wings, ribs, and chicken salad. There were other days, like today, that she had a taste for the home cooking of Sinai House's kitchen. It was five o'clock when she stepped off of the bus on Friday and made her way across the street to the shelter. Shandi could smell the fried chicken as soon as she entered. By the time she showered and changed into her regular clothes, it was time to gather for grace.

Today, Avery was working in the kitchen instead of standing in the serving line. Shandi could see him behind the half wall that divided the cooking area from the serving area and she hoped to catch his eye, but he never looked in her direction.

"Umph, umph, umph," Velma said out loud as she bit into the drumstick she held in her hand. "I'm shore gonna miss the way y'all boys back there cook when Junior come to pick me up tomorrow 'cause that chile of mine can't cook a lick. I might need y'all to fix me a to-go plate."

Junior, pleeeease come tomorrow, Shandi pleaded inwardly. It was a futile desire and she knew it. She'd concluded earlier in the week that Velma's claim was one that had been made often. Other than Shandi, no one else even seemed bothered by her constant detachment from reality. The men in the serving line displayed broad smiles and agreed to do so as though they genuinely thought there was a chance that they'd ever have the opportunity to fix the takeout order for the delusional woman.

Generally, after the men in the kitchen and in the serving line finished their duties, they would join the others in the dining area and take part in the meal that they'd prepared. Shandi had eaten at the shelter two days this week and on neither day did Avery come out. She knew he was avoiding her and she understood why. While she couldn't pretend that the fact that he'd served time didn't frighten her just a bit, Shandi knew that her blatant display of shock was enough to offend anyone in his situation.

When dinner was over and everyone had cleared the dining area, Shandi made the walk back up the hall to see if Avery was among those still cleaning up. She asked one of the other men about him and he pointed her towards the kitchen, which was off-limits to everyone except assigned workers. Ignoring the sign that was in plain view, Shandi walked behind the wall and rounded the corner, where she saw Avery and another man tying up the garbage bags. She didn't know his name, but had seen him enter the workout room with Avery on more than one occasion. Both men turned to face her when they heard the unfamiliar light footsteps approaching.

"Hey," Shandi said, looking directly at Avery. "You got a minute?"

"Ma'am, you're not supposed to be back here," the other man spoke.

"Please?" Shandi never took her eyes off of the one she'd come to see.

"It's a'aiht, dog," Avery said to his coworker. "I'll finish this up and take it to the Dumpster."

Once the man disappeared from the area, Avery resumed gathering the garbage bags as if Shandi wasn't present. She felt a bit foolish just standing there watching him, but was enjoying the scenery. Avery's physical makeup coupled with his criminal record gave him a commanding presence that was almost intimidating; but strangely enough, it was nonthreatening all at the same time. Shandi felt nervous and somewhat uneasy being in the secluded back room with him, but she experienced no fear for her safety.

"Did you want something?"

His question was saturated with irritation and it snapped her from her trance. Shandi had been so absorbed in her thoughts that she hadn't noticed that he'd finished his task and had been waiting for her to speak.

"I've been in jail, you know," he said sardonically. "You might not want to be back here where nobody will be able to hear your screams."

"Okay, I deserved that," Shandi said.

"No kidding?"

"Avery . . ."

"What right do you have to look down on me?" he demanded. "Yeah, I'm in this shelter, but so are you, Shandi. Yeah, I did something that messed me up enough to make me have to start my life back over from scratch, but so did you. Okay, maybe you didn't do time, but you don't know my story no more than I know yours. How you gonna judge me like that?"

Shandi had never felt more ashamed of herself than she did at this moment. She didn't even have a defense to offer because everything he was saying made sense. Her whole life people had done nothing but be judgmental of her about one thing or another and it always made her feel insignificant. Knowing the scars she still carried from years of belittling comments and actions from classmates, teachers, and even her parents, Shandi couldn't believe she'd done the same thing to another human being.

"And you know what's funny?" Avery said. "I didn't even care what your reasons were for being here. It didn't even matter because I was looking at who you are today, not who you used to be, that might have got you here. But since who I *was*, is so important to you, let me lay it out on the line."

"No, Avery. You don't have to do that."

Ignoring her statement he continued. "I was a sixteen-year-old honor student who was tired of seeing my stepfather beat the crap out of my mama every other day. I'd seen it happen for five years and I was sick of seeing her swollen and hearing her lying to her friends about how she got like that. So one night when her husband was out drinking, I loaded his gun 'cause I knew when he got home, my mama was gonna look like a punching bag to him through his drunken eyes. That day, he decided he was gonna strangle her with a necktie and I disagreed with that decision. Because I loaded the gun in advance of the crime for the purpose of using it, the system said it was premeditated and they gave me ten years for paralyzing a would-be murderer. I had to settle for a GED because of it and that wasn't fair, but you know what? I did my time. That's who I *was*, Shandi.

"Who I *am*, is a hard-working man who is well on his way to getting his life back together. Every day while you're at work, I'm at Morehouse working on a degree in physical education. Some of these fellas found Christ while they were locked up and that's how they ended up here. I didn't. Last fall, I met one of Mount Sinai's members during my first semester at Morehouse and he convinced me to visit one Sunday. I heard Pastor Griffin preach that day and my whole life changed. That was nearly a year ago and I've been coming ever since. I'm here in this center because I'm a part of the Prison Ministry and I like being hands-on with the guys. I like being here and working for the ministry because I'm with other people just like me who I can relate to and who can relate to me. This is who I *am*. Now, if you can't deal with who I am because of who I was, then this conversation is already over."

"I'm sorry." Shandi's voice was just above a whisper. "I didn't mean to judge you; I just wasn't prepared for what you said that day. I wasn't expecting it."

"You think I was expecting it?" Avery asked. "You think I expected to be thrown into the system with common criminals? That kind of stuff can really play on the mind of a kid as young as I was. In order to survive, I had to adopt a prison mentality. I had never been in a real fight in my life before being locked up, but I can't even tell you how many I had to be involved in by the time I was released. You see this?"

He rolled up his short sleeves and showed her the tattoo that she'd noticed the first day they spoke in the lunch line.

"This was something I did for my own protection. The Daggers were a prison gang that I joined so I wouldn't have to fight my own battles all by myself. They protected me and as ironic as it may sound, they made the last five years of my incarceration much more bearable."

"I'm so sorry," Shandi apologized again.

"Do you see me as a bad person?" he asked, looking at her as though her opinion of him meant the world.

Shandi shook her head from side to side. Her quivering lips were a prelude to the impending spill that flooded her eyes. "No, I think you're great. You saved your mom's life, Avery. How can you be a bad person? You're great. Your mother is alive because of you. I wish I could have saved mine."

Avery stepped closer to her and pulled her to his chest. Shandi remembered many days and nights of crying about situations in her life, but she couldn't remember the last time someone had held and comforted her while she did. In Avery's arms she felt free to release every tear she'd ever held back.

6

I.O.U. Me

In response to his stroking, DJ could feel his daughter moving inside of Traci's belly. He kissed his wife's forehead as she slept next to him in the secluded comfort that the Stone Mountain Inn offered. After their heated exchange, DJ decided that he and his wife needed some quiet time alone, prompting him to book a three-night stay at the nineteenth-century plantation replica that was located inside the historic Georgia Stone Mountain Park. It had been just what they needed. Hand in hand the expectant parents had taken daily walks on the nature trail, and while wrapped in one another's arms, their nights in Room 216 had been filled with passion.

With DJ's growing duties at Mount Sinai, it had been quite a while since they had been able to spend this much uninterrupted time together. The on-site restaurant gave Traci a break from her daily dinner preparation and the extended, obligation-free time gave them a chance to relax, enjoy each other's company, and talk about everything on their minds—except Shandi.

In spite of the extra mile DJ had gone to give his wife the vacation that she deserved and the time with him that she longed for, he couldn't erase the thoughts of Shandi that lingered on his mind daily. He wanted to be able to discuss his feelings with Traci, but DJ knew it was the last conversation his wife wanted to have, and he couldn't blame her for that.

DJ hoped it would go away; he'd even prayed for God to take it—whatever *it* was—away, but nothing had changed. Ever since the day the lovely lady had stepped foot in his office, she'd been in his thoughts and constantly in his prayers. What he wanted to explain to Traci was that his emotional attachment to Shandi wasn't a threat to their marriage. He loved his wife unconditionally and would never consider leaving her or being unfaithful to her. Still, Shandi had somehow etched what felt like a permanent place in DJ's heart.

He eased out of the bed, attempting not to wake his wife who stirred beneath the warm blanket. Putting on a pair of jeans and a shirt, DJ slipped on his bedroom slippers and walked to the restaurant for coffee and the Danish that he'd fallen in love with. Sitting at a table for two, he sipped on the hot liquid and returned to his thoughts.

When he presented the idea to Traci that they share a few days of solitude together, she readily agreed. The short trip to spend time at Stone Mountain felt as perfect to her as it had to him. Traci laughed for the first time in days when she saw him pull the packed suitcases out of the closet. DJ told her that he knew she'd agree and that was why he'd already prepared for the days ahead.

What he didn't tell her was that he'd stopped by the shelter to see Shandi the previous evening while he was out running errands. They'd talked over tea again and she seemed more content than before. Seeing her smile made him happy, and finding out that her attitude had improved concerning her job and her stay at the center made DJ feel better about leaving and being unavailable to her and the other people of Mount Sinai for the next three days.

Although he knew his attraction to Shandi wasn't sexual, DJ constantly hoped and prayed that it wasn't somehow still sinful in nature. Never before had he been in a place where he felt an emotional connection with another woman. And the one for Shandi was stronger than he wanted to admit. It felt a lot like love, and for him it was frightening. DJ was on his second cup of coffee and had just finished his third Danish pastry when his time of isolation ended.

"Hey, you, I knew I'd find you here."

DJ turned at the sound of his wife's voice and stood to greet her as she approached the table.

"I taste icing," Traci responded, rolling her tongue around the surface of her lips after he'd kissed her. "You've been eating those sweet rolls again, haven't you?"

"Aw, baby, you know that's just the natural taste of my kisses."

"Yeah, right." She laughed after sitting in the chair across from him. "You're hooked on those pastries."

"They are so good," DJ said, eyeing the counter where the remaining treats were on display. "Plus, I think the sugar gives me energy," he added with a wink.

"Right, DJ." Traci was unconvinced. "I'm pregnant, so I have a reason for being fat. What do you plan to tell people about your weight gain if you keep eating that junk?"

"I can't get fat. I got my father's naturally trim build."

"Oh yeah?" Traci challenged. "How do you know? Think about that for a minute."

DJ laughed, immediately picking up on her allusion.

"You want something to drink?" he offered. "I'll bet these pastries would taste great with milk."

"Well, you'll never know, because we both know that as much as you love milk, it doesn't feel the same way about you; and since I have to sleep with you tonight. . . ."

DJ laughed again. "Don't worry, love. I wouldn't do you like that. They have some juice over there, if you want some."

Traci shook her head and pushed his empty cup and saucer aside so that she could hold his hands from across the table. She stared quietly for a moment at their connected hands before speaking.

"Do we really have to leave tomorrow?"

"Well, I have about two hundred twenty-five people who will be expecting to hear me preach in the morning, so I think it's best that we do."

"You could let Minister Gray preach," she suggested.

"He taught Bible Study for me on Thursday night."

"What about Elder Richards?"

"Why don't you want to leave? Aren't you ready to be back at home? You're the one who's always saying that there's no bed like your own."

"I know," Traci said through a faint smile.

"I'm glad you've enjoyed it so much that you don't want to leave," DJ said. "I promise we'll do it again soon. In another six weeks or so, we'll have Taylor to keep us from getting any sleep, so maybe in a month we'll book this same hotel, request the same room, and enjoy our last few days of peacefulness."

Traci seemed to light up at the idea of returning. She smiled and brought the back of his hands to her lips for a kiss.

"I love you, sweetie," DJ told her.

"I know." The hint of tears appeared in her eyes as she whispered the words.

"You okay?"

"I'm scared, DJ."

The look in her eyes told him that the subject he'd succeeding in avoiding for the past two-and-a-half days hadn't been absent from her mind anymore than it had been from his. The last thing DJ wanted was to end their minivacation on a sour note, but he knew there was more Traci wanted to say.

"I'm scared because I know that it wasn't me that you were deep in thought about when I walked in and saw you staring into space."

He wanted to deny her suspicions, but that would be lying. DJ tightened his hold on her hands and looked down at the table in front of him to avoid having to watch the lone tear that streamed from her eye.

"What is it, DJ? Is it that she's prettier than me? Or taller than me? Is it because I'm not a size six anymore?"

"Stop, baby," he interrupted, now looking her directly in the eyes and leaning across the table as close as he could to her face. "Don't even go there. You know me better than that."

"Then what is it? Why can't you shake yourself of her?"

DJ felt trapped. In one sense he wanted to talk about this but in another, he knew he couldn't give answers that would make it go away or even make his wife feel better about this awkward situation. He reached out and wiped her tears with his fingertips.

"I don't know, baby," he whispered. "I wish I did, but as God is my witness, I don't know. But the one thing I know for sure is that I'm in love with you and *only* you. I don't know why I feel this special *thing* for Shandi, but I know I'm not in love with her. You have to believe me. I've been praying about this and God hasn't given me any answers yet, but I know my heart, Traci, and *you* are my heart. I love you with everything that I am. From the day I visited my cousin at Spelman College and saw you walking towards Laura Spelman Hall, I knew you were the woman I'd spend the rest of my life with.

"You've given me so much love and happiness, baby, and I would never do anything to hurt you. You deserve my love, you deserve my devotion. Traci, I owe you me."

"I don't want you to be with me out of obligation, DJ."

"That's not what I meant," DJ quickly explained. "When I say I owe you me, what I'm saying is I'm the best that I got. The man that God made me is all that I am and that's what I want to give you because you deserve nothing less than the best I have to offer."

DJ used his hand to brush more moisture from her cheeks. He didn't know if what he'd said even made sense to her, but it had come from his heart. They sat in silence for several moments. DJ wanted to say more, something, anything at all that might drive his point home, but he couldn't find the words.

Traci was the first to move as she slipped out of her seat and turned to walk away. DJ's eyes stayed fixed to the table in front of him.

"Prove it."

She'd stopped after taking only a few steps. Confused by her words, DJ looked up at her in search of an explanation.

"We've got one night left here," she added, wiping the residue of moisture from her face. "Prove to me that I deserve all you've got."

DJ wasn't sure if he'd ever before seen the look that he now saw in Traci's eyes. He got up from the spot he'd been sitting in for the past two hours and joined her, placing a soft but lingering kiss on her lips. As they passed the buffet counter, he stopped and put three of the pastries on a napkin.

"What are you doing?" Traci asked.

"I don't know, baby, but I got the feeling I might need a little help tonight."

Traci laughed out loud as he took her by the hand and led the way back to Room 216.

7

Mender of Broken Hearts

Shandi sat and looked out the window of the MARTA bus at the scenery that had become very familiar over the past month. It had been a busy shift at Chili's and from inside her shoes she tried to wiggle away the throbbing ache from her feet. Buying some more supportive shoes was high on her priority list this week.

Mentally, she calculated the funds that she'd saved since beginning her job and figured that in another month, by Thanksgiving at the latest, she'd be able to move from Sinai House into an apartment of her own. She could hardly wait. The people who ran the center were nice and the people who lived there were too, but she didn't know how much longer she could stomach living in a homeless shelter. *Homeless*. It just sounded so depressing.

Getting to know Avery had made it much better, though. Shandi had hoped that by now, he would have asked her out on a date. Unlike many of the residents there, Avery had a vehicle and it would be easy for them to go out to a movie or to dinner. She knew he liked her. Shandi could see it in his eyes every time they spoke, but he hadn't taken the initiative of inviting her to share an evening out on the town with him.

Avery was such a gentleman. Even though they weren't officially a couple, he treated her far better than any boyfriend had in her past. Shandi had only had a couple of real boyfriends, but they were all the same—not caring about her feelings or what she had to say. It was always about them. Avery was different. He was the only person in the world she'd shared the details of her whole existence with, and she believed him when he said he'd keep her secrets. She wasn't quite ready for the world to know all of her past and the details of her life that placed her at this point.

The night after he'd made his life an open book to her while talking by the garbage cans behind the kitchen wall, they sat out on the lawn of the shelter and watched the stars while she told him her story. Avery didn't return the favor of making her feel worthless as she'd initially done him. Instead, he listened and said things to her that caused her to feel good about herself. When she told him how Peaches never even took her home from the hospital, Avery said it was her mother's loss. No one had ever said that to her before. Shandi had always felt that she'd missed out on growing up with her real mother. Avery told her that it was her mother who missed out on seeing her daughter grow up. No man had ever shown her genuine kindness before except Avery . . . and Pastor Griffin.

Shandi smiled when she thought about the man who officially became her pastor last Sunday. He had done nothing but make her feel welcome since the day she walked into his office. Since then, she noticed how he always smiled when she walked into the service on Sunday mornings and how he'd made it a point to stop by the center at least once every week. Sometimes she'd see him twice a week. Pastor Griffin always took the time to speak to every tenant at Sinai House, but Shandi noticed that he seemed to take out more time with her.

She enjoyed their late-evening chats over tea and when she didn't see him for a few days, she felt a strange emptiness. He was a married man, and Shandi was well aware of that, but she couldn't pretend that she didn't feel a calming when he was near. It was like he brought peacefulness with him. When they talked two nights ago, she found out that they had a lot in common, from their love for classic movies to their low tolerance for dairy. Pastor Griffin was almost as easy to talk to as Avery.

Finally at her stop, Shandi stepped off of the bus and quickly crossed the street. The construction crew was hard at work, still building the addition to the shelter, which was nearing capacity. By the time they finished, she planned not to be around to know what the expanded version looked like from the inside. The food that had been prepared for the day smelled heavenly, but since Shandi had already eaten before leaving work, she didn't mind that most of the people were almost finished with their meal when she arrived.

Shandi showered and took advantage of the few minutes of peace and quiet in her room to count up her monies. It was only a matter of time before Velma would make her appearance, and Shandi wanted to have her money placed back into its secret hiding place behind the dresser by that time. She worked five days a week at Chili's, and in three weeks she'd saved nearly $800 in tips, spending money for only necessities. Next Sunday, she would do what she'd refused to do over the past three weeks. She would give the ten percent that was asked of the people taking advantage of the graciousness of the Homeless Ministry. It was only right after all they had done for her. She had just wedged her wallet in the small space between the wall and the dresser when the room door opened.

"Chile, you missed a good meal tonight," Velma said.

"I ate at work," Shandi told Velma as she opened and closed the drawers of her dresser, pretending that she'd just put something inside.

"Well, as skinny as you is, you could've stood to eat some more. How tall are you, anyway?" Velma asked, walking closer so she could measure Shandi against her own height.

"What you? 'Bout six-one?"

"Not hardly, Velma."

"Well, you tall, I know that. I bet Junior would like you, Shandi. He's tall, too. He was the star on his high school's basketball team, six-three and full of talent." Velma stuck out her chest while she spoke as though she was literally swelling with pride. "Oooh wee, that boy could make some touchdowns."

"Field goals," Shandi corrected.

"Yeah, them too, honey. He was *real* good. I bet the two of you would hit it off right off the bat. He ain't married and he done made something of himself too. You know what?" Velma snapped her finger like a lightbulb had suddenly gone off in her head. "Maybe when he come pick me up tomorrow, I can introduce y'all to each other. Wouldn't that be something if me and you both could leave together? We roommates today and we could be family tomorrow! Chile, wouldn't you just die?" she added with a satisfied laugh.

"Yes, I would, Velma," Shandi said, knowing the woman wouldn't pick up on her sarcasm.

The knock to their room door was a welcome sound. Shandi didn't think she could take one more minute of the thought of her marrying Velma's make-believe son. When she opened the door, she was even more relieved to see Avery standing on the other side.

"Hey. Can you come out for a minute?"

"Sure."

Shandi was more than happy to follow Avery into the dining area. He had already poured them both a glass of orange juice and there was a folder in front of the place where he sat. Initially, she thought this might be the night that Avery would ask her out, but from the look of things, this seemed more like a meeting for business.

At first, there was small talk between sips from their glasses. Avery asked her about her day at work and all the while Shandi was talking to him, her eyes gravitated towards the manila folder on the table. When she finished telling him about her day, Avery talked about his. He was excited about a high test score in one of his classes and about one of his classmates who had agreed to come to church the following Sunday. Shandi listened, but curiosity about the folder kept her from giving him her full attention.

"Over the last few days, I've been contacking some people that I knew and pulling a few strings," he said as he slowly picked up the folder and held it in his hands. "From the things you told me, I don't know if this will be news that you'll be cool with, sad about, or maybe not care one way or the other."

"What is it?" Shandi's heart pounded in her chest. She'd told Avery so much stuff that she wasn't sure what he was referring to.

"I found out some information on your mom."

Shandi's eyes locked onto the folder that he still held. What had he found out? Between the flaps of the closed folder, were there answers to all the questions she'd had her whole life? Shandi had a million questions but she couldn't voice any of them at the moment. It felt as though her lips were wired shut and her tongue had been glued to the roof of her mouth.

"Do you want me to continue? Do you want to know what I found out?"

Her face still paralyzed from fear and anticipation, Shandi nodded and watched intently as Avery opened the folder and laid it on the table in front of her. For several minutes, Shandi's eyes scanned over the paperwork that had been copied from official files that had been found somewhere. Shandi had no desire to know where Avery had gotten the information; she was just glad to be able to get some of the answers she never thought she'd find.

There was a copy of an official Grady Hospital birth certificate that revealed her mother's given name, Leona Smith. According to her date of birth, she was barely nineteen when she had had Shandi. Taking the liberty of flipping to the next few sheets of paper, Avery showed her three photos of her mother. One was of her dancing, scantily clad in what looked like a two-piece swimsuit covered in red fur. She had a pretty smile and a body that was self-explanatory as to why her career as a stripper had been so successful. Another showed a more innocent side of Leona, as a youngster standing with a group of girls in front of a school. On the last one, she appeared a bit frail as she smoked a cigarette, sitting at a bar with a shot glass in front of her. All of the photos showed her at different stages in her life, but in every one of them, Shandi could see a strong resemblance to herself.

When Avery flipped over to the final page, she gasped and covered her mouth. Through vision distorted by unexpected tears, Shandi silently read the certificate that verified her mother's death almost three years ago. In the space marked "Cause of Death" was a single word: AIDS.

Shandi felt Avery's arms around her. He'd moved from the chair where he'd sat across from her onto the vacant one by her side. She pressed her face into his chest and soaked the shirt that he'd changed into following his kitchen duties.

"It's gonna be okay, Shandi," he whispered. "It's gonna be okay."

"I don't have anybody now," Shandi wailed, trying to keep her voice at a level that wouldn't draw any of the others into the room. "How could she do this to me? I don't have anybody."

Avery pulled away from her and cupped her face in his hands, forcing her to look at him.

"Don't you ever say that, you hear me?" he demanded. "You are not alone now, nor have you ever been. Remember last Sunday's sermon? Remember Psalms 27:10?"

Shandi nodded.

"You're not alone," Avery repeated. "Yes, this is painful and I can see that this is breaking your heart, but that's one of the many things that Jesus does, Shandi. He makes stuff like this easier to deal with. He can fix everything for you if you just let Him into your life and allow Him to take care of this and everything else that you're trying to deal with on your own. You understand what I'm saying?"

Shandi nodded again and Avery brought her head back to his chest and hugged her tight. Though her tears seemed to multiply and saturate both her face and Avery's shirt, Shandi began feeling a strange sense of tranquility. She felt his face close to hers and could hear him whispering. At first, she thought he was trying to comfort her with soft words, but she soon realized that it wasn't her that he was talking to. Avery was talking to God, praying for her while he held her in his arms. Shandi closed her eyes, clinging both to Avery and every word he uttered.

8

The Lord's Prayer

DeShawn Griffin Sr. stood in front of the full-length mirror and readjusted his necktie for the third time. From the time he was a child, he'd never liked wearing suits, not even on Sunday mornings. DeShawn had grown up the son of a proud sanitary worker who left the house bright and early every morning, heading for his job with a smile on his face. He was as happy as any high-ranking executive making five or even ten times his salary. Knowing he could provide for his family was all the reward that his father needed, and he passed the profession on to his only son with as much satisfaction as any millionaire would have had in grooming his offspring to take over the family business.

"Ain't you got that tie right yet, DeShawn? You gonna make us late for church," Alice remarked as she passed by her husband on the way to the living room to sit and wait.

"Woman, you just be glad I'm wearing one."

"You *better* wear one," Alice called from the adjoining room. "What you gonna look like—the pastor's daddy, and you ain't got on no tie like the other men in the church who ain't even related."

DeShawn laughed quietly. This wasn't about DJ. His son couldn't care less whether he wore a tie or not. It was Alice who wanted him dressed like a showpiece every Sunday morning and he'd grown to love doing it just for her. When they met over forty years ago, he was grungy and smelled of whatever refuse he and his father had collected and thrown on the back of their truck. He still remembered the day like it was yesterday.

Alice Jane Taylor was one of six children born to Evan and

Maxine Taylor, one of the few well-to-do black couples living in Atlanta back in those days. That day, she wore a yellow-and-white dress that masked the fullness of her young developing hips, white bobby socks, and black patent leather shoes that looked like they'd been spit shinned. A yellow ribbon held her hair in the neatest ponytail DeShawn had ever seen. He spoke to her as she walked towards the front porch of her family's home. She was kind enough to return his greeting, but barely even looked at the man who collected the neighborhood trash.

DeShawn made up his mind on that day that no matter what it took, he would get the pretty, dark-skinned girl to give him full attention. Although she lived several blocks north of his low-income neighborhood, DeShawn began going out of his way to pass her house on any given day. Some days he was fortunate enough to catch a glimpse of her and other days he had to settle for seeing one of her five sisters and brothers.

In his search to find another way to capture her interest, DeShawn found out that Alice's family attended the white wooden church that stood on a corner lot near her community. Convincing his parents to allow him to "go visiting," DeShawn polished his best pair of dress shoes and put on the only suit he owned and made his way to the church. After service had ended and all dressed up in his Sunday best, DeShawn got the courage to introduce himself to the plump and pretty seventeen-year-old girl, and for the first time, she looked at him and smiled.

Until the day he died, Mr. Taylor detested the fact that his baby daughter had chosen to "marry down." He never accepted DeShawn as his son-in-law, and never would come and visit the humble home that his monies as a sanitation worker could afford. DeShawn wasn't welcome in his father-in-law's home, either, although Alice was allowed to visit whenever she liked. But for the grungy garbage collector whose pride had been securely instilled by his father, it didn't matter. He had captured the heart of the woman he'd longed for and she loved him unconditionally.

"What do ya think?" DeShawn said, stepping out into the living room for Alice to see the finished product.

A broad smile crossed her face and she applauded and bobbed her head up and down in approval.

"Look at you—all dressed up and looking like the president of the United States!"

It was the reaction that made wearing a suit and tying and retying his necktie worth the discomfort. DeShawn turned to a decorative mirror on the living room wall for a last check to be sure that his salt-and-pepper hair was well groomed.

"Is DJ starting to look a little like me or is it just wishful thinking? I was looking at him during Bible Study a couple of nights ago and for the first time, I could see a little bit of me in the boy."

Alice laughed, hearing the pride in her husband's voice as he talked about the child God had given them twenty-five years ago. Having been married for fifteen years without being able to conceive, the Griffins had just about given up on being parents when they got the news about the baby. It was the happiest day of both their lives. Their desire was to have two children, and a little girl to match their son would have been perfect. When the second miracle didn't happen, they embraced the one gift they had and raised him the best they knew how.

"He got your height and your big feet," Alice responded. "He might as well have your good looks too."

"Well, now the good looks, he might've got from both of us."

In forty years, DeShawn and Alice had certainly had their share of arguments, misunderstandings, and fallings out. Their different upbringings and diverse exposures had given them separate opinions on the things of daily life, including politics and money matters. But regardless of outside issues, no one could challenge the love that they had for one another or the love they had for their son.

Walking into Mount Sinai gave them even more reasons to be grateful and proud. When they joined the church some thirty years ago, they had no idea that one day their son would be serving as pastor. DJ had done so much to revive the church when it was on the verge of dying along with its former pastor. When DJ was still a baby, Alice and DeShawn had prayed over him and promised God that as He had given the child to them, they were giving him back to be used however the Lord desired. They had no idea that this would be their son's purpose in life, but they couldn't have asked for a better future for him.

The members loved him and every Sunday they seemed more enthused than the one before. DeShawn watched as DJ entered from the side of the pulpit as the choir began singing. Today, DJ had chosen not to wear his ministerial robe. Instead he sported a burgundy suit with a gray tie-and-handkerchief set. Without even communicating with one another ahead of time, the ensembles of the father and son matched almost to perfection. DeShawn and Alice exchanged smiles.

"Our Father which art in heaven . . . hallowed be, hallowed be, hallowed be, hallowed be . . . Thy name!"

The choir sang the words a cappella, in four-part harmony, and in a powerful fashion that brought the congregation to its feet. The bass guitar, the keyboard, and the drums joined in and before long even DJ had to place his Bible aside and come to a standing position. The structure of the building seemed to rock under the pressure of the foot-stomping worshippers who grooved to the rhythm.

Everything hadn't always been this invigorating. When the membership first began growing, DeShawn and Alice worried and had their doubts about whether or not it was God who was orchestrating the expansion. They remembered a time when godly love wasn't the only kind of love that was being offered to their son. Under this younger, handsome leader, more college-age and professional females were starting to take interest in the church. The structure had been there before most of them were born, but until DJ took the reins, they'd not seemed interested in attending.

DeShawn was proud of how his son had set the record straight from the start. Because of his sincerity and devotion, DJ was able to stay focused, and for that reason the church's growth was not stalled and he gained the respect of the founding and current members as well as the newcomers.

As DJ took the stand to bring the message of the day, everyone settled in their seats and sat in expectation of what their pastor would enlighten them with this Sunday. From his seat, DeShawn Sr. scanned the crowd around him. There were faces that he'd not seen before, which was a sign of God's continued favor. He also saw familiar faces who never seemed to miss a Sunday. From executives to ex-cons and from residents of gated neighborhoods to residents of Sinai House—they all came to listen to the boy God had given him and his wife.

When DeShawn opened his Bible to turn to the scripture that DJ had instructed, he stopped at the folded slip of paper tucked in the section that had divided the Old Testament from the New Testament for twenty-five years. It was a copy of DJ's birth certificate. On days like this when he felt nostalgic and overwhelmingly grateful, DeShawn liked to read the paper displaying the name DeShawn Griffin Jr. and the names of his parents, Alice Griffin and DeShawn Griffin Sr.

9

That's What I Believe

"Do you ever wonder why some people get all the good luck and other people don't?"

Since accepting Christ a few nights ago, Shandi had come to depend on Avery as more than just a friend; he had become somewhat of a mentor to her both spiritually and mentally. She had so many questions about Christianity and about life in general, and since Avery was more experienced in both, he was able to give her the answers that she needed. Many times he would revert to scripture passages, and Shandi was amazed at how he could pull one out of his head on the spot, without having to look it up in the Bible.

Sitting next to Avery in his late-model Honda Accord, Shandi brushed her hair away from her face. It was the first chance she'd gotten to ride with him and although she was ecstatic to finally have the experience, the situation surrounding it all put a damper on her spirits. This wasn't the occasion that she'd envisioned in her mind.

"Luck, my foot." Avery grimaced. "If you want to take over the payments, you can have it."

Despite her earlier sadness, Shandi laughed. She could understand how he might have misread her words, but it was funny just the same.

"I'm not talking about you, silly. Me and you, we're two of the ones who haven't gotten all the breaks. You had ten years of your life, including a part of your childhood, taken away because of the legal system. At twenty-eight, you're just starting your sophomore year in college when you should have been finished and maybe working as a major league coach or something. And me, well, I don't even have to go there. I think I would have rather been locked up than to have gone through what I've been through."

"Be careful what you pray for, Shandi," Avery said, throwing her a look of warning before returning his eyes back to the road in front of him. "I wouldn't wish jail on nobody who didn't deserve to go there."

They rode in silence for several minutes. A couple of days ago, Avery had been able to find out where Leona Smith—or Peaches, as most people seemed to have known her—had been buried. Shandi took the day off from work and he missed a day of classes so that he could go with her to put closure on a relationship that she never really had. It was obvious that Leona had died poor. In the cemetery there were beautiful marble headstones everywhere. Some were cut in the shape of Bibles, some in the shape of hearts, and Shandi had even seen a few that had the deceased person's photograph set inside the headstone. On some of the eye-catching tributes, scriptures were displayed, and on others loving farewell words were engraved. Leona's spot didn't even have an upright piece showcasing her final resting place. Instead, her name and dates of birth and death were carved in the flat concrete that covered her place of burial. Shandi and Avery never would have seen it had they not used their hands and feet to sweep away the leaves and dirt that hid it from plain view.

Although she never knew her mother and had spent most of her life hating her or blaming her for one thing or another, Shandi couldn't hold back the tears. To know that she didn't even have the option of meeting the woman who chose not to keep her was disheartening. As a child, she used to imagine what her mom was like or how the woman would react if she ever had the opportunity to reunite with her estranged daughter. Now she'd never know.

Avery had been nice and kind enough to buy an arrangement of silk flowers and they left them there. It was probably the first time in three years that anyone had bothered to do so. The flowers were the only bright spot on the otherwise dismal gravesite.

"I mean people like Sister Traci," Shandi said, continuing the conversation as if the minutes of silence had never existed. "If you put me and her side by side it's like comparing fresh oranges and rotten apples. But why? Why couldn't I have been the one with her life? Why couldn't I have had parents who pushed me to go to college? Why couldn't it be me who is getting ready to start a family of my own? How come she gets to be the one to live in a nice house with a gorgeous, sexy man who's not only licensed to practice law, but licensed to preach in front of crowds of people every Sunday and tell them about Jesus and a better life? What criteria did she meet that I missed that got me sharing a room with a woman who is one sleeve short of a straitjacket, and her sharing one with this incredibly amazing guy who gives her all the attention she needs and more. I just believe that something's not quite right about that."

With the exception of the sound of the cool fall air that came through the small openings in the car windows, the car was silent. Shandi stared through the glass beside her at the outside world. As they drove along the busy Atlanta street, weaving through the lunch-hour traffic, she noticed people in suits coming in and out restaurants, and just yards away there were others who sat on MARTA bus benches and stood on street corners, looking dejected and confused.

"You know," Avery said, ending the quietness, "I noticed recently that you talk quite a bit about Pastor Griffin. Do you like him?"

Shandi looked at him and replied, "Don't you?"

"Yeah, I do. I like him very much, but more like in a spiritual and brotherhood kind of way."

"What are you saying?"

"I'm saying that when I talk about him, I use words like true man of God or great preacher or highly anointed. That's a whole lot different than words like gorgeous, incredibly amazing, or sexy, don't you think? I mean, that sounds like a whole different kind of liking him than the way I like him."

Shandi detected a twinge of irritation in Avery's voice. Under other circumstances that would most likely have angered her. If it had been any other man who was taking her words and drawing premature conclusions, she would have been annoyed. With Avery, it gave her a sense of confirmation of what she knew she felt in her heart for him. His reaction answered lingering questions she had as to whether her attraction to him was mutual.

"Why, Avery Bevels, are you jealous?" Shandi asked in her best Southern belle imitation.

"I ain't said all that now," he said, shrugging his shoulders in a nonchalant fashion. "I'm just saying that those words might not be the best words to use when you're talking about your married pastor, that's all. I mean, you could say them in front of the wrong person and it might start unnecessary confusion in the church or something."

Shandi turned her face back to the side window and tried to conceal the smile that stretched her lips.

"So, why didn't you answer my question?" Avery challenged after a few moments had passed.

Shandi laughed, but his eyes were serious when he glanced in her direction before making the turn onto the street that would lead them back to Sinai House.

"No, I don't like him like that!" she said, slapping Avery on his arm as though scolding him for asking such a foolish question. "I mean, I can't deny that I do think he's cute and all and he's been nothing but nice to me; but it's not like I want to get with him."

Avery remained quiet as he found an available space in the center's parking lot and climbed out of the vehicle. Shandi got out too, and walked around to the side of the car where he was kicking the front tire, checking for air pressure.

"You didn't answer *my* question, either," she said.

Avery stood up straight and thought for a moment before facing her for clarification.

Shandi refreshed his memory. "I asked you if you were jealous."

"I did answer that."

"No, what you said was, 'I ain't said all that.' " Shandi mimicked his voice and his shrug as she repeated his words to her.

Avery smiled at her theatrics, and then folded his arms, leaned back against the car, and watched the security guard in the distance as he paced at the entrance of the lot. The cool, late-October breeze chilled Shandi's arms through her sweater, but in the short-sleeved shirt that displayed his muscles, Avery seemed unfazed. For a brief while the guard stopped walking back and forth and returned Avery's stare, seemingly curious as to why they were still standing at the car. After a few seconds, he waved in their direction, turned away, and continued his duties.

"Maybe a little bit," Avery at long last admitted. "I mean, I've seen him come to the center and I've seen the two of you off in the corner in your own little conversation, laughing and drinking tea. I ain't trying to say that he would go for you if you went for him; I'm just saying that he's human. And yeah, I know he's a preacher and all, but he's still a man and I could see why he might be attracted to you, and you wouldn't be the first woman in the congregation who caught a case of the hots for him. It's just 'cause he's happily married and ain't available that they're not really chasing after him."

"Well, Pastor Griffin's not my type," Shandi told him, happy to hear Avery hint that he thought she was attractive. "He's easy to talk to so he'd probably make for a great friend, but nothing more. He's too much like me. You know they say that opposites attract and we're not opposites so we wouldn't make a good match even if he was available."

Avery stared at his shoes as he spoke. "You know when you talked earlier about Sister Traci having all the luck, I was thinking just the opposite. I believe Pastor—and all the other men in the church who were blessed enough to avoid the troubles that people like me and the guys who work in the kitchen have had—are the fortunate ones. They meet a great girl and they can tell her about their future and their past with no worries that they'll be seen as second-rate. Guys like me meet a girl and wonder what we should or should not say. Even if we've made a full three-sixty and are doing everything that we know God wants us to do, we've been there enough times to know that if we say too much we'll miss out. But we also know that if we can't be honest, then what we get probably won't last long anyway. So, in the end, if a girl has the choice of a man like Pastor Griffin or a dude like me, who do you really believe she's gonna choose?"

"Why don't you ask her and find out?"

Shandi posed the question and then watched Avery's face as his eyes redirected themselves and slowly locked into hers. Unfolding his arms, he reached out and touched a stray strand of hair that the wind had blown into her face and gently smoothed it back into place, and then used the same hand to caress her cheek. The fine bumps that broke out on the skin of her arms had nothing to do with the cool breeze that now caused fallen leaves to skate across the paved lot.

"Go ahead," Shandi whispered. "Ask."

"Okay," Avery said with a boyish smirk. "If you had a . . ."

"You," Shandi said before he could finish. "I'd choose you."

10

Speak To My Heart

Most women nearing their date of delivery would want little more than to be able to sit back, prop their feet up, and relax. DJ laughed as he looked out of the sliding glass door that separated him from his backyard where dozens of his congregation played a variety of games or lounged around, enjoying the cool but sunny day. The Fall Fun Day at the home of the pastor had been the brainchild of his wife, who was just over three weeks away from delivery. The backyard that Traci had described as too big when they moved into the house last year, had now proved to be quite convenient.

Early November had brought with it cooler temperatures, but that didn't stop the children from shedding their sweaters and jackets and chasing each other across the lawn. The young men too had come out of their pullover sweaters and windbreakers and now wiped away the beads of sweat that they had worked up on the basketball court. The older men opted for the less strenuous game of horseshoes, and the teenagers of both sexes gravitated towards the volleyball net and played with as much spirit as did the members of the 2004 Olympic team. Most of the women sat in lawn chairs or on blankets on the grass and enjoyed exhilarating conversations that would die down every time DJ neared.

"You know, I'm gonna start thinking that you ladies are talking about me," he said, handing Traci a glass filled with strawberry lemonade.

"All good stuff, Pastor," Mother Milsap assured him above the laughter of the others. "All good stuff."

"Pastor DJ!" one of the older teenaged boys called, holding the basketball in his hand. "We need one more. Come on and show us some of your skills, yo!"

DJ waved in his direction and gave the thumbs-up signal before bending to place a kiss on his wife's lips, drawing coos from the on-lookers who surrounded them.

"You okay?" he asked. "Are you warm enough?"

Traci smiled and replied, "Yes, sweetie. I'm fine, thanks."

"Sister Traci, you better enjoy this while you can," one of the ladies advised, " 'cause after the baby comes, *she's* gonna be the one getting all his attention, not you."

Another chimed in. "I know that's right. When my water broke with LaCreflon, I was scooping it up with my hand and trying to put it back in. I was tired of being fat, but I was loving the attention and I wasn't ready to give it up."

"I bet that po' chile wished she could go back in too when she found out what her name was," Velma said, shaking her head. "That's why when my son was born, I just named him Junior. I knew he'd love that name all his life and he still does. If you don't believe me, you can ask him when he comes to pick me up tomor-row. Ask him," she urged.

"Well, my son was giving Traci attention before she got preg-nant," Alice spoke up. "I raised him well, so I know it ain't gonna stop when the baby gets here."

DJ nodded in agreement. "That's right, my dear sisters, so you all can put away all the fables and personal testimonies. When Taylor gets here, the only thing that will mean is that I'll have two women to adore instead of one. And it will be double the pleasure."

"Thank you, sweetie," Traci beamed, accepting one last kiss. Bringing her lips to his ears, she whispered, "You just earned your-self a shower partner for the night."

Smiling in anticipation of what was to come, DJ left the women to their soft-spoken admirations and girly giggles. He walked back into the house to change into clothes that would allow him more freedom to take on the challenge of the men on the court. As he passed the large window that faced his front yard, he stopped and watched as Avery parked and got out of his car, followed by Shandi, who climbed from the passenger side. DJ had noticed them sitting together at church last Sunday and talking afterward on the church lawn. He'd wondered then if there was a spark igniting between the two, and seeing Avery embrace Shandi before taking her hand and leading her towards his backyard was enough to end his curiosity.

Avery was a good man, and DJ knew it. He remembered well the night during Bible Study a little more than a year ago that he and the others prayed with Avery, introducing him to a personal relationship with Christ. Still, DJ wasn't sure about him being the right one for Shandi. Having lost both her parents recently, she was probably vulnerable, and DJ was certain that Avery was far more streetwise than she.

When DJ lost sight of them from the front window, he walked into his bedroom and continued to watch the couple as they strolled along the side of the house and into the backyard with the other guests. He almost hated the thought that Shandi and Avery looked good together. Even more, he hated the fact that how they looked together even mattered to him. DJ turned from the window and tried to change his point of focus. A spirited game of basketball with the boys was just what he needed.

"Show 'em how it's done, baby!" Traci called out from her chair when DJ emerged from the house clad in athletic gear.

DJ's presence seemed to spark a higher level of competitiveness in the men. The original group of six quickly expanded to ten, the same number allowed on the floor of an NBA game. Those who weren't interested in playing gathered to watch as teams were assigned, dividing the men in half. What started out as a friendly competition seemed to turn into an intense match that consisted of two major players: DJ and Avery.

The two men, serving on opposing teams, dominated the game, hustling to get the ball from one another's hands, each blocking to keep the other from making a shot, and once even scuffling on the ground, both determined to take possession of the loose ball.

When the volleyball game came to an end, many of the women vacated their seats and joined the crowd of basketball onlookers. DeShawn Sr. and the other deacons put their game of horseshoes on hold, and even the children became engrossed while watching the ten men—two of them in particular—battle it out as though a hefty purse was on the line.

There were a few cheers for Avery, but most of the members rooted for their pastor, and when DJ's team outscored Avery's by a mere three points, it was to the delight of almost everyone. Everyone, that is, except Traci.

"What was that?" she demanded as soon as the last guests had gotten into their cars and left the premises.

The festivities had gone on until the skies started to darken and the temperatures began to drop. DJ had gotten only a few minutes with Shandi, but he had been pleased to find out that things were still going well for her. He had even felt better about her closeness with Avery when she told him that Avery had been helping her with scriptures and praying with her daily. When he saw the two preparing to leave, DJ made it his business to shake Avery's hand and congratulate him on a game well played. Although it was clearly a match that had lost its friendly competitiveness, Avery appeared satisfied with his pastor's praise.

Still, DJ had seen the look on his wife's face after the game finally ended and he knew that she wasn't happy. In spite of the fact that all of the games and the fellowship returned to normal for the rest of the day, DJ could hear Traci's lingering displeasure in her quietness, and he could only wish that the hours that passed after the rivalry would erase the memories from her mind by the time the outing came to a close. He knew it was a long shot, but he hoped for a miracle.

"DJ," Traci called, when there was no answer to her earlier question. "What was that all about out there?"

Playing stupid had never been his practice, but desperate times called for desperate measures.

"What?" he asked, trying to put on his most innocent, confused face. "What are you talking about?"

"DJ, please don't insult my intelligence. You know what I'm talking about."

His wife's facial expression was a clear signal that she wasn't in the mood for games. DJ dropped the façade and decided that it was best to just answer her question and hope for leniency.

"It was a friendly game of basketball, Traci."

"Friendly? Was that what you call that, DJ?"

"The boys wanted a challenge and I gave them one."

"They wanted a challenge in our backyard, DJ. If they wanted to play Antoine Walker, they would have taken it to Phillips Arena. And if you had really been playing the *boys*, we wouldn't be having this conversation, would we? You weren't playing the boys, you were playing *one* boy and that was Avery Bevels."

"That was a coincidence. He just happened to be the only one on their team who was challenging my skills."

"And he also happened to be the only one on the team who is seeing Shandi. Is that a coincidence too, DJ?"

"Traci . . ."

"No, DJ," Traci said as she held up her hand to stop him. She took a deep breath before continuing. "Look, I know you love me and I've heard every word you've told me about this thing you have for Shandi Manning. I'm trying to understand it, all the while hoping that it will go away. Well, after nearly two months, I don't and it hasn't. So, please forgive me for copping an attitude. I'm just having a hard time dealing with the fact that in the name of fun, my husband just nearly killed himself and somebody else all because of another woman."

Upon hearing the bedroom door close behind her, DJ sank onto the floor in front of the living room sofa and stared at the blank screen of the television against the wall across from him. The dirt embedded in the fibers of his clothes was a direct result of his power struggle with Avery. His worthy opponent had won that round, slapping the ball away from DJ and tossing it to another teammate for two points. In the end, though, DJ sealed the win, breaking the tie with a three-point shot; however, the victory that tasted sweet two hours ago now was anything but. Once again, Traci was right and despite the fact that he didn't voice it, DJ was well aware of just how right she was. How could he expect her to understand something that escaped his own ability to reason?

In the distance, DJ heard the sound of water running from the shower in the bathroom, but he knew that this was no time to try and cash in on Traci's earlier offer. Disappointed in himself for his own inability to define his emotions, DJ buried his face in his hands.

"Okay, God, it's on you," he whispered. "You've got to help me with this one. Please give me some answers before all the questions destroy my family. Please, God. Talk to me."

11

The Question Is

In recent days, Shandi had traded her novels in for textbooks in pursuit of the diploma that she'd let slip her grasp the first time around. One of the local high schools offered GED classes in the evening hours, extending a second chance to her and other adults who had made the mistake of not taking advantage of the free public education that was offered them in their teen years. Because she still worked her full shift at Chili's, Shandi was already feeling the effects of the two-and-a-half extra hours, three nights a week, that were added to her schedule.

By the end of the first class, she was already prepared to throw in the towel, but Avery kept her motivated. His pride in her for taking the initiative to complete the high school equivalency course was the incentive that kept her determined to go the distance. He was already looking six months ahead to her graduation, adding more encouragement by promising to fly his mother in from Pennsylvania to enjoy that time with them. Shandi couldn't pass up the chance to meet the woman she'd come to know as Mama Pearl.

Despite the fact that Avery's unfortunate incarceration had been due to his quest to save his mother's life, there had been no animosity on his part against her. He'd told Shandi that his mom had come to visit him almost every day of the ten years he'd been behind bars. A year ago Mama Pearl had moved to Philadelphia to take care of her aging, sickly aunt, and since then, she and Avery had kept in contact only by weekly phone calls. He sounded excited every time he spoke of seeing his mother again and introducing her to his best girl.

Hearing Avery talk about his mom made Shandi long for hers.

Even in realizing that Leona gave her away and knowing that she was dead, there was still a feeling of incompleteness that lingered inside of Shandi. One day, she wanted to have children of her own, and since she would not be able to give them a maternal grandmother, she would at least like to be able to tell them something about her. There had to be more to the life of Leona Smith than just the fact that she had made her money dancing on stages, tabletops, and the laps of seedy men.

Shandi chewed on the bottom of her ink pen as she stared straight ahead at her instructor. The next thing she knew, her classmates were gathering their belongings. Her mind had drifted so far away that she hadn't even heard the permission to dismiss. She grabbed her books and headed towards the parking lot where Avery was sitting in his car waiting for her, as usual. As soon as she climbed into the seat next to him, Shandi handed him a folded sheet of paper.

"Oh, baby, this is good!" Avery said as he saw the score on her first graded assignment.

Shandi leaned in to deliver the kiss he beckoned for and said, "I knew you'd like that."

"You were right," he said. "Let's frame it."

Shandi laughed at his enthusiasm and buckled herself in while Avery navigated his car onto the street. At this late hour, the traffic was light and Shandi leaned back in her seat and gazed at the scenery. The landscape of downtown Atlanta was so beautiful during the night hours. All of the tall buildings clustered together and the lights that could be seen miles before reaching their source were beautiful against the darkness of the nighttime canvas. A city so beautiful and resourceful shouldn't be so riddled with crime and poverty. Nor should it have graveyards so cluttered with the bodies of people like Leona.

"You're mighty quiet," Avery noted. "What's on your mind?"

"Peaches."

"What about her?"

"I need to know more, Avery," Shandi said. "I need to know what happened to get her from being a regular kid to being a nightclub stripper. I need to know why she gave me up and why she lived such a reckless life. The first time I attended Mount Sinai, Pastor Griffin preached a message about God not having favorites and how He passed out blessings and goodness to everybody. When I look back over my life, I don't see where He passed out any on my side of the tracks."

"You're here, aren't you?" Avery said, placing his right hand on top of hers. "Sometimes we have to go through things in life to get us to a certain point where God wants us to be. If your adoptive parents hadn't died, you probably never would have returned to Atlanta and had you not done that, you never would have stepped foot in Mount Sinai. You're who you are right now because of that decision that you made on that Sunday morning. We're together now because of that, so don't say God hasn't done anything good in your life, Shandi. I would hope that if nothing else, you'd see where we are right now as a good thing."

Shandi wrapped both of her hands around Avery's hand and squeezed. She loved the way he adored her and she cherished their young, budding relationship.

"I do, Avery. I'm real thankful that He brought us together, but I still have so many questions about my life. I need to know stuff that was before you, before Mount Sinai, and even before Felix and Justine Manning. I know it sounds crazy, but I need to know about me before I was even born. I need to know about Leona."

"It doesn't sound crazy at all, baby."

Shandi tossed in bed that night, only sleeping minutes at a time before being awakened by mild nighttime commotions that generally didn't stir her. Rustling leaves outside her window, the sound of footsteps as the security guards did their hourly walkthrough, Velma's periodic snorts when she repositioned herself in the bed just a few feet away—all these noises happened every night, but tonight they disrupted her already unsound sleep.

As usual, she was up at seven o'clock in the morning, preparing for the long day ahead. With today being Friday, at least she had no classes to attend after work. Shandi felt dead on her feet as she worked her shift on less than three hours' sleep, but she remained cheerful and attentive to her customers. Their tips were needed if she was going to stick to her plan of moving soon. It seemed that five o'clock would never come, but when it did, Shandi gathered her takeout order and her purse and fished for her MARTA card as she walked out the door. The sound of a car's persistent horn caught her attention and she turned to see Avery pulling up beside her.

"'Sup, Shawty? What's yo' name?" he teased while hanging out the driver's window sporting a pair of shades that suited his face well.

Laughing, Shandi scampered around to the passenger side and got in. Because of his dinner duties at Sinai House, Avery had never been able to pick her up from her job. Seeing him today was a pleasant surprise.

"What are you doing here? Shouldn't you be cooking or serving right about now?"

"I took the night off, so you're gonna have to share whatever it is that smells so good in that bag. Earlier today, I put a call in to a friend who has a friend who has a friend and I found out some stuff about your mom that I thought you might want to follow up on."

Shandi turned in the seat to face Avery. Before responding, she took a moment to see if his face showed any signs that he was kidding. It seemed too unreal that he would have found new information since yesterday. Avery noticed her look of disbelief.

"I guess some good came out of my incarceration," he added. "I know people now that I wouldn't have known otherwise."

"Is this legal?" The last thing Shandi wanted to do was get Avery in trouble because of his desire to help her.

"All I did was ask," Avery shrugged. "How they got the information, I don't know, nor do I want to find out. I just know what I was told."

"Which was?"

"Leona worked at The Cat's Meow," he told her. "It's actually an upscale club near Midtown and the crowd it draws is kind of elite, so she wasn't dancing for cheap, I'm sure. I figure we could drive over there and maybe talk to somebody who knew something about her that they could tell you."

Shandi brought her hands to her chest to try and stop the fluttering. Sitting back in her seat, a million thoughts ran through her head. This could be the break that she needed. If someone could tell her about Leona—where she lived, what other profession she may have had . . . anything, Shandi would be grateful. Maybe they could even tell her who her father was. If her father was still living, maybe she could contact him and maybe he would be happy to meet her. Maybe, just maybe, she could have the family she'd longed for after all.

The Cat's Meow was already open for business when they arrived. In her mind, Shandi had always imagined her mother dancing in a smoke-filled room with grungy, horny truck drivers and drunkards shouting filthy obscenities at her and demanding special favors. The Cat's Meow had the luxurious appearance of a five-star restaurant. After Avery paid the cover charge for them to enter and their IDs had been checked, they were allowed inside. Looking around, Shandi felt underdressed in the shirt and slacks that she'd worked in for the past eight hours. She nervously checked to be sure her top was tucked in neatly and followed closely behind Avery as he went to the bar and asked for the manager.

For several minutes they stood and waited for the supervisor to make his appearance. The Cat's Meow may have looked like a normal fine-dining restaurant, but it wasn't. This was definitely a gentlemen's club in its truest sense. Waitresses in suggestive cat suits served the guests and dancers, aiming to tease and please, and were beginning to bare all to the more than three hundred onlookers.

"Want a drink while you wait?" the bartender asked.

Looking more uncomfortable than Shandi had ever seen him, Avery shook his head and turned his back to the tables where the action was in progress. Tears welled in Shandi's eyes as she watched the women move in the most suggestive and disgusting ways she'd ever seen. The sight of it made her nauseated. She imagined one of them being her mom and thought of how likely it was that a man just like one of these well-to-do, educated, professional men had given her mom the disease that took her life.

"I'm Chase Barron. How can I help you folks?"

The manager was stylishly dressed, just as Shandi had expected. He was a white gentleman who appeared to be in his early forties and he flashed a warm smile as he shook both their hands.

"Can we talk somewhere in private?" Avery asked.

"Sure we can."

Another well-dressed man, who was unmistakably a bodyguard, followed the three of them into an office where Chase closed the door behind them and offered them seats. The bodyguard remained standing.

"Are the two of you here in response to the ad we placed in the paper? We do still have a bouncer position available and we're always looking for more kittens," he said, flashing a smile at Shandi.

"Naw, potna, see it ain't even like that." Avery's tone caused the guard to come to attention.

Fearing they would be made to leave without the information she needed, Shandi jumped in and said, "Mr. Barron, we're actually here to try and find out some details about my mom. She used to dance here. If you could please, please help us, I'd really appreciate it."

"Your mom?" Chase said. "You're what—twenty, twenty-one?"

"It was a while back," Shandi explained.

"Well, I've been managing this place for the last fifteen years. If it was further back than that, I probably won't be able to help you. We generally clean house when the girls get around thirty-five to make room for a younger crew."

"She didn't raise me, so there's a lot I don't know about her. I don't know how long she danced, but her name was Leona Smith, if that rings a bell."

Chase thought for a brief moment, and then shook his head.

"Nope. Sorry," he said. "You have to keep in mind that on average, we have about forty girls employed here at the same time. Some of them come and stay a while and some of them don't. Names may not stick with me."

With a heavy sigh, Shandi closed her eyes and settled back in her seat. It felt as though she would spend the rest of her life chasing roads that her mother had traveled that all would lead to dead ends.

"Her stage name was Peaches," Avery said. "What about that? Does that help at all?"

The look on Chase's face told them that the name had turned on a light switch in his head.

"Peaches? The only Peaches that worked here died a few years ago."

"Yes, that's her!" Shandi said, leaning forward with renewed excitement.

"Well, that's pretty much all I can tell you," Chase said. "She started dancing here when my dad ran this place and she worked about fifteen years. She stopped working about ten or eleven years ago. Next time I heard anything about her it was when I heard she'd died."

Chase paused and smiled, nodding his head slowly as he continued to recollect.

"So, you're her daughter that folks around here wondered what happened to. My dad said she got herself pregnant right after she started working here and he had to let her go. After giving birth, she bounced back in shape and returned to the stage stronger than ever, making a name for herself in a very short time. Yeah, that Peaches was something else. When she left, she was approaching her thirty-fifth birthday but in my opinion, she could still give any of the younger girls a run for their money. I couldn't talk her into staying, though. She'd met some guy who promised her the world and she chose him over us. I hear he died a few years before she did."

He reached into a drawer and pulled out a photo album, flipping through the pages until he got to a section that was reserved just for the popular dancer. He looked from the photo on the page in front of him to Shandi, who sat across from him, and then back at the picture again.

"Well, I'll be dogged," Chase said, sliding the album across the desk so that they could get a better view. "It's just like looking in a mirror for you, isn't it?"

Avery and Shandi scrolled through ten pages of nothing but photos of Peaches posing with the other dancers or her dancing for the establishment's clients. Although it was hard to look at the snapshots of her mother in action, Shandi was glad to see more images of the woman she never knew, but missed just the same. She wiped a stream of tears from her cheek and handed the album back to the manager.

"She was beautiful, wasn't she?" Chase said as he closed the album and tucked it back in his drawer.

"Do you know who my father was?"

Chase shook his head. "No, I don't. I don't think anybody ever knew that, including Peaches and the man who got her pregnant. If she was telling the truth to my dad, she got raped after her show one night on her way home. She never saw the guy, and once he was done fulfilling the fantasy I'm sure he got while watching her show, he took off. She never saw his face and since she got terminated a couple of months later, even if he came back to the club to watch her dance he probably never knew she was pregnant."

Shandi closed her eyes to try and block out the images that Chase's words were forming in her head. Her earlier thoughts of wanting to know her father diminished abruptly. Now she prayed that his identity would never be made known to her. She prayed that over the years, he'd had to pay for his selfish act of violence against her mother. She hoped that he wasn't allowed to live while her mother lay dead in a poorly marked grave.

"What about family? Did she have family in this area?" Avery asked.

"I'm not sure, but I doubt it seriously," Chase said. "Peaches was sort of like a drifter. She lived on the streets for a while, but with the money she made here, she was able to get an apartment. But she never talked about family. I think the other kittens here were about as much family as she ever had."

Shandi felt Avery's hand on her arm, stroking it lightly to console her. A steady flow of tears had been streaming from her eyes ever since she'd seen the photos, and the tears had gotten heavier after hearing of her mother's ordeal.

"Let's go," Avery whispered.

Nodding in silent agreement, the two of them stood to leave. Avery thanked Chase for his help, and after shaking his hand, Chase extended his hand to Shandi. He seemed to feel genuinely sorry for her as he spoke.

"Look, finding the family of a woman who gave you up for adoption and has been dead for years can be like looking for a needle in a haystack. I'm sorry I couldn't help you more, but in this business, we tend not to get too close to the hired help. I've told you all I know. This might be one that you and your brother will just have to let rest in the grave with Peaches."

"I'm not her brother," Avery said.

"I don't mean you. I mean her brother."

"I don't have a brother," Shandi said.

"Sure you do," Chase said. "Peaches had a girl *and* a boy—a set of twins. If you didn't know that, now you know," he said, seemingly finding satisfaction in feeling that he'd been the one to disclose the information that might help her further. "He's a preacher . . . runs that church on the East Side that the old man who used to preach on the street corners used to pastor."

12

Can You Reach My Friend

On Sunday morning, when DJ walked through the side entrance that led to the pulpit, one of the first things he noticed was the stranger sitting beside Avery in the spot that was normally filled by Shandi. After a quick scan of the crowd showed no signs of her sitting elsewhere, he began to wonder where she could be. She hadn't missed a Sunday since the first time she visited and inwardly he looked forward to seeing her enjoying the service along with the others.

Switching his focus to Traci, who squirmed a little in the front row in an attempt to achieve a comfortable position, DJ was glad that the sermon he had prepared would be an abbreviated one. He knew she was tired and probably more uncomfortable than usual due to lack of sleep. Last night she tossed quite a bit, even waking him a few times with her restlessness. Friday, at their appointment to see her doctor, they found out that Traci had already begun to dilate and was measuring at two centimeters. Dr. Canton told them that the big day was now only days away. Her original date of delivery had been November 30, but now it seemed that little Taylor wasn't going to wait that long. Following the doctor's recommendation, DJ had already put Traci's packed bags in the trunk of the car in preparation for what might be the early arrival of their daughter.

Yesterday some of the sisters from the church had gotten together for a planned baby shower. The nursery that DJ and Traci had set up months ago was now filled with toys, clothes, Pampers, and baby gadgets that Taylor would enjoy for years to come. The past nine months had seemed everlasting, and both parents were now ready for the arrival of their bundle of joy.

As the choir was singing, an usher, dressed as usual in her white nurse's uniform, stepped up onto the pulpit and slipped a piece of paper into DJ's hand. Generally, if there were any special prayer requests, they were given to him at the close of the service and he'd include them in his prayers throughout the week. Only when a person told the attendants that it was pressing would they give it to him during services. DJ nodded his head to thank her for the delivery and then proceeded to open the folded note. The scribbled words were written in red ink and seemed to jump from the paper:

Pastor Griffin,
   I need to speak to you as soon church is out. I hope today isn't a bad time for you because this really can't wait.
PLEASE.

Thank you.

The short note was signed by Avery and had a distinct feel of urgency to it. His heart pounding within the walls of his chest, DJ read the note again, immediately knowing that something was wrong. So many questions swarmed together in his head that he couldn't decipher any of them. The sense that something terrible had happened, was happening, or was about to happen to Shandi almost overwhelmed him. It was as if God was telling him that today his ministry was needed in a different capacity.

Elaine Collins was one of only two female ministers on the staff of seven at Mount Sinai. Her smile was broad as she readily accepted DJ's offer to yield the pulpit to her on this Sunday morning. The pastor beckoned for his wife before whispering in the usher's ear and disappearing back through the same door that he'd made his entrance from just minutes earlier.

"What's the matter?" Traci asked, entering his office in time to see him shedding his ministerial robe and hanging it back in his closet.

"I'm not sure. I just wanted you to be in here for this meeting."

"What meeting?"

As soon as she'd posed the question, the office door opened and Avery walked in, followed by Alice Griffin. She had seen the sudden chain of events and had come to see if her assistance was needed. DJ motioned for Avery to sit in the vacant seat beside Traci, but he opted to stand. Alice sat in the chair instead.

"I thought maybe we could talk in private," Avery said, glancing at the women before turning back to DJ.

"Would you rather I asked them to leave?"

Avery looked back at the women again and decided that maybe it was best that they all heard it from him. The news he had in some way would affect all of them and the element of surprise wouldn't be any less if they learned about Shandi's connection to them later. His main concern was whether or not his pastor even knew he was adopted. If he dropped this bomb on him in front of his mother, it could cause a problem. But Avery couldn't be worried about that now. Alice Griffin had followed him uninvited. He could only hope that she and her husband had been straightforward with their son about his family history.

"This is about Shandi, isn't it?" DJ asked.

Avery nodded and said, "Yeah, it is. I don't know how much you know about her past and why she moved to Atlanta."

"She told me about the death of her parents, if that's what you're referring to."

"Did she tell you how they died?"

"Yes, she did," DJ said, careful not to volunteer any information in case Avery's motives were to find out for himself.

"Did she tell you that they weren't her real folks and that she was adopted?"

DJ paused for a moment. To him, this was new information. Other than the fact that her parents had both suffered drug-related deaths, he had no idea of the details of Shandi's life back in Chicago. He answered Avery with a silent shake of his head. Alice and Traci sat quietly, confused as to the reason behind Avery's interrogation.

"When's your birthday, Pastor?" Avery asked.

"Why are you asking me that, Avery?"

"Because I need to know," he said. "For Shandi's sake, I need to know."

It was DJ's turn to look confused. When he didn't immediately answer, Avery spoke again.

"Are you adopted?"

DJ's adoption was never a matter that he discussed with his church members. Alice and DeShawn Sr. were the only parents he'd ever known. They'd told him early in his life, around about the time he started first grade, that they had adopted him. Back then he hadn't even known what the word meant, but they explained to him how God had given him to them in a different way than most parents got their children. It was a while later before he fully understood what they meant, but knowing he wasn't born to them meant nothing to DJ. Alice and DeShawn Sr. loved him, nurtured him, protected him, and made sure all of his needs were met. To him, they were his parents.

Avery's last question had made Alice uncomfortable. She stood from her seat and faced Avery, who stood several inches taller than she.

"You getting mighty personal, Brother Avery. What this got to do with anything?"

"It's okay, Mama," DJ said as he raised his hand to quiet her.

"Are you?" Avery pressed, never taking his attention from his pastor.

"Yes, I am."

"Is your birthday June fourth?"

"Yes, it is. Why are you asking me this, Avery?" DJ asked for the second time.

After a tense pause that seemed to last much longer than it actually did, Avery looked at him. His voice was barely above a whisper, but they all heard him say, "She's your sister."

"What?" DJ and Traci said in one voice.

"Her mother had a set of twins and she gave them both up for adoption," Avery explained. "The folks who adopted Shandi got one kid and I guess you all got the other one," he said, looking briefly at Alice.

"That's it," Traci whispered, looking relieved that both her and her husband's questions about his emotional attachment to Shandi had been answered. "That's why you've been feeling like you have."

Noting his mother's quietness and downcast eyes, DJ suspected that this wasn't the first she'd heard of him having a twin sister. He felt numb from the inside out and slowly walked behind his desk where he would be directly in front of his mother.

"Did you know about this, Mama?" he asked, realizing deep inside that he already knew the answer. "Did you and Daddy know I had a sister?"

At a snail's pace, Alice sank back into her chair. Despite the fact that her eyes were closed, tears formed at the corners and rolled down her cheeks. DJ sat too, feeling that his trembling legs could no longer hold up the weight of his body. He slid open the drawer beside him and pulled out the box of tissues. No one had used them since his meeting with Shandi back in September. Traci pulled out a few for Alice and a few for herself as well.

The resonating sounds of Minister Collins preaching in the sanctuary of the church seemed to reverberate in the office, where no one spoke a word.

"Why didn't you tell me, Mama?" DJ asked.

"We wanted to get both of you," she started. "Your sister's adoptive parents were supposed to get both of you at first, but they had a change of heart for some reason and decided they just wanted the little girl. That opened up the door for me and your daddy to get you. When we found out what happened, we asked the folks there if there was any way we could get both of you so that you wouldn't be separated. We were told that the papers had already been signed for your twin, so you were all we could get."

"But why didn't you tell me?" DJ insisted. "When I was a kid, I used to wish I had a kid brother or sister. Now I'm finding out that I had one all the while?"

"I don't know why we didn't tell you, son," Alice said. "I guess in a way we were afraid of what might happen. Maybe me and DeShawn was scared that you'd go looking for her and maybe we were just scared of what might happen if you found her. We had prayed so hard for you, baby. We didn't want nothing to happen that would make us lose you. I'm so sorry. You should've never found out this way. I'm so sorry."

DJ reached across his desk for Alice's hands. As displeased as he was about the situation as a whole, he didn't feel any anger towards his parents. An array of emotions was brewing inside of him, but anger didn't seem to be in the mix. As with Traci, a part of him felt relieved to finally have an answer for his questionable need to protect Shandi and be a part of her life. In another sense, he felt happy to know that he had been reunited with a part of his biological self that he never knew existed. Then there were the butterflies in his stomach that signified his nervousness from not knowing what to expect of this newfound discovery.

"Pastor Griffin," Avery said, disrupting the family moment. "I need you to talk to her."

"I know this news had to blow her away," DJ said. "It's a lot to digest without sorting through the confusion."

"She's more than confused," Avery explained. "Shandi is hurt and very angry right now. That's why she's not here today. She couldn't bear the thought of looking at you."

"Why? Does she think I knew about this and didn't tell her?"

"Look at your life, Pastor, and then look at hers. I don't know if she's blaming you or blaming God, but she's searching for somebody to blame for what she feels was an unfair deal. All of a sudden she can't stand Atlanta or anything associated with it, including me. You've got to talk to her and make her understand. I couldn't find the right words to say, but I know you can, Pastor Griffin."

DJ didn't want to admit that he was at a loss for words. He needed a few days to cope with this himself before trying to explain it to Shandi. Avery's next words made him realize that his mental request for time had been denied.

"I know she's gonna be angry at me for even mentioning this, but I don't want her to leave. If we don't do something to stop her . . . if *you* don't do something to stop her, she's gonna be on a plane to God knows where by tomorrow. Y'all might see this as some kind of miracle or something to celebrate about, but Shandi doesn't and I'm gonna lose her if you don't talk to her. We're all gonna lose her."

13

Still My Child

Sunday morning was the only day of the week that there was almost complete peacefulness at Sinai House. As Shandi walked through her shared room, emptying her drawers and stuffing items back into the rolling suitcase she'd unloaded them from two months ago, she wondered why she ever started spending her Sundays in church. If she had any sense, she would have been spending them in her room, getting stuff done that she couldn't get done during the week due to Velma's mindless chatter or other goings-on in the center for the God-rejected.

As she walked across the carpeted floor, Shandi passed a mirror that was mounted on the bedroom wall and paused to look at her reflection. Her eyes were pink and puffy from lack of sleep and the abundance of tears she'd shed over the past several hours. In Chicago, her entire life had been spent scraping, scrounging, and sometimes stealing just to survive, while she had a brother seven hundred miles away living like he was Donald Trump's secret black child.

In anger, she punched at the clothes that wouldn't lie flat in the overflowing suitcase. She had bought a few items since moving to Atlanta, mostly clothes for church. Now the luggage that she could once fit all of her belongings in was inadequate. Frustrated, she pulled some of the items out and tossed them on the floor so that she could close the zipper.

Now that everything that could fit inside was packed, Shandi slipped her hand behind the dresser and moved it about in the narrow space until she felt the wallet that held the money that would get her far away from this nightmare that she'd gotten herself into. Carefully, and through tear-distorted vision, she counted out every dollar she'd saved from her shifts at Chili's. Her plan to find a place here in the city had been scratched and replaced with a plan to catch the first flight that would take her as far away from here as possible.

Shandi buried her face in the dollar bills and wept. She didn't want to leave Atlanta, but she knew she couldn't stay here. She'd escaped Chicago to get away from memories of her forsaken childhood and now, just when she thought she was getting it all together, she was slapped in the face again, this time by the two she trusted most: her pastor and God. Shandi was so engrossed in her own pity and tears that she didn't hear the knock at her door.

"Shandi."

Through half-blinded, watery eyes, Shandi looked up to see the man she now knew as her brother, standing in her doorway dressed in a black suit that he, no doubt, had purchased with money that his good life had afforded him. She quickly gathered her money and her wallet and stuffed them in her purse. As much as she had come to trust Avery, she knew the chance that he would keep all of this to himself was slim to none. But nothing was going to change her mind. She was already prepared for this.

"Can we talk?" DJ asked, approaching with caution.

"Talk about *what*?" Shandi asked with new anger surfacing as she spoke.

She watched DJ bend down and scoop up her tossed-aside articles of clothing. By the time he picked up the last piece, only about ten inches separated the two of them. When he stood, they looked one another straight in the eyes. For the first time, Shandi saw eyes that looked just like hers and she swallowed back the fresh batch of tears that threatened to show themselves. In DJ's eyes, she saw evidence that he'd been crying too.

"About us, Shandi," DJ said, placing the clothes on her bed and turning again to face her. "I'd love to talk about us. I've had a sister for twenty-five years and I never knew it. There's so much I want to know and I know you have questions for me. We'll never know anything about each other if you take off and leave like this."

DJ's eyes were pleading and a part of Shandi wanted to reach out and embrace him, but her jealousy and resentment wouldn't allow her to.

"I think I know everything I need to know about you, Pastor Griffin," she said, trying unsuccessfully to hide the hostility in her tone. "You were adopted by good parents who loved you and gave you a good life. You graduated high school, went to college, and got married, and now you're about to have a baby. You have a beautiful home in a classy neighborhood and a church full of people who are crazy about you. That's who you are.

"Now, you wanna know who I am? I'm the cursed, betrayed, and forsaken one. I'm the one God didn't think was good enough to be placed with a family like yours. I'm the one who had to fight every day at school because kids picked on me for wearing the same clothes over and over again. I'm the one who had to drop out of school to try and bring money into the house that wasn't going to be smoked from a pipe, shot through a needle, or drunk from a bottle. I'm the one who *stupidly* came to Atlanta to try and find and make amends with my natural mother, only to find out that she was so selfish that she didn't even bother to bring her children home from the hospital. She spent her nights shaking her naked behind in front of rich men, but she died poor, sick, and lonely. I'm the one who is living in a homeless shelter having to share my space with a lunatic who talks about a rich son who she ain't never had because I can't afford my own private roof over my head. I'm the one . . ."

"She's dead?" DJ interrupted Shandi's speech, making her lose her train of thought.

"What?"

"Our mother," DJ clarified. "You said she died."

"Three years ago," Shandi said, wiping from her cheeks water that had begun dripping from her chin.

"Who was she? What happened?"

"Does it matter now?" Shandi lashed out again. "She never wanted neither one of us, Pastor Griffin, so why should it matter? I don't even know why I came here looking for her. All I know is that I've got to get up out of here before I really lose my mind."

For the first time, DJ touched her. Shandi looked down at his hands as he grabbed her by both arms to stop her from turning away.

"Please don't leave," he begged.

Needing both of his hands, DJ released Shandi and stripped himself of his suit jacket and tossed it on the bed with her clothes.

"Look at me, Shandi," he said, grasping her arms again. "I'm not Pastor Griffin anymore, I'm just DJ. Do you understand that? I'm your brother. When it comes to biological blood relatives, we're all we've got. I'm sorry about all that you had to go through, but don't hold that against me. I can't be responsible for the wrong that our mother did. We need to wipe the slate clean and start from today. As far as you and I are concerned, our life as siblings started today. Stay here, Shandi. Stay here and I will help you get on your feet. You can move in with me and Traci and stay as long as you like. We'll make sure . . ."

"Listen to yourself!" Shandi screamed, pushing him away. "You're talking just like the twin that God chose to bless! It's easy for you to wipe the slate clean because you ain't had to share your house with roaches and rats. You weren't the one who had to slide your dresser in front of the door at night because you were afraid your daddy might get high or drunk and would try and come in your bedroom and mess with you! Thank you very much, but I don't need your help. I've been a charity case for you since the day I moved in here. And you think I want to move in your house now? I'd rather keep sharing this room with the harebrained moron that I stay with now. You think I don't know your wife don't like me? I guess I'm too low-class for her. I see it in her eyes every time she looks at me . . . like she's too good or something. I don't mean no disrespect to you as a preacher or nothing. You've been nice to me, but she hasn't."

"That was my fault, Shandi," DJ defended. "I'm sorry you were made to feel that way, but I promise it's not a personal thing."

"I don't even want to talk about it. It don't matter none now, anyway. I don't need her and nobody else." Shandi's tears broke again. "You preached that Sunday in September that God didn't play favorites and He passed blessings around to everybody. I've been trying to figure that one out since the day I heard you preach it and this right here proves that you were wrong. All I've ever been is beat down, lied to, and misunderstood. I ain't never had nothing that didn't just about cost me my life to get. And every time I think I got something, it gets taken away. I thought I was gonna be happy here. I thought I had a future here at Mount Sinai and maybe even a future with Avery, but now all that is messed up."

"It's not messed up, Shandi. The church needs you, Avery needs you, and God knows I need you. Please, Shandi, just give it some time. Don't do this to me."

Shandi picked up DJ's jacket from her bed and handed it to him. "My mind is made up. All my life I've done stuff for other people. I'm tired now. This time I have to do what's right for me."

He took the jacket from her hand and Shandi turned her back to him when she saw a tear trickle from DJ's eye. She knew his heart was in the right place, but she had to leave. He couldn't understand her, nor could anyone else. After not hearing him leave, she glanced over her shoulder and saw DJ standing with his head down, staring at the suit jacket in his hand. Silent tears were flowing now and he made no attempt to hide them. Shandi turned her back to him again and prayed that he'd leave as she folded the remaining clothes that he'd picked up from the floor earlier.

"Shandi."

She heard him, but did not turn to face him. Shandi could hear him sniffling in an attempt to regain control of his emotions. There was a quiet moment that blanketed the room, and then he continued.

"Shandi, I wish I could go back in time and make things turn out differently, but I don't think it would be God's will for me to do that, even if I could. I don't know why God chose to allow things to happen as they did, but no matter what, I'll never believe that God is not true to His Word. We go through things in life for a reason. From the time I was born and left behind by our birth mother, I believe God was grooming me to revive a church that was all but dead. I believe He anointed me to be the one to build on the strong foundation that Reverend Battles started. I think I had to be adopted by DeShawn and Alice Griffin and brought up in the manner that I was in order to do that.

"But you were no mistake, either. Who you are, where you've been, and what you've experienced weren't haphazard events. I don't know what God is grooming you for, Shandi, but I'm certain that He allowed you to go through everything for a reason. There's a ministry inside of you and there is no way that you would have been prepared to take it on, had you not first endured. As cruel as it may sound, you had to be adopted by the family that took you in, in order for you to be able to carry out the purpose that God has for you. And whatever you may believe about His fairness, you can always believe this. It didn't matter who gave birth to you or who adopted you. From the very beginning, Shandi, you were always God's child and you always will be His child. You can leave here and run to Africa and you'll still belong to Him. In the end, sweetheart, that's all that really matters. It's not about who our natural parents are, it's about who our heavenly Father is."

Complete silence followed his words, but from the sound of his voice, Shandi knew that he'd been stepping closer and closer to her as he spoke. Knowing he was now only inches behind her, she didn't move from her position. When she felt his arms wrap around her, she gasped—not in surprise, but in an attempt to hold back the onset of more tears. His embrace seemed to last forever, and Shandi felt a tear from his face touch her cheek. She wanted to turn around and throw her arms around his neck, but she couldn't.

"I've missed you my whole life," he whispered. "Wherever you go from this point on, you'll never be able to say that nobody loves you."

His arms slipped from around her, and seconds later Shandi heard the door opening.

"How are you gonna say you love me?" she asked, turning to face him. "You don't even know me. I've been here for two months and you just found out that we shared our mother's stomach at the same time, and now all of a sudden you love me? You don't love me no more than Leona Smith did."

"Leona Smith." DJ repeated the name with little emotion, but Shandi knew from his expression that he was glad to know it. He looked at the floor for a brief moment and then turned his eyes to Shandi.

"I didn't just come to find out that I love you, Shandi," he said. "I just came to find out *why* I love you. Love isn't determined by how well or how long you've known someone; it's about an emotional connection that we sometimes don't understand. Leona Smith, in her limited knowledge of what love was, may have loved us as well. Her giving us away may have put you in a bad place, but it took that to put you in *this* place. Love is too deep to measure with a shallow ruler, Shandi. The woman you refer to as a moron knows that better than most people. Velma is no lunatic. She didn't invent Junior."

Shandi looked at him in surprise at his last statement.

"Junior really is her son. He died in a house fire in Austin, Texas, during the Christmas holidays last year. Velma's not crazy, Velma is in love. She's in love with a son who she can't bear to picture as dead and buried. So, she keeps him alive in her mind and that's how she copes with the fact that she's the one who fell asleep with the grease heating up on the stove. It may not make sense to us, but sometimes love is unexplainable. When Jesus died, He died for the sins of the whole world. He even died for the men who spat on Him and beat Him and nailed Him to the cross. If He could love them and even turn around and love us before we were even born, then don't tell me that I can't love you."

Shandi watched him turn away and walk out of her room. When she was absolutely sure that he was gone, she released the deep sobs that racked her insides.

14

Feels Like Rain

Taylor's birth early on Tuesday afternoon served only as a bandage to slow the heavy bleeding of DJ's heart that Shandi's leaving on Monday morning had caused. He had gone to the shelter to sit and talk with Avery, and they were in the middle of their conversation when he got the call that Traci's water had broken. Thinking that DJ might be too nervous to keep a level head, Avery drove him to his house to pick up his waiting wife. With Traci's contractions already just five minutes apart, Avery continued to serve in the capacity of chauffeur so that DJ could give Traci all the attention she needed. Once they reached the hospital, the couple's fame, good insurance, and preadmittance gave them immediate consideration and allowed them to be attended to soon after their arrival.

It seemed that their daughter was as anxious to meet her parents as they were to meet her. Just over an hour after Traci had been placed in the delivery room, DJ was holding his eight-and-a-half-pound daughter in his arms, kissing her tiny hands as she slept in the warm blanket she'd been given. Had she been born just a few days earlier, DJ wouldn't have needed Avery to tell him that Shandi was his twin, because Taylor came out looking very much like her absent aunt.

Later that night, the newborn was being admired by more well-wishers and onlookers through the window of the nursery. Traci's parents had flown in from Trenton, New Jersey, and were proud to welcome their first granddaughter into the family. Up until this point, they'd had only grandsons, courtesy of their older daughter and son, who'd each had two boys. Throughout the afternoon and into the evening, both family and church members came and went, all anxiously awaiting the chance when they could have their turn at holding the little girl.

By nightfall, they'd all gone home to allow both mother and daughter the rest that they needed. After Traci had breastfed Taylor, an attendant came and took the baby to the nursery so that her mother could get some sleep. DJ sat by the bed and held Traci's hand, telling her over and over again how proud he had been of the way she braved the challenge of natural childbirth. When he saw her drifting off to sleep, DJ turned his attention to the television and an old episode of *Andy Griffith*. The volume was low, but loud enough for DJ to hear the antics between Sheriff Andy Taylor and Deputy Barney Fife.

"I'm sorry about Shandi, DJ."

Because DJ thought Traci was asleep, Traci's words startled him. He turned and looked at her through the grayness of the dimly lit room. When he made no attempt to respond, she reached over the lowered bed railing for his hand, linking her fingers through his.

"I need you to know that I never doubted your love for me," she continued. "I just didn't understand what it was about her that drew you. I'm sorry that I was so difficult about the whole thing."

"Baby, neither one of us understood what I was going through. I don't blame you for how you felt about it," DJ said.

"I know you don't blame me, DJ. But I'm still sorry. I think I'm sorry most of all because I didn't even allow myself to get to know her. When I became First Lady of Mount Sinai, I'd asked God to give me an open mind and heart when it came to the people who served and worshipped there. I saw early on that your ministry was going to draw all types of people and I prayed that whoever came, as long as their intentions were honorable, that I would receive them with open arms. I didn't do that for Shandi, DJ. Other than the very first day when she came to talk to you, I don't think I showed her any warmth at all. She came to Christ and joined the church only because of the love that you and Avery showed her."

Traci's voice trembled as she continued talking. "I even intentionally left her off the list of names that I gave the girls to invite to the baby shower. I left her out of her own niece's celebration, DJ. I don't know, nobody else may have noticed my coldness towards her, but I'm sure Shandi did. If I helped to do anything at all, it was to run her away. I am so sorry."

The thoughts of Shandi's bitterness and anger at the time she left, and the things she told him, resurfaced in DJ's mind, but he kept them to himself. This was no time to burden Traci even more by revealing how hurt Shandi was by her rejection. Besides, with or without acceptance from Traci, DJ was sure that his sister would have still opted to leave. The picture was so much broader than the unaddressed strain between the women.

After Traci finally drifted off to sleep, DJ took the walk from her private room to the hospital's nursery. It appeared as though Piedmont Hospital had experienced a baby boom. Like other fathers and family members who were gathering at the nursery, DJ admired other babies through the glass on his way to the area where he knew his own newborn had been placed. When he approached the corner where Taylor could be seen, he first saw Avery, with his hands shoved in his pockets, staring at the sleeping child.

"Looks a lot like Shandi, doesn't she?" DJ whispered.

Avery turned slightly at the sound of his pastor's voice, and then smiled and nodded in agreement. The two men stood in silence for several moments, admiring the nineteen-inch bundle whose head was covered in a pink cap to match the socks that covered her hands and feet.

"You know where she is, don't you?" DJ asked.

"Yes."

Avery's quick honesty drew DJ's eyes away from the glass.

"Pastor Griffin, please don't ask me where she is because I can't tell you," Avery said.

"Avery . . ."

"She made me give her my word this time," Avery said. "If I tell you where she is, she'll move again, and this time she won't even tell me. I can't chance that. I already feel empty not being able to see her every day like I used to, but at least I know that I can go and see her when I get a break. I know you want to know where she is and I know that not knowing is ripping you up inside, but you have to understand the position I'm in, Pastor. I love that girl and I can't risk losing her forever."

Fighting emotions, DJ turned back to the window and exhaled heavily before nodding his head. He did understand Avery's plight, but it didn't lessen his anguish, and apparently his body language gave away the pain he tried to conceal.

"I'm sorry, Pastor Griffin," Avery said. "I know this ain't easy for you."

"I've never wanted for anything, Avery," DJ said. "My parents sometimes went without so that I could have whatever it was I needed to get me the best of everything. I had more clothes than I could wear, more toys than I could play with, and more love than I had room to receive. I think the only thing in life I ever longed for that I didn't have was a sibling to share it all with."

DJ paused to wipe a lone tear that ran down his left cheek. He dabbed at each eye with a handkerchief he pulled from his pocket, and then continued.

"Whoever said it is better to have loved and lost than never to have loved at all was wrong. I would rather have never met Shandi or found out that she was my sister than to have found her only to lose her. I was doing just fine before she walked through the doors of Mount Sinai. As senseless at it may sound, I think I fell in love with her, as my sister, on the very first day I met her."

"You ain't got to convince me," Avery said knowingly.

"I think I could live with it all much easier if she wasn't so angry with me when she left. She felt wronged by me somehow and knowing that she left with so much animosity against me is hard to deal with. That alone has left such a thick cloud over my head. It's like I'm living in an ongoing rainstorm that only God can end."

DJ watched as his daughter made a sudden movement, and then calmed again. It was almost time for another feeding and the periodic smacking of her lips was a sign that Taylor would be prepared. A nurse passed the window and noticed DJ standing there looking. She motioned an invitation for him to enter, but DJ shook his head. He would wait until she was brought back in the room later. When he held his daughter, he didn't want it to be in front of onlookers through a showcase window. He wanted it to be in the privacy of Traci's room so that any emotions that stirred inside of him could be shown without discomfort.

"I wish I could tell you where she was," Avery spoke up. "I *want* to tell you where she is, but I can't. I gave her my word that I wouldn't."

DJ turned to him once more. He knew that keeping the information from him was difficult for Avery. DJ could see the struggle on Avery's face and knew that if he pressed hard enough and used Avery's conscience as a target, he could probably at least get a hint that would give away where his sister had retreated. But as badly as he wanted to know, DJ didn't pursue the issue any further.

"As a man of my word, Avery, I couldn't, in good conscience, ask you to break your vow to Shandi. But when you talk to her, please tell her I love her."

Delivering a gentle pat to Avery's back, DJ turned away and walked back to the room to say good night to his wife before leaving for home.

15

At The Table

"Baby, you didn't inconvenience us none," Peggy Taylor told her daughter as she took her newest grandchild from Traci's arms. "This right here is a whole lot better than me and your daddy spending Thanksgiving at home by ourselves."

Traci and Taylor had been allowed to go home on Thanksgiving morning, just in time for the yearly dinner that Mount Sinai held at the homeless shelter. Although DJ's intention was to take her straight home, his wife wanted to be at the shelter to watch everyone pitch in to get all of the food prepared and the table set for the dinner they all shared together at what was called "The Family Table." Her mother had fussed about her being out in the fall air just two days after delivery, but Traci insisted.

Avery and the others who generally manned the kitchen were hard at work, nearly tripling their normal recipes to accommodate not only the center's residents but many of the other church members as well. The expansion of Sinai House had been completed just in time to afford them the additional room needed for the extra tables and chairs that were being brought in. With her mother and husband not allowing her to lift a finger to help, Traci sat back and watched the reconstructed dining hall transformed into a place that would feel like an oversized home dining room to all the people who were taking part in the festivities. She closed her eyes and inhaled. The whole center smelled of turkey, ham, dressing, collard greens, macaroni and cheese, and sweet potato pies.

The timer on the oven in the kitchen sent a piercing signal that meal preparation was nearing an end. From the reclining sofa chair where she sat, Traci could see both her mother and mother-in-law fussing over Taylor while her father and father-in-law helped DJ and several of the other men bring in the last of the new couches that had been donated by a local furniture store. Traci looked at the clock on the wall. Time was passing swiftly and six o'clock was less than an hour away. She hoped everything turned out as planned. After his recent ordeal, DJ needed today to be perfect.

By now, nearly everyone in the congregation had gotten the shocking news about DJ and Shandi's family ties. Just the word of their pastor being an adopted child was surprising enough. Traci couldn't remember how many times she'd heard someone in the congregation tell DJ that he looked just like his daddy. Aside from them both being tall, handsome black men, Traci didn't see any resemblance, and she was sure that many of those who'd made the comparison felt a bit foolish now at knowing the truth.

Like any grapevine news, the one of DJ and Shandi had many variations. The most repeated one was that they were born Siamese twins and had to be surgically separated. In one version of the Siamese story, one of Shandi's arms was prosthetic because in the separation, DJ got the "good arms."

He wasn't ready to talk about it yet, so DJ allowed them to guess and wonder. No one had proof who had gotten the incorrect version started, but Alice Griffin couldn't be convinced that it wasn't Mother Milsap.

"It was her," Alice had insisted on yesterday. "Just as sure as her wigs don't cost but five dollars, it was her. She gossip during the week just about as much as she shout on Sunday morning. She's the one who put it out that Sister Nichols was pregnant. Who ever heard such a thing? The woman was near 'bout fifty-five years old and just 'cause of Gertrude Milsap's mouth, she had to try to convince folks that all she was was fat. I'm telling you, if you ever want to get a rumor started, just telephone, telegraph, or tele-Gertrude."

Traci didn't want to jump on the blaming bandwagon, but she was inclined to agree with Alice. When he wasn't by her and Taylor's side, DJ had been spending some time with Avery, who had shared the pictures of Leona and details of her life that he'd gathered during his quest to help Shandi find their mother. DJ had had copies of the pictures and the death certificate made, and had placed them in a photo album he'd purchased just for storing memories of the woman who had given him life. Traci promised him that she'd go with him to the gravesite whenever he decided to visit, but DJ didn't seem to be in any hurry.

"I don't feel any great sense of loss," he had told her last night after they had put Taylor to sleep. "I mean, I guess it would have been nice to have at least met her, but I don't feel that I missed anything having not had that opportunity. Shandi seemed so broken up about everything and I guess the difference is that I had a very capable mother who raised me like her own. She didn't have that, so between the woman who gave birth to her and the woman who adopted her, it's like she never had a mother at all."

He may not have felt a loss without Leona, but Traci knew that DJ felt extremely incomplete without Shandi. He found comfort in the simplest things. Before leaving the hospital, while thumbing through a book of babies' names, DJ found that both his and Shandi's names were of African American origin and they both meant "God is gracious." He thought there must have been a divine reason why two sets of adoptive parents, who knew nothing of each other, would each have given their child a name that had the same meaning as the other's.

"You got somewhere to be?" DJ's voice interrupted her clock-staring.

"Huh?" Traci turned to face her husband, who looked surprisingly handsome in the blue coveralls he'd been working in.

"I didn't mean to scare you. I just saw you staring at the clock on the wall and wondered if you were planning on going somewhere."

"As if I could if I wanted to," Traci said, rubbing her still swollen stomach. "I'm hungry, though. I hope dinner is about ready to be served."

"Not quite," DJ said. "So, what do you think?" He pointed towards the finished product in the dining area.

"It looks great, sweetheart. You all did a superb job in a short time. Reverend Jacob Battles would be proud."

DJ smiled and said, "Thanks. We're gonna all run home and get cleaned up. By the time we all get back, it will be time to eat. If you want something before then, I'll have the guys fix you a little something to tie you over."

"No, I'll be fine."

Traci watched him walk towards the exit door, stopping briefly to kiss his daughter's forehead before dashing to catch up with the others.

With the workers leaving and the staff disappearing into their separate rooms, Traci was left alone in the corner where her chair was situated. Peggy and Alice sat in the lounging area talking and laughing while passing Taylor from one to the other. Traci had come to accept the fact that she wouldn't get much quality time with her baby until her mother went back to New Jersey. At least then she'd have only one grandmother to compete with. Though quiet times alone with her daughter were few right now, she welcomed the extra help.

The crowd around Taylor grew as people began trickling in to share in the annual spiritual family gathering. For some, it was their first glimpse of the newest member of their pastor's family. Traci smiled in appreciation as she watched her mother instruct them to stand back.

"Y'all gonna give my grandbaby a cold or something. Whatever you can't see from right there, you won't see."

Traci directed her attention back on the door and watched as each person entered. Some were dressed as though they were coming for Sunday morning service and others were in casual pants and sweaters. The coatrack at the entrance area quickly filled, and the security guard who monitored the door began using one of the front rooms to house the growing mound of wool, leather, pleather, and other artificial material.

Pots and pans began rattling in the kitchen area as Avery joined the other capable hands in preparing the buffet. While bringing out one tray of sliced turkey, he looked across the room at Traci and smiled before disappearing once again behind closed doors. As the minutes passed, the noise level rose, and Traci was forced to divide her attention between her door-watching and the well-wishers who hadn't seen her since last Sunday's church service.

It was nearly six-thirty by the time DJ returned with both his father and hers. He called for everyone to gather at the tables, and Traci joined him as everyone held hands for family prayer and grace. At one point, DJ's prayer became more emotional than usual and everyone knew why.

The line was longer than it had ever been. It was a sign of how many souls God had added to the church from last Thanksgiving until this year. There were at least one hundred twenty-five adults and children. Had all the church members come instead of traveling out of town to visit family members, there would not have been enough seats. But even with the increase in numbers, there was plenty of food to feed everyone. And DJ had already decided that any food left over this year would be taken to a public homeless shelter located twenty miles from Sinai House.

As soon as everyone was seated and had begun enjoying their meal, the security guard from the front door walked into the dining hall. He paused for a moment and stepped to the side, causing DJ to drop his fork on his plate. Traci turned and looked at Avery and the two shared smiles broadened with relief. Shandi was an hour later than she'd said she would be. Traci had begun worrying that she had, for some reason, changed her mind. None of that was important now. All that mattered was that she was here.

"Shandi," DJ whispered.

Avery got up from his table and walked over to hug her. It had been only four days since he'd last seen her, but they'd felt like the longest four days of his life. By the time he released her, DJ was standing beside both of them.

"She made me promise not to tell *you*," Avery said. "She didn't say nothing about not telling Sister Griffin."

DJ turned to look at his wife. The tears in her eyes prevented her from seeing the tears in his, but Traci knew that they were there. She didn't know if her phone call to Shandi would bring her home, but once she knew how to contact her, she had had to try. Traci picked up her napkin to wipe her tears, and when she looked up again DJ and Shandi were sharing an emotional embrace. DJ was holding on to his sister as if he was afraid that she'd leave again if he released her. They were talking to one another as they held one another, but the words were too muffled for their audience to hear. There was barely a dry eye at the table. Even the men had been touched by the heartfelt reunion.

One voice finally ended the stillness that had lingered for the past several moments.

"Oooh wee! Thank you Jesus," Velma said with both her hands raised above her head. "Ain't the Lord good? I am *so* glad I was here to see this. See how God works, y'all? If this here would have happened tomorrow, I would've missed it, 'cause you know Junior's gonna be here bright and early. . . ."

A Healing of the Hearts

Maxine Billings

1

"Big Momma, Janae's appointment is at eight forty-five," thirty-year-old Kenya Jamison kindly reminded her maternal grandmother, Paulette Callahan, as they made their way to the front door of the Jamison home in Temple, Georgia. "She's just getting her teeth cleaned so it shouldn't take long. They already have our insurance information."

Paulette was an attractive, petite woman with smooth milk chocolate skin that put one in mind of a creamy Hershey's chocolate bar. She kept her waist-length hair plated and twisted in a large bun at the nape of her neck. Though her hair was completely gray, she appeared much younger than her eighty-one years.

Paulette grinned at her nervous granddaughter. "I know, Kenya. You told me a thousand times already. Remember?"

Not paying her grandmother any attention, Kenya rattled on, "Can you still take her to school afterwards? I have five tapes to transcribe for Dr. Green. I wish he wouldn't do so many at one time. He knows how that stresses me out."

Five-year-old Janae tugged on the leg of her mother's stone-washed jeans. "Momma, do I have to go to school today? Why can't I stay home with you? I'll help you work."

Kenya had been listening to her young daughter whine all morning about her desire not to go to school. It wasn't like Janae to beg to stay home. Kenya had too many other things on her mind at the moment and couldn't deal with her whimpering little girl. Since Janae had not implied even once that she was sick, Kenya figured that whatever it was couldn't be all that serious.

She sternly repeated what she'd said earlier more than once,

"Janae, you're not sick. You're going to school so stop whining." Turning her attention back to her grandmother, Kenya asked again, "You can take her to school when you leave the dentist? She can ride the bus home with Kourtnie as usual."

Paulette hated seeing Kenya so edgy. Kenya had started her medical transcription business from home about two years ago and needed Paulette's assistance from time to time with her young daughters. Paulette didn't mind one bit helping Kenya and her husband, Trent, with the girls, for she loved being a great-grandmother, especially now that she was retired and could devote more time to them. Kenya had informed her last night that one of the local doctors had bestowed on her a pile of tapes to be transcribed. Kenya took pride in the fact that the doctors she worked for were always extremely pleased with her work. However, there were still occasional moments when the stress would overwhelm her, like today.

Paulette gently placed her hand on Kenya's arm. "Honey, yes. I thought we worked all this out last night when we talked on the phone. Calm down and stop worrying. I know what to do. Now go do what you need to do. Me and Nae'll be fine." Glancing quickly at her great-granddaughter, she inquired, "Won't we, Nae?"

Again, Janae reminded the two grown-ups, as she held her little round face up and stared at them both pitifully, "I don't wanna go to school. I wanna stay home."

As she painstakingly clutched the child's hand, Paulette responded gleefully, "We'll talk in the car. Give your Momma some good-bye sugar."

The little girl obeyed, but not because she wanted to. Then she and her great grandmother were out the door.

Briefly, Kenya stood in the doorway as the cool, damp moisture of the March morning swept across her face. With spring due to arrive in a little under two weeks, the surroundings had already begun to burst forth with vivid colors. She inhaled a cool breath of fresh air prior to stepping back inside and shutting the door.

Before going to her office to start her day's tasks, Kenya strolled into the bathroom to splash a sprinkling of warm water onto her face to prepare herself for what she prayed would wind down to a stress-free day. In the back of her mind, however, she doubted that that would happen with all the tapes the good doctor had heaped on her. She reached over and grabbed a fluffy Caribbean-blue hand towel from an antique brass towel ring and gently pressed it to her face a few times.

As she stared at her reflection in the bathroom mirror, Kenya was reminded of how much she resembled her father. She loved styling her hair in pigtails like the ones she wore now, one on each side of her head. She'd always felt like the oddball who walked to the beat of her own drum and sensed that other people viewed her as such also. As a child, she found herself admiring Zaire, her twin sister, and wanting to be just like her.

Their parents' wedding anniversary was yesterday. If they were alive, it would have been their thirty-sixth. Perhaps that was another reason Kenya was so uptight this morning, for the day had awakened in her memories of her lost childhood with her mother and father. Yesterday morning before church, she, Trent, Kourtnie, Janae, and Paulette had strolled over to the gravesite on the church property and placed her mother's favorite flowers on the graves. Jonquils is what their mother and the older generation called them— better known to the younger age groups as daffodils. Whatever you called them, the cluster of bright yellow perennials was beautiful. Shaking her head, Kenya brought herself out of her reverie and proceeded to her office to work on the tapes.

It was a few minutes after twelve o'clock. Kenya had been working nonstop on the tapes and had finally paused for a bathroom break and a quick bite of lunch. She decided to call her grandmother to see how Janae was when she'd been dropped off at school. Though her girls were still young, she wanted them to learn to face their problems, and not always run home like scared little puppies with their tails tucked between their legs. Nevertheless, she felt guilty that she had not taken the time this morning to address Janae's problem instead of just brushing off her little girl.

Paulette's telephone was answered on the first ring by a wee voice that sounded a lot like—*Janae*!

Kenya threw empathy for her daughter to the wind as she screamed into the phone, "Janae! Why aren't you in school? You're supposed to be at school."

The next voice Kenya heard over the receiver was that of her grandmother. "Hello."

"Big Momma!" Kenya squealed in a rather unpleasant tone.

"What is Janae doing out of school? I specifically asked you to take her to school after her cleaning."

Paulette had not been expecting Kenya's call. If she had, she would have given her little great granddaughter explicit instructions not to answer the telephone if it rang. They'd been caught. "Now, Kenya, just calm down," she stated diplomatically. "Let me explain."

Kenya was seething with anger, yet she attempted to control her temper, for this was her grandmother, whom she dearly loved. Paulette was such a softie when it came to her great-grandchildren. She certainly hadn't been that way with Kenya and Zaire. To them, their grandmother was mean compared with their friends' parents, who allowed their children to do what they wanted and go where they wished without any questions. Now that she was older and had children of her own, though, Kenya appreciated the manner in which Paulette had reared her and her sister. From her adult eyes, she no longer saw her grandmother ways back then as mean; Paulette just didn't take any mess from them, the way parents did from their children nowadays. However, she still felt there were times when her grandmother was too easygoing with Kourtnie and Janae.

"Go ahead, Big Momma, explain," Kenya stated rigidly.

Paulette began, "Kenya, she was so upset after we got through at the dentist. She kept saying she didn't wanna go to school 'cause the teacher doesn't like her. She was crying and going on so I let her stay here with me. I know I was wrong to go behind your back, but I couldn't take her to school in that condition. I just couldn't."

"Well, you should have called and talked to me instead of just taking it upon yourself to keep her out of school."

Paulette defended her actions. "I knew you were busy, and I didn't wanna bother you."

"Big Momma, she's my child," Kenya respectfully reminded her grandmother. "You should have consulted me. Tell her to get her lil self ready because I'm coming right now to pick her up and take her to school."

"Oh, Kenya," Paulette moaned, "can't you just let her stay here? The day's half-gone."

Kenya shook her head. "No, I can't do that. Janae has to learn that she can't always pick and choose what she does and doesn't wanna do."

Paulette further objected, "But, Kenya . . ."

Kenya stated adamantly, "No buts, Big Momma. I'll see you in a few minutes."

Paulette was still holding the telephone to her ear when she heard a gentle click. "Well, okay then," she replied into the lifeless receiver. Placing the phone back into its cradle, she warned the scared little tot beside her about her mother's upcoming arrival. "Nae, your Momma's a little upset with us 'cause I didn't take you to school. She's coming to pick you up and take you."

Throwing her arms around her great grandmother, Janae cried, "But I don't wanna go, Big Momma."

Paulette returned the child's embrace, gently patting her back as she spoke. "I know, baby, but your Momma's right. You have to go to school if you're not sick. It's the law. I was wrong to keep you out without her permission. Did you know that parents can go to jail for not sending their children to school for no good reason?"

Paulette heard a muffled, "No."

"Well, we don't want your Momma to get in trouble, do we?"

Janae answered, "No." She half-wished that she'd faked a stomachache or something in order to have her wish granted, but she knew better than to do that. Lying was on the list of no-no's in her family's house. The time or two she and Kourtnie had been found guilty of it, they had been severely punished—no television, telephone, or video games for a week or two had seemed like life sentences to them.

"No, we don't. So here's what I want you to do. Com'ere." Removing the little girl's arms from around her, Paulette gently pulled Janae back against the cushions of her recently upholstered orange floral thirty-year-old settee. Reaching inside the pocket of her sweater, she pulled out a soft white handkerchief with pink-and-red embroidered flowers amidst bright green leaves. "Here, take this. Wipe your face and blow your nose."

Janae did as she was instructed.

Paulette said, "When your momma gets here, tell her what's bothering you. She'll help you work it out. Okay?"

Janae whispered, "Okay." Remembering what her parents had taught her and her sister about how to address their elders, she said, "Yes, ma'am."

Paulette smiled as she gave Janae a squeeze. "That's my big girl."

Paulette said a silent prayer thanking God that she'd finally been able to soothe her great granddaughter's nerves.

Thirty-year-old Zaire Dickinson sat at the desk of her plush suburban Atlanta fashion design office, sipping her cup of chocolate mocha cappuccino. The hot steam warmed her nose every time she lifted the sweet creamy delicious liquid to her mouth.

Her assistant, Nicolette Williams, downed a Diet Sprite as they listened to the sweet jazzy sounds of Kenny G's "Passages."

Casting a beautiful smile at Zaire, Nicolette commented warmly, "I love this one. It's a great piece for the fashion show this Saturday. What d'you think?"

Zaire was in her own little world, anxiously contemplating the telephone call she'd decided to make today. She hoped she could actually go through with it this time. In the past, she had picked up the phone only to put it back down for fear that she would be rejected again. She sorely missed her family. Eleven years of not seeing or talking to them had left an enormous hole in her heart. If only she'd had the courage to stay when tragedy had struck their family a second time, perhaps things would be different.

Nicolette was concerned about her friend. This morning, Zaire lacked her usual cheery disposition. When Zaire simply bestowed a bewildered look her way, Nicolette said, "The music—do you like it?"

Zaire's expression remained serious. "Yes, I love it. What about the scenario for the stage? Did we get the palm trees for the beachwear line?"

Nicolette nodded. "Yes, they came last Friday. Everything's all set. So this music's okay for beachwear?"

"Yeah, sure."

"Okay. Anything else?"

Zaire smiled, her dimples sinking deep into her polished toffee complexion. "No, that's it."

"All righty, then. I'm right outside the door if you need me."

"Thanks." As an afterthought, Zaire added, "Oh, Nicolette, will you ask Jenny to please hold my calls?"

"Sure," Nicolette cheerily answered as she closed the door behind her.

Zaire's brow wrinkled with anxiety. Whirling her black leather high-back chair around to face the tall, black bookcase, she leaned forward and reached for a silver-plated, five-by-seven picture frame. Smiling gently, she lightly brushed her fingertips across the matte finish glass where underneath lay a photo of her with two of the most precious children on earth.

She and her twelve-year-old twins, Shawn and Amili, had just recently taken a family portrait. Zaire felt it was time for her youngsters to meet their extended family. When she had paid her sister and grandmother an unexpected visit eleven years ago, the twins were only five months old. However, Zaire had not taken them along with her. Kenya and Paulette were not even aware that she had children. Zaire had planned to tell them during her visit, though, which went totally sour when Kenya refused to see her or speak to her. To make matters worse, before she could tell her grandmother about Shawn and Amili, Paulette had a relapse right before her very eyes, which had sent Zaire running again.

Although it hurt her deeply, Zaire understood why Kenya hated her. They were only ten years old when the worst tragedy imaginable had struck their family. Ever since that terrible day, she found herself, against her will, periodically replaying the catastrophe over and over in her head. It had happened on Thanksgiving, Zaire's favorite holiday. Their entire family, including aunts, uncles, cousins, and grandparents, always got together for the special occasion. That year, the dinner had been at Kenya and Zaire's house. Their father said the blessing. Then they ate, and everyone told what they were most thankful for. Afterward, they played games and ate some more.

Later that evening, she and Kenya had gone to spend the night at their grandmother's house with some of their cousins. The next thing Zaire remembered was them all being awakened in the middle of the night and hearing a lot of commotion and crying. Various family members removed their cousins from the room. One aunt remained behind and, as delicately as she could, told them that their mother and father were gone. By overhearing their relatives talking and whispering among themselves, Zaire and Kenya learned a few days later that their father had shot their mother, and then himself. To this day, Zaire didn't understand what had gone wrong, for she had never once seen or heard her parents argue.

Although Paulette was a widow, she had taken in her daughter and son-in-law's children and raised them as her own. For the next eight years, Kenya and Zaire lived and grew up together, and planned their future in connection with the other. They made a pact to always be there for each other no matter what. However, when their grandmother developed a brain tumor during their senior year in high school, the thought of losing someone else she loved overwhelmed Zaire, and she left town with her boyfriend. She had thought she was in love. It didn't take long for her to realize that she had left with him for all the wrong reasons. The next thing she knew, she was pregnant and alone in a huge and unfamiliar city.

She didn't know what kind of reception she'd receive this time, but she was willing to take a chance.

It was almost one o'clock when Kenya returned home. She was so upset at her grandmother that she had no idea how she would be able to concentrate on the tapes now. She decided to take a bathroom break before she got started, hoping she'd be able to work without further interruptions until the girls got home from school.

The telephone rang as she made her way back through the bedroom. She wondered who it could be. This was one of those days when she didn't need to get stuck on the telephone with anyone. She had been meaning to get a caller ID unit for the bedroom. Fearing that it might be the school calling about Janae, Kenya decided to answer the call without prior knowledge of who was on the other end.

"Hello." Kenya's emotions were racing as she prayed that Janae was all right.

The tranquil voice on the other end spoke. "Hello. Kenya?"

The voice had a vague familiarity to it, but Kenya couldn't recall who it might be. "Yes, this is Kenya," she answered, curiosity lacing her response.

The caller knew no other approach than to just be straightforward. "Kenya, this is Zaire."

Kenya came close to going into shock. All she could do was plop down onto the bed with the receiver still to her ear.

"Kenya, are you there? It's Zaire."

Kenya attempted to dam up her emotions, but she couldn't. Suddenly, all the pain and anguish of the past eleven years came bubbling forth like the waters of a mighty flood. Finally able to speak, she demanded in a tone full of venom, "What do you want?"

Zaire answered hopefully, "I just thought it was time for us to get back together. Yesterday was Momma and Daddy's wedding anniversary, and—"

Kenya abruptly interjected, "Their anniversary has been coming around every year that you've been gone, and all of a sudden, you want us to be a family again?"

Zaire came close to reminding her sister that she had refused to see her or talk to her when she'd visited eleven years ago and had also failed to respond to any of the cards and letters she'd sent her over the years. Instead, she replied regretfully, "Kenya, I know you're angry with me, and you have every right to be. I shouldn't have walked out on you and Big Momma the way I did when she got sick, but I was so scared."

In a tone edged with contempt, Kenya pronounced, "I was scared too, but I didn't walk away like you. And now that *you* think it's a good time for us to get back together, I'm supposed to just welcome you back with open arms? Well, you're too late! I don't wanna hear it. Don't call here again." Without uttering another word, she slammed the phone back onto the receiver.

Kenya felt as though her world had come to an abrupt standstill. The pounding in her chest felt like someone was trying to stomp the life from her. Falling back onto the bed, she envisioned her and Zaire when they were just ten years old. Zaire had promised to help take care of their grandmother after their parents' tragic deaths. Their little hearts had ached every day for their parents, but through it all, they had grown closer than two peas in a pod. However, when Paulette was diagnosed with a brain tumor, Zaire had flown the coop. Even when she showed up a year later, right away she disappeared again. Thankfully, the growth was treatable, and their grandmother had recovered after a couple of years.

When Zaire had shown up out of the blue, Paulette had been totally ecstatic about her return. Kenya, however, was not the least bit impressed. Throughout the years, the cards and letters Zaire sent also made no impression upon Kenya's heart; she had burned every single one without even opening them.

Kenya had looked up to her sister. Zaire had been everything she wanted to be. They had planned their future lives together. Then, when Paulette had gotten sick, Zaire had left Kenya to hold their grandmother's bedside vigils without her. While Zaire was off enjoying herself, Kenya was worrying day and night about whether Paulette would live or die. Zaire was nothing but a coward, and every ounce of love and respect Kenya had had for her had walked out the door with her when she abandoned their family.

2

Despite the painful memories that had resurfaced, Kenya emerged from the bed, but she couldn't sit down and concentrate on the tapes. When most people were troubled by something, they lost their energy and stamina. She was quite the opposite; she became very industrious. She got into one of her cleaning frenzies and tidied up the house. Afterwards, she cooked a hearty meal of salmon patties, homemade biscuits, coleslaw, and banana pudding—the kind of pudding her grandmother used to make where you cooked the creamy filling on the stove and topped the dessert with real whipped topping made from egg whites.

"Hey, Momma," ten-year-old Kourtnie announced cheerfully as she entered the kitchen where her mother was almost done preparing supper.

Without turning her attention away from the salmon patties sizzling away in the black iron skillet, Kenya replied, "Hey, sweetie. How was your day?"

"Fine," her daughter answered. "How was yours?"

After removing the last two patties from the hot oil and placing them on the paper-toweled baking sheet with the others, Kenya looked at Kourtnie. She had all the family she needed right here. Zaire could just crawl back under whatever rock she had come from for all she cared. "My day was fine," she lied. "Thanks for asking. You got homework?"

Kourtnie answered, "Just a few math problems I didn't finish at school."

"Need some help?"

"No, I can do 'em."

Kenya smiled, relieved that she wouldn't have to spend most of the night with her head in her daughter's math book, trying to assist her. "Where's Janae?"

"In her room. She told me on the bus she had a bad day, but she wouldn't tell me what happened."

Kourtnie's answer was as Kenya had expected, considering the circumstances earlier in the day. Not coming to greet her mother after school was a sure sign that Janae was still in a bad mood.

Kenya showed no emotion as she responded, "She'll be okay. I'll talk to her. Your Daddy'll be home in a bit. Go finish your homework while I talk to Janae."

"Yes, ma'am."

Kenya found her youngest child in her room, playing with her stuffed animals. She joined Janae on top of the plush ladybug comforter.

"How was your day?"

Not looking up from her stuffed friends, Janae answered, "Okay."

Janae was a tough cookie. However, Kenya was a bit concerned. "So after I talked to Mrs. Evans and left, everything was fine?"

Janae was still a little miffed at her mother for taking her to school, but she realized she had to be careful about showing it. Looking up momentarily with big, brown glassy eyes, she replied, "Yes, ma'am."

Kenya grinned, leaned over, and planted a kiss on Janae's left cheek. "Good. Daddy should be home soon. Do you want a snack before supper?"

Janae shook her head. Remembering to mind her manners, she responded, "No, thank you."

"Okay. You can play a few more minutes. Then you have to wash up for supper." Kenya's smile was thoughtful. In an effort to cheer up her young daughter, she added, "We're having your favorite—salmon patties."

Although her nostrils had already taken in the heavenly aroma as she and her sister had walked through the door, at the mention of her favorite food, Janae grinned. "Did you make biscuits, too?" She loved her mother's salmon patties slathered with mustard and slapped between her melt-in-your-mouth biscuits.

Kenya smiled. "Yes, they're in the oven." Rising, she added, "I'll see you later."

"Yes, ma'am," Janae muttered as she went back to playing.

As soon as Trent got home from work, he knew something was wrong. The house was spotless, and supper consisted of more than the usual light meal they had during the week. He supposed cleaning and cooking was Kenya's way of destressing herself.

Kenya immediately cornered him in their bedroom. "Guess what Big Momma and *your* daughter did today."

Attempting to lighten her mood, her husband asked teasingly, "Which daughter?"

Frustrated, Kenya began, "Which . . ." Then letting out a heavy sigh, she said, with just enough seriousness that he'd know she was not in the mood for his wisecracks, "You know which one—Janae. Who else? You know how she has Big Momma eating out of the palm of her little narrow hand."

Pulling on a navy blue T-shirt, Trent apologized after sensing his wife's seriousness. "Sorry. I was just playing." However, against his better judgement, he graciously added, "Loosen up."

Why was he always telling her to loosen up? Truancy was a serious matter. Kenya eyed her husband. His boyish face made him appear much younger than his thirty-two years. His flawless coffee complexion and low-cut head of hair made him look as though he was barely out of his teens. He was nice looking. Many times, stares from young girls in public had made her put a few of them back in their proper place.

Trent pulled his shirt down around his waist as he asked, "What did they do?"

Kenya plopped down onto the black wrought iron queen-size bed, which was covered with a red-and-white floral quilted bedding ensemble. She looked up at her husband as she relayed to him what had transpired.

Before he could stop it, Trent let out a snicker. Paulette and Janae were always doing something and getting caught smack dab in the middle of it. One would think they'd have learned how to cover their tracks by now. He reflected back to the time when Kourtnie was Janae's age. Something had happened at school, and the teacher had informed the students that the entire class would be punished as a result. Kourtnie was upset because she had not been guilty of the mischievous act and, therefore, did not want to be punished for something she hadn't done. He and Kenya had tried to explain to her that sometimes in life the innocent were punished along with the one committing the wrongdoing if it wasn't known who the guilty party was.

Kourtnie could not accept their explanation. When she told Paulette what her teacher was going to do, Paulette had written the teacher a note bluntly instructing her not to be punishing her great grandchild for something she didn't do. However, he and Kenya knew nothing of the letter until Kourtnie's teacher had called Kenya in reference to it. Of course, Kenya had been agitated with their daughter and her grandmother, just as she was now.

Shocked and upset that Trent found the situation amusing, Kenya's eyes widened as she expressed rather sternly, "Trent, it's not funny. You think playing hooky is funny? Not to mention I had to leave *my* work, go pick her up, and take her to school. If it happens again, I'll call you at the pharmacy and let *you* be the one to have to get off work to take her."

The act itself was not humorous in the least. It just tickled Trent when he pictured Paulette and Janae getting caught. He would have given anything to have been a fly on Paulette's wall and to have seen the look on their faces when they realized they were in deep trouble.

Sitting down beside his wife, Trent put his arm around Kenya and pulled her close. "I'm sorry. You're right. This is serious, but I'm sure Big Momma didn't mean any harm. You know how she is when it comes to the kids."

Kenya was quick to say, "Yeah, I know, and that's the problem. She's gotta stop doing stuff like that. I know she loves them, but I don't want them spoiled. They've got to learn how to make it in the real world. Her petting and pampering them isn't going to help."

Trent agreed, "I know. You're right. You want me to talk to her?" he kindly offered.

"I already did. 'Course it never seems to do any good. Let's just drop it for now. I just had to vent."

Kenya thought about mentioning Zaire's phone call to Trent but changed her mind. He already knew they had issues. Kenya had made it unquestionably clear to her sister that she had no desire to talk to her. Since she thought Zaire would make no further effort to contact her, there was no need to mention the call to Trent.

*   *   *

Paulette gazed down at the fingernails of her right hand while holding the telephone to her ear with her left. "You still mad at me?" Her tone was cordial.

Having just put the girls on their school bus, Kenya scurried about with the cordless phone to her ear in an effort to tidy up the kitchen before starting on her transcription tapes. Having to break away from her work the day before had put her behind. She had missed the helping hand Trent always gave her in the mornings. He was a pharmacist at a nearby pharmacy, and today he had had to arrive earlier than usual for a meeting.

Yes, she was still a little agitated at her grandmother, but she never could stay mad at her for too long. "Big Momma, you have to be firm with Janae. You give her an inch, she'll take a foot. You were very strict with me—and Zaire," she added, without even wanting to mention her sister's name, "when we were growing up."

Paulette felt a slight headache coming on but attempted to ignore it. She readily admitted, "Yeah, but times were different then. I couldn't let y'all run wild like other kids. You'd lost both your parents, and I was trying to do the best job I could to raise you the way I thought your momma and daddy would've."

Kenya politely interjected, "Exactly, Big Momma. So you should understand how I feel. I'm trying to do the same thing for my kids."

"I know," Paulette agreed, "but Janae's just a baby. I know I was wrong for keeping her out of school without your permission, but I felt so bad for her."

Kenya loved what a compassionate soul her grandmother was, which was why the nursing profession had been the perfect field for Paulette. She responded with a chuckle that warmed her heart. "You're just a big ol' soft, squishy marshmallow."

Paulette tried not to interfere with how Kenya and Trent raised the girls. Kenya was a tough disciplinarian, but Paulette realized that it was she who had instilled that attitude in her granddaughter, since it was how she had reared Kenya and Zaire. She did not doubt that Kenya wanted to bring her children up right, to be God-fearing. However, she felt Kenya was way too rigid, not just with her own children, but with everyone and especially when it came to her sister.

Paulette laughed as she wholeheartedly agreed, "Yeah, I am a marshmallow when it comes to my babies."

Kenya stated earnestly, "I know you love them, and you worry about them just like I do. You raised me and Zaire the best way you could. Now you have to let me raise my kids the best way I can. Okay?"

Paulette concurred, "You're right. From now on, I'll keep my mouth shut."

Grinning, Kenya rolled her eyes heavenward as she respectfully replied, "No, you won't, but I'll remind you of this conversation later when the time comes."

The two women laughed heartily and called a truce.

Paulette responded facetiously, "I'm sure you will, smarty." She had hoped that during the course of their conversation Kenya would tell her about Zaire's call yesterday. She wished they would make amends. Zaire wanted to, but Kenya was still living in the past.

Probing delicately, Paulette asked soberly, "Kenya, is there anything else you wanna talk to me about?"

Right away, Kenya sensed that her grandmother knew about Zaire's call. "No. Why?"

Paulette saw no need to further beat around the bush. "I know Zaire called you yesterday. She called me last night. She really wants the two of you to get together and talk. She wants to see us. She lives in Atlanta now. I'm gonna meet her at Red Lobster in Douglasville this Sunday after church. Kenya, she's been gone eleven years. I didn't teach y'all to hold grudges." Attempting not to sound preachy, she added practically, "You know what the Bible says about forgiveness. Won't you come with me?"

Choking back her emotions, Kenya stated smoothly, "No, Big Momma, I'm not going. Please don't pressure me on this."

"Kenya, you can't run away from your problems forever. You're always talking about how your girls need to face their fears. What about you? When are you gonna face yours?"

Kenya wasn't afraid to talk to Zaire; she simply had no desire to do so. Zaire was the one who had walked out on them during their time of need—not once, but twice. No amount of talking or anything else would erase what she'd done.

Paulette tapped gently on the hospital room door and entered after being told to come in. Her smile broadened as she pushed the wheelchair toward the bed where the new mother and baby were waiting. As a retired nurse, she loved volunteering her time and services at the hospital. She was quick to tell everyone that keeping active in her church and community kept her from rusting away at home.

"Good morning, Mrs. Dupree." Paulette's cheerful voice echoed through the air. She also acknowledged the woman's husband, who stood nearby. "Mr. Dupree, good morning."

The young couple smiled as they greeted the kindhearted woman, whom they'd both fallen in love with in just the short while they'd known her.

Paulette stated jovially, "So you and little Amelia get to go home today. Are you excited?"

The woman grinned uneasily. "Yes. A little nervous, too."

The man carefully removed the sleeping baby from his wife's arms while Paulette assisted her to the wheelchair. Paulette assured her, "That's a natural feeling for first-time parents. You and Mr. Dupree will do a fine job. Stop fretting."

After securing the newborn into the carrier car seat, Mr. Dupree grabbed the carrier by the handle with one hand and his wife's bag in the other, and followed them out the room to the elevator. They chatted away on the ride down to the first floor.

Paulette and Mrs. Dupree waited under the awning as a light mist of rain began to descend while the man took the baby and his wife's overnight bag with him to their car. When he drove up, Paulette pushed the chair a little closer to the vehicle. Before he helped his wife into the car, Paulette gave the couple a warm hug. They waved one last time before the car pulled away.

Paulette felt a great sense of fulfillment. Her mind drifted back in time thirty years to the day her daughter and son-in-law had become parents to twin girls. Outside of the day Paulette had given birth herself, it had been the happiest day of her life. Angelique and Reginald had been happy, it seemed. Paulette, too often wondered what had gone wrong. Neither of them had ever confided to her about any problems they may have been experiencing. Though the *incident*, as everyone discreetly referred to it, had happened twenty years ago, sometimes it still felt like it was yesterday.

To this day, she still could not believe that Reginald had put an end to her daughter's life and then taken his own. She always expected to wake up from this terrible nightmare any moment, yet never did. Suddenly, Paulette began to feel lightheaded. She quickly grabbed hold of the railing and lowered her body slowly to the bench under the canopy. She hadn't had a dizzy spell strike her in years. Concluding in her mind that it was triggered by the painful memories of the past, she redirected her attention to more pleasant thoughts as she carefully lifted herself up and made her way back inside the hospital.

3

After Sunday morning service everyone scattered about, conversing with one another and complimenting the minister on his sermon.

As Paulette shook the hand of the young preacher, just barely out of his twenties, she smiled warmly. "Pastor Humphries, I really enjoyed your sermon on endurance. And the way you drove it home with the scripture from 1 Corinthians 15:58 truly touched my heart." Grinning and shaking her head slowly from side to side, she continued, "It's so good to know when we're doing the Lord's work that it's not in vain."

A woman who resembled Paulette reached out and grabbed the minister's hand in both of hers and began shaking it up and down like she was pumping water at a well. "Yes, you did a good job," she enthused. "You keep it up."

The dark-skinned, handsome young man smiled gently, revealing the most beautiful pearly whites the two women had ever seen. The entire congregation was extremely proud of young Jaleel, because he was a good example for not only the younger ones but all those in the congregation.

"Thank you, sisters. I'm always nervous before I give a sermon, but when I see your and the other members' faces looking back at me, it helps alleviate my anxieties. And of course, relying on our heavenly Father helps tremendously."

The women smiled with pride. Jaleel was well educated and expressed himself extremely well, but he had a very humble spirit.

Paulette declared, "Well, relying on God is the right thing to do, isn't it, Dorothy Mae?"

Still holding on to Jaleel's hand, Paulette's sister of seventy years agreed, "It sure is."

Not wanting to take up all of the pastor's time, the two women politely excused themselves. As they walked toward the other side of the church, Janae ran to greet them.

Wrapping her short arms as far around her great grandmother's waist as she could, she squealed excitedly, "Big Momma!"

Leaning down, Paulette returned the child's loving embrace. She wouldn't mind staying encased in her great granddaughter's little soft brown arms for the rest of her life. "Hey, precious. You doing okay?"

"Yes, ma'am." Not forgetting her great-great-aunt, Janae removed her arms and hugged Dorothy. "Hey, Aunt Dorothy Mae."

Dorothy exclaimed, "Hey, sweetness. It's good to see you. How you doing?"

Janae awarded Dorothy a big wide grin. "I'm fine."

Kenya and Kourtnie appeared.

Kourtnie greeted her elderly relatives pleasantly and hugged them both.

"My, my," Dorothy cried out, "you girls are getting so big. Kourtnie, how old are you now?"

Kourtnie laughed easily. "Ten."

"Ten," Dorothy repeated. "A few more years and you'll be a teenager."

Kourtnie grinned proudly as her mother insisted, "Don't remind me."

They chuckled and talked a few minutes more.

Finally, Dorothy said, "I better be going. I'll talk to y'all later."

They bade Dorothy farewell and made their way to the opposite side of the church toward the front exit.

Once outside, Kenya instructed her youngsters to go to the car where their father was waiting. Then she queried her grandmother, "You're still gonna meet her?"

"Yes, I am," Paulette firmly responded.

Kenya was quick to express her discontent. "I can't believe you're gonna see her."

"She wants to see you, too," Paulette politely reminded her granddaughter.

"Big Momma, I already told you I'm not going."

"Well, that's your decision, and I've already told you I'm going.

I'll talk to you later." Paulette left Kenya standing there and walked toward her car.

How could her grandmother do this to her? Zaire was the one who had abandoned Big Momma during her illness, while Kenya had stayed by her side. Zaire couldn't stick around when the going got tough. Now she wanted to just waltz back into their lives as though the past had never happened. What stronger bond was there than that of family? Wasn't blood thicker than water? Not if you were Zaire.

4

Paulette couldn't believe she was sitting an arm's length away from the grandchild she hadn't seen or spoken to in eleven years. As she stared into Zaire's cocoa-colored eyes surrounded by nut-brown skin, Paulette simply drank in her presence. This was her other baby. Kenya and Zaire had come from her daughter's womb, but in raising and caring for them, Paulette felt as though she'd given birth to them herself.

"Big Momma, thank you so much for coming. You look great," Zaire exclaimed over dessert at Douglasville's Red Lobster. Awarding her grandmother a dimpled smile, she enthused, "It's hard to believe you're eighty-one. You look so much younger." As she eyed her grandmother longingly, it was as though Zaire's mother had been resurrected and was sitting across from her.

Paulette reached across the table and affectionately squeezed her granddaughter's hand. "Well, look at you with your hair all swooped up on top of your head looking all pretty. I can't believe you're actually here." She tenderly touched Zaire's right cheek with her left hand. "God has answered my prayers." Her smile broadened. "He may not come when you want Him, but He's always right on time."

Zaire still didn't understand that saying although she'd grown up hearing it on a regular basis. How could somebody be on time for you if they didn't come when you wanted them? She was thirty years old, yet it made no sense whatsoever to her. It didn't matter, though. She wasn't even sure anymore if God existed. If He did, where was He twenty years ago when her mother was murdered by her father, after which time he had committed suicide? The God she had been brought up to believe in would not have allowed something so terrible to happen and especially not at a little innocent child's favorite time of year. And then eight years later, the same God had struck her grandmother with a brain tumor. The celebration she held so dear no longer had any meaning for her, for with it came too many painful memories. After the death of her parents, her relatives had attempted to carry on their family tradition; however, it was never the same. Zaire's days of giving thanks were over.

In an effort to pull herself from her discouraging thoughts, Zaire squirmed excitedly in her seat. "You told me on the phone that I have two nieces. Do you have any pictures? Do you have some of Kenya and her husband—what's his name—Trent?"

Paulette smiled as she proudly responded, "Yes, I have some pictures. And yes, Kenya's husband's name is Trent." She opened up her pocketbook on the seat beside her and pulled out her miniphoto album. She opened it to a family portrait she had had taken with the foursome just last summer. "Here's one of all of us taken last year. There's some older ones in there too you can look at."

Passing the album to Zaire, Paulette watched as her long-lost granddaughter happily scanned each and every photo, stopping every now and then to ask questions concerning the pictures.

Zaire exclaimed, "The girls are beautiful—just like Kenya, but they favor Trent, too." She hated to part with the album, especially since Kenya obviously still wanted nothing to do with her. When she had seen her grandmother enter the restaurant alone, her heart had dropped. She closed the album and hesitantly returned it to her grandmother.

Sensing that Zaire was having difficulty parting with the pictures, Paulette carefully removed the family portrait from the album and offered it to her.

Surprised, Zaire's hand slowly went for the picture as she questioned, "You're giving this to me?"

"Yes, it's yours."

With all her heart, Zaire wanted the picture but didn't feel right depriving her grandmother of it. "No, Big Momma, I can't. It's yours." She offered it back to Paulette.

Paulette refused to take the picture. "You keep it. I want you to have it. I have an eight by ten at home on my wall. I can get another wallet-size one made. Keep it."

An appreciative grin spread over the width of Zaire's oval-shaped face. "Thank you."

"You're welcome, baby."

As the two women sat there talking, their hearts were bubbling over with an indescribable sensation.

As soon as Trent and the girls walked through the door from their ice cream outing, he noticed the aroma of household cleaning products that filled the air—a sure sign that Kenya was upset about something. They followed the noise coming from the kitchen and found Kenya on her knees scrubbing the inside of the oven.

Kourtnie happily announced, "Momma, we brought you some ice cream."

Janae added, "It's your favorite—strawberry cheesecake."

Without ceasing her task, Kenya said, "Thank you. Will you put it in the freezer for me?"

"Yes, ma'am," Kourtnie responded as she went over to the refrigerator and placed the cup in the freezer compartment.

Trent told his daughters, "You two need to go wash off. You're all sticky."

The girls did as they were told.

Trent's brow creased with worry. Slowly, he made his way toward his wife. "Are you okay?"

With her head inside the oven, Kenya said, "Yeah."

"Are you sure?"

"Yes, I'm sure."

"Kenya, you've been acting strange ever since Monday when Big Momma didn't take Janae to school. Whenever something's bothering you, you always get into a cleaning frenzy. Now I know you can't still be upset about that. I'm sensing something else is on your mind. What is it? Let's talk."

Kenya finally came up for air and dipped her gloved hands in the sink full of lukewarm and now dingy water. Pulling the stopper from the sink, she allowed the water to drain. Afterwards, she squirted a small amount of dishwashing liquid onto a sponge, wiped it over the inside of the sink, and rinsed the sink clean. Tearing off two paper towels from the holder on the counter, she vigorously wiped her gloved hands, dropped the damp towels into the trash bin, removed the gloves, and placed them on the counter. "Talk about what? I told you I'm fine."

The look Trent gave her was laden with agitation. They were now standing face-to-face as he tenderly gripped her hands in his and lifted them up between their chests. He gazed into her deep brown eyes as the love he felt for her surged through his heart. "I know you. We've been married eleven years. I know you like I know the back of my hand." He shook his head. "Don't tell me you're fine when I know you're not."

Kenya's heart began to race. She loved Trent and knew with every fiber of her being that he loved her as he had just so reverently reaffirmed. Nevertheless, she didn't care to discuss her sister with him. Her words tumbled from her lips. "I'm fine."

Trent dropped his head and let out a quick, soft sigh, not out of anger but sheer disappointment that Kenya would not confide in him. They were supposed to be partners, best friends. Sometimes she just clammed up and wouldn't talk to him. He hated it when she did that.

Gently pulling her hands from his, Kenya pecked Trent's cheek and walked away, leaving him alone with his thoughts.

Zaire downed the last of her key lime pie. "Mmmm, that was good." It had been scrumptious, but nobody could cook like her grandmother. She could almost smell the luscious odors that she remembered from her childhood of her grandmother's home cooking. She was reminded of the nice little comfortable home she and Kenya grew up in. "Do you still have the weeping willow tree in the front yard? Please tell me you do. Oh, I loved that tree."

Paulette laughed hysterically at her granddaughter's childlike enthusiasm. Zaire had always been a free-spirited, outgoing creature. "Yes, I still have my weeping willow tree."

Kenya solemnly mused, "I think the weeping willow is the most beautiful tree on the face of the earth. I love the way the branches droop down. And the leaves—so thin and narrow with just a hint of white."

Zaire's heartfelt appreciation for God's creation deeply touched Paulette. When she was young, Zaire had regularly expressed admiration regarding the beautiful things the Creator had brought into existence. She had such a deep spiritual conviction.

Paulette encouraged, "Tell me some more about your fashion design business."

"Well, I just relocated to Atlanta in January, and my business is really doing well. My line is women's everyday and evening wear. My children's line will be out this summer."

Paulette beamed. "I'm so proud of you. Sounds like you're doing good. The Lord has truly blessed you. I can't wait to tell Kenya about our visit."

Zaire simply smiled. How her heart craved the love her sister once poured over her like sweet maple syrup over a stack of their grandmother's delicious homemade pancakes. "I can understand why she doesn't want to see me. I shouldn't have left." Her mood suddenly turned somber as she stressed with heartfelt remorse, "Big Momma, I'm so sorry for walking out on you at a time when you needed me the most. I was so scared of losing you like Momma and Daddy. I just couldn't take seeing you suffer. I—"

"I know, baby." Paulette gave Zaire a sympathetic look. "You told me in your letters, and I understand. Don't make yourself suffer anymore than you already have by continuing to relive it. As for Kenya, she's still hanging on to the past. Give her some time. She'll come around."

Zaire's heart still felt heavy. She blinked back tears that felt like the mighty waters about to erupt from a thundercloud. "Big Momma, I have something to tell you, and I don't know quite how to put it except to just say it. When I left home and went to New York with Malcolm, I was four weeks pregnant, but I didn't know it at the time. I found out when we got to New York."

Paulette's entire body felt as though it had been run over by a Mack truck. She did not want to believe what she'd just heard. For the first time ever in her eighty-one years, she was at a complete loss for words.

Zaire mistook her grandmother's silence for downright disappointment and disapproval. She felt Paulette about to give her the hard lecture she hadn't been able to issue eleven years earlier.

5

Paulette remained silent as Zaire finished her story. Paulette had never liked Malcolm Powers. Strike one was that neither he nor his family went to church. She gave him two strikes the day he had the nerve to tell her that he didn't believe in marriage and felt a man and woman should first live together to see if they were compatible. The moment those wicked words spilled from his lips, she had almost thrown him out of her house. The more she expressed her condemnation of him, the more in love with him Zaire seemed to be.

Zaire explained, "Malcolm said we could both go to school—me up until I had the baby—and he'd get a job. When I told him I was pregnant, he said he wanted us to get married. He promised me the moon, the sky, and the stars, and I believed him. I believed every word he said because I loved him, and I thought he loved me. A couple of months went by, and he never mentioned marriage again. Every time I brought it up, he got angry. I wanted us to be a real family, not just living together. One day when I asked him when we were getting married, he hit me in my face so hard that it knocked me unconscious. When I came to, all I could think about was Momma and Daddy and my baby—how I or my baby or both of us were gonna end up dead if I didn't get away from him. I packed up my stuff and left."

At last, Paulette was able to speak. The thought of her baby pregnant and all alone in a huge, unfamiliar city so far away from her home and her family made her ask, "Where'd you go?"

Zaire answered, "I found a shelter. I worked and went to school until I had the babies. Afterwards, I was able to go back to school and managed to stay until I graduated. It was hard, but I did it."

Paulette wondered, *Did she say "babies"?* She'd get back to that later. For now, she needed to know something else. "Why didn't you let me know what was happening to you? Why didn't you tell me this when you came to visit or in the cards and letters you sent?"

Zaire painfully recalled the last time she'd seen her grandmother. "I was going to tell you, but you had a relapse and had to be put in the hospital. I thought you were gonna die, and I got scared and ran again."

Paulette remembered what her granddaughter had just said from some of her letters.

Zaire went on, "So after I left, I didn't see any point in telling you, not even in the cards and letters I sent."

Paulette felt a jolt in her heart from the mental image of Zaire struggling to get on with her life. Finally, she queried, "You said *babies*. You've been pregnant more than once?" Imagining her child going through this agony more than one time caused an additional pang in her heart.

Zaire shook her head, looking as deep into her grandmother's eyes as she could. "No, I've only been pregnant once. I have twins— a boy and a girl—twelve years old. They were five months old when I came to see you. I left them with some friends in New York when I visited."

Paulette thought her heart would explode. Smiling, she reached across the table and took Zaire's hand in hers. "Are you serious? My baby has twins?"

Now Zaire was smiling, too, as the tears she'd managed to somehow hold inside now came rushing out like the rain bursting down from the sky on a dark, stormy day. "Yes, Shawn and Amili. I have pictures, too. You wanna see?"

"Do I wanna see?" Paulette teased. "Of course I do."

Zaire reached inside her purse and pulled out her wallet. After flipping to the picture taken of the twins for their family portrait, she handed the wallet to her grandmother.

Like a child's Popsicle on a sunny day in the midst of summer, Paulette's heart began to melt. "They're beautiful children." There was one thing she didn't like, though. She let out a grunt as she smiled mischievously. "Too bad they look like their ol' knucklehead daddy."

Zaire laughed heartily before expressing mournfully, "You tried to warn me about Malcolm, but I wouldn't listen. I thought I loved him. At the time, I did, but I was so young and stupid and hard-headed."

Paulette commented honestly, "You weren't stupid, and you weren't hardheaded. You were young and in love. Believe it or not, I remember what that feels like. Let's not cry over the past any-more." She smiled as she inquired, "When do I get to meet my great-grandbabies?"

"Soon, I hope. They can't wait to meet you." Reluctantly, Zaire added, "And the rest of the family." Speaking excitedly, her words gushed from her lips. "We live on the outskirts of Atlanta. It'd be great if you could come to the house one day. I can pick you up. Or if you prefer, we can come to your house. It doesn't matter—what-ever you want to do."

Paulette was beside herself with glee at her newfound knowledge that she had two more great grandchildren. "Doesn't matter to me, but I would love to see where you live so why don't we say your house?"

Her excitement caused Zaire to bounce forward a little in her seat. "Great. When?"

"Well, I take Kourtnie and Janae out every Saturday so how 'bout next Saturday?"

"Sounds good." Suddenly, Zaire thought about her sister's posi-tion and how she might not go along with all they were planning. Her enthusiasm dissipated. "There's just one problem, though."

Paulette kindly uttered, "Don't worry about your sister. I'll talk to her."

That was all Zaire needed to hear. She remembered her grand-mother being a strong woman who could move mountains. She and Kenya had discovered that when they were young, for Paulette had overcome many obstacles in providing everything they needed. It felt so good to be home again.

As soon as Kenya opened the door, Paulette voiced firmly, "Kenya, I need to talk to you about your sister."

Hoping she didn't seem disrespectful to the woman who'd raised her like a mother, Kenya held her left hand up, palm out, in front of her. "Big Momma, please don't start that again. I don't want to talk about Zaire."

Paulette suddenly felt herself switching from feeling tender and compassionate toward Kenya to rough and harsh. She was tired of this foolishness. "Don't you hold your hand up at me, Missy," she sternly warned her granddaughter.

Kenya didn't know what had gotten into her grandmother. She hadn't seen Paulette this riled up in years. She let her hand fall back down to her side as she apologized, "I'm sorry. I wasn't trying to be disrespectful, but Big Momma, I asked you not to pressure me on this."

Paulette stepped inside and closed the door just as Trent was approaching. "Who is it, baby?"

Kenya turned slightly, attempting a smile. "It's Big Momma."

Paulette and Trent greeted each other and embraced before all three headed to the living room and sat down. Kenya felt extremely uncomfortable. She didn't want Trent to know about Zaire's telephone call or the fact that she had refused to go with her grandmother to meet Zaire.

Trent said, "Big Momma, we missed you at dinner today."

Paulette apologized, "I'm sorry I couldn't make it. I had a previous engagement."

Kenya inconspicuously eyed her grandmother, her look begging her not to mention Zaire. Paulette wanted to be as discreet as she possibly could, but she had to talk to Kenya now. For the moment, she complied with her granddaughter's unspoken request.

Trent sensed some tension between the two women unlike any he had ever seen before. When Kenya suddenly asked him if he could give her and her grandmother a moment alone, he knew he had surmised correctly. Lifting himself from his seat, he kindly responded, "Sure."

Kenya decided that the quicker she allowed her grandmother to have her say, the faster she'd be done. She waited until Trent had gone before she stated, "Go ahead. Say what you gotta say."

As Paulette joyfully relayed to Kenya the afternoon she'd shared with Zaire, Kenya showed no emotion whatsoever. However, when she learned that Zaire had children, her heart began to thump inside her chest. She couldn't believe her sister had a set of twelve-year-old twins. But she still had no empathy for her sister. For what

Zaire had done to their family, she'd gotten exactly what she deserved. She never would have had to suffer had she stayed with her family. Kenya would never forgive her for walking away. She respectfully allowed her grandmother to speak and said nothing until Paulette finally stopped for air.

Kenya's tone was frigid as she stared at Paulette. "Big Momma, do you think that what you just told me is going to make me change my mind about seeing Zaire? After what she did to us—walking out like she did? Then she has the audacity to show up like we're supposed to just pick up where we left off. She shouldn't be able to just waltz back into our lives as though she's been on a week-long vacation."

Paulette stared at her granddaughter sorrowfully. "Kenya, that's not the attitude you should have. You know that's not how the Lord expects you to act. His Word tells us to be forgiving of others just as we want Him to forgive us. Have you forgotten Matthew 6:14 and 15? If we forgive each other our trespasses, God will forgive us, but if we don't forgive others, neither will He forgive us. Your sister was scared. She made a mistake. We all do. We're all imperfect and need each other's forgiveness from time to time. You're expecting perfection from an imperfect creature just like yourself and me and everybody else."

All Kenya would say was, "As I recall, Zaire made more than one mistake. She walked out on us twice. I was scared, too, but I didn't leave."

Paulette couldn't understand why she was unable to get through to Kenya. How could someone who was so loving toward everyone else be so heartless toward her own sister? It had torn her up too when Zaire left, but Paulette was an old woman who wasn't getting any younger; she wanted her family back together. How could a person hold a grudge for so long?

Paulette appealed to her granddaughter's levelheadedness. "Kenya, our time on this earth is short. We never know from one minute to the next what might happen. I'm not condoning what Zaire did, but you've got to put it behind you so you can move on. You've got to make peace with her while you still can."

This time, Kenya said nothing.

Paulette continued, "Zaire wants us to get together. I thought this Saturday when I have the girls will be a good time."

Kenya's eyes grew huge as she vehemently responded, "No,

you're not taking Kourtnie and Janae to see her. I don't want them anywhere near her."

Paulette objected, "But Kenya, she's their aunt, and her children are their cousins. You're actually refusing to let them see each other because your heart's so full of hatred? Regardless of what Zaire did, you need to let go of the past. Otherwise, how will your heart ever heal? Think about it. Won't it be nice for us all—you, Trent, the girls, and me—to go to Zaire's this weekend and spend some time together?"

Kenya shook her head adamantly. "That's not going to happen. You go if you want to, but keep us out of it." She rose and walked away, leaving her grandmother alone.

Later the same evening, Trent found Kenya scrubbing the bathtub. She had just cleaned it yesterday. Something was obviously causing her some tension. As a pharmacist, he filled prescriptions almost every day for some type of antidepressant, high blood pressure medication, or other stress-related problem. Everyone had their way of handling life's problems. Whatever was bothering his wife, she was trying to deal with it herself and would not allow him to help her.

He sat on the opposite end of the tub. "Can we talk?"

Kenya didn't respond but just kept right on cleaning the tub.

Trent carefully placed his hand on the arm she was scrubbing with in order to get her to discontinue her motions. Kenya stopped but didn't speak or look at him.

His voice was tenderly compassionate. "I don't know exactly what's going on, but it's obvious that something's upsetting you. Let's talk about it. Maybe I can help."

Without looking at her husband, Kenya replied in a tone that was laced with acridness, "It's a family matter. You can't help."

Trent was somewhat offended but objected as delicately as he could. "The last time I checked, I was family. All week long, you haven't been yourself. At first, I thought you were just still upset about Big Momma not taking Janae to school, but I know now it's more than that. I'm not going to pressure you anymore to talk to me about something you don't want to discuss with me, but if you change your mind, let me know."

With that said, Trent stood and walked away. Kenya returned to her scrubbing.

6

The next afternoon, Trent stopped by Paulette's on his way home from work. He had decided that since he couldn't get any answers from Kenya, he'd see what information he could obtain from her grandmother.

"She's hiding something from me. I know it." He looked sorrowfully at Paulette. "Big Momma, what is it? What did the two of you talk about last night when you stopped by?"

The expression on Paulette's face was thoughtful. As much as she wanted to tell him, she felt that it was her granddaughter's place to talk to her husband about the matter. "Trent, you need to talk to Kenya."

The poor man looked so distressed as he spoke. "I've tried. She refuses to talk to me."

Paulette suddenly wondered—since she couldn't get her granddaughter to change her mind about seeing Zaire, perhaps Trent could. Should she tell him? Kenya would probably be very angry at her if she did. Against her better judgment, she said, "Last week, Kenya's sister, Zaire, called her. They haven't seen or talked to each other in years. The last time Zaire was here was eleven years ago shortly before you and Kenya got married."

Trent watched Paulette in stony silence as she spoke. He couldn't believe Kenya had not shared this exciting bit of news with him. This was good. Here was the opportunity for them to reunite.

Paulette continued, "Zaire lives near Atlanta now and wants to see Kenya, but Kenya refuses."

A veil of despondency covered Trent's face. "Are you serious?"

Paulette nodded. "Yes. Just like eleven years ago when Zaire showed up, Kenya still refuses to see her."

Trent didn't understand. He knew how hurt Kenya was when Zaire left, but he couldn't imagine his wife allowing something that happened when they were teenagers to continue to widen the gap between them.

Paulette went on. "Yesterday I met Zaire at a restaurant in Douglasville where we had lunch." She filled Trent in on the details of Zaire's past. When she was finished, she said, "Anyway, Zaire wants us all to get together, and I was hoping this Saturday we could go to her house."

Trent smiled. "That's great. I'll talk to Kenya. Maybe I can get her to change her mind."

Paulette was glad she'd told Trent. She felt very optimistic that he could have some positive influence on her granddaughter.

Kenya was furious at her grandmother. As she pulled the covers back on the bed, she expressed to Trent as he stood, simply observing her reaction, "Big Momma had no right to tell you anything. If I'd wanted you to know, I would've told you myself. She has such a big mouth."

Trent attempted to calm his wife. "Kenya, don't say that about your grandmother. If you want to be angry at someone, be mad at me. I'm the one who went to her. I could tell she didn't want to tell me."

Kenya jumped into bed and turned off the bedside lamp, leaving her husband still standing beside the bed in the dark. "Yeah, right," she mumbled. "If she was having such a hard time telling you, she never would've said anything. If either of you think you're going to get me to change my mind, then you're both sadly mistaken."

Trent eased into bed and snuggled up beside Kenya, gently placing his arm around her. He whispered in her ear, "Why are you so angry? Zaire's your sister."

Suddenly, Kenya reached over, turned on the light, and sat up in the bed. Glaring at her husband, she admonished, "You know, Trent, I don't need you to tell me Zaire's my sister. I also don't need any pressure from you about this. It's none of your business, and you just need to stay out of it."

Trent sat up in bed beside Kenya. He had never seen his wife behave so irrationally, and neither had he witnessed this fierce side of her. He was reasonable and didn't press Kenya on too many issues, but he would not give in to her this time. He didn't like arguing so he kept his tone amiable although firm. "It *is* my business. I'm Kourtnie and Janae's father, and I say they have a right to meet their aunt and cousins. You, on the other hand, are a grown woman, and I can't make you do anything you don't want to do. But Saturday, the girls, Big Momma, and I are going to see Zaire and her children."

Shocked that her husband was going against her wishes, Kenya strained her neck in an effort to see if he was serious. The fixed look on his face gave her the answer to her question. Without uttering another word, she climbed out of bed and left the room.

Trent called out after her. "Where are you going?"

Kenya refused to grant him a reply. When he caught a glimpse of her walking past the bedroom door, he got his answer when he saw her carrying a blanket and a pillow she had evidently retrieved from the hall closet. Perhaps he should go after her. No, whenever she got like this, it was best to leave her be for the moment.

Kenya went to the living room where she curled up on the sofa. She was so upset with her grandmother. Why had she told Trent anything? She should have kept quiet. Kenya decided that she would express her displeasure to Paulette the first thing the next morning but immediately changed her mind. There was someone else she could talk to who would understand.

The next day, Kenya met her second cousin, Melva Wilson, for lunch. Melva was thirty-one, still single, and fourteen months older than Kenya and Zaire; both of Melva's parents were deceased. Her mother had been the youngest of Paulette and Dorothy's siblings.

Melva could vividly recall how close her twin cousins had been, but in an instant, their bond had been broken. She listened intently as Kenya filled her in on all the details of the latest family saga—although she already knew, since Dorothy had briefed Melva after she had spoken with Paulette.

Kenya was saying, "I don't know why she couldn't have just stayed where she was. Big Momma just wants to forgive and forget like nothing ever happened. Trent went by her house last night, and you know how she is when she gets to talking. She told him about Zaire's call. Now not only is she on my back about seeing Zaire, but he is, too. And do you know what he had the nerve to tell me? He's taking Kourtnie and Janae with them Saturday to Zaire's."

Melva asked, "You really don't want to see her?"

Kenya shamelessly admitted, "No, I don't. Melva, she walked out on us. You know that."

"I know, but she's still your sister."

Kenya took a sip of water and placed her glass back on the table. "It doesn't matter. I can't forgive her for what she did."

Curious, Melva asked, "Don't you even want to see her children?"

Kenya purposely ignored her cousin's question. When her grandmother had told her that Zaire had children, her heart had swelled with exhilaration; however, Kenya would never admit that to anyone. Of course she wanted to see Zaire's children, but that didn't change how she felt about Zaire.

Melva hated seeing Kenya in this state of mind. "You're stressed out." She eagerly proposed, "Why don't I come over Saturday while Trent and the girls are gone? We'll give ourselves a spa treatment—facials, pedicures, the works. It'll make you feel better."

Despite feeling defeated, Kenya managed to let out a chuckle. Her cousin was an independent beauty consultant for a large cosmetics company. Every time they talked, Melva attempted to get her to host a show.

"Come over if you want to, but let me remind you that I'm not hosting a party. I don't know how many times I have to tell you that."

"I didn't say anything about you hosting a party. You should pamper yourself a little—destress. We can watch a movie and eat some popcorn. Now doesn't that sound good?"

Kenya's smile broadened. "I guess so."

"So what d'you say? Are we on, or what?"

Kenya's face became brighter. "We're on."

Kenya could always count on Melva to boost her spirits. However, in the back of her mind, she wished Saturday would never come.

7

Despite her displeasure at the meeting that would soon be taking place, Kenya instructed her youngsters, "You two behave."

Kourtnie replied, "We will."

Janae wanted to know, "Momma, how come you're not coming?"

A very uncomfortable feeling washed over Kenya. Rushing the two children along in an effort to avoid responding to Janae's innocent question, Kenya put a hand on each of their backs, saying, "Come on. Daddy and Big Momma are waiting."

They went into the living room where Trent and Paulette were sitting patiently. Paulette's face lit up when she saw her great grandchildren.

She asked, "You ready to go?"

"Yes, ma'am," the girls answered in unison.

"Okey dokey," Paulette said. Grabbing Kourtnie and Janae by their hands, she led them outside.

Trent stood and walked over to Kenya. Wrapping his arms around her waist, he warmly implored, "I wish you'd change your mind and come with us."

Kenya slowly wiggled herself free of his embrace. At the moment, she wasn't feeling any love for him.

Trent stared woefully at her. Her action had hurt him. "She's your sister. You haven't seen each other since you were teenagers. She has children you didn't even know about until recently. Regardless of what happened between the two of you, they're your family. She's trying to make amends. Can't you at least meet her halfway?"

The thick coat of ice covering Kenya's heart would not melt. Trent waited for her response. After several seconds of silence, he attempted to kiss her, but she turned away before his endearment could land on her lips.

Why was she acting this way toward him? He was simply trying to unite himself and their children with her family. What was wrong with that? He drank in the sight of her, not understanding the change that had taken over.

Whispering softly, "We'll see you later," Trent turned and walked away with a feeling of total rejection.

The girls were extremely excited about meeting their aunt and twin cousins. Their questions and lively conversation on the way to Zaire's house made the hour-long drive whiz by.

Trent glanced down at the MapQuest directions to Zaire's house as he approached a red brick circular driveway next to a white picket fence. Sitting off in the distance stood an immensely beautiful white-and-brick, two-story home with black shutters, a huge front porch, and a balcony overhead.

Trent happily announced, "I think this is it."

He turned the steering wheel of his red Tahoe to the left and glided down the driveway toward the house. Kourtnie and Janae could hardly wait for the vehicle to stop so that they could get out and meet their new family. They quickly unfastened their seatbelts and jumped out.

Before anyone else could make it up the steps of the house, Janae was already on the porch greeting her aunt and cousins. They allowed her to finish making the introductions.

"And this is my sister, Kourtnie." Taking Paulette's hand gently in hers, Janae announced to her cousins, "This is Big Momma." Then she released her great grandmother's hand, took hold of her father's, and proudly announced, "And this is my daddy."

Zaire gave them each a warm hug and introduced her children. "This is Shawn and Amili."

The children smiled and said hello. Taking their cousins by the hands, Shawn and Amili escorted them inside with the grown-ups tagging behind.

Paulette felt a huge sense of pride and happiness. She was blessed to have such a beautiful family. Angelique and Reginald would have been proud, too. Paulette's only wish was that Kenya was here. She didn't know how she'd do it, but she would get the two sisters together somehow.

"Hey over there," Melva said to her cousin as they sat at the Jamisons's kitchen table, their faces covered in pastel-colored facial masks. "You still with me?"

Kenya looked at Melva. "Yeah."

Melva had hoped their spa day would put her cousin at ease, but it obviously wasn't working. "You know, you should've just gone with them."

"What?"

"I said you should've gone with them to see Zaire and meet her kids."

Kenya pursed her lips. "I don't want to see them."

"Aren't you even curious?"

"About what?"

"What she looks like after all these years. I mean, y'all were still teenagers when she left, and when she did come back, you wouldn't see her. And what about her children? They've got your blood running through their veins, too. Don't you want to see them at least? You know, they had nothing to do with what happened between you and Zaire. They're two little innocent children."

Kenya pushed her chair back, rose, took her washcloth over to the sink, and wet it under some warm water. After wringing out the liquid, she returned to her seat. "I didn't say they had anything to do with it." The warm wet cloth felt so good on her face. She pressed on it for a few seconds before gently wiping away the mask.

Melva went to the sink and moistened her own washcloth. Turning around, she politely reminded her cousin, "Aunt Angie and Uncle Reggie wouldn't be happy with the way things have turned out between you and Zaire."

Kenya looked at Melva and callously replied, "Melva, don't throw Momma and Daddy in my face like that. You think you're gonna make me feel guilty so I'll see Zaire?"

Melva honestly denied, "I'm not trying to make you feel guilty. I just think it's sad that when your momma and daddy died, you and Zaire were so close, and now you've grown apart. This isn't how they wanted things to turn out."

Over the years, Melva had always seemed to understand why

Kenya was so upset with Zaire. During Paulette's illness, she had even expressed displeasure toward Zaire for leaving. Why was Melva also turning against Kenya? Zaire had everyone she loved opposing her. Kenya didn't understand; she was the one who had stayed and helped take care of their grandmother while her sister had deserted them.

Frustrated, Kenya said, "Melva, I don't wanna talk about this anymore. I thought you came over here to cheer me up. You're stressing me out even more."

Melva felt terrible. In her heart, she felt that Kenya had every right to be upset with Zaire. However, she thought Kenya should humble herself to the point of forgiveness. "I'm sorry. I didn't mean to. I'll shut up if that's what you want." She eyed her cousin.

"Thank you."

Melva burst out laughing.

Eyeing her cousin as though she'd gone crazy, Kenya asked, "What's so funny?"

"I said I'd shut up if you wanted me to, and you just said 'thank you.' "

Kenya squirted a small amount of moisturizer in her palm, rubbed her hands together, and gently rubbed it over her face. As she smoothed on the cream, she replied, "Well, I was saying thank you to your apology, but if you want to apply it to your generous offer to shut up, then that's fine by me, too."

In the next instant, Kenya and Melva were laughing themselves silly. It used to be this way with Zaire. Kenya thought momentarily about how the three of them used to hang out together and have so much fun, but those days were long gone.

The first day of spring was only one day away, but springtime was already in the air. It was a warm, sunshiny day. Zaire's home and property were breathtaking. As they sat around the table on the patio near the pool eating lunch and getting to know one another better, Paulette and her family were surrounded by luscious gardens of trees and flowers.

Trent said, "So, Zaire, Big Momma tells me you're a clothing designer. Is that what you always wanted to do?"

Zaire smiled. "Pretty much. Big Momma taught me and Kenya to sew when we were young. I used to design and make clothes for our Barbie dolls. Right now, I only have a women's line. I'm starting up a children's line this spring." Casting a loving glance at her twins, she added, "Shawn and Amili were my inspiration for that. Ever since they learned to talk and came to understand more of what I do for a living, they were constantly asking me when I was going to come up with something they could wear."

"That's great," Trent acknowledged. "What about a men's line? Have you thought about designing clothes for men?" He grinned as he teased his sister-in-law, "We like to look good, too, you know."

Zaire admitted, "I haven't really thought about it." With a mirthful grin, she added, "But now that you've brought it to my attention, I'll certainly consider it. Enough about me. Big Momma tells me you're a pharmacist. You help the sick just like her. That's nice." Her smile grew wider as she threw a loving glance in her grandmother's direction before looking back at Trent. "What do you like most about your job?"

Trent could talk all day and night about his work, for he loved it. He grinned as he leaned back in his chair. "I love working with the doctors, nurses, and patients, and assisting them with the patients' healthcare needs. Sometimes I advise people regarding the selection of nonprescription drugs. It makes me feel good when I see them again and they're smiling because they're feeling better, and they thank me for taking the time to help them."

Zaire commented warmly, "That's good. You sound like a people person."

Trent's smile was proud yet reserved. "I am."

Amili implored, "Excuse me. Momma, is it okay if we play badminton now? We're through eating."

"Sure, honey," Zaire replied.

All four youngsters jumped out of their chairs and ran to the middle of the backyard where the net was already set up.

Zaire bragged, "Your kids are beautiful. They're so sweet."

Trent said, "Thanks. So are Shawn and Amili. Thanks for inviting us. I think it's important that the kids get to know each other. I'm sorry Kenya wouldn't—couldn't come." He hoped Zaire hadn't caught his slip of the tongue.

Ignoring Trent's indiscretion, Zaire commented from her heart, "I appreciate you and the girls coming with Big Momma. As for Kenya, there's no need for you to apologize. I blame myself for her not coming. We're not the friends or sisters we used to be, and it's all my fault."

Paulette felt now was the time for her to speak. "Zaire, Kenya's a grown woman now. She needs to quit holding on to the past."

Trent, although he loved his wife, silently agreed.

8

"Momma, we had so much fun." Janae had been talking nonstop all evening regarding the trip to Zaire's. She had instantly fallen in love with her cousins and her Aunt Zaire. Kenya's jaws were tired from the fake smiles she had been plastering on her face.

"That's good, honey. I'm glad," Kenya said as she pulled the comforter up over her daughter. "You better go to sleep. We've got to get up early in the morning."

"Can you come with us next time? Why didn't you come? When can we go again? They have a swimming pool. Aunt Zaire said next time we can go swimming."

Kenya wished there wouldn't be any more next times. She reminded her daughter, "Yes, I know. You told me. Go to sleep now." She leaned over and kissed Janae's cheek. "Good night."

"Good night. I love you."

"I love you, too."

Kenya went to tuck in Kourtnie and had to listen to a repetition of everything Janae had happily shared with her and then some. "Momma, Aunt Zaire is so nice. Did you know she designs clothes? She's gonna start doing clothes for kids, too. That must be so cool to have everybody wearing your clothes. She said she used to make clothes for her Barbie dolls. Did you sew, too?"

Kenya supplied her daughter with the briefest answer she could think of to only her last question. "I did a little." In an effort to put an end to Kourtnie's praises about Zaire, Kenya offered her a gentle reminder. "That's enough talking for now. Go to sleep. We've got to get up early in the morning."

"Yes, ma'am. Good night."

Kenya leaned over and kissed her daughter's forehead. "Good night. I love you."

"I love you, too."

Kenya turned out the light and went to the master bedroom where she found Trent in bed reading. As she got ready for bed, he apologized, "Sorry—they're pretty wired up, huh?"

"Yeah, they are, especially Janae. She was throwing a million questions at me. She asked if I'm coming next time. Trent, I hope you and Big Momma didn't plan another one of these little get-togethers. I'm not changing my mind."

Trent cheerily announced, "We're meeting at Big Momma's next week."

Kenya stifled a heavy sigh, but he could tell from the expression on her face that she wasn't happy. In an effort to get her to open up to him, Trent asked, "What?"

Perturbed that their little family gatherings would continue, Kenya simply stated, "Nothing."

Trent stared at his wife and asked with gentle curiosity, "Kenya, is what your sister did so terrible in your eyes that you don't want to see her or your niece and nephew, whom you've never met? She made a mistake, but she finally got up the courage to contact you. She's trying to make amends. Won't you at least meet her halfway?"

Kenya allowed her sigh to tumble out this time. "Trent, I don't wanna talk about it. It's between me and Zaire, and I'd appreciate it if you'd just stay out of it."

Trent refused to back down. "You're always talking about how the girls need to learn to face their problems head on, but look at you. You're a grown woman who refuses to talk to your own sister over something that happened years ago."

Kenya fired back, "I have a right to feel however I want to." She hopped onto her side of the bed with her back to him.

Trent closed his book and laid it gently on the bed beside him. Turning aside, he tried once more to reason with his wife. As he lovingly put his arm around her, he began, "Kenya—"

Kenya's tone was subdued as she immediately charged, pausing between each word, so there would be no misunderstanding about her desire. "*Don't* touch me."

Realizing now that Kenya was more upset with him than he'd initially thought, Trent attempted to reconcile. He carefully responded, "It's obvious you're upset and very angry with Zaire. If you don't talk to her, you'll never be able to rid your mind and heart of the resentment you feel. I know it's hard to let go of animosity when people hurt us, especially people we love. You know, the Bible says if a person wrongs us, we should go to that individual and talk to him about it. I can tell this is tearing you apart. You'll never have peace of mind if you don't make peace with her."

Trent waited a brief moment for Kenya to respond. When she didn't, he placed the book he'd been reading on the nightstand, turned off the lamp, and dropped his head onto his pillow.

When Paulette attempted to get up the next morning for church, she had a terrible headache accompanied by nausea. She was determined not to let her sudden illness keep her from her Father's house; therefore, she pulled herself out of bed. Perhaps, she thought, if she ate some breakfast and took some headache medicine, she'd feel better.

She was successful in taking only a few steps. Having difficulty walking, she decided to get back into bed. She'd never experienced anything like this before. She'd noticed for the past several weeks she'd been suffering from headaches and dizziness that were usually worse in the morning and seemed to ease during the day. Although her symptoms were similar to the ones she had had years ago, she figured she was just tired. She decided to stay in today, although she felt guilty for not going to church. She rarely missed a service, especially since she was basically a healthy individual despite her age. It had been several years since she had been seriously ill.

After the service, the Jamisons stopped by Paulette's. Kenya and Trent knew she had to be sick when they didn't see her at church. When Paulette failed to answer the door, Kenya used the key her grandmother had given her to get into the house.

As Kenya, Trent, and the girls walked through each room, they called out, "Big Momma!"

Paulette's eyelids fluttered open until they were focused on her granddaughter. She smiled when she saw Kenya. Her headache and the nausea had subsided, and she was feeling much better. She slowly muttered Kenya's name.

Kenya was deeply concerned. "Big Momma, are you all right? When we didn't see you at church, we got worried. What's wrong? Are you sick? Why didn't you call us?"

Paulette smiled at Kenya's barrage of questions.

Kenya heard her husband call out her name. Without turning around, she announced, "Trent, I found her. She's in bed."

When Paulette spotted Trent, Kourtnie, and Janae, she welcomed them. "Y'all can come in." When she attempted to sit up, Kenya and Trent rushed to her side and assisted her so that she could rise up and sit back comfortably in her bed against the pillows. "I'm fine. I wasn't feeling too good this morning so I decided to stay home. I'm okay now."

Kenya politely demanded, "What was wrong?"

Paulette didn't want her granddaughter to worry. "I just had a headache and was feeling a little dizzy and nauseated."

Kenya was concerned. Her grandmother had to be pretty sick to stay home from church. She needed medical attention. "Maybe we should take you to the emergency room."

"No," Paulette quickly responded. "I told you I'm fine."

"Big Momma . . ." Kenya began.

"I'm okay. Stop fretting."

Kenya stared at Paulette for a moment. Her grandmother was a strong woman, but she was eighty-one years old even though she wanted to act like she was twenty-one. Although Paulette hadn't had any serious health problems since her cancer diagnosis years earlier, Kenya was still worried. "I'll fix you some dinner. Have you eaten anything?"

Paulette shook her head. "No." Sliding back the covers, she started to climb out of bed.

Kenya asked, "Where are you going?"

"To the bathroom. Is it okay if I take a bath and put on some clothes?" Paulette teasingly inquired.

"You want me to help you?"

Stunned, Paulette crossed her eyes at Kenya. "Help me what?"

"With your bath."

Paulette playfully reminded her granddaughter, "Kenya, I'm not a baby. I'm eighty-one years old. I've been bathing myself since I was knee-high to a grasshopper. I think I'm capable of washing myself. Besides, I don't want you seeing me naked."

Trent, Kourtnie, and Janae giggled. Trent convinced himself that Paulette had to be all right since she still had her sense of humor, although he was a little concerned, too.

Kenya looked at her family and grinned. "Well, okay, Big Momma.

You don't have to jump down my throat," she said teasingly. "I'll start dinner. What do you have a taste for?"

"Well, there's some ground beef in the refrigerator. I was gonna make some patties and gravy. Whatever you wanna fix to go with that'll be fine."

Kenya, Trent, and the girls left Paulette so that she could take her bath. Kourtnie and Janae played while Kenya and Trent started dinner. Trent peeled some potatoes, cut and rinsed them, and got them boiling in a pot of water while Kenya started browning the hamburger patties. After she washed and cut up a cabbage and began steaming it, she finished browning the patties and made the gravy. When the meal was complete, Kenya called everyone to the table. Trent passed the blessing, and they dived into their food.

Paulette felt extremely blessed to have her family with her. If only she could get Kenya to change her mind about Zaire, her family circle would be complete. When they finished eating, Trent suggested that the ladies sit down and relax while he and the girls clean up the kitchen.

Paulette gratefully expressed, "Thanks for dinner. You and Trent sure know how to whip up a delicious meal quick."

Kenya smiled warmly. "Thank you, but it's because of you that I am able to do it." Before she realized it, she began reminiscing. "Do you remember how you used to let me and Zaire help you cook? We weren't bigger than ants, but you'd have us in the kitchen standing on stools, whipping, mixing, and baking. Then Zaire would . . ." She stopped when she became aware that she was getting caught up in the moment. She had no idea why she had started talking about the good old days.

Paulette looked at Kenya, hoping she would finish her story. Perhaps Kenya's heart was beginning to relent toward Zaire. Paulette urged, "What, baby? What would Zaire do?"

Kenya refused to complete her journey down memory lane. "Nothing," she mumbled. She was disappointed that she'd even mentioned her sister. She didn't want anyone to think she was going to change her mind about seeing Zaire.

Paulette sensed Kenya's dismay. "Kenya, don't be so hard on people, especially your loved ones, that you push them away. I know Zaire hurt you; she hurt me, too, but she wants to make things right. When people hurt us or make us angry, we stop seeing the good in them and all we see are the things we don't like. Remember when you girls were younger how close you were, how you looked up to Zaire? Can you recall the things you liked about her? Yes, she made some mistakes. We all do, but are we worthless in God's eyes? He sees the good in us despite our imperfections.

"It's true we can't see hearts like He can, but if we just stop and look at each other, I think we'll find a lot of good things. Of course, we'll find some not-so-good things, too. But if God doesn't dwell on our faults, who are we as imperfect creatures to feel that we know each other's heart better than Him?"

Kenya didn't respond to Paulette's remarks. No matter what her grandmother or anyone else said, she would never forgive Zaire.

As Zaire wheeled her black TrailBlazer through the city limits of the small town of Temple, in northwestern Georgia, she noticed that the place had grown a little since the last time she'd visited. As she drove past the two huge shopping centers on both sides of Highway 113 directly off Interstate 20, Shawn inquired from the backseat, "Mom, *this* is where you grew up?"

Zaire turned slightly, smiling at her son as she answered, "Yes, it is. What d'you think of it?"

"It's all right, I guess. It's small."

Zaire grinned. Her children were accustomed to living in larger cities. However, they were still down-to-earth kids so she was sure Shawn and Amili would fit right in. She remembered that even as a child she hated the little bitty town and couldn't wait to grow up and move to a big city.

Now Zaire was missing home. It could never be like it was, though—not with her parents gone. She wanted her children to have some knowledge of their family's history, but some of it was just too grisly. A part of her desired to drive by the house she and Kenya had lived in with their parents and show it to her children. However, the past was so dreadfully painful. For the past twenty years, she always got depressed around Thanksgiving, as memories of that tragic day returned to haunt her.

Zaire agreed, "Yes, it is small compared to what you and Amili are used to." She eyed her daughter. "Well, Amili, what d'you think of my native home?"

Amili seriously asked, with a touch of innocence, as her eyes traveled over the small town, "Where's the mall?"

Zaire was vastly amused as she let out a hearty laugh. "We just passed it about twenty miles back in Douglasville."

Amili's mouth fell open. "You mean they have to drive *twenty miles* to the mall?"

Zaire smiled. "It's not *that* far. Just wait 'til you see where Big Momma lives. You and Shawn'll love it."

Amili gave her mother a warm smile before refocusing her attention back to the book she had been reading and thought to herself, *Whatever you say, Mama.*

Zaire could hear the sounds coming from Shawn's video game in the back. Her children were young, and she didn't mind them finding some pleasure in the wholesome things that interested them, but she wanted desperately for them to get to know their family. She and Kenya had grown up hearing their grandmother's tales and various life stories. Shawn and Amili needed a piece of that legacy. She now deeply regretted that she had not returned sooner. Perhaps they could catch up. If only Kenya would allow them in her life, that would put the icing on the cake.

Zaire turned off the road, driving slowly down her grandmother's driveway. There stood the weeping willow tree she remembered from her childhood. Stopping the vehicle, she said, "Okay, guys. We're here."

Zaire couldn't believe she was actually home again.

9

It was dusk, and Paulette was running through the yard with her four great grandchildren catching lightning bugs in jars. This was Shawn and Amili's first efforts at capturing the glowing insects, and they were extremely excited. Zaire was simply amazed at her grandmother's enthusiastic spirit and high level of energy. Paulette had been firm yet loving toward her and Kenya, but she'd never run around the yard playing with them like she was doing now. Zaire supposed it was the times they had lived in and the circumstances. When the twins' parents died, their grandmother was a widow who had just lost her only child, and at the age of sixty-one, took in her two young granddaughters to raise on her own.

As she reflected back on their family situation, Zaire totally understood why her grandmother couldn't amuse them like their friends' parents could them. To see her whimsical, eighty-one-year-old grandmother now was truly awe-inspiring. Zaire loved seeing her this way.

Paulette had earlier shared some stories about Zaire and Kenya's childhood with the children. Shawn and Amili had gotten a humongous kick out of hearing about some of the funny things their mother and aunt used to do. Paulette also briefed them on her own childhood. It made Zaire's heart glad that her children could now readily have moments to seize some historical knowledge of at least the maternal side of their family.

As she and Trent chatted while they sat on the front porch, Zaire happily announced, "Today has been so wonderful." Inhaling a deep breath of the country air, she added, "I can't believe I stayed away so long. I've missed this place. Most of all, I've missed the people." She dared to ask, "How's Kenya?"

Trent wished he knew. "She's okay. Sometimes she puts up this wall and won't let me in."

Zaire felt horribly guilty because she felt Kenya's barrier was her fault.

Trent continued, "She puts up a hard fight to be tough, but I think she does it mostly for the girls. She wants them to grow up to be strong and able to fend for themselves, and she feels she has to set the ultimate example. I admire her strength, but sometimes I think it's just a front."

Zaire reflected on what her sister was like coming up: very conservative and serious-minded, always making the safe choices. Zaire, on the other hand, was the adventurer, the creative spirit, who didn't mind taking chances.

Zaire said, "It's obvious that your family's important to Kenya. We teach by our example, and I admire her for trying to instill good qualities in Kourtnie and Janae. But after getting to know you, I see she doesn't do it alone. It's obvious to me that you're a good husband to Kenya and a wonderful father to Kourtnie and Janae."

Trent smiled modestly. "Thank you. I appreciate that."

Zaire confessed, "Shawn and Amili's father has never seen them. I was four weeks pregnant when I left him after he started abusing me, and that was the last I ever saw of him. He knew I was pregnant, but neither of us had any idea I was having twins."

Trent couldn't believe a man would just disregard his own flesh and blood. It tore him apart just thinking about it. "He never contacted you to check on you and the baby?"

An awkward smile appeared on Zaire's face as she shook her head. "No."

"Do Shawn and Amili ever ask about him?"

"They used to."

"What did you tell them?" Trent suddenly remembered it was none of his business. "I'm sorry. I shouldn't have asked."

Zaire gave him a look that was filled with sincerity. "No, it's okay. I don't mind your asking. They were about eight, I guess, when I told them the truth. I tried to keep it short and simple. I just told them that their daddy and I were very young when I got pregnant with them and that when he started hitting me, I got scared and left. I've tried to teach Shawn to never abuse a woman, physically or verbally—anyone, for that matter—to always show people love and respect. And I tell Amili if she's ever in an abusive situation to get away quickly and find someone to help her. I don't want them to experience what I did.

"I guess you know what happened to our parents." Zaire eyed Trent as he nodded. "I've heard stories of how some women have been abused for years by their husband or boyfriend. The first time Malcolm hit me, I didn't think twice about leaving him. I immediately had flashbacks of the day we got the news about Momma and Daddy. I didn't want to end up like that.

"Everyone was shocked at what Daddy did because no one had ever seen or heard of any violent moments between them. If they had any, Kenya and I never knew about them. The way I figured it was that if my daddy, whom I'd only seen shower love on my momma, could do something so terrible to her, then Malcolm could and probably would do the same thing to me; so I left, and I didn't think twice about it."

Trent contemplated the situation in his mind.

Zaire continued, "Sometimes I wonder because there's a history of violence in my family with Daddy, and then Malcolm, does that mean my children will inherit that awful quality? They're so sweet and innocent now that I just can't imagine them doing anything horribly wrong, but look at all the people in the world who started off that way and later turned into monsters."

Trent tried to give his sister-in-law some encouragement. "It's true that humans can inherit a lot of things and sometimes do, but for the most part, how we turn out has to do with our upbringing and what we're exposed to. I see Shawn and Amili just as you do—sweet and innocent. I see Kourtnie and Janae that way, too. As parents, we have our faults just like everybody else, but we try to raise our children to be God-fearing and to live their lives in ways that please God.

"Sometimes things can and do go wrong. Even if that happens, it doesn't mean all hope is lost. People can change. God sees our potential, the person we are on the inside. We can't see hearts like He can, so all we have to go by is what we see people do. So if someone makes a mistake, we just have to be like God in the sense that we're willing to forgive them, because we all sin."

Zaire took in Trent's words like a sponge soaking up water. She couldn't take credit for having instilled the fear of God in her children, as she hadn't had anything to do with God in years. She had, however, tried to plant seeds of goodness in their hearts.

Trent's heart went out to his sister-in-law. Perhaps if given another opportunity, Kenya would reconsider and see her sister. Zaire had been through so much. What could he do to reunite the two?

Zaire felt very uneasy as Trent pulled his vehicle into his and Kenya's driveway. At first, Zaire had thought his suggestion was a good idea, but not anymore. She had allowed him to convince her to leave their children at Paulette's while they paid Kenya a surprise visit. When they'd informed Paulette of their decision, she had gone along, hoping it was what Kenya needed to move her to absolution.

"Trent, I'm not sure about this now. Kenya's already made it pretty clear that she doesn't want to see me. No matter how much I want us to reunite, I have to respect her wishes."

Trent was sure that once Kenya saw Zaire, she would come to her senses. "It's the only choice we have right now. She may not change her mind otherwise."

"That's just it. I want her to change her mind on her own. I don't want to try to force her."

"You're not trying to force her. It was my idea. I'll let her know that."

Trent opened his door, climbed out, and walked around to open Zaire's door. Reluctantly, she got out and followed him up the sidewalk to the front door. The beating of her heart was so intense that Zaire felt as though someone was dribbling a basketball inside her chest. A voice inside her head ordered her to turn around and run as far away from the house as she could, but her feet commanded her to keep going. Like a scared little child, she stood out of sight behind Trent in the darkness of the evening.

Trent unlocked the door and entered the house. Stepping over the threshold, Zaire followed him. She couldn't believe that after years of being estranged from her sister she was now standing inside the home Kenya shared with her husband and children.

As she looked around, Zaire admired the room's decor. This appeared to be the family room. A white entertainment center sat in a corner accentuated by deep yellow walls with white trim. A plush sofa in off-white with huge floral pillows sat in the middle of the room. A gold floor lamp with a black shade and a glass-topped black wrought iron coffee table complemented the white fireplace, which had a dark marble interior. Suddenly, all of Zaire's doubts dissipated as she basked in the warmth of her sister's home.

"Kenya!" Trent called out. He instructed Zaire, "Have a seat. I'll be right back."

Zaire smiled as she made her way to the sofa, which seemed to be inviting her to sit a spell. As she waited, she contemplated the sweet reunion with her sister.

Without any warning, it seemed as though everything started moving in fast motion. When she heard a noise behind her, Zaire stood and swirled around to stare dead into the face of her sister. Smiling, she started toward Kenya but stopped when she saw the hateful scowl on her sister's face.

Kenya felt as though she were in the twilight zone. This wasn't happening. Zaire was not standing here in her family room after years of them not seeing each other.

Kenya vehemently spat out, "What are you doing here? I told you I didn't want to see you." Then she gave Trent a cold, hard stare that could have bored holes straight through him. "Trent, what's going on? Did you bring her here?"

Trent was totally disappointed in Kenya's reaction. "Yes, I did. I just thought you should see each other and talk."

Kenya lashed out, "Oh, so you're making decisions for me now? You know, you gave me no choice when you decided you would take Kourtnie and Janae with you on your little get-together, but don't think you're going to start making decisions for me."

Kenya turned back to Zaire. "You've got a lot of nerve. I can't believe you came here after I specifically told you on the phone I didn't want to see you or talk to you."

Zaire's mouth fell open but no words escaped at first. "Kenya, I'm sorry. You're right. You told me you didn't want to see me, and I shouldn't have come. I'm sorry." Without uttering another word, she slowly turned on her heels. She felt like running but somehow managed to walk. As she made her way to the door, she envisioned Kenya's eyes on her back, blazing full of fire. She could almost feel the heat racing up and down her spine. Before closing the door behind her, Zaire heard Trent chastising Kenya for her rude behavior.

Zaire climbed back into the car and waited for Trent. After a minute or two, he returned. He felt horrible. His plan had gone nothing like he had hoped.

As he drove back to Paulette's, Trent expressed his heartfelt apologies. "Zaire, I'm so sorry. I had no idea Kenya would react like that. I feel awful."

It wasn't Trent's fault, as he had only been trying to help. Zaire blamed herself. In her heart, she knew it was exactly how Kenya would receive her. She had somehow fooled herself into thinking the reception would be warm. She chalked it up to wishful thinking.

"It's okay. I knew it was how she would react, but I fooled myself into believing differently. I knew how she felt, and I went anyway. It showed a total lack of respect for her and her feelings."

Trent offered, "I'll talk to her. I'll get her to—"

Zaire immediately said, "No. Please don't say anything else to her about it. Just leave her alone. If and when Kenya decides to see me, it has to be her decision. It won't be genuine if people try to coerce her, and that's not how I want us to reconcile. I know you were trying to help, and I appreciate it, but Kenya and I have to work this out ourselves."

Zaire could kick herself for agreeing to go see Kenya. She supposed it was a demonstration of the length one would go to in order to gain back a loved one they'd lost. Although she hadn't prayed in a very long time, she found herself beseeching God that she and Kenya would get back together soon.

Kenya was terribly upset. After finally getting the girls into bed, she approached Trent in the family room.

She strongly admonished him, "You had no right bringing Zaire here. How could you go against my wishes and do that?"

Trent had been deep in thought, pondering his wife's outrageous reaction to her sister's visit. He looked at Kenya. "I was trying to help. Why do you have to be so hard on her? Why are you so rigid with everybody? You act like if you bend a little you're gonna break in two."

Kenya didn't appreciate him trying to find fault with her. "I'm not rigid with everybody. I've already told you that what happened between me and Zaire is between us, and I'd appreciate it if you'd just stay out of it."

Ignoring her request to not get involved, Trent commented, "I don't understand you." He rose and walked toward her, stopping in front of her.

As he gazed into the depths of Kenya's beautiful deep brown eyes, he lovingly but firmly grasped her arms. "You're not the cold-hearted person you want your sister to think you are. I know because that's not the woman I fell in love with. The woman I fell in love with was kind, caring, and considerate; she still is. This division between you and Zaire is going to tear you further apart. I wish you'd just meet her halfway and try to close it. Family is so important. You know I'm an only child and both my parents are dead. You, our girls, Big Momma, Aunt Dorothy Mae, and Melva are my family—and now, Zaire and her children."

At the mention of Zaire being his family, Kenya flinched.

Trent continued, "Don't keep shutting her out. Pray and ask God to help you close the gap. I'll pray for you, too. I'll even pray with you. I always talk with God about our family, and I know you do, too. Maybe you can include Zaire in your prayers."

Kenya's heart remained cold and unresponsive. She supposed Trent thought his little speech was going to get her to change her mind about Zaire. Well, it wasn't. She said nothing as she callously removed herself from his hold and walked away.

The next morning, Kenya was cooking breakfast when Trent came in. Perhaps he'd pushed her too hard. He desired to make up with her. Walking up behind her as she stood over the stove, scrambling a pan of eggs, he lovingly wrapped his arms around her waist and kissed her neck. She was still seething and pulled away slightly. She wished he would just go somewhere and leave her alone. There was no need for him to attempt to get back on her good side, as he'd messed up big time when he'd butted his nose where it didn't belong.

"Good morning," Trent cheerily greeted his wife.

"Mornin'," Kenya mumbled begrudgingly.

"Need some help?" he asked.

She didn't even want to talk to him. Kenya simply shook her head.

"Want me to do the toast?"

What Kenya wanted was for him to just leave her alone. Before she realized it, she spat out, "I told you I don't need any help. Can you just leave me alone?"

Removing his arms from around her waist and stepping to stand beside her, Trent looked at Kenya as he spoke tenderly. "It's obvious you're still angry. I'm sorry I upset you. Are you gonna stay mad at me forever?"

Kenya felt like screaming. She didn't like being angry at him. He was her husband and a good one. She loved him. She also desired to respect him as the family head, but he had overstepped his boundaries.

Without looking away from her task, Kenya informed her husband, "Trent, I really don't wanna talk about this anymore. Will you please go wake the girls so we can eat breakfast and get ready for church?"

"Sure." Trent turned and walked away, praying for guidance in the matter of Kenya and Zaire.

10

Spring had said farewell, and summer would soon be departing. For the past several months, Trent, Kourtnie, Janae, and Paulette had continued their get-togethers with Zaire and her children. Dorothy and Melva had also joined them on a few of their outings.

Kenya still was not thrilled with how her grandmother had allowed Zaire such easy access back into her life. As for Melva, who had been Kenya's stronghold after Zaire's departure, she and Kenya remained close, although Kenya frequently reminded her that she felt like she was being betrayed all over again.

Paulette was almost fifteen minutes late picking up Kourtnie and Janae for their Saturday together. Kenya began to grow concerned, for her grandmother was always prompt. When Paulette failed to answer both her home and cellular phones, Kenya's anxiety increased. As she hung up the telephone, all kinds of tragic pictures of her grandmother in distress raced through her mind. She wished Trent hadn't had to go to the pharmacy today. After quickly gathering up the girls, she drove to Paulette's house.

Paulette's car was in the driveway. Kenya didn't bother to knock. She hastily inserted her key into the lock and turned the key. She, Kourtnie, and Janae rushed through the house repeatedly calling out, "Big Momma!"

Finally, they heard a muffled, "I'm in the kitchen."

They ran to the kitchen where they located Paulette on the floor beside the table.

"Big Momma!" the three screamed at once as they ran over to assist Paulette.

"Big Momma," Janae squealed, "are you hurt?"

Paulette smiled a happy sigh of relief that she had been rescued. "I'm fine, sweetie."

"What happened?" Kenya wanted to know.

As the three helped her up, Paulette replied, "All of a sudden, my legs just gave out on me. The next thing I knew I was on the floor, and I couldn't get up."

They helped her to sit down.

Kenya announced, "I'm taking you to the emergency room."

Paulette politely put up her hand. "Kenya, I'm fine. I just need to sit down a few minutes."

Kenya protested, "Big Momma, you're a retired nurse. You know yourself that you should get checked out. You may as well come on because I'm taking you even if I have to do it with you kicking and screaming."

Kourtnie gave her great grandmother a serious look. "That's right, Big Momma." Remembering one of Paulette's sayings, she added, "Now do you wanna do it the hard way or the easy way?"

Paulette snickered. "Well, Kourtnie, since you put it like that, I think I'd like to do it the easy way." She eyed Janae, waiting for her to get in her say.

Janae replied, "Good choice, Big Momma."

They managed to get Paulette to the car. Kenya felt very optimistic that her grandmother was just suffering from the ravages of getting older. Nevertheless, she would feel much better after a professional opinion.

The attending physician had requested to speak with Kenya and Paulette alone, so Kenya had called Melva and asked her to come and sit with Kourtnie and Janae. Now, as she sat in a chair beside her grandmother's bed, Kenya felt her entire body go numb. How could her grandmother's brain tumor from years ago have recurred? She felt as though she was in a thick fog. She heard the doctor saying something about a neurological examination, a CAT scan, and a biopsy. She couldn't believe they were living the nightmare all over again.

Kenya was finally able to look at her grandmother, who had such a serene look about her. She didn't understand how Paulette could remain so calm. She'd just been told that her brain tumor had returned, yet Paulette maintained her rugged demeanor.

As soon as Kenya was alone with her grandmother, she sat down on the side of the bed, threw her arms around Paulette, and sobbed. "Oh, Big Momma, I'm so sorry. How could this happen again?"

Paulette remained calm despite seeing her granddaughter in so much emotional pain. She put her arms around Kenya and patted her back. "It's okay, baby."

Kenya trembled. "No, it's not okay. Why you? I wish it was me."

Paulette tenderly countered, "Don't say that. You're still young, and you have two young children. I'd never admit it otherwise, but I'm an old woman who God has blessed with eighty-one years of life. All I ever asked Him to do was help me to raise you and Zaire right and let me see you grow up. He's done that. I can't ask for more."

Paulette was talking as though she was going to die. She had beaten this thing once. Modern medicine was a lot more advanced than it was back then. She could conquer it again. All Kenya could do was shed more tears.

Later that night, Kenya cried some more as she told Trent, "I should've taken her to the doctor sooner. That day when she complained about having headaches and being dizzy, I should've taken her then. I should've known something was wrong. How could I have been so stupid?"

Trent pulled his wife into his arms. "Stop. You're not stupid. You couldn't have known. Stop torturing yourself. Remember you wanted to take her to the emergency room, but she wouldn't go."

"She's been through this once before. The symptoms were similar. A bell should have gone off inside my head. I should have made her go. We could have put her in the car and taken her anyway."

Trent thought about Paulette's tenaciousness. "No, I don't think so. We would have had a fight on our hands. She let you take her today. Be glad that you got there when you did. Don't torment yourself over things you have no control over. What we have to do now is be there for her."

Kenya could only sob more. Trent was right, they had to be there for her grandmother. She prayed that the diagnosis wouldn't be as bleak as she feared.

A few days later, Kenya, Trent, and Dorothy sat with Paulette in the doctor's office as he explained the results of Paulette's tests. Paulette was advised that the tumor was massive yet possibly treatable. Treatment options and their side effects were then explained. When Kenya boldly stated that they would like a second opinion, Paulette proclaimed just as brazenly that she didn't need a second opinion because she didn't want to be poked and prodded on anymore.

Kenya thought she was dreaming when she heard her grandmother telling the doctor that she did not desire to undergo any treatment whatsoever, as she wanted what time she had remaining to be as painless and comfortable as possible. She had been through it years ago, and it was an unpleasant and draining experience. When Paulette had advised her family of her decision, Kenya had tried to convince her grandmother to accept the treatment; however, Paulette had remained steadfast. Even though her announcement had not come as a surprise, it pained Kenya deeply to actually hear her grandmother express her wishes to the doctor.

After being given a life expectancy of about three months, Paulette expressed her desire for Hospice care. Paulette had always been a fighter. Now, however, it seemed to Kenya that her grandmother was giving up on herself and life. Trent had told Kenya that whatever Paulette decided, they had to respect her decision and be supportive. His words echoed thunderously in her head.

Later that evening, Kenya sorrowfully shook her head as she and Paulette sat on the sofa in Paulette's living room. "I can't believe this is happening."

Without warning, Paulette brazenly announced, "We need to tell Zaire. I think it'll be nice for us to come together as a family."

Kenya wanted to tell her grandmother that her illness was no cause for a family reunion with Zaire, but she kept quiet.

11

Five days later, the family met at Paulette's after church and discussed each family member's schedule to help provide care for their loved one. Afterwards, Kenya sneaked outside for a breath of fresh air. Perhaps in the backyard, no one would find her as she sat nestled on one of her grandmother's Adirondack chairs.

Hearing a noise behind her, Kenya turned to look directly into the face of her sister. She quickly spun her head back around to stare off across the field of flowers at the lower edge of the yard. She wanted to be alone. She desired to talk to no one, especially Zaire. She had said all she had to say and only what was necessary regarding their grandmother's care. Just because Paulette was terminally ill, it didn't mean the two of them were going to become bosom buddies again.

Zaire slowly made her way to another chair and sat down facing her sister. "Kenya, please talk to me. You've only spoken a few words to me since I've been here, and those were concerning Big Momma's care. Can't we talk about us? If I could rewind our lives back to the day I first left and start afresh, I would. I'm sorry I left the way I did and especially at a time when you and Big Momma needed me the most. You have every right to be angry with me, but can't we at least talk about it?"

Staring off into the distance, Kenya dryly replied, "There's nothing to talk about. Don't think because you're here now that it's going to change things between us. The only reason you're here is because it's what Big Momma wants. I love her, and I want her last days to be pleasant, so if it means me having to be around you, I'll do it for her."

"So that's really the way you want it?"

"Yeah."

Zaire waited a brief moment, half-expecting Kenya to say something on a positive note. When it didn't come, she got up and walked away. Before she had made the effort to come back into her family's life, she had figured it wouldn't be easy. She just hadn't realized how difficult until now. Their grandmother, the woman who had raised them as though they were her children, was dying, and her own sister couldn't stand the sight of her.

Zaire found herself growing angry at the God everyone wanted her to believe in. The God who had allowed her parents to die such horrible deaths twenty years earlier and the same One who let her grandmother redevelop this terrible malady. If He did exist, perhaps He was using Kenya's hatred of her and of Paulette's illness to punish her further for the sins she'd committed. Maybe she should just leave and never come back. No, she couldn't do that. She'd come too far to turn around now.

As Kenya stood at her kitchen sink, she peeked out the window at the colors of autumn. Thanksgiving was next month. Her mind drifted to her childhood when everything seemed good. It was her grandmother's dream for their family to be whole again before she passed away. Now that she would soon be gone, Kenya wanted very much to grant Paulette's wishes. Yet every day, she found it more and more difficult to forgive Zaire. All the scriptures on forgiveness did nothing to move her to action. She prayed to God to help her to do the right thing, but her heart remained in turmoil.

Kenya was so confused. She didn't understand why she couldn't will herself to change her attitude. She contemplated the things her grandmother had said in her living room that day she'd been sick, when the two of them talked while Trent and the girls were cleaning the kitchen. Something about looking for the good in people. Kenya had looked up to Zaire when they were younger. Zaire had such a lively spirit. Everyone liked her; they just flocked to her like bees to honey.

Without Zaire around during Paulette's first bout with cancer, Kenya was alone except for their other relatives who helped with her care. Kenya was just a scared teenager at the time, just like Zaire. They'd shared a bond. Her sister had broken it when she walked out on the two people she should have loved the most. In

Kenya's eyes, any good that was there was now gone. Trent had told her more than once to meet Zaire halfway. Could she do it?

For the past four weeks, Zaire had been spending every weekend with their grandmother. However, Kenya still maintained a safe distance from her sister except in cases of necessity. The Hospice care staff had been extremely diligent in providing services, which helped Paulette and her family. Home health aides, church members, and community volunteers were very generous with their time by helping out with such things as basic bedside care, daily living activities, and even freeing up time for the family to go out or just get a break from caregiving.

Thanksgiving had always been Zaire's favorite time of year. Perhaps they could rekindle the family togetherness they once shared before it was too late. Too many lives had been taken from them already. What if something happened to her or Zaire before they made amends? Kenya was taken aback when she suddenly realized that she would not be able to stand it if anything ever happened to the sister she no longer cherished.

Before she realized it, Kenya was preparing to go to her grandmother's house so that she could talk to her betrayer. She still had no penetrating desire to speak with Zaire, yet it seemed that some force was making her decisions and movements for her. She had no idea what she would say and quickly uttered a brief silent prayer to God for His guidance. She informed Trent where she'd be and asked him to keep an eye on the kids. She smiled as she watched the cousins spread out on the family room floor eating popcorn and watching a video. The picture so reminded her of herself and her cousins when they were younger and got together at Paulette's house, playing games like hopscotch, hide-and-seek, and Red Rover.

Zaire granted Kenya the privilege of spending a few minutes alone with their grandmother. Afterward, Kenya found her in the kitchen where she'd sat down to have a bite to eat.

Kenya hesitantly approached her sister. Why did she feel so nervous? It didn't use to be this way. "Can we talk?"

Surprised, yet pleased that Kenya finally wanted to talk to her, Zaire cheerily answered, "Sure."

Kenya pulled out a chair and sat down. "I know it's a little early, but I just wanted to ask if you and Shawn and Amili can come spend Thanksgiving with the family—you know, like we did when we were kids."

Zaire was touched that her sister thought enough of her to invite her and the children, but she no longer viewed the holiday as a day of celebration. Every time she thought about the tragic events of the day twenty years ago, the pain was too unbearable. It had taken every ounce of strength she could muster to keep returning every weekend for the last four weeks to their grandmother's side. She hadn't been able to stick around in the past. She wondered why she was getting the boldness to do it now. She felt herself growing afraid again, along with the urge to swiftly withdraw again from her family's lives. She was trying to be there for them this time, but she didn't know if she could. She hadn't expected this to happen again. Paulette was not in too bad a state at the moment. What would Zaire do when things got worse?

Zaire could not bear to look at her sister for fear Kenya would see the apathy in her eyes. "Thank you, but we won't be able to come."

Kenya was shocked that Zaire had turned down her invitation. Did she know how hard it had been for her to get up the nerve to come over and ask her? Zaire had said she wanted them to talk, but when Kenya finally reached out to her, she was rejected. Her sister hadn't changed one bit. She was still just as selfish as she was when she'd decided to abandon her family on a whim. Kenya should have known.

Kenya shook her head in disbelief. "What? Why not?"

Zaire answered reluctantly, "We just can't."

"I don't understand. Why not?"

Zaire could not stay seated. She jumped up from her seat, rushed over to the sink, and stared out the window. *Please don't ask me anymore questions.* She thought she was ready to talk to her sister about the past. She was—but only certain parts. "Kenya, please don't keep asking me that. We can't come."

Kenya rose. "You know, you've got a lotta nerve. You had me fooled into thinking that you wanted to make things better between us. Then I try to reach out to you and you reject me. Why'd you even come back? I wish you'd just stayed where you were." Abruptly, she turned and walked away.

With her head hung low, Zaire sobbed uncontrollably. Why had she thought she could just come back and pick up where they'd left off? The pains of the past had destroyed their lives forever.

*   *   *

When Kenya returned home, she was visibly upset. She told Trent about her conversation with Zaire.

Trent advised, "You've got to give her time. She has to get used to being a family again."

Kenya snapped, "She didn't have any trouble being a family when it came to the little get-togethers she had with everybody a few months ago. She's still selfish. I ask her to do one little thing for the family and she won't do it. You told me to meet her halfway. You see what it got me?"

"Kenya, this is a very emotional time for all of us. Big Momma is ill, and we don't know how much longer she'll be with us. If she senses all this negativity, it won't be good for her. Make her last days peaceful ones. Try to get along with Zaire."

"I am trying. I don't understand her. As kids, Thanksgiving was her favorite time of year because that's when all our family got together, and we had such a good time."

"Thanksgiving was also a tragic day for you and Zaire. Maybe the holiday brings back too many sad memories for her."

"Well, what about me? They were my parents, too, but I still want to keep the tradition alive."

"I know you do, but baby, you can't force your wishes on her. Give her time. Maybe one day she'll change her mind. Right now, you *and* Zaire have to be there for Big Momma because she needs you."

Kenya fell into the warmth of her husband's arms and cried. "Oh, Trent, I don't know how much more my heart can take. Why is this happening to Big Momma? It's so unfair. I'm so tired. I can't take anymore."

Trent took his hand and lifted Kenya's chin so that they were looking directly into each other's eyes. His tone was firm yet gentle. "Don't say that." He remembered the scripture at 2 Corinthians 4:7. "I know you're hurting, but God will supply you the power you need to go on." He found himself quickly recalling the verse at Isaiah 40:29. "He knows you're tired. He'll increase your strength."

Kenya's lips trembled as she spoke, tears streaming down her face. "I just feel like my heart is breaking in two. It's the same feeling I had when Momma and Daddy died, then when Zaire left. I don't wanna hurt like this anymore."

Trent took his hands and wiped Kenya's face and kissed both her cheeks. He whispered, "I know you don't." Another Bible verse came to mind: Psalms 34:18. "God knows your heart is breaking, and He won't leave you. He'll stay close to you, and so will I."

He held his wife in his arms and allowed her to cry as he tried to soothe her spirit. He said a silent prayer for the family and especially for Kenya and Zaire's hearts to be healed of their past and present afflictions.

12

Zaire was surprised when Kenya showed up early at their grand-mother's house the next morning. Kenya followed her sister into the kitchen.

Zaire asked, "Would you like a cup of coffee and some break-fast? There's a few grits and eggs left over. I was able to get Big Momma to eat a little bit."

"No, thank you," Kenya answered. She soberly inquired, "How is she?"

"She's resting."

They sat down at the table. Trent had encouraged Kenya to ap-proach her sister once again. She was trying to reach out but didn't know quite what to say, so she asked, "Would you like to come to church with us this morning?"

Zaire felt relieved that she had a good excuse not to attend. "No, I have to stay with Big Momma."

"It's still early. We can call up someone to stay with her."

She'd been caught off guard. Zaire replied, "I'll stay with her. It's my turn, and I want to do my share."

Kenya complained, "You never come to church with us."

Zaire felt that Kenya had always been more spiritual than she was. Perhaps that was why she had become indifferent and Kenya hadn't. She'd thought a lot about how upset Kenya had gotten with her yesterday. Zaire had come to make peace, not more war. For years, she had been yearning for the opportunity to sit down and talk to her sister about her errors, and she'd messed it up. Maybe she should come clean regarding the apathy which had replaced her belief in God.

Zaire asked solemnly, "Do you remember when Momma and Daddy died and you asked me if I thought they were in heaven?"

"Yeah."

"Do you remember what I said?"

Kenya shrugged her shoulders. "I think you said you didn't know."

"Yes, that's what I said. And I said it because at that point, I wasn't sure anymore if God or heaven existed."

Kenya was shocked. "How could you think such a thing?"

"Because of what happened to Momma and Daddy—and on Thanksgiving no less. I couldn't understand—I still don't understand—how a loving God could allow something so terrible to happen to our family and especially at our favorite time of year. I no longer wanted to believe He existed because if He did, how could He let that happen?"

Kenya didn't want to hear anymore of her sister's crazy theories. She was appalled! "How can you ask those kinds of questions? We were raised to believe in God, and when something bad happened, you turned your back on Him. How can you just change your views like that? You need to let Him back in your life. No wonder you did what you did to me and Big Momma."

Zaire had thought she could open up her heart to her sister. She had not expected to be judged, criticized, and condemned. Never before had she shared those feelings of indifference with anyone, and the one person she used to be able to tell all her secrets to seemed to have turned even more against her.

Zaire glared at her sister. Up until this point, she had been able to remain calm despite Kenya's aloofness toward her. "How could you say something so terrible to me?"

"Well, if you hadn't been wondering stuff like that, do you think you would've turned into an atheist and walked out on your family?"

As she rose, Zaire's piercing eyes beamed down at Kenya. "Don't you dare sit there and try to judge me. You're a self-righteous snob who thinks you're better than everyone else. You sit there preaching the gospel to me when you don't even practice what you preach."

Kenya was standing up now, too. "What are you talking about?"

"You've got all the answers except when it comes to yourself. You know, I may not be a churchgoing fanatic like you, but I remember a thing or two about the Bible. Like forgiving people who wrong you. I know what I did to you and Big Momma was terrible. I wrote you letters. I sent you cards. And not once did you respond. Even when I came back, you refused to see me." Zaire threw up her hands. Coming back had been a huge mistake. She had tried to make amends with her sister, but she knew now that it was no use. "You know what? I don't need this. I'm through begging for your forgiveness. As soon as Big Momma's gone, I'm out of your life for good. That's what you want, isn't it?"

Kenya responded, without the tiniest bit of remorse, "You do what you wanna do." Then she was gone.

Over a month had passed since the eruption between Kenya and Zaire. For their grandmother and family's sake, they tried to be civil with one another. Paulette was now in the preactive phase of death, which the family had been told might last approximately two weeks. However, they'd also been advised that some patients show signs of the preactive stage of dying for a month or longer. Everyone was exhausted. They were very grateful for the Hospice workers and also for their church family and friends who graciously continued volunteering their assistance so that they could replenish their energies.

After church, Trent and Zaire took the children on a hayride. Kenya was in no mood to venture anywhere. Melva decided to stay in with her. They chatted as they sat comfortably in the Jamisons' family room.

Kenya somberly informed her cousin, "Zaire says she's leaving as soon as Big Momma's gone."

Melva asked, "*Leaving*—you mean for good?"

"Yeah. She says she'll be out of my life."

"Is that what you want?"

Kenya shook her head and shrugged her shoulders. "I don't know what I want anymore. My life will never be the same without Big Momma. When Momma and Daddy died, everything just started going downhill, and nothing's ever been the same."

Melva reached over and gently touched her cousin's hand. "Nothing's the same because you had a very drastic change take place in your life, and now you're about to have another one."

Kenya nodded. "Yeah."

They were silent for a moment.

Kenya said, "Zaire was always so carefree and outgoing. Everybody's right about me—I've always been rigid and no fun to be around. I don't know why I'm like this. Trent's always telling me to loosen up. I try, but I can't. It's like there's something within me holding me back."

Melva's mind digressed back to a time when the three young cousins were happy and carefree. She recalled their slumber parties and how their laughter filled the air. She kindly reminded her cousin, "You haven't always been that way. You, Zaire, and I used to have so much fun together. Then Aunt Angie and Uncle Reggie died. Even though we were young, I noticed then that that's when you began to shut down while Zaire seemed to just keep being herself. Maybe what's holding you back is the pain inside."

Kenya didn't offer her cousin a response but mulled over what Melva had just said.

When Trent and the children returned from their hayride, Kenya went to her grandmother's house to talk to Zaire. She peeked inside Paulette's bedroom. Zaire was sitting beside the bed talking to Paulette in a smooth, gentle tone. Paulette had begun having increased periods of lethargy, but the family still spoke to her often. Kenya didn't say a word as she entered and took a seat in a corner.

Although she was aware she'd get no verbal response, Zaire whispered to her grandmother, "Are you warm enough?" She gently pulled up the covers a little. Reaching over and grabbing a bottle from the nightstand, she squeezed a bit of lotion into the palm of her hand and rubbed her hands together. Then she tenderly massaged the cream over her grandmother's hands. "Gotta keep your hands soft and pretty. You always did have such beautiful hands." Drawing one of Paulette's hands to her lips, she brushed it with a delicate kiss.

Kenya was touched by the tender compassion her sister showed toward their grandmother. Zaire hadn't run away this time as she had in the past. Kenya began to think about the things she'd always liked about her sister—*the good.*

A few moments later, Zaire left the room so Kenya could be with their grandmother. After a brief visit, Kenya found her sister sitting in the living room and asked if they could talk. Although a little reluctant, Zaire agreed, and Kenya joined her on the sofa.

Kenya had tears in her eyes and wasted no time in expressing what she'd come to say. "When you left, I started to hate you. Nothing you could do or say would change the way I felt. Although I had Melva, Aunt Dorothy Mae, and some of our other relatives, I was so alone without you. I felt abandoned and betrayed. You weren't around for any of the bedside vigils for Big Momma, and I became very bitter toward you. I'm not telling you this to make you feel bad. I've been hiding from my feelings for too long, and I'm tired of hiding. I didn't like feeling that way. It frightened me to feel like that about my own sister. It was scary.

"I was afraid I would turn out like Daddy—not to the point of physically hurting you—it's just that I was consumed with so much hatred that I didn't know what I'd do or say, so I avoided you. I've had these feelings for years and didn't know how to deal with them. When I think about what Daddy did to Momma, it frightens me to death. I'm so afraid I may turn out like him. Maybe I already have. Look at how I've treated you." Kenya's lips began to tremble as the tears spilled down her face. "I'm so sorry. Can you ever forgive me?" she asked hopefully.

Zaire quickly got up from her spot on the sofa and moved closer to her sister, pulling Kenya into her arms. She said, "There's nothing to forgive. We were young. It doesn't matter anymore."

Kenya countered through her weeping, "It matters to me. I was wrong. We're adults now, and I've been acting so childish."

Zaire's response was laced with love. "I forgive you, Kenya." Pausing briefly, she went on, "When Big Momma was diagnosed with cancer, I couldn't take the thought of losing someone else again. Long before that, I lost my faith in God, though, when Momma and Daddy died. I never mentioned it to anybody and went to church because I knew it was what Big Momma expected.

"To this day, Thanksgiving just isn't the same. That's why I got so upset when you invited me and the kids for Thanksgiving dinner. While you stayed and tried to deal with your feelings as best you could, my solution is to always run away. The only problem with that is the feelings follow you wherever you go. I'm sorry for leaving like I did and not being there for you and Big Momma. Will you please forgive me?"

Kenya cried harder as she hugged Zaire with all her might. "Yes, I forgive you, Zaire."

Kenya and Zaire felt that everything had come full circle. Although they had loved ones who were no longer living and were about to lose another one, they sensed that the gaps had closed. And Zaire now had the chance to redeem herself and be by her grandmother's side as Paulette battled another illness.

Epilogue

It was the first Thanksgiving Zaire had spent with her family since she left home years ago. It was good to be with them again, and she was especially glad her children had become a part of her grandmother's legacy. Even after twenty-one years, it still pained her when she thought about the tragic events of the last Thanksgiving she and Kenya had shared with their parents. However, she was now looking forward to the time when painful memories would not be called to mind. Kenya had shared this scripture at Isaiah 65:17 with her.

After everyone's bellies were full, the children went outside to play. Dorothy went in to sit with her sister while Kenya and Melva cleaned up the kitchen. Zaire took a stroll into her and Kenya's old room. She opened up the closet and began rummaging through some of their old stuff that was still packed away.

Kenya and Melva were finishing up in the kitchen when Zaire came bursting in carrying a shoe box full of cassette tapes she'd discovered in the closet. "Look what I found. Remember these?"

Curious, Kenya questioned as she dried a plate, "What are they?"

Zaire replied, "They're the tapes you, me, and Melva made of us singing when we were young. Don't you remember?"

Melva started grinning as she came over to remove one of the tapes from the box. "Yeah, I remember these. Kenya, you remember."

Kenya responded, "Oh, yeah. How old were we when we made these? Fourteen, fifteen?"

Zaire answered, "Yeah, I think so. Let's put one in the cassette player."

Melva went over to the kitchen counter where her aunt kept her cassette player and popped in the tape. The first voice they heard was Zaire's singing "A Lovely Day." Then came Kenya and next was Melva. Soon the three women were singing along with the tape at the top of their lungs and dancing all over the kitchen floor. In a matter of seconds, Trent and the children had joined them; they, too burst into song and began to shimmy.

The next day, Kenya and Zaire took the tape and cassette player into their grandmother's room and played it for her. Afterwards, they sat on either side of Paulette's bed holding her hands and talking to her. They hoped she was cognizant of what they were saying. The Hospice care workers had told them Paulette would be able to hear them up until the very end even though she could not respond by speaking. They had been assured that their loving presence at their grandmother's bedside would help her to feel calmer and more at peace until she died.

Kenya assured Paulette, "Zaire and I are okay now, Big Momma. We know you're tired, and we know you're ready to go. We love you, and we're gonna miss you. You've lived a good life, and we know we'll see you again."

Zaire stated warmly, "Big Momma, I love you. I've always loved you. I'm sorry for leaving like I did years ago. I just thank God that He brought us back together before it was too late. I wish we had more time, but in the future we'll have forever. And that's a guarantee because like you always say, 'Our God don't lie.' "

Zaire now understood what she'd always heard her grandmother and others say about God always being on time even though He sometimes didn't come when you wanted Him to. Although she'd had her doubts about Him, He had seen her heart and helped her to make it back home to her family before it was too late.

Kenya had been harboring hatred and fear for years and was finally learning to let it go. And just like her grandmother had said, once she began looking, she had been able to take notice of the good in Zaire.

Kenya and Zaire thought they felt their grandmother squeeze their hands. It was a time of joy and sadness.

Paulette felt she could now let go. She was at peace with her Maker, and her girls were at peace with one another. They had been reunited. In God's due time, they would all be reconciled again. At last, her family had begun to experience a healing of the hearts that only God could provide.

The Devil's Advocate

Linda Hudson-Smith

1

As Stephanie Trudeaux perused the special-delivery letter she held
in her small hands, tears splashed downward from her lovely
autumn-brown eyes, leaving salty tracks on her pretty sienna-brown
face. After refolding the piece of registered mail, Stephanie tossed it
onto the teakwood coffee table, her thoughts in utter turmoil over
what she'd just read.

Feeling emotionally abused, Stephanie swept her tears away
with the back of her hand. "Why?" she shouted into the empty
room. "Why now, after all these years?"

Picking up the telephone receiver, Stephanie hit the memory dial
code that would connect her with her twin brother, Stephen, whom
she positively loved and adored. Stephen didn't live that far away,
but she knew he'd come running to her rescue no matter the distance.

Stephanie resided in the family home in Houston, Texas, in the
southeast portion of the fourth largest city in the United States.
Stephen Trudeaux, a single firefighter, lived nearby in his newly built
home in League City, which was also in the southeast section of
town. The Houston home the twins grew up in was located in Harris
County, and Stephen's new house was in Galveston County. Their
deceased mother, Doreen, had left the family home to both twins.

Twenty-eight-year-old Stephen was the elder twin by a mere five
minutes, but he acted as though he was several years older than his
mirror-image sibling. Stephen thought of Stephanie as his baby sister, often referring to her as his "darling angel." Long ago, when he
became old enough to understand his role as the only male in the

Trudeaux family, he had vowed to protect his mother and little sister at all costs and to stand by their side through thick and thin.

"Hello," Stephen greeted cheerfully.

Stephanie forced a smile to her generous lips when she heard her brother's familiar, silky-smooth Texas drawl. She also possessed a Southern accent, but it wasn't quite as distinct as Stephen's. "It's just me, Stephen."

Upon hearing his sister's whispery voice, Stephen dropped down on his king-size bed, clad only in a black silk robe. Stephanie always sounded like she was just waking up from a long winter's nap. She had the kind of wispy-soft voice men seemed to love.

Where six foot three, rock-hard muscled Stephen was rugged and drop-dead gorgeous, possessing the same skin, hair, and eye color as his twin sister, five foot six Stephanie was petite, soft, and delicately pretty. Despite being of the opposite sex, they looked very much alike.

"Hey, darling angel, what's cooking in your part of the city?"

Rolling her eyes to the back of her head, Stephanie moaned softly. "A very big pot of unsavory stew. Did you receive any special-delivery mail today, Stephen?"

Stephen glanced over at the coffee table, where a week's worth of mail was piled high. "No special deliveries here. And I've already received my regular mail today. I've sorted through it, but nothing particularly interesting caught my eye."

Stephanie battled fresh tears. "Well, I did." Her full lips trembled as she drew in a deep breath. "I received a letter from a law firm representing Malachi Trudeaux, our long-lost father."

Stephanie had expected the deafening silence, the dark abyss of nothingness. She kept her voice stilled out of respect for her twin. Stephen was at war with his emotions and she could feel all that he felt. He detested Malachi Trudeaux, despised the man who'd run out on their mother shortly before their birth, constantly voicing the deep hatred he felt for their biological father.

The long period of silence had Stephanie totally unnerved. "Stephen," she finally called out softly, "talk to me, Stephen."

Bravely fighting off his unstable emotions by clenching and gnashing his teeth, Stephen swiped at the tears pooling in the corners of his autumn-brown eyes. "What exactly did the letter say, Stephanie?"

Stephanie snorted. "A lot of rhetoric, as far as I'm concerned. It seems that Malachi is requesting our presence. He wants us to come to New Orleans and meet with him. I can't believe you didn't receive a letter too. It doesn't make sense that he'd send one only to me."

Stephen made a hissing sound into the phone. "That old man better think twice before he comes messing with me. According to Mama, I have the same hotheaded temper as him, so he'd do well to watch himself. Since twenty-eight years has passed us all by, what could he possibly have to say to either of us, Stephanie? What in the devil could he want from us?"

Stephanie shook her head from side to side. "I don't know. Mama's been dead for over a month now. The fact that he didn't bother to show up at the funeral makes me wonder why it's so important for him to contact us now. Maybe he doesn't even know that she's dead." Stephanie suddenly felt bitter and cold inside. It seemed to her that their mother's deep, abiding love for Malachi had all been in vain. She had simply loved a man who hadn't been able to love her back.

Stephen mumbled a few expletives. "Maybe he's finally developed a conscience. I don't know what's going on with him and I could care less. I just know that I don't want anything to do with the man. Disregarding my feelings, how do you feel about the situation, Stephanie?"

Nervously fingering the hemline of her denim shirt, Stephanie bit down on her lower lip, seriously pondering Stephen's question. "I don't know. I believe Mama died still loving him, so I'm kind of curious to know what she saw in him. If she loved him, and we know she did, there had to be some goodness in him at one time. Mama didn't give her love easily." Succumbing to the unyielding grief she still felt over her mother's untimely death, Stephanie's voice broke, and then she began to sob. "How dare he do this to us so soon after Mama's funeral?"

As if it were his very own misery, Stephen deeply felt Stephanie's. It broke him up inside when she cried. The two siblings had always been able to feel each other's emotions, and right now was no exception. "Come on now, Stephanie, don't cry. I'm here to take care of you, darling angel. You hold on tight. Soon as I get dressed, I'm on my way over there."

Once Stephen disconnected the line, Stephanie cradled the phone. After dropping down onto the creamy beige damask sofa, she curled her legs up under her. Looking around the spacious living room, she gave a cursory glance to some of the material fruits of her labor. None of what Stephanie possessed had come easy. As an entrepreneur of a home interior design studio, she constantly had to work doubly hard to keep her successful business up and running.

Before it was ever delivered to the home Stephanie had then shared with her mother, the sectional couch had been in layaway for six months, along with the two matching chairs. The teakwood coffee and end tables had been purchased during a clearance sale. Unmarred by wear or tear, the elegant antique cherrywood dining room set had been given to her mother by one of her rich employers. The newer furniture had been purchased as a surprise birthday present for her mother from her and Stephen, but Doreen Trudeaux hadn't lived long enough to enjoy it. After her heart had failed her for the first time, Doreen's death had come suddenly and swiftly.

It often amazed the twins that their mother had continued to work mainly as a domestic in this day and age, especially when there were so many other kinds of jobs that she could've trained for and done very well at. Doreen had so many jobs that her children couldn't even sum up her occupation in a word. She was a jack-of-all-trades and a master of many. She took in laundry, cleaned houses and offices, stacked and dusted books on the bookshelves at the local library, and also cooked special meals for several community churches.

The only day Doreen ever rested was on the Lord's Day. She had taught her children that a personal relationship with God, a solid roof over their heads, a clean place to sleep, daily bread, and healthy minds and bodies made them wealthier than most. Doreen had lived long enough to see both of her kids finish college and enter the workforce with respectable jobs.

Stephanie was so in awe of her mother and the way in which she handled everything with such diplomacy. Nothing ever seemed too hard for Doreen. She never spoke ill of her runaway husband, nor would she allow her kids to do so. As far back as Stephanie could remember, her mother hadn't ever made any excuses for Malachi's desertion of his family, but she never blamed him for it, either, at least not verbally. Stephanie often wondered how Doreen really felt.

Even when Stephanie had tried to outdo Stephen, which happened quite often, Doreen had taught them that it was okay to be competitive, but to never rival each other. Stephen was Doreen's boy-man and he had taken very seriously his status as man-of-the-house. She had taught her boy and girl all about hard work and the fringe benefits that could be reaped from such, yet Doreen had never completely indulged herself in the good things life had to offer.

Doreen had lived for her kids, and had died knowing they'd be well taken care of, which had been evident in the tidy sum of money she'd left for them. During the reading of the will, the twins had been astonished at the amount of money they were to receive, surprised that their mother even had a will, as poor as they'd been. As far as Stephanie and Stephen knew, Malachi had never paid one dime in child support to their mother, but that was something Doreen had never confirmed nor denied for them. As a very private person, Doreen often kept things inside.

Wanting desperately to understand why it suddenly seemed so important for their father to make contact with them after so many years had passed by, Stephanie picked up the letter and reread it. Seeing the gold-embossed name of the prestigious law firm representing Malachi gave Stephanie the impression that he must be doing very well for himself. It certainly didn't seem as if he was pinching pennies. She'd heard and read plenty about the New Orleans–based Saxtons, all of it very positive. A father-and-son team ran the nationally known law firm.

Upon hearing the key inserted into the lock, Stephanie looked over at the front door. Stephen stepped inside at the same time he flung back the door. Smiling charmingly at his sister, he blew her a kiss from across the room. Stephen then removed his jacket and hung it on one of the brass hooks on the mahogany hall tree. Long strides quickly brought him over to the sofa, where he sat down next to Stephanie and pulled her head against his chest. "Is this the letter?" he asked, removing it from her shaking hand.

Stephanie looked up at him and nodded. "Maybe you should take an aspirin before reading it. The content certainly has my head splitting." She smiled halfheartedly.

Stephen laughed as he lightly tousled Stephanie's hair. "I did that before I left home. Just hearing you mention Malachi's name instantly caused my head to throb. That old coot has some nerve. What makes him think we'd be at his beck and call?"

Stephanie shrugged. "Your guess is as good as mine, Stephen."

As if he somehow expected the content to change, Stephen continued to stare at the letter he'd already read three times. "I'm not going to even try and guess at Malachi's motives. It would be a waste of time, anyway. There's nothing he can do or say to convince me to come see him. He's the last person I want to lay eyes on. This situation has me so freaking angry."

Hoping to calm him down a bit, Stephanie squeezed Stephen's fingers. "Don't go getting yourself all worked up over this. If you don't want to go see him, I can understand that. But my curiosity won't let me stay away. Nor do I want to miss out on the opportunity to ask him all the questions I've repeatedly rehearsed in my head. I have to let him know just how I feel about his absence in our lives." She lifted herself up from the sofa. "Want something to snack on?"

Stephen finally looked up from the letter. "Thanks, Stephanie, but I'd just finished eating breakfast when you phoned me. I'm still pretty full right now. Have you eaten?"

Stephanie sighed hard as she moved toward the kitchen. "I'm going to get a little something now. I'm not overly hungry, but I could eat. I'll be right back."

Stephen looked after Stephanie with concern. Although she hadn't been dieting, she had recently lost quite a few pounds, weight that she really couldn't afford to lose off her mere one-hundred-ten-pound frame. It bugged Stephen to see how much their mother's death had taken a toll on her. He'd never seen his sister looking so poorly and it had him worried.

The new upgrades of shiny stainless steel appliances, granite countertops, burnt sienna maple cabinets, and earth-toned tiled flooring and matching backsplash made the spacious, island-style kitchen very warm and quite appealing to the eye. A round solid wood table and four chairs sat atop a beautiful round Asian-style rug done in a variation of browns and rich gold tones. Beige-and-white cell shades graced the kitchen's bay and two slender side windows.

Stephen stepped into the room just as Stephanie filled a tall glass with a mixture of cranberry and orange juices. When he slammed his fist down on the breakfast bar, she flinched, nearly dropping the drink from her hand. Seeing the deep pain in her brother's eyes tore at her heartstrings. Stephen was in so much emotional pain, but she couldn't ease his agony.

Stephen began to pace, waving his hands wildly about. "I can't believe this guy," he shouted. "Where was Malachi Trudeaux when Mama was working her fingers to the bone? Where was he when we really needed him? Who knew where he was when you and I were working our butts off and going to school at the same time? Where was he all those nights we heard Mama crying herself to sleep, Stephanie? Where?"

Stephanie sat the glass down on the counter and reached for her brother's hand. As he pulled away from her grasp, she realized how angry he'd gotten. His rage upset her. In a silent prayer she asked that God restore Stephen's calm to him, along with a truckload of compassion.

"Now that we've managed to haul our behinds off the rocks, off the jagged stones that kept our feet bleeding profusely, he wants to see his children. That no-good jerk must be sick or dying. As a fire-fighter, I've saved many lives and numerous dwellings, but I'll rot to death before I rescue Malachi from his sudden attack of guilt. He can burn in hell for all I care."

Stephanie gently coerced Stephen into sitting down on one of the stools at the breakfast bar. "Don't let him do this to you, Stephen. Your emotions are snowballing out of control. We can't let his un-caring attitude with us dictate our actions toward him. Mama would want us to go see him, especially if he's ill. 'Be true to your-selves.' Mama always told us to do that. We can't let this incident change who and what we are inside. We're good people, Stephen."

Looking into the eyes of his sister, Stephen wiped his tears away with the paper napkin Stephanie had handed him. "Sorry for losing control, Sis. I just couldn't help it."

She ran her fingers through his thick waves. "That's okay. But Malachi has to answer to God, not to us. Leave his judgment up to his Maker. It's not up to us to mete out his punishment. Stephen, we're nothing like Malachi, so let's not start behaving like him."

Pushing his glass of juice around on the counter, Stephen eyed Stephanie with open skepticism. "How do you know we're not like him? We don't even know who he is. When you think about it, Mama didn't say that much about him, except that he'd probably return one day. Well, we know how that turned out. He didn't even show his face at her funeral. Heck, we really don't know anyone from his side of the family. All of the Trudeauxs have deserted us."

Stephanie shook her head from side to side. "We don't know

that for sure, Stephen. His parents could've already been dead when we were born. Maybe he's an only child. We just don't know, but I think we owe it to ourselves to find out. We'll never have complete serenity until we get the answers from our father. If he is ill or dying, this may be our last chance to get at the truth and reconcile our differences. Will you go to New Orleans with me, Stephen?"

Stephen closed his eyes, wishing Stephanie hadn't asked him that particular question. He hated denying her anything within reason. He didn't need to look at her to know she was close to tears. Her sorrow and pain was in her voice. Her sorrow was his sorrow. Her pain was every bit his pain. It had always been like that and he couldn't imagine it ever changing. "Oh, Stephanie," he moaned, "you're one of the most successful businesswomen that I personally know, and I'm darn good at what I do for a living. Why do we need to do this for him, darling angel? There's no room for Malachi in our lives. We've got each other. That's all the family we need."

Stephanie leaned over and rested her chin atop Stephen's head. He had made some valid points, but she just couldn't concede. They had to see Malachi, had to learn as much as they could about their father, their background, which was their heritage. She didn't want anything he had to offer, monetary or otherwise, but she did want to know what caused this man to run off and leave his wife alone with newborn twins. She also desired to know if they had other siblings, grandparents, aunts, and uncles. If they didn't honor Malachi's request, they'd never know.

Stephanie crossed her hands on top of her head. "Don't be so hard, Stephen. I've never seen you act this cold and bitter. Just give yourself a couple of days to think it over. But Stephen, I have to tell you, I believe we should go."

Stephen smiled lazily. "It's not that I'm so hard. It's just that you have a big old marshmallow for a heart. No matter how many times someone spears your heart and then plunges it into the fire, you recover, and then you go and expose it all over again. You give up your heart too easily, Stephanie. Malachi's not worthy of your love. Nor is he worthy of mine. I'm sorry, but I can't go to New Orleans. If you want to go, I won't try to talk you out of it. But please don't ask me to be thrilled about it, because I can't be."

Stephanie's displeasure showed in her eyes. "Is that your final word, Stephen?" Stephanie knew she could get Stephen to do just about anything for her, but she wasn't going to press him on this one. She deeply respected her brother but knew where to draw the line with her requests. She wouldn't want her brother to do something he was totally against. By the stubborn set of his jaw, she could easily see that Stephen was totally against meeting Malachi.

Hating to disappoint her in any way, Stephen got to his feet and warmly embraced his sister. "It is, Stephanie. I've got to run now. Are you going to be okay?"

Stephanie took hold of both her brother's hands, strong hands that had literally been through fire. "I'll be just fine. I'm glad you came over. Where are you running off to?"

"I'm taking Darcy to the movies, a matinee. I don't know what we're going to see, but I'm sure she has something already picked out. Want to come with us?"

Darcella Coleman, a registered nurse, had been Stephen's love interest for the past three years. Due to their mother's bad experience with marriage, neither twin was interested in going through the rituals of matrimony. Stephanie was terrified of just the word itself, and Stephen had the tendency to steer clear of any conversation geared toward forever after.

"Not today, big brother. I've got some important paperwork to catch up on. Tomorrow is Friday, and I can hardly wait for the weekend to begin. You and Darcy enjoy yourselves."

"Thanks, Stephanie. We will. Come on and walk me to the door."

Smiling softly, Stephanie gestured for her brother to scoot. "You know the way out, boy. Call me later, before I shut down for the night."

The doorbell rang just as Stephen was about to exit. He opened the door to find a stranger standing on his sister's doorstep. "How can I help you, brother?"

Smiling, the man extended a mocha brown hand toward Stephen. After a firm handshake, he reached into his breast pocket and took out a business card, which he handed to Stephen. "I'm looking for Miss Stephanie Trudeaux. I represent Mr. Malachi Trudeaux."

Stephan carefully studied the gold-embossed card. He then turned to go back inside to get Stephanie, noticing instantly that she had already stepped into the hallway, though out of sight of the man inquiring about her. She had obviously heard the doorbell.

"This gentleman is the 'devil's advocate,' Stephanie. Are you interested in seeing him?"

"I'm only one of Mr. Trudeaux's attorneys," the man said with undisguised indignation. "I didn't attend college all those years to be referred to as a 'devil's advocate.' I can assure you, sir, that everyone in our law firm is quite ethical."

As Stephen sniffed arrogantly, Stephanie stepped forward, giving her brother a scolding glance. She'd never known Stephen to be rude to anyone, especially someone he'd never met before. His nose was seriously out of joint over this, she mused. "Hello," she said politely, extending her hand to the handsome, muscular stranger, who possessed crystal-clear eyes, the color of smoked topaz. "I'm Stephanie Trudeaux. What can I do for you?"

"Gregory Saxton, Miss Trudeaux. Most folks call me Tré, as I'm the third Gregory in the family." Before letting go of her hand, Gregory held on to it for a few brief moments, appearing slightly stunned. He had let his professionalism fly right out the window, which had him thoroughly embarrassed. This woman could probably not care less about what anyone called him.

Though Gregory was no longer touching her, Stephanie was shaking from the fleeting encounter. As his smoky gaze held her captive, his heated touch had sent a blaze of fire right up her spine. Stephanie quickly turned her attention to Stephen, breaking the mesmerizing spell she'd fallen under. "I'd like to hear what Mr. Saxton has to say, Stephen. I want you to stay and hear him out as well. Can you please do that for me?"

Although he didn't want to hear anything Malachi's henchman had to say, Stephen wouldn't think of leaving his sister alone in her house with a stranger.

Upon hearing Stephanie call Stephen by name, Gregory stepped into the hallway. Looking back and forth between the two siblings, he realized these were the Trudeaux twins. That meant he didn't have to take his mission any further than this one address.

Gregory stroked his chin. "Actually, I needed to see you both." He looked Stephen dead in the eye. "I was going to call on you after I left here, Mr. Trudeaux. Can you stay and join us?"

Stephen pursed his lips. "I guess you wouldn't have found me at home, since I'm here. I can make this meeting short and to the point, Mr. Saxton. I'm not interested in anything your client has asked you to convey. As far as I'm concerned, the devil of a man is just a sperm donor, nothing more or less. But I will stay and support my sister. Shall we go into the living room?" As he led the way, Stephen draped his arm around Stephanie's slender shoulders.

Gregory followed the twins into the living room, seating himself on the short end of the L-shaped sectional sofa. Stephanie and Stephen sat at the opposite end.

After opening his briefcase, Gregory removed two sets of stapled papers and handed a set to each of the siblings. As Stephanie and Stephen perused the documents, Gregory crossed his legs, dragging his eyes ever so slowly over the very attractive Stephanie. If the circumstances were different, and had they lived in the same state, he knew he could go for her in a big way.

Once he read the papers, Stephen made an airplane out of one and then sailed it across the room. "Tell Malachi he's wasting his time on us. My sister and I aren't up for sale. We know how to take care of ourselves. We've practically done it all our lives, Mr. Saxton."

Stephanie squeezed Stephen's hand pretty hard, her way of trying to keep him in check. "What makes you think he's trying to buy us, Stephen? There's no mention of money in these documents. None whatsoever."

As he raised himself up from the sofa, Stephen's laughter was derisive. "You have to learn to read between the lines, darling angel. These documents are more about what they don't say than what's actually spelled out in black and white. Isn't that right, Mr. Saxton?"

Gregory stood also. "Whatever you say, Mr. Trudeaux. I'm not here to agree or disagree with you. The Saxton firm represents your father. Seeing that you and your sister received these letters comes with the job. Normally we send out any important correspondence by registered mail, but our client requested they be delivered in person. That's the deal in a nutshell."

Stephanie rose to her feet and stood alongside Stephen. "Now that you've done your job, Mr. Saxton, I'll see you to the door. My brother and I need to talk in private. I'll be back in contact with you as soon as possible. Are you leaving Houston right away?"

Gregory raised an eyebrow, mentally noting that the lady wasn't one to mince words. For all her angelic looks and seemingly timid personality, Gregory now had a totally different read on her from his initial impression. Instead of shy and weak, he saw that she possessed quiet strength and a strong will. He liked strong women, especially assertive ones.

Gregory trapped Stephanie within his warm gaze. "I'll be in town until late tomorrow evening, Miss Trudeaux. I'm staying at the Hobby Airport Hilton should you need to contact me. The phone number of the hotel is penciled in on the back of my business card." Gregory bent over and closed his briefcase, gripping the handle tightly. "I hope to hear from you soon."

Stephen opened his mouth to protest, until Stephanie squeezed his hand hard again.

Gregory clearly read Stephen's expression. "I know where you stand, Mr. Trudeaux, but your sister hasn't committed one way or the other." Gregory smiled at Stephanie. "Good evening, Miss Trudeaux, Mr. Trudeaux. I can find my own way out." His parting glance showed his desire to get to know Stephanie better. He hoped he'd made his interest in her perfectly clear.

Stephanie listened for the door to catch before she clicked her tongue disapprovingly at her brother. "There was no need for you to be so rude, Stephen. He's only doing his job."

A boyish grin tugged at Stephen's lips. "Yes, and by the look of things, he's snagged you in the process. You could barely keep your eyes off him, Stephanie. You're smitten with *the devil's advocate*. Watch yourself, darling angel. Gregory Saxton may have come here to represent Malachi, but he left here desperately wanting Malachi's only daughter. That is, the only daughter we know of."

Rolling her eyes, Stephanie pointed toward the hallway. "Should I offer to escort you to the door, too, Stephen? If you keep talking like that, I'm going to toss you out of here on your ear. Gregory Saxton doesn't even know I'm alive, at least not in the romantic sense."

Stephen laughed at the thought of his sister tossing him anywhere, since she weighed in only at a mere one hundred and ten pounds. She had a hard time keeping her weight above a hundred and five, which was always a big concern for him since she ate like a horse. "Oh, he knows you're alive all right. If I read him correctly, he's just dying to take your pulse."

Dropping down on the sofa, Stephanie swatted at her brother playfully. "Go home, Stephen. The muggy heat has gotten to you." She laughed at Stephen's pouting expression. "I know you mentioned going to an early movie with Darcy, but aren't you on duty tonight?"

"Yeah, I go in at midnight. I'll be on duty for four nights straight and then I'll be off for several days. When do you start your vacation?"

"At the end of next week. I hope I can finish up everything before then. I have several interior design projects to complete. Business is good, so I have no complaints."

"You'll get it all done, Stephanie. You're one of the most efficient persons I know." Stephen dropped down next to his sister. "What do you think of the meeting we just had?"

Stephanie shrugged. "We don't know too much more than we knew before Mr. Saxton showed up. The papers pretty much say the same as the letter I have. Something's definitely up, but I just don't know what. Malachi has a reason for summoning us to New Orleans."

"You can bet the farm on that one. The man is up to something. I understand all your reasons for wanting to see him, Stephanie, but none of them is compelling enough for me to consider it. We've done without him all these years and I see no reason why we have to suddenly make room for him in our lives. He'll be nothing more than a big interruption. If he had come to us when we were a lot younger, it might make sense to me. We're no longer children."

Stephanie smiled weakly, the usual brilliance missing from her eyes. "I know how you feel, Stephen, and I understand it. At any rate, I'm going to give a lot of thought to visiting him. If I end up wanting to get to know him, you can later learn who he is through me. Is that okay?"

Stephen frowned lightly. "Yeah, it's okay. I just don't want to see you get hurt." He bent over the sofa and kissed her brow. "See you later, Stephanie. I'll call you from work."

Stephanie got up from the sofa, but she didn't follow Stephen out. Formalities were rarely practiced between the two, yet they normally called each other before showing up on the other's doorstep. The welcome mat was always out, as both were free to come and go as they pleased. As long as one sibling had a home, the other one would never be homeless.

Despite their closeness Stephanie was terribly afraid that her decision to meet Malachi might come between them. If she somehow had to choose between her father and brother—though she hoped it wouldn't come down to that—Stephen would win hands down. There would be no contest in that instance. Her brother was the only male who'd always been there for her.

Stephanie closed her eyes and sent up a quiet supplication, asking God to work everything out for both her and Stephen. If it was His will for her to meet her father, she asked to be given some sort of sign. She also prayed that her desire to see Malachi wouldn't put a wedge between her and Stephen.

2

Stephanie pushed back the sliding glass door and stepped out onto the patio. Stephen had laid the concrete slab all by himself, covering it with a shingled roof. Gray Hardy plank decking complemented the large patio, along with comfortable outdoor furniture, including a wooden swing. Large clay pots housed a variety of plants and colorful blooms.

In less than a few seconds humidity had Stephanie surrounded. She immediately felt beads of moisture forming on her skin. The curls around her face and nape had become instantly damp. One corner of the patio always received a cool breeze at night, which helped to relieve her overheated flesh, but nothing but a good rain could squelch the burning heat of this fall day.

At the same moment Stephanie stretched out in the chaise lounge, she heard the side gate open and close. Coming from around the side of the house at breakneck speed was Farrah Freeman, Stephanie's lifelong friend, next-door neighbor, and part-time employee.

Upon spotting Stephanie on the lounge, Farrah smiled brightly. "I thought I'd find you back here. I rang that bell too many times for you not to hear it if you were inside. I knew you were home. You need to have Stephen wire the doorbell so it rings out here. You might miss some important company one day. I know, I know. I've already said that a thousand times."

Farrah took a moment to catch her breath, causing Stephanie to crack up. Sometimes she talked so fast that she'd run out of steam, which seemed to be the case now. There was rarely a dull moment when she was around. Farrah was always the life of the party.

Stephanie and Farrah's loyalty to each other was so amazing. The two women were friends for life.

Sassy, sleek, and slender Farrah dropped down on the swing hard enough to make it move back and forth. "Speaking of company, who was the fine brother that just left your house? I thought Muhammad Ali was old and retired. And as far as I know, I don't think he has a son!" In anticipation of Stephanie's response, Farrah wrapped one of her reddish-brown curls around her nut-brown finger. "Who was he, Stephanie? I'm dying to know."

No longer having to figure out who Gregory reminded her of, Stephanie snapped her finger, grinning widely. She definitely had to agree with Farrah. He did look very much like a younger version of Muhammad Ali. "Gregory Saxton, the devil's advocate. He's a member of the New Orleans law firm Saxton & Saxton. I'm sure you've heard about them."

Whistling loudly, Farrah stretched her shimmering ebony eyes. The unexpected shrill sound nearly jarred Stephanie's bones, making her wince. "Of course I have. Saxton & Saxton," Farrah reiterated, frowning with curiosity, "why are those rich folks coming to see you?"

With her bright mood quickly fading, Stephanie rolled her eyes upward. "They represent the devil himself, Malachi Trudeaux, who suddenly wants to see his kids." Stephanie laid out the entire saga for Farrah, her tone lacking its normal enthusiasm.

Stephanie sighed hard. "I'd like to meet him, too, just to see what he's all about. I'd also like to know what he looks like. Unfortunately Stephen wants nothing to do with him."

Stephanie thought it was so sad that she and Stephen didn't even know what Malachi looked like. There hadn't been a single photograph of him anywhere in the house. It seemed as though he were a phantom of some sort. When the twins would ask Doreen what he looked like, she would always say, "He'll be back one day, then you can see for yourselves."

Doreen had been right about him coming back, but she hadn't lived to see that day.

Often when their mother wasn't home, the siblings would look through her personal effects, which had been hidden away in an old cedar chest. But they hadn't been able to find anything to do with Malachi, not even their parents' marriage certificate or anything akin to divorce papers. However, Malachi was listed as the biological father on their birth certificates.

Until the letters from Malachi had arrived, Stephanie had begun to believe he was a figment of their mother's imagination, and that Doreen might not even know who their father was. Because Doreen had never had a relationship with another man, Stephanie knew that her mother wasn't a promiscuous woman. But there were all sorts of circumstances out there in the world, those where women were taken total advantage of, and then left all alone and pregnant. That was the very scenario Stephanie had entertained quite often. It was the only one that made any sense.

Farrah moved off the swing and onto one of the lawn chairs. "Stephanie, you've been wondering about this man since forever, so I think you should see him. Stephen is a male, a prideful one. It's probably hard for him to let his ego make a compromise with his heart. If this meeting is ever going to happen, Stephanie, you'll have to be the one to take the lead. Stephen won't, so don't expect him to. But I do believe he'll come around in due time."

Stephanie stood up and began pacing the deck. "I just hate to go to New Orleans alone, Farrah, but I guess I'll have to. Of course I'm going to give the whole idea a lot more thought, but I believe my mind's already made up. At the very least, Malachi owes us an explanation. And more than anything else, I want to know why he didn't attend Mama's funeral."

"You deserve an explanation, Stephanie. I'd go to New Orleans with you, but I'm not taking any vacation days until around the Christmas holidays. You should be glad the weather has started to cool off, though it's hot today. Much like Houston, New Orleans is like Hades in the fall. I've been so eager to feel much cooler days. How long do you plan to be gone?"

Stephanie pursed her lips. "I'm thinking three or four days, max. One day to see Malachi. On the other ones I plan to see the sights and hear the sounds of New Orleans. Mama took Stephen and me there when we were around twelve, but I haven't been back since. Those memories are very dim now. I was too young then to understand the rich history of the city. I'll appreciate it a lot more now that I know some of what it's all about."

"Sounds like fun to me. If you're only going to be gone a few days, I might try to go with you. I'll check the vacation schedule tomorrow. If no one is scheduled off, I'll see what I can do. I'll still have plenty of time left for the holidays. I rarely take all my vacation days."

Farrah worked full time as a physical therapist at a local hospital and was also a part-time accountant for Stephanie's home interior business. The girl truly had a way with numbers.

Stephanie rushed over and hugged Farrah. "That would be super, girl. We could catch some jazz on Bourbon Street—and we just might catch the roving eye of one or more hot-blooded males. Southern men are often touted as the good ones, great catches."

Rolling her eyes, Farrah sucked her teeth. "I wouldn't know. The only thing I'm likely to catch in New Orleans is a cold. You know my track record with men. Simply put, the ones that I want don't want me, like that fine-behind brother of yours."

Knowing of her deep infatuation with Stephen, Stephanie shot Farrah a sympathetic look.

"Don't look at me like that, Stephanie Trudeaux! I don't want your sympathy or your pity. I just want a man. Not just any man, a real good one." Farrah released a heavy sigh.

Stephanie hated to see her friend looking so unhappy. Neither of them had had very good luck with men. They always seemed to run into the wrong kind of guys, the ones with the worst agendas. It seemed like most of the men they encountered were looking for a woman they could move in with and be taken care of by. A lot had changed with the dating scene.

Stephanie dated occasionally, but she wasn't interested in getting into another long-term relationship. It had been almost two years since she and Ramón Collier had called it quits after dating exclusively for two years. Although they still remained friends, the couple had just outgrown each other. All the things they once seemed to have in common had somehow up and disappeared. The breakup had been by mutual agreement. Ramón still had high hopes of rekindling their burnt-out romance, but Stephanie saw no chance for such an occurrence. She had moved way past all stages leading up to reconciliation with him.

Farrah got to her feet and stepped off the edge of the patio.

"Are you leaving already, Farrah? You just got here."

"I'm afraid so, dear friend. My day off will be over before you know it. I have to iron something to wear to work tomorrow. I'm not organized like you. If I had a week's wardrobe all figured out,

I'd think I had finally cracked under the pressure of not having a man in my life."

Farrah laughed along with Stephanie.

"If it's not too late when I'm through with everything, I'll come back over. Otherwise, we'll talk tomorrow, Stephen's darling angel."

"Whatever you decide, I'll be here. See you or talk to you later, Farrah."

Stephanie smiled inwardly at Farrah's parting comment. Everyone who knew the twins was aware of the name Stephen affectionately called his sister. Stephanie could clearly remember the first time her brother had dubbed her as his darling angel. After stretching her body out fully on the chaise, she then lowered the top of the lounge so that her head rested back comfortably. Still smiling over that memory, Stephanie closed her eyes.

That summer day in Houston had been hot and insufferably muggy. The twins had been at the local playground, happily riding the merry-go-round. The swirling air, though relatively hot, had given them a brief respite from the clinging heat. Several of Stephen's male friends had been pushing the ride while Stephanie had sat in the middle of it, atop the bars. The speed of the merry-go-round, coupled with the heat, had caused Stephanie to become dizzy. A horrible feeling of nausea had formed in her stomach just before she'd toppled from the bars and hit her head hard on the wooden platform.

Stephen had screamed for the boys to stop pushing the playground ride, but it had taken a long time before they'd heard him because of all the laughter and gleeful shouting. As soon as the merry-go-round had slowed enough to mount, Stephen had made a mad dash for his sister. Once he had her safely cradled in his arms, he kissed the growing lump on her left temple, frowning at the rapid change in the color surrounding the bruise.

"It's okay, darling angel," he'd soothed, repeating it over and over again. Tears welled in Stephanie's eyes as she revisited the long ago tender moment between the siblings. She and Stephen were more than siblings, more than twins. They were each other's best friend. That didn't mean there weren't any verbal fights or major disagreements between them, because there'd been plenty of spats over the past twenty-eight years. Just as their mother had taught them not to rival each other, she'd also taught them not to hold grudges. Doreen was forever preaching on forgiveness.

Stephen was Stephanie's knight in shining armor, whether she wanted him to be or not. Most of his friends hated to have their sisters tagging along behind them, but Stephen had insisted on it, thwarting their taunts to leave her at home. Never once had he resented the responsibility that Doreen had placed on him in looking after Stephanie while she was away. Stephen's emotional maturity was so much more advanced than Stephanie's had been when they were younger, which had made him all the more protective of her.

Stephanie welcomed the peace that now engulfed her. The morning hours had been very trying and she hoped the rest of the day would go much better. Her thoughts then turned to Gregory Saxton. She couldn't help wondering what type of man he was. He had certainly been polite and gentlemanly toward her. Remembering how his hackles had risen at the derogatory name Stephen had called him had revealed to her that he was no pushover. She liked a man who knew how to stand up for himself in the face of adversity. She had an inkling that Gregory had earned Stephen's respect by his swift response to her brother's rudeness, but Stephen would never admit to that. Right now all he saw Mr. Saxton as was just another adversary from the enemy's camp.

Now that she'd made up her mind to go to New Orleans, Stephanie thought of phoning Gregory to let him know of her decision. He had informed her that he'd make all the necessary arrangements for her trip should she decide to go. She didn't know where she was supposed to stay while in Louisiana, but she hoped hotel accommodations would be chosen. She couldn't imagine herself staying in the home of a stranger, even if the stranger was her own father.

There were so many things she wanted to say to Malachi, so many things she was dying to learn about his family and him. Her biggest concern was how she was going to react to her father. How was she supposed to react to a man who'd deserted his family? Just thinking about coming face-to-face with her father gave her a bad case of the shivers. She certainly couldn't see herself rushing into his arms like a love-deprived orphan, a person who just wanted to belong to someone, anyone. No, it wouldn't be like that, she silently vowed.

Malachi would never know how needy Stephanie really was for the love of her father.

The more thought Stephanie gave to the visit, the easier it became for her to convince herself that meeting her father for the first time could actually be a very exciting prospect. She was aware that it could be even more so if only she and Stephen were of one accord. This was a monumental event, one they should face together, instead of being at odds over it.

Since she and Stephen resembled their mother, she couldn't even conjure up an image of what Malachi might look like. She remembered the one time when she and Stephen had pressed Doreen hard to describe him for them. Once again, Doreen's answer had been sort of off-the-wall. She'd told them that Malachi was tall, dark, and extremely beautiful, and looked pretty much like the description given of the rebellious angel, Lucifer.

The two males certainly had a lot in common, Stephanie thought churlishly. An errant Lucifer was kicked out of heaven, taking a third of the angels with him, while Malachi had run off willingly, leaving behind his entire family, forsaking heaven in the process. She'd only read in the Bible about Lucifer's deviousness, but she'd experienced Malachi's evil deeds firsthand.

Stephanie wanted so much to keep an open mind where Malachi was concerned, but she found it exceedingly hard to do so. She couldn't find any acceptable excuse for such cowardly behavior, yet she was willing to hear her father out and would try to give him the benefit of the doubt.

Was it possible that she and Stephen had Malachi figured out all wrong? Could there have been a set of highly unusual circumstances surrounding his decision to leave Houston? Just another burning question, she mused, one that'd she'd never know the answer to if she didn't make the trip to New Orleans. Since Stephen wanted no part of discovering anything about the man who'd fathered them, she'd have to be the one to do it for both their sakes. Their dreams for the future would never be fulfilled until all the facts of the past were known, and then put to rest.

Since Malachi was the only living being that could supply her with all the answers, Stephanie once again deemed the journey as imperative.

With all systems on go, Stephanie pulled out Gregory's business card. She then called the Hilton Hotel. Thinking she'd probably have to leave a message for him, she was surprised when he answered the phone. It took her a couple of seconds to find her voice, since his did strange things to her. "Mr. Saxton, this is Miss Trudeaux.

I'm calling to let you know that I've decided to see my father. I'd like for you to get the ball rolling and get back to me on the details."

"I'm happy to hear that, Miss Trudeaux. But let me ask you something. This Miss and Mr. thing sounds a bit too formal to me. Do you think we could ease things up a bit since we'll be conversing on a regular basis, at least for a short time? I have no objection to you calling me Gregory, Greg, or even Tré. Is my suggestion okay with you?"

Stephanie snorted under her breath. The last thing she needed was to become overly familiar with Malachi's legal counsel. Then she gave his congenial suggestion another thought, quickly deciding there was no harm in them being on a first-name basis. "That's fine with me, Gregory. I'll be waiting to hear back from you on travel arrangements."

Gregory made a couple of more comments regarding travel plans before ringing off.

After the electric gate was opened from inside by the mistress of the place, Eliza Beth Tobias, affectionately known as Liza, Stephanie parked her midnight blue Volvo convertible in the circular driveway of the spectacular Tudor-style estate home. Although she'd been in numerous estate-size homes and even inside several mansions, she was always mesmerized. That there were so many black people who actually lived like royalty never ceased to amaze her. Since it was so far from her own reality, Stephanie had never even dared to daydream about living in a mansion, but she loved to visit her clients who did. These homes were a decorator's dream.

With a good grip on her briefcase, Stephanie moved toward the towering front door. Just as she reached the top step of the landing, Eliza Beth appeared in the entryway, smiling broadly.

"Hi, Stephanie," Eliza Beth gushed merrily. "Come on in. I took the liberty of having Ms. Sarah fix us an early supper before taking her leave for the evening."

Stephanie smiled back at her wealthy client, the gorgeous, classy wife of world-renowned cardiovascular surgeon, Lemanz Tobias. Stephanie normally didn't get too chummy with her clients, but Eliza Beth was one of those bubbly women who hardly anyone could resist. Their business relationship had turned into a nice friendship over the past several months, yet Stephanie had never shared any deep confidences with anyone other than Stephen and Farrah. On occasion Stephanie and Eliza Beth went shopping, had luncheon dates, and had taken in a few movies. Their love for interior design was what they mostly had in common.

Stephanie chuckled, rubbing her stomach. "You didn't need to have Ms. Sarah go to all that trouble, Liza. But since you did, I don't mind telling you I'm more than a bit hungry. The snack I had earlier this morning is gone with the wind."

Eliza Beth cupped her hand under Stephanie's elbow. "In that case, we can go straight back to the kitchen. I don't know how much business we'll feel like doing after devouring a plate of Ms. Sarah's delicious soul food, but we can worry about that later."

Stephanie's eyes danced with joy. "What did Ms. Sarah fix this time?" Stephanie had instantly taken a shine to the fifty-three-year-old Sarah Watson, the Tobias's chef and nutritionist. Ms. Sarah was just as taken with Stephanie. Having had a daughter who'd died in her early teens, Ms. Sarah loved to dote on her employer and her group of friends. She often wished her daughter was still around for her to love and pamper. Ms. Sarah was also a widow of five years.

Eliza Beth hunched her shoulders. "I don't know. I only requested soul food. I rarely go in there when she's working on her masterpieces. I love to take a taste of this and a pinch of that, which is very annoying to her. After she threatened to quit on me if I didn't stay out of her pots and pans, I do my best to keep myself away from her food until it's ready to be served."

Stephanie grinned. "I feel you on that. Whatever it is, I know it's going to be delicious."

Out in the mammoth-size, bright, and cheerful kitchen Stephanie and Eliza Beth wasted no time in filling their plates with collard greens, yams, and macaroni and cheese. The delectable scent of cornbread muffins was still in the air. Smothered steak and onions, along with thick brown gravy, and a roasting pan full of braised lamb chops appeared cooked to perfection. A huge tossed garden salad rounded out the meal. Freshly baked peach cobbler had been prepared for dessert. The piecrust had been toasted to a golden brown and sprinkled lightly with sugar.

Weight issues hounded Eliza Beth from time to time, but that didn't stop the hostess from digging into her food with gusto. So that her weight didn't become a major problem, she had employed a personal trainer to keep her in check. Matthew Parker came to the house twice a week to put Eliza Beth through a vigorous work-out program he'd designed especially for her. Not only was the Tobias gym outfitted with every kind of exercise machine ever made, along with a wet and dry sauna, and a massive indoor whirlpool, but an Olympic-size lap pool was also housed on the property.

Settled down at the kitchen table, which was large enough to seat eight, Eliza Beth passed the blessing. Stephanie joined in on giving a hearty amen at the end of the humble prayer.

Stephanie closed her eyes after the first bite. "This is so yummy. If Ms. Sarah were still here, I'd give her a big hug. She sure knows how to throw down in the kitchen."

Eliza Beth laughed. "I know that's right. I love all the different cheeses she puts into the macaroni dish, but that's one dairy product that doesn't always love me. But I don't have the same problem with plain milk. Go figure. I won't eat too much of the macaroni so I can keep my stomach from suffering later." Despite her comment Eliza Beth filled her fork with the cheesy dish and popped it into her mouth, closing her eyes to savor the delectable taste.

Eliza Beth waved her fork in the air as her eyes popped open. "What's been happening in your exciting life? Have you done any celebrities lately?"

Stephanie nearly choked on the iced tea she had taken a large swallow of. After taking a minute to make sure all the drink went down the right way, she looked at Eliza Beth and cracked up. "You need to learn how to phrase things a little more delicately. I know what you meant, but someone else might not have. No, I don't have any celebrity clients right now. However, I have had a consultation with a young brother who's going places in the music world. He's a songwriter and producer. He was just contracted to write several songs for a couple of superstar divas. He goes simply by S. B. Smith. Only twenty-five years old, the young man is having a home built out in Whispering Lakes, right off the I-45 South, not too far from Galveston."

Eliza Beth nodded. "I know exactly where Whispering Lakes is. I have a friend who's building out there. Housing is going up every-where around this city. It won't be long before Houston will be charging California-type real estate prices. Speaking of houses, how's that fantastic-looking twin brother of yours doing with his new one? And is he free yet?"

"Stephen loves his new house, loves all the suggestions I made for decorating it to fit his great personality—and that "I'm every-man" persona of his. He's very happy living in League City. And he's still very much involved with Darcy Coleman, who is really a great person. With a great husband like Lemanz, why do you even care about Stephen's marital status?"

Eliza Beth batted her eyelashes. "I don't. It's just that I have a couple of girlfriends in mind for him if things don't work out with Darcy. Now, if I were single, he simply wouldn't be with his current love interest. He'd be all mine," she said with unwavering confidence.

Laughing, Stephanie raised an eyebrow, "I'll say! Pretty confident about that, huh?"

"For sure! I can't think of one thing that I ever wanted and didn't get. I'm what you call a go-getter. Most people think I'm a gold digger, but that's so far from the truth it makes me laugh. When a woman possesses confidence, knows exactly what she wants, and then proceeds to go after it, others see her goals in life as cold and calculating. I'm neither frosty nor scheming. I just set high standards for myself. Is there anything wrong with that?"

Stephanie shook her head in the negative. "No, nothing at all. That is, if we don't step on anyone's fingers and toes while clawing our way to the top."

Eliza laid down her fork and stared down at her plate, looking as if she was contemplating her next response. "I don't think I've ever stepped on anyone during my quest for my success to meet up with someone else's success, but I can't say that I'm not capable of it. I'm definitely guilty of moving a few obstacles out of my way, like Lemanz's ex-girlfriend, Tiffany . . . whatever her last name is. But my assertion is a simple one. If she had been an immovable fixture in his life, I wouldn't have him. You think?"

Stephanie couldn't stop herself from laughing. Eliza Beth had such a way with words. She was funny even when she wasn't trying to be. She possessed a PhD, but had worked only two years in her field before marrying the charming Lemanz Tobias. She hadn't worked a day since she'd become his wife, nor had she ever seemed bothered by it.

"Girlfriend, you ought to stop clowning, but I see your point. And you *do* have him! I can't argue with you on that fact, Liza."

"What about a scoop of ice cream to go with the peach cobbler?" Eliza Beth asked.

Stephanie frowned slightly. "As good as it looks, I don't think I'm going to have any dessert. I'm already too full from the entrees."

Eliza Beth sucked her teeth. "Oh, so you're just going to sit over there and make me look like an overdosing Miss Piggy, 'cause I can't imagine not devouring a bowl full of cobbler, with lots of ice cream. Come on, have just a dab or two with me. It won't hurt to have a taste."

"That would be 'Mrs. Piggy,'" Stephanie joked, laughing. "Misery *does* love company. Okay, just a little dish of it if that'll make you happy, but without the ice cream. I don't want to have to make a bathroom stop on my way home. Dairy products aggravate my stomach, too."

Eliza Beth pumped a fist in the air. "Now you're talking good sense, my sister."

Stephanie's mind wandered to her trip to New Orleans while Liza Beth pulled out the ice cream carton from the freezer. Gregory had sounded so pleased that she'd agreed to her father's request for a visit, telling her that he didn't think she'd ever have to regret her decision. He then informed her that he'd make all the arrangements and that she'd hear from him with some sort of travel confirmation within the next twenty-four hours or so. For a reason she didn't understand at all, she was quite eager to hear from Gregory again.

After placing the two bowls of dessert on the table, Eliza Beth sat back down, eyeing Stephanie curiously. "You look as if you're in another world. What's up with the glistening eyes? Are you thinking of something delicious besides the cobbler? Perhaps a someone?"

Not daring to answer either question in depth, Stephanie shrugged nonchalantly. "Just thinking about an upcoming trip, that's all."

"That's all! You looked as if your thoughts were extremely pleasant ones. Your eyes had that seventh-heaven kind of look. Where are you off to, Stephanie, and for how long?"

Stephanie decided to ignore Eliza Beth's comments for fear of opening up a certain can of worms. Mrs. Tobias happened to be a hopeless matchmaker. If she thought for one second that Stephanie had been thinking about a man, the probing questions would be endless. She would then do everything in her power to seek out Gregory Saxton—and the matchmaking would begin. "New Orleans, but only for a few days. Business and pleasure."

Eliza Beth raised an eyebrow. "Do you have a decorating assignment down there?"

Stephanie shook her head in the negative. "No, just going down there to meet someone."

Eliza Beth lifted both eyebrows this time, making Stephanie immediately realize she'd unwittingly opened up the very can she'd hoped to keep the lid on.

Leaning forward in the chair, placing both elbows on the table, Eliza Beth wiggled her eyebrows suggestively. "A man?"

Stephanie saw no use in trying to skirt the issue. Liza Beth would not stop until she knew everything there was to know about the trip. "I'm going to meet my father. He lives there."

Eliza Beth smiled. "Oh, that should be fun. How often do you visit your dad?"

Stephanie sighed, wishing there was a way out of what she knew was going to turn into a little heart-to-heart session. "This will be our first visit ever. I've never met him."

Eliza Beth looked as though she could be knocked over by a feather. "I'm surprised to hear that. I know we don't get too deep into our personal lives, but I never would've guessed that. If you don't mind my asking, why haven't you ever met him?"

Stephanie once again prepared herself to lunge into a topic she found disturbing, to say the least. She revealed to Eliza Beth as much as she could without going into a lot of heavy details. The fact that she didn't know very much about her father was rather an embarrassing thing to disclose, yet talking about it helped her to affirm what she had to do.

People had the tendency to form their own opinions. That those views might not favor her mother was a big concern for Stephanie, especially since there was very limited information to share. For some unknown reason men involved in this type of situation always seemed to come out smelling like a fresh rose; the women often came out smelling like a dead one.

After Stephanie finished the last line of her parental saga, Eliza Beth got up from her chair and came around the table. She then knelt down in front of Stephanie. "I can only imagine how tough this has been on you. I want you to know that I'll be here for you if you ever need to talk or to just have someone to sit in silence with. We haven't known each other all that long, but I really feel like we've become good friends. Anything you've told me will stay with me. I won't even share it with Lemanz." Eliza Beth raised three fingers. "Girlfriend's honor."

Stephanie leaned forward and hugged Eliza Beth. "Thank you for saying that, Liza. Lemanz is your husband and I don't mind if you share it with him. But I appreciate you not sharing it with anyone else, not that we have any other friends in common."

Eliza Beth reclaimed her seat. "We have Ms. Sarah, but I won't breathe a word to her."

"Oh, yes, Ms. Sarah. How did I ever forget her? Thanks for keeping my confidences, Liza. It means a lot to me. However, I'm going to be just fine. I'm Texas tough. This meeting is long overdue. I'm going to take the bull by the horns and hope and pray he's a tame one. If not, I'll get on and ride him until he throws me off. I'm also letting God lead out on this one. He's never once failed to dance me onto the right path. He won't fail me now."

Eliza Beth smiled warmly. "You speak of God so often in your conversations. It must be really nice to have an up-close and personal relationship with him. I believe in God, but I don't think I am where you are in your faith. What did it take for you to get all the way there?"

Stephanie inwardly disagreed with Eliza Beth's comments about her Christian status. Although she'd grown up in the church, had been constantly spoon-fed Bible truths, she was still a babe in her faith. It was one thing for church personnel to teach you about Jesus, but as an adult, Stephanie thought it was necessary for her to confirm what she'd been taught as a child.

"To answer your question in part, it takes lots of humbling prayers, and putting God first in all we do. But I'm not even close to being all the way there. Everyone comes to understand and apply Bible principles at different times, mostly in God's time. Believing in Him is a big plus. Then comes trusting in Him. I know that I have a very long way to go in my Christian walk, but I've come to understand that sanctification is a work of a lifetime. I do read the Bible and closely study His word, but I rely a lot on the Holy Spirit to guide my way. I always listen for that little voice inside my heart to tell me what to do next. Life is much easier that way."

"That's an interesting comment. Care to expound?"

Stephanie clapped her palms together. "It's rather simple. The little voice that some of us call our conscience is so much more than just that. I believe it's our communication with the Holy Spirit. One of the problems is this: we don't often hear our internal voice, or if we do hear it we choose to ignore it. Because we've learned to tune out our natural instincts—God's instructions, which are communicated to us in so many ways—we get knee-deep into trouble."

Eliza Beth nodded her head up and down. "I like what you have to say. Maybe we can study the Bible together when you have time. I think I can learn a lot from you. When you get all your personal issues settled, perhaps we could hold Bible Study lessons here once a week. I have several close girlfriends who might like to join us."

Stephanie nodded her agreement. "I'd like that very much, Liza. I don't know how much you'll learn from me; every day brings about a new revelation, but I'm willing to share with you what I believe in. I *will* respect your beliefs, whether they're the same as mine or not. It's up to us as individuals to decide what type of relationship we want to have with God and how we want to go about achieving it. No one can do that for us."

Stephanie looked down at her watch. "Time has really gotten away. We'd better get down to discussing all the great ideas I've come up with for redecorating your six bathrooms." Stephanie laughed heartily. "Six bathrooms. Oh, how I wish!"

3

Stephanie had been nervous from the moment she'd learned that Gregory was going to personally drive her to New Orleans. While in the process of packing her suitcase, her hands had trembled something fierce just from the very idea of it. All sorts of romantic thoughts about the charming attorney had ripped haphazardly through her mind, making her wish she'd never met him. A five- to six-hour drive in such close proximity to one Mr. Saxton had her quite shook up. That she was extremely attracted to him had her feeling completely off-kilter.

Gregory's shocking announcement about the travel arrangements had come over the telephone, but only after he'd already arrived back in Houston, leaving her no chance to voice an objection. Farrah hadn't been able to make the trip. Stephanie had been aware that she'd be leaving for Louisiana the next day, but she'd expected to receive an e-ticket via the Internet.

"You've gone back into your shell of silence, Stephanie. Still worried that I might be a kidnapper?" Gregory joked, smiling tenderly.

Stephanie felt ashamed of her earlier remarks. The truth was that she didn't know who he was. Other than being aware of his law firm through various forms of media, she really didn't have firsthand knowledge about him as a person. He could've been a kidnapper for all she knew.

The fact that Stephen had already had Gregory thoroughly checked out was the only reason Stephanie was seated next to him in his fancy car, a silver BMW. From all the pertinent information Stephen had come up with on Gregory, it seemed that the young lawyer was an upstanding citizen and a very respected man in both his professional and personal life.

Stephanie smiled back at him, thinking it would be nice if she had the skills of a Houdini. "I've already apologized for saying that you could be a kidnapper. If I truly thought that, do you think I'd be in this car with you?"

Keeping his eyes trained on the road, Gregory shrugged. "I guess not. We were having a great conversation when you suddenly went silent on me, so I was left to wonder. How are you doing so far? Hungry? Need to stretch your legs or take a bathroom break?"

Nodding her head, Stephanie laughed. "All of the above would be nice. We have been in this car for over two hours, you know."

Gregory glanced at the dashboard clock. "Yeah, we have. I could use a break myself. I'm used to driving long distances, but I'm all for stopping every couple of hours." He pointed at the large advertising sign on the side of the road. "There are a lot of restaurants coming up soon, just a few exits away. We'll stop then. I have a half tank of gas, but I'll go ahead and fill her up."

Seated in a booth inside Burger King, Stephanie poured sweet onion dressing over her fire-grilled chicken salad. There had been many restaurants to choose from, but she'd had a taste for the salad she often ordered from the Burger King nearest her house. Gregory had ordered one of the combo meals, which included a fish sandwich, large fries, and a soft drink.

Gregory studied her profile, wondering if she was really okay with meeting her dad, especially without her twin brother. Gregory had tried to talk Stephen into making the trip with them, or even coming down to New Orleans later, but Stephen had been adamant in his refusal.

Stephanie looked up from her meal and caught Gregory staring at her, though she'd already felt his eyes riveted upon her. "I hope you like what you see." Unable to control it, she blushed, her cheeks turning a shade darker. "Why are you staring at me like that, Gregory?"

Gregory felt no shame in being caught in the act. He really hadn't been looking at Stephanie in an intimate way. He was just worried about her. "I'm concerned, that's all."

Surprised by his response, Stephanie lifted an eyebrow. "Concerned about what?"

After laying down his sandwich, Gregory folded his hands and then placed them out in front of him. "How you're really feeling about meeting your dad for the first time. Stephanie, I may be Malachi's lawyer, but that doesn't keep me from taking a personal interest in what you might be going through emotionally. I have an idea that this isn't a walk in the park for you."

Stephanie was totally touched by Gregory's sensitivity to her feelings. His concern wasn't something she'd expected. He simply had a job to do for a client who'd hired him. She felt that his comment had been a sincere one and had not come as a result of any personal interest in her. He had instantly earned her respect.

Soon after wiping her mouth with a paper napkin, Stephanie took a quick swig of her soft drink. "Thanks for your concern. And you're absolutely right. This isn't easy for me. Had Stephen agreed to come along I'd probably be feeling a lot less tense. How much do you know about our situation with our father, Gregory?"

Gregory hunched his shoulders. "Not much more than the fact he's been an absent parent most of your lives. He has mentioned to me the regret he feels over it. He hopes to make things up to you and your brother. He definitely realizes he can't make up for lost time. Your dad just doesn't want to lose any more precious time. Getting to know you is his top priority."

Stephanie thought that Malachi should have put his children at the top of his list long before now, but she decided not to comment. Gregory didn't need to know how bitter she was. It would serve no purpose to vent her true feelings to him. "Do you know Malachi on a personal level or is it just a professional relationship?"

"Both. He's not only one of my father's best friends, he's also my godfather. I grew up around him. He's a good man. But this is my take on it, Stephanie. If he stayed away from his own kids, there must've been some serious mitigating circumstances. He's always taken a personal interest in me. He was present at most of the important events in my life. I can't begin to imagine why he wouldn't have done the same with his own flesh and blood. By the way, I refer to him as Uncle Malachi. It's always been that way."

Stephanie began feeling uncomfortable at getting too deep into her personal business with Gregory. For whatever reason, it didn't shock her to learn that Gregory was Malachi's godson, but it did make her feel quite sorry for her brother, who hadn't had the pleasure of knowing his father on any level. That Malachi could offer such support to a godson when he had a flesh-and-blood son of his own was downright unsettling for her. Sorry that she'd opened up this particular conversation, Stephanie tried to come up with a good reason for wanting to shut it down. It didn't take her long to come up with one. The truth always worked for her.

Trying to dissolve the lump in her throat, Stephanie swallowed hard. "I don't think I want to get any deeper into this discussion. I'm afraid I don't have the stomach for it. I hope to have all the answers soon enough—and they really should come from Malachi. Sorry I asked the questions I did. Is it okay for us to go back to talking about things a lot less personal?"

Gregory turned his mouth down at the corners. "Whatever you like, Stephanie. We don't have to talk about anything to do with Malachi, but I'd like to get a little personal." He grinned. "I'm hoping you'll let me show you around my great city, the Big Easy. We don't have to look at it as a date if you don't want to. I'm a fantastic tour guide."

Stephanie smiled warmly. "If you don't mind, I'd like to take a little time to think about it. I do want to explore as much of New Orleans as time permits, but we'll have to wait and see how I plan to do it. Meeting my father is the only thing I can give serious thought to right now."

"I do mind, but I respect your wishes more. To help you make up your mind about me as a tour guide I'm going to tell you all about my colorful birthplace. When I finish painting this unbelievable portrait of my city for you, you're going to feel as if you're living right smack dab in the middle of it."

Stephanie grinned broadly. "Sounds like I'm in for a real treat. Let the painting begin!"

Stephanie felt as if a thousand frogs had suddenly invaded her throat. The more she tried to swallow, the larger the lump grew. Her palms felt as sweaty as her forehead did and she discreetly wiped them on her dark slacks. Breathing had suddenly become a chore.

As she listened to her shallow breaths, Stephanie wished she could just open her mouth and gulp in some fresh air without it being noticed. If this was what dying for air felt like, it was a horrific feeling. She could only imagine that her face was drained of all color. It was easy for Stephanie to admit that this was the most terrifying moment she'd ever experienced.

The tall, handsome man standing before her was an enigma, yet he looked very familiar. It seemed as if she'd seen him somewhere before, but *where* the sighting had occurred was the twenty-million-dollar question of the moment. She racked her brain trying to figure it out.

As much as Stephanie had thought she and Stephen looked a lot like their mother, anyone could easily guess that Malachi was their father or somehow closely related to the twins. It was an uncanny thought, but Doreen and Malachi could've passed for brother and sister. The resemblance was downright remarkable.

Although his skin and eye coloring were different, Stephen was very much the mirror image of the handsome man possessing smooth, smoky-dark skin and wavy, silver hair. It was quite the contrast, yet his mustache and eyebrows were jet black, without a single strand of silver thread among the thick, neatly trimmed hairs. Thoughts of Lucifer came to mind. Malachi was every bit as beautiful as the angel had been described.

Stephanie could clearly see how her mother may've gone absolutely gaga over this fascinating-looking man. His athletic build was that of a man much younger in years than himself. Muscles were bulging out everywhere on his anatomy. He had such a strong presence, almost formidable, and he probably commandeered attention wherever he happened to be. And those beautiful dark, eyes . . . What could she say about his hypnotic eyes when they simply defied description? Wise and mysterious would definitely fit into the equation.

While looking into the wisdom-filled eyes of the man who had fathered her, Stephanie didn't know whether to laugh or cry. Her surging emotions were so jagged it was hard for her to remain in control of them. Tears would be more appropriate, she finally considered, since this occasion was hardly a laughing matter.

Malachi stepped closer to Stephanie, causing her to take a step back. "Hello, young lady. I'm so glad you could come to New Orleans. I'm so pleased to have you here. How are you?"

The deep bass voice sliced into Stephanie's musings, warming her through and through. The gentleness and eloquence of his tone surprised her. She'd somehow expected him to be gruff and rude.

But why had she expected that when she really had nothing to go on in that sense?

"Hello," she finally managed to say, feeling as though she should curtsy in front of him, too. From the looks of things, the man appeared to be just as rich and regal as anyone she'd ever come into contact with in her interior design business. It felt like being in the presence of royalty.

His residence was by far the largest, classiest estate home she'd ever stepped foot in. Malachi looked and lived the part of a wealthy man. *How well-to-do?* She wasn't sure, but by the expensive furnishings and elegant accents she'd guess that he was filthy rich.

Reining in her thoughts, Stephanie forced herself to smile gently, hoping her face wouldn't crack from the exerted pressure. "I'm doing just fine. How about you?"

Malachi grinned broadly, looking so pleased to see her. "Very well, my dear. Please have a seat. I'm sure you must be extremely tired after such a long car journey. I trust that Mr. Saxton took very good care of you during the road trip."

Stephanie looked all around the luxurious setting of the formal living room before settling down on an elegantly fashioned but comfortable wingback chair. "Yes, yes, he did. The trip was long but rather pleasant. I learned a lot about New Orleans from Mr. Saxton. He loves his native city with a passion. He even offered to show me around before I return to Houston."

"I'm happy to hear that." Malachi grew curious about the utter look of intrigue in his daughter's eyes when she'd spoken of the godson he very much loved, admired, and respected. *Had Gregory stolen Stephanie's heart before he himself could find a loving place within it?*

Malachi made direct eye contact with Stephanie, marveling at the color of her eyes, which were nearly the same autumn hue as her mother's. "You're a beautiful young woman, Stephanie." Malachi kept his eyes trained on his daughter as he seated himself in the matching chair, only separated from hers by a beautiful, highly polished antique mahogany table. "You remind me a lot of Doreen, especially when she was your age. Oh, Doreen! What a looker."

Stephanie was once again surprised by the gentleness of his tone. He'd also said her mother's name as if it was sweet and dear to him. The twinkle in his eyes was filled with warmth and affection when he'd called Doreen's name . . . and the look of love was on his face.

How could that be? Stephanie had to wonder. Hadn't he left Doreen all alone to fend for herself and his two children? Stephanie couldn't wait to hear his side of the story, which was actually the only side, since her mother had refused to reveal the nature of their breakup.

Malachi continued to eye Stephanie openly, unashamedly. He thirstily drank in her beauty, as though he was indulging himself in a tall, cool, refreshing drink of some sort. He couldn't seem to stop himself from staring at her. "If you're not too tired, would you like to see the rest of the estate, my dear?"

Stephanie quickly shook her head in the negative. "I don't think you invited me here to see all the wealth you possess. At least, I hope not. This isn't a social visit for me, either. Can we just get down to what's been on your mind, Mr. Trudeaux?"

Malachi was visibly shaken by the formal way in which Stephanie had addressed him. It sounded terribly disrespectful to his ears, yet he knew her intent was not so. *What else had he expected her to call him?* Father or Dad would've been so nice, he admitted to himself.

Hopefully Stephanie would one day come around to thinking of him as such, Malachi mused. If it was within his power to make it happen, he was going to do everything he could to build a solid, loving, and trusting relationship with his kids. His thoughts turned to his only son, causing his eyes to mist up.

Stephen may not be accessible to him now, but with God in control of the situation, Malachi had every reason to believe his son would eventually want him to be a part of his life. It might take a miracle, but God was in the business of working miracles on a daily basis. Malachi trusted and believed in God wholeheartedly, trusted and believed in His promises.

Feeling a sudden nervousness, Malachi cleared his throat. He was used to addressing men of wealth and power on a regular basis, yet this slip of a girl had him so unnerved. "Stephanie, I know you don't know much about me, if anything at all, and I hope that'll change. There are a lot of things I could tell you, but I don't ever want to dishonor the memory of your precious mother. Secrets are often sacred to the secret keeper."

Stephanie raised an eyebrow. "Unless that was your intent, why would you think you'd be discrediting her?"

Looking rather sad, Malachi scratched the center of his head with his forefinger. "The relationship I had with your mother was very complicated. I'd rather not get into any of the troubling details. I respect Doreen very much. I respect what she believed she had to do, though I vehemently disagreed with the way she wanted to handle things."

"Disagreed with what?"

Malachi shook his head from side to side. "I'm sorry, Stephanie, I shouldn't be confusing you. I guess it's best that I just get down to why I asked you here. I'd very much like for you and Stephen to take over the day-to-day operation of my multimillion-dollar company, S.S.M. Trudeaux Corporation, a giant among communication conglomerates. I need youthful legs and fresh perspectives to continue to be competitive further on into the twenty-first century.

"Everyone at the company seems so close to retirement age. We've recently hired a few youngsters, but we don't nearly have enough bright minds working in the company. Our strength will only remain inexhaustible if we have youthful innovators onboard. Since it will all be yours one day, I've decided to turn it over to you and your brother while my mind is still sound enough to guide you through the takeover process. I know you two will do this company proud."

With her mind racing like a Category 3 hurricane, Stephanie was astounded by Malachi's suggestion. *How in the world would he know that?* He couldn't possibly know that for sure. "Are you ill? Is that what this is all about?"

Even Malachi's outburst of laughter was gentle to Stephanie's ears. This man was a bagful of surprises, inasmuch as he was totally different from what she'd imagined. Not only was he extremely good-looking—and despite her question regarding illness, appeared strong and healthy—he also seemed quite sensitive to Stephanie.

Then what in the dickens had been the problem between him and Doreen? What had made this seemingly caring man desert his family, especially in time of such great need? If he wasn't ill, why had he bothered to contact them at all?

His laughter now under control, Malachi stroked his chin thoughtfully. "Dear girl, I'm healthier than I've ever been in my life. I have the heart rate of a man in his early twenties—that is, according to my doctor. I work out every single day and I jog around this entire ten-acre estate before the sun hits the sky. No, Stephanie, I'm not ill. Quite the contrary."

Stephanie didn't even try to hide her perplexity. "Then I guess I don't understand. Why would you want Stephen and me to take over your company if you can still run it yourself?"

Malachi shrugged. "Just for the very reasons I've already stated—youthful minds, my dear. Besides that, S.S.M. Inc. already belongs to you on paper. Helping you to learn the day-to-day operations would be easier on you and Stephen than if you were to inherit it after my death."

"What makes you think we'd even accept the company now or even after your death?"

Malachi shifted his body to a more comfortable position. He wasn't used to squirming, but he hadn't ever been seated next to his daughter. "I don't happen to think that at all. That's one of the reasons I invited you here. Because I really don't want you to sell your birthright, that's why I'm asking you to take over while I'm still alive. Should you both decide to accept the offer, the transition might otherwise prove to be a bear if you do it later rather than sooner."

Stephanie felt highly offended. "Birthright! How can you even speak of such when you've never been a part of our lives? It's repulsive to hear you say that to me."

Malachi flinched inwardly. Stephanie's anger made him somewhat uneasy, but he wouldn't let it show. He could only hope that she didn't have the same fiery temper that Doreen had once possessed. Doreen was the most stubborn woman he'd ever known.

To Stephanie, Malachi didn't appear the least bit chagrined, which didn't set too well with her. She thought he should be looking like the cat that just got caught in the act of eating the canary. His demeanor wasn't what she'd call smug, but she didn't like his calmness.

"I understand why you'd say that, but I beg to differ, Stephanie. I've been very much a part of your lives, but only at a distance. I attended most of your grade- and middle-school functions, your graduations from both high school and college, and Stephen's induction as a firefighter. I've been at most every important event in your lives, including parent/teacher conferences. I just did them separately from Doreen. I even saw you, Stephen, and your dates on your high school prom nights." Malachi went on to name the date of every event he'd ever attended in their behalf. Though he'd been careful to remain in the background, he'd been there.

Stephanie was truly flabbergasted. That Malachi had rattled off the exact date of each event was mindboggling for her. *Who was this man, really? And why had he done everything so covertly?* It seemed that his children had been important to him, but a lot of good it had done them when they hadn't been made aware of any of it. Stephanie then wondered how he'd known about all their events. *Had Doreen kept him abreast of everything?* It all seemed so strange.

Malachi got up from the sofa and strolled over to the window to give Stephanie time to digest what he'd just told her. Her shocked expression let him know how much he'd stunned her.

All Stephanie could do was stare at his retreating back. Malachi's unbelievable revelations had left her speechless and feeling completely numb.

Then suddenly Stephanie's heart nearly stopped beating as a stark memory entered her mind. A black stretch limousine sped into her thoughts, causing her to tremble slightly. Seeing Malachi standing with his back to her brought back in full effect the memory of where and when she'd seen him. He'd had his back to her on that afternoon, too. Everything to do with the sighting had suddenly been brought into sharp focus.

Stephanie's eyes filled with tears as she recognized Malachi's back as the back of the stranger getting into the limousine at the cemetery, the day of her mother's funeral. She recalled fleetingly wondering who he was, since she hadn't ever seen him before. She'd been way too grief-stricken to give the man's presence any more thought at the time, but she'd mulled it over in her mind many times since. So, Malachi *had* been at Doreen's funeral. For whatever reason, that revelation brought Stephanie a tremendous amount of comfort and relief.

Stephanie and Stephen had known all of their mother's close friends, which had been very few in number. Doreen wasn't a social person. Church, catering parties, and shopping was about as social as it had ever gotten for her. The limousine and the man had seemed totally out of place to Stephanie. Even though Doreen had worked for quite a few rich families, most of her employers had been Caucasian, not African American. One of Doreen's wealthy employer's cohorts paying his last respects was what she'd eventually chalked up the incident to.

Stephanie intently watched Malachi as he returned to his seat.

The buildup of moisture in his eyes had her wondering if he'd been crying. The sad expression on his face lent more credence to her thoughts. The thought of him shedding tears had her wanting to put her arms around him to bring him some semblance of comfort. This man wasn't at all a stranger to pain and suffering, she suddenly realized. It seemed to her that he'd also been deeply hurt before.

After shaking off her bout of empathy, Stephanie put her index finger to her left temple. "You know something, disrespectful or not, you need to come clean with me. If you choose not to, I choose not to listen to another word you have to say. I need the truth from you, plain and simple. Why weren't you active in our lives? In front of our eyes, not behind our backs."

Feeling terribly sick on the inside, Malachi rubbed his large palm across his forehead. "Stephanie, it won't change a thing for me to answer that question. We can't go back and undo any part of the past . . ."

Stephanie held up her hand in a halting position. "Enough said, Mr. Trudeaux." She got to her feet. "Please have someone take me back to Houston or perhaps to a hotel for the night. If I have to wait until tomorrow morning to leave I can make my own arrangements to get home. This meeting is over and done with." Stephanie's body shook with the force of her anger.

If the pain crushing Malachi's heart wasn't caused by a heart attack, it sure felt like it. A dagger forced into his chest couldn't have hurt more. His doctor may've recently given him a clean bill of health, but his heart was in big trouble right now. He couldn't let his daughter walk out now, not after seeing her and loving her the way he did. He needed her too much for that.

Malachi looked grieved as he stood up. The alternative to letting Stephanie walk away was one heck of a kicker, though. Secrets didn't always die when the soul departed from the body. Doreen was deceased now. But he was very much alive, wanting desperately to live out the rest of his life surrounded by his two children—and eventually their children. Telling Stephanie the truth just might undermine Doreen in the eyes of her daughter. He didn't want to do that, but it didn't seem as if he had a choice in the matter, not if he wanted to be in his daughter's life. And he did want that, desperately so. Malachi couldn't think of anything he wanted more.

Malachi walked over to Stephanie and put both his hands on her shoulders. Hoping she wouldn't pull away, he dared to briefly touch his forehead to hers. Warmth instantly spread throughout his body, bringing tears to his eyes. If only he could hug her, squeeze her tightly. He'd never had the chance to do that, not even when she was first born. Although his heart had beat strongly all these years while apart from this children, he'd often felt dead inside. Death was the only thing that might've been worse than the sentence Doreen had handed out to him.

"Let me tell my story from beginning to end before commenting? Can you agree to that?"

Although Stephanie was no longer sure she wanted to hear the truth, now that she was darn near face-to-face with it, she reluctantly decided it was best to agree to his terms. Would it be hurtful? Undoubtedly. She could stop him before he got started, demand that she be taken home, but running away from things wasn't her method of operation. In fact, confronting the truth was the only reason she was in New Orleans. It was her belief that refusing to see Malachi would be like retreating from what might finally set her and Stephen free.

Stephanie only wished that Stephen felt the same way about seeing Malachi as she did. He hated that she'd decided to go to New Orleans, but he hadn't tried to stop her. He had wanted Stephanie to get her needs met, since she so desperately wanted to confront Malachi about his absence. Getting through to her brother had been the most impossible task she'd ever taken on, one that had been to no avail. Maybe he was also afraid of knowing the truth, especially after not knowing the facts for such a long time. The truth could be very scary indeed. She was definitely terrified of hearing it right now, yet hoping that Malachi would be perfectly honest with her.

Stephanie's big, bad, firefighter brother was often fearless, especially when it came down to doing his job. But when it involved matters of the heart—the heavy, emotional stuff—he often lost his tough edge. Stephen always accused her of having a marshmallow for a heart, but there were times when he was an absolute cream puff himself.

Stephanie looked up at her father. "I agree to your conditions, Mr. Trudeaux. I came to your home to hear you out. I'm very eager to hear what you have to say."

Knowing that what he had to say was probably going to devastate his daughter in more ways than one, Malachi eyed her somberly. "Thank you, Miss Stephanie. Thank you."

All settled down into one of Malachi's guestrooms, magnificent in décor and size, Stephanie was stretched out on the king-size canopy bed, wrapped up in one of the fluffiest towels she'd ever used. She had been assigned to a suite of rooms located in an entirely different wing from where Malachi slept. Malachi lived in grand style, a lifestyle of the rich and famous.

Wondering if Stephen was at home or at work, so she could put a phone call into him, Stephanie glanced at the fancy clock on the wall. There was a time when she'd known his work schedule right down to the minute, but her ever-growing business didn't leave her much time to keep close tabs on the brother she adored and was adored by.

Maybe phoning Stephen wasn't such a good idea after all. Just a phone call wouldn't suffice in this extreme case. He needed to be seated next to her when she revealed to him Malachi's incredible story. There was no doubt in her mind that Stephen would call their father a bold-faced liar. He'd fly into a rabid rage and she'd spend the next half hour or so trying to calm him down. The same thing had happened practically every time they'd discussed Malachi.

Stephanie's cell phone rang, causing her to jump up from the bed and dash across the apartment-size room to retrieve it from the round mahogany dining table. The caller ID revealed Stephen's number. Thinking of how their thoughts ran so much alike, she laughed. Hoping she could get through the conversation without giving away too much of what Malachi had told her, Stephanie warmly greeted her brother.

"I just called to see if you're okay, Stephanie. You were supposed to call me when you got to New Orleans. It seems as if the rolling-stone devil has you wrapped up tightly already."

Palming her forehead, Stephanie grimaced. "Oh gosh, Stephen, I'm sorry. I forgot. Ever since I got here things have been going at a whirlwind pace. However, your little sarcastic statement is completely wrong. Malachi has been nothing short of a perfect host and he doesn't have me all wrapped up. Are you on duty?"

"Yeah, I am. I wasn't scheduled, but I was called in to work some overtime. How was your trip? By the way, sorry for the sarcasm. I'm sure you could've done without it."

"I accept your apology, big brother. The trip was just fine. Gregory is very charming. And you were right, he does have somewhat of a personal interest in me. He's asking to show me all around New Orleans. He also wants to take me down to the French Quarter for dinner, on any evening of my choice."

"What did you say to that, sister dearest?"

Stephanie grinned. "I told him I'd think about it, and then let him know."

"Well, are you going to accept his invitation?"

Stephanie switched the receiver to her left ear. "I wasn't so sure earlier, because I didn't know if I'd be staying on in Louisiana past my initial meeting with Malachi. Now that I've thought about it and have decided to stay on for a while longer, I'm going to take him up on his offer. I really want to visit the French Quarter. With a native as a tour guide it should be a very interesting outing. Does accepting his offer bother you?"

Stephen sucked his teeth. "I think you already know the answer to that one. But since you have a good head on your shoulders and your instincts are very sharp, I'm not too worried about you. You're also a pretty good judge of character. If Gregory Saxton is a big, fat rat, I believe you would've already smelled the stench."

Stephanie smiled at Stephen's offhanded comments. "Thanks for that!"

"Speaking of instincts, what's your read on Malachi, Stephanie?"

Stephanie ran her fingers through her hair. "I'm not completely sure about him yet. But I don't think he's a bad man. Not at all." Stephanie closed her eyes for a moment, pondering her next remarks to her brother. "Stephen, won't you please change your mind about coming down here? I think you really need to talk to Malachi and hear for yourself what he has to say. I'm sure he'll be forthcoming with you. I sense that he's an honest man."

Stephen let go with a loud expletive. "What honest man does what he did to us? Maybe I'd better rethink all the credit I gave you a couple of minutes ago. You're not talking with your head. I can tell that your heart has been exposed to Malachi already. And he's using your charitable spirit for all it's worth. I've got to go, Stephanie. The fire bell is sounding."

"Wait a minute, Stephen," she yelled into the now dead phone line.

Deciding that it would do no good to call him right back,

Stephanie clicked off the phone and began to pace the room. Stephen had lied to her. She knew it. The fire bell hadn't gone off. There's no way she wouldn't have heard it, since it would've been so loud that she or anyone else could've heard it through the phone. Totally dismayed by the conversation ending so abruptly, Stephanie shook her head from side to side.

What was she to do now? It was imperative for Stephen and Malachi to at least meet and talk, even if it happened only once. That couldn't hurt anymore than what had already occurred. "Stephen," Stephanie whispered into the air, "please come to your senses. Like it or not, Malachi is our biological father."

4

A soft knock on the door caused Stephanie to roll over and look at the bedside clock. The bright red digital numbers read six AM. She then glanced toward the entryway. After getting out of bed, she draped her silk nightgown-clad body in the matching powder blue robe. As she slowly crossed the room, her mind still half-asleep, Stephanie hoped the visitor wasn't Malachi. Before seeing him again, she needed more time to think about the shocking things he'd already revealed to her . . . and then figure out how to relay them to Stephen in a less distressing manner.

The young woman standing before Stephanie wore a big smile on her pretty, milk chocolate face. She appeared to be in her early twenties, if not a tad younger than that. Stephanie took the soft hand extended to her and shook it briefly.

"Good morning, Miss Stephanie. I'm happy to meet you. My name is Candice Moreau. I'm a member of Mr. Trudeaux's housekeeping staff. Is everything to your satisfaction?"

Stephanie rubbed her hands together, now understanding why the woman was at her door so early. "Hello Candice, nice to meet you, too. Everything is just fine. Thanks for asking."

"You're welcome. Mr. Trudeaux takes his morning meal in the main kitchen at seven thirty—and he has invited you to join him. However, if you're not ready to get up and at 'em, he said to tell you that he fully understands. If you can't make breakfast, he hopes you'll join him for lunch in the informal dining room around noontime."

Stephanie felt a sudden rush of relief for the gracious way out. "That's good to know. I think I'd like to lie in bed a little longer.

Please give him my sincere regrets for breakfast, but tell him I'll see him for lunch." Stephanie laughed, feeling a bit silly. "I hope he knows I need an escort. There's no way I can find my way around this palatial house on my own."

Candice laughed, too. "I'll let Mr. Trudeaux know you'll need someone to show you around the place before lunch. This house is probably a lot bigger than you've even imagined. It has endless corridors and innumerable rooms. Before I go, is there anything I can get you?"

Stephanie briefly thought about the question Candice had asked. "I'd really like a cup of hot tea. Is that something you can make happen?"

Candice nodded. "Absolutely. If you'll allow me to come in, I can show you all the convenient gadgets in the kitchen. But if you prefer room service, that's not a problem, either."

Stephanie looked downright puzzled. "The kitchen! Are you saying there's a kitchen inside this suite? If so, I can't imagine where it is. I was sure I'd seen everything."

Candice laughed at Stephanie's expression of utter disbelief. "Yes, ma'am, there is. If you so desired, you'd never have to leave this room. May I come in and show you around?"

Stephanie stepped aside, making a sweeping gesture. "By all means, Candice. Please do."

Candice moved into the suite's foyer. "Follow me, Miss Stephanie," Candice said cheerfully, quickly moving toward the back of the room.

Stephanie grinned when Candice opened the large double doors with a key she'd retrieved from a nearby cabinet. The same doors Stephanie had wondered about, but hadn't dared to venture beyond. She'd thought it was just another guestroom on the other side.

Candice waved her arms about. "This is your own personal kitchen. By early afternoon it'll be fully stocked to your pleasure." Candice pointed at another door. "That door leads out into the corridor. The housekeeping staff enters from there to keep from disturbing the guests. Don't worry about a surprise visit from anyone. You'll get a schedule sheet that lists the times for the daily cleanings and all other necessary visits to your suite by the staff."

The mammoth-size room surpassed anything Stephanie had even imagined. Eliza Beth's huge kitchen would pale in comparison to the size of this one—and it wasn't even the main one in Malachi's home. Stephanie couldn't help wondering if every suite was equipped like this one.

Candice opened up one of the polished maple cabinets, showing off an array of beverages for brewing or stovetop heating. "What kind of tea would you like?"

Stephanie blinked hard, astonished by what she saw. "Now that I know I have use of this magnificent kitchen, I can fix my own tea. It might take me a few minutes to make up my mind, since I have so many choices. Thanks for the offer, but I think I can take it from here, Candice."

Candice started backing out the room. "In that case, I'll take my leave. Before I go, if you need anything at all, there's a self-explanatory list of extensions on the telephones. You don't have to want for anything while you're a guest in Mr. Trudeaux's home."

Stephanie frowned slightly. "I don't consider myself a guest in this house. I'm Mr. Trudeaux's daughter." Stephanie had surprised herself with that announcement, especially since she'd never completely thought of herself as such, at least not with so much conviction.

Candice appeared troubled. "I'm sorry, I didn't mean to imply anything sinister. All the staff knows exactly who you are, Miss Stephanie. The boss couldn't contain his joy when he heard you were coming for a visit. He has all but shouted the news from off the rooftop."

Not knowing how she should respond, Stephanie just stared straight ahead for several seconds. "That's nice to hear, Candice," she finally said, hoping this visit would be all that she needed to get on with her life. Stephanie wanted nothing more than to be free of her burdens.

Candice once again started for the exit. "I'll leave you now. Enjoy exploring the kitchen. Remember to call if you can't find something you want. Good day, Miss Stephanie."

"Thanks for everything, Candice. And it would please me a lot if you'd just simply call me Stephanie. Everyone else does."

"Thanks for the honor, Stephanie." Candice bowed at the waist as she left the room.

Alone again, Stephanie somehow felt much calmer about being in Malachi's home without Stephen. Candice had helped to put her at ease. If the rest of the staff was as nice and accommodating as Candice had been, Stephanie felt that her stay would be a pleasant one.

Starting from the left side of the room, which was equipped with all stainless steel appliances, Stephanie opened each cabinet to take inventory of its stock. It appeared to her that the pantry was already full. When she opened the stainless steel refrigerator, it was bare of food items, but plenty of soft drinks and juices filled the lower shelf. The fridge definitely needed stocking, she mused, frowning at the absence of milk, which she drank a lot, as she'd also done as a child. Stephanie was in the habit of having milk with most of her meals.

After selecting an herbal blend of lemon tea, Stephanie turned on the gas under the kettle. Looking around at all the fancy gadgets, she noticed that the coffeemaker could be operated with just a touch of a button. It appeared that the clear coffee vial was the only thing that had to be replaced. Modern technology and modern times at its finest, she mused. "Wonder if there'll come a time when all you have to do is glance at something to operate it," she remarked, laughing.

After preparing her tea to her liking, Stephanie carried the cup of hot liquid back into the bedroom, where she sat down on the side of the bed, placing her beverage on the lace doily-protected nightstand. She then stretched out on the bed and made herself comfortable.

Upon surveying her cheerful surroundings, a few new decorating ideas came to mind. All the rooms in the suite, from the living room to the kitchen, were decorated lavishly. The color scheme was a simple one. Everything was fashioned in white and various colors of beige, which complimented the dark mahogany bedroom furniture and dinette set. The sofa, loveseat, barrel chairs, and matching ottomans were covered in a soft beige microfiber material.

A few sips of the tea had put Stephanie in a relaxed mood. Despite her desire to brainstorm the previous night's conversation with Malachi, her eyes still felt heavy with sleep. It was so unlike her to stay in bed after six o'clock in the morning, but the long car journey had her feeling completely worn out.

Stephanie didn't believe in burning daylight. She had a purpose for every second of the day, but she'd lately come to realize that all her time was spent on business. With no man to share her downtime with, her social calendar often went begging. The outings with Stephen and Darcy, Farrah, and the recent ones with Eliza Beth were the only fun events Stephanie could lay claim to. Boring wasn't a strong enough word to describe her limited time alone.

Stephanie had to smile when she thought of Gregory. Although he'd revealed only a few personal facts to her, she found him intriguing. He had attended law school in California, but had returned home to Louisiana to go into practice with his father.

Witty as well as charming, Gregory had kept Stephanie laughing, which wasn't an easy feat. Stephen often accused her of being too serious and too stiff. But she'd been so relaxed in Gregory's company, surprisingly enough. She couldn't remember the last time she'd had a date. That made her even more eager to take Gregory up on at least his dinner invitation.

No man had possessed what she was looking for, at least out of the few she'd met over the past year. She wanted a Christian man, someone who'd love and respect her as much as she loved and respected herself. Stephanie knew that she had a lot to offer a lifelong partner, but the man she planned to spend the rest of her life with had to be able to give the very same in return.

Even though just the thought of marriage frightened Stephanie, marrying a Christian man was extremely important to her, if she ever decided to do so. Her profound love for God and her unwavering faith in Him had to be shared by her mate. Stephanie couldn't imagine being with any man who didn't share her Christian values.

Stephanie didn't know if Gregory was a man of God or not, since neither of them had broached the subject of their religious and spiritual beliefs. If she kept her eyes and ears open, Stephanie believed he'd eventually reveal his true character to her. People always did reveal their true selves, sooner or later. Since they didn't have much time, it would have to be sooner.

The clothes Malachi had chosen to wear gave a new meaning to the word 'casual.' Stephanie couldn't believe how regal he looked in his black-and-gray designer sportswear. His black Nike shoes looked brand new. Among his other very charismatic attributes, his powerful build was a major attraction. *He's such a graceful man, too,* she mused, admiring his confident stride. Stephanie marveled openly at how dark and handsome he was. Every silver hair was in place and his clean-shaven face looked smooth and baby-soft.

That Malachi had never even considered a second marriage astonished her. She was certain that a lack of female admirers had nothing to do with his decision not to marry again. So many of the things he'd told her still had her in disbelief, yet Stephanie didn't think of him as a liar. In fact, Malachi had been more forthcoming than she'd ever expected him to be.

As Malachi strode toward her, his large hands outstretched, Stephanie couldn't help smiling, her heart completely softened by the warm expression he wore on his face. His eyes appeared to be filled with such pride. Was this the way a loving father looked at his daughter when he thought of her as his pride and joy? Stephanie could only wonder.

Feeling very confident about building a meaningful relationship with his daughter, Malachi eagerly took hold of Stephanie's hands and brought her into his tender embrace. Seconds later he held her slightly away from him, placing his hands on her arms. He then took the liberty of kissing her forehead ever so tenderly. "I trust that you slept well, my dear."

Stephanie smiled and nodded, thoroughly warmed by his gentle affection. "I slept like the dead, but my body is still so tired from the long ride. I actually could've stayed in bed all day. The pillow-top mattress is heavenly and I could go on and on about the exquisite linens. I've never slept on anything so soft. There's not a thing in that magnificent suite I won't be raving about for months to come. Thanks for making things so comfortable for me."

"Your sincere comments have made me a very happy man. Candice told me you needed an escort, so that's why I'm here." He then crooked his arm and held it out for his daughter to take. "Lunch will be served shortly after we get downstairs. Are you hungry?"

Stephanie stretched her eyes, rolling them expressively. "Ravenous."

Malachi gently patted her hand, the one holding on to his arm. "Great. I'm sorry to hear you're so tired. After lunch you can come back upstairs and lounge all day if you'd like. I've completely cleared my calendar for your visit, but there are many things I can do if you'd just like to relax. We'll still have tomorrow, at least I hope so."

Stephanie heard the uncertainty in Malachi's voice. She could tell that for a man so full of confidence, he wasn't at all sure if she'd stay on as his guest. "Of course we'll have tomorrow, and perhaps a day or two after that. Then I have to get back to Houston. I have a business to run."

Stephanie suddenly felt awkward as she strolled alongside her father. What to call this man was puzzling her, since referring to him as *Mr. Trudeaux* no longer seemed appropriate. Something good and heartwarming had happened between them the previous night and she didn't want to risk offending him by keeping things so formal. Stopping dead in her tracks, she looked up at him. "I have a problem and I need to solicit your help."

Malachi looked concerned, his brows furrowing. "If at all possible, I'll help you in any way I can. What is it, my dear?"

Happy and content with his response, Stephanie smiled sweetly. "I'd like to discuss my dilemma over lunch. That is, if you don't mind."

"Not in the least bit. I can hardly wait for us to get into it, Miss Stephanie."

The long mahogany table, beautifully adorned with the finest linen, looked as if it had been set for a king and queen and their entire court. Using fine china, silver, and crystal for informal meals was unheard of in Stephanie's world. Her eyes bulged at what she thought of as the unimaginable. Malachi's financial standing was apparent in every nook and cranny of his home that she'd seen so far. If he ran his business the same way as he ran his home, Stephanie figured it had to be a splendid corporation. Considering all his wealth and prestige, she couldn't help wondering how he'd managed to stay so down-to-earth, or was everything about Malachi just a façade? Time would tell. Her thoughts fleetingly turned to Stephen, wishing he was there to see how well Malachi lived and to hear everything firsthand that their father had to say.

Malachi pulled out a chair for Stephanie, and then seated himself to the left of her at the head of the table. No sooner had he taken another breath then a couple of members from his staff appeared, carrying on silver trays stacks of petite sandwiches, a tureen of hot soup, a bowl filled with a variety of salad greens and cherry tomatoes, and a glass pitcher of freshly squeezed lemonade. The condiments were already on the table, along with a tray of kosher dill slices and an abundance of black and green olives. Considering

Malachi's size, Stephanie had somehow expected a larger fanfare, even though there was nothing meager about the meal set before them.

The very moment the two women took their leave Malachi said a blessing over the food.

Malachi grinned as he poured a glass of lemonade for both his daughter and himself. He then picked up his fork. "Let's dig in?"

"By all means." Stephanie first prepared a salad to her liking, and then she chose a couple of turkey sandwiches and a few filled with a delicious-looking chicken spread. The sandwiches were so small that Stephanie thought she could probably eat a dozen and still be hungry.

Stephanie moaned lowly upon taking the first bite of her sandwich. The turkey turned out to be smoked, which was one of her favorite meats. "This turkey is so flavorful and tender," she expressed to Malachi, rolling her eyes to show her pleasure.

"I'm so glad you like the sandwiches. The chicken salad is delicious, too. Don't be shy now, Miss Stephanie. There's plenty more where those came from."

The rest of the meal was eaten virtually in silence, but Stephanie didn't feel the least bit bothered by it. She felt very comfortable with Malachi, although she'd only known him for less than twenty-four hours. She found him unpretentious and easy to converse with. He'd certainly poured his guts out to her last evening. Never once had she gotten the impression he was being less than truthful with her. Malachi's honesty was what had endeared him to her. She didn't know how she knew he'd been telling the truth, but she was convinced that he'd told her no lies.

Malachi wiped his mouth on the linen napkin, and then placed it on the table. After a couple of long swallows of lemonade, he gulped down a glass of ice water. "Now that we've finished our meal, Stephanie, why don't you tell me about the problem you mentioned earlier."

Stephanie folded her hands and placed them in her lap. She looked down at her plate for a moment, and then lifted her head to make direct eye contact with her father. "I saw how much it disturbed you yesterday when I referred to you as Mr. Trudeaux, so I've been trying to think of something less formal to call you by and still remain respectful. Do you have any suggestions?"

Malachi was quite surprised by the nature of her problem, which he didn't see as a major one. He was her father and nothing could ever change that. "I assume that it might be troubling for you to call me dad or father. Am I right?"

Stephanie nodded. "It doesn't seem appropriate, somehow. I really don't know you as such, but that doesn't change the fact that you're my father. Dad is normally an earned title, in my opinion, since anyone can father a child. But from what you told me last night, it seems that you have been a dad, even if it was from a distance. Calling you just Malachi isn't an option for me. Mom would kill me if she heard me call you by your first name. She raised us much better than that. I'm so sorry things didn't work out between you two. Stephen and I have missed out on so much by your absence. We longed to have both parents in our lives while growing up. I'd love to refer to you as dad, but it may take a bit of getting used to. Can you live with me calling you Mr. Malachi for now?"

The pain in Malachi's eyes was visible. Years had been lost to him, too, precious time that none of them could ever retrieve. He had longed to be a father to his children every bit as much as they'd wanted him to be there for them. As much as he wanted Stephanie to call him dad, he knew this wasn't something she could force herself to do. Nor would he want that. It was up to him to shower her with all the deep love he felt inside, so that she would be left with no doubt about his feelings. He desperately wanted her to know that he was for real. Malachi didn't want to do anything that might alienate him from his darling Stephanie. The family circle wouldn't be complete without Stephen, but he knew he'd have to be patient there as well.

Malachi reached over and covered his daughter's hand with his. "I can certainly live with your choice, Stephanie. I know you need to take baby steps with me. I'm just so grateful that you're here. I love you very much. I *am* your father and you *are* my daughter. Hopefully the rest will come naturally, after you get to know me a little better. Patience is a must in this instance."

Stephanie leaned over and kissed his smooth cheek. "Thank you." She let go of a nervous giggle, relieved to have that conversation out of the way. "Your comments mean a lot to me."

Malachi's face beamed with heartfelt emotion. How many times had he longed to have his children's love and affection? That was the first kiss he'd ever received from his daughter and he hoped it wouldn't be the last. "You're certainly welcome, my dear. Ready for dessert?"

"Would you mind if we had dessert after you show me around your home? I'm eager to see the rest of the place. If it's anything like what I've already seen, I'm in for a grand tour. This is like experiencing a touch of heaven for an interior designer."

The old plantation home had been refurbished inside and out and had been turned into a splendid architectural work of art. Stephanie had lost count of the number of rooms in the house only minutes into the tour. It appeared that no expense had been spared on furnishing Malachi's grand mansion. A heavy European influence was very much present in the magnificent décor. There were some areas in the house that looked as if they'd never been used; the formal living room was just one of many. Picture perfect, the impeccably tasteful salon would've beautifully graced the front cover of any number of popular home magazines.

Spaced all around the massive front porch, the majestic white columns gleamed in the bright sunshine. Extremely well-maintained lawns, a riot of colorful blooms, and innumerable trees, green plants, and bushes practically overran the ten-acre estate. The massive dollar sign–shaped pool and seemingly endless flagstone decking was breathtaking. Malachi also had a fully equipped gym, outfitted with a Jacuzzi tub, and both wet and dry saunas.

As they walked back toward the main entryway to the house, Stephanie looked up at Malachi and smiled. "This is quite a place you have here, which is a gross understatement. I've never seen such magnificence. It seems that you've done very well for yourself. Your company must be invaluable. You're virtually surrounded by the enormity of your success."

Malachi nodded, lowering his lashes. "Success doesn't always equal happiness, Stephanie. I would've given all this up just to be with my kids. I have forgiven Doreen, and she me, but I often find myself wondering what it could've been like had I not made the biggest mistake of my life. Seeing you and Stephen all grown up reminds me of how much I've missed out on. How difficult a task do you think it'll be for me to reach out to your brother?"

Folding her arms across her chest, Stephanie's mouth turned

down at the corners. "I wish I could be more encouraging, but I can't. Stephen is chock-full of anger. It won't be easy to get through to him. You can consider my reaction to your letters as mild compared to how Stephen has reacted to you making contact with us. I didn't think I should tell him on the telephone everything you've told me, so I'm going to talk with him about it as soon as I get home. If anyone can change his mind, I can, yet I'm not very optimistic."

Malachi flung his arm loosely around Stephanie's shoulder, pondering her comments carefully. "I appreciate your desire to change Stephen's mind, but I'm not sure it's a good idea. I don't want to put undue stress on the loving relationship you two share. I'll have to figure this one out on my own." Malachi sighed hard. "I had high hopes of us spending our first Thanksgiving together as a family. I can't tell you how many holidays I've spent alone because I couldn't be with my children. No one else's company would ever do."

It disturbed and saddened Stephanie to think of Malachi all alone during festive times. He was a living example that money couldn't buy happiness. He had so much material-wise, yet he hadn't been able to have in his life what would've made him the happiest. It seemed to her that if Malachi had had open access to his family, his life would've been more complete. He'd obviously suffered through years of loneliness, just as Doreen had done. How could two people who had loved each other so much have let pride and hardened hearts get in the way of utter fulfillment? So many good years had been wasted on being angry and unable to forgive. She hated to admit it, but Stephanie believed that Stephen's anger could also become his undoing.

Stephanie's eyes grew bright with curiosity. "What about other relatives? Are there any?"

"Only one brother, Stephanie. If he gets back into town in time, he's coming out here to meet you. Your Uncle Maxwell is a long-distance trucker."

Stephanie looked surprised. "Since your company is such a huge success, why doesn't he work there with you?"

Malachi chuckled. "Maxwell Trudeaux is a free spirit. No stuffy suit and strangling tie for him. Chaining him to a desk would kill him. He's very successful in his own right. Although he owns the trucking company and employs numerous truckers, he'd never give up driving to take on administrative duties. He has a very capable staff for that. Max loves the open road, which is the main reason he can't give up driving the big rigs."

Stephanie grinned. "He sounds like a very interesting man. Does he have a family?"

Malachi threw his head back and laughed heartily. "A woman in every truck stop is his motto. He especially goes for the female short-order cooks and waitress types since he loves to eat. Max is just a huge old softie with a great big heart. He'd never hurt a fly intentionally."

"Who's the oldest, you or him?"

"Max has two years on me. He's fifty-five and I'm fifty-three. But I'm the better-looking brother," Malachi joked. "If Max heard me say that, he'd take serious exception. He just happens to think he's the cat's meow. Would you like to see some family pictures?"

Stephanie's eyes sparkled. She was thrilled at the prospect of seeing the family she'd never gotten to know. "That would be nice. What about your parents?"

"They died long before you and Stephen were born. Your grandparents, Joseph and Marquisa Trudeaux, would've worshipped you and your brother. I was a very young man when they passed away, only two years apart. Diabetes plagued Mom and heart disease killed Dad."

Stephanie reached up and gently squeezed the large hand still resting on her shoulder. "I'm deeply sorry for your loss. Wish I had gotten to know them."

Malachi bent down and kissed the top of Stephanie's head, making her feel even more secure in his presence. "Thank you for that." He then pointed at the silver BMW in the driveway as they drew closer to the house. "Looks like we have a visitor." He grinned. "I wonder if Gregory is here to see me or you. I guess you already know he's rather taken with you, my dear. Have you decided to go out to dinner with him?"

Stephanie frowned slightly. "Only as a casual friend. My life is too complicated right now to get into anything heavy with anyone. Besides, long distance relationships rarely work. Gregory seems like a really nice man, but is he a spiritual one?"

"I believe that he his. He was brought up in the church and still attends services every week. I know that for a fact because we belong to the same parish. He's a good man, Stephanie, dependable as they come. Now Grant, that brother of his, is a horse of a different color."

Stephanie raised an eyebrow. "Brother? He never mentioned having a brother to me, and we were in the car together for several hours. I find that odd. Don't you?"

"No, because I know their unfortunate circumstances. Grant is insanely jealous of Gregory because of his success as an attorney, yet he had the same opportunities afforded his younger brother. Those two are like oil and water. They just don't mix. Believing that Gregory is the favorite son, Grant tries to compete with Gregory at every turn. Gregory no longer bothers to enter the game he has no desire to play. Their father, Gregory II, has just about lost all hope for them to come together in peace. He loves both of his sons with a passion, but he's sorely disappointed in the older one's shiftlessness and arrogance. Gregory II is also a good man."

Malachi opened one side of the massive double doors and allowed Stephanie to precede him into the house. Before locating Gregory, Malachi took his daughter into his arms. "I just can't seem to get it through my head that I'm not asleep and this is not a dream. Hugging you every now and then lets me know I'm very much awake, Stephanie. I hope you don't mind."

Stephanie allowed herself to really feel Malachi's arms about her, her eyes welling with tears. His warmth felt so good to her that she never wanted the loving embrace to end. For her it was like a dream, too. How many days and nights had she dreamed about her father, wishing he was there to love and comfort her?

"I don't mind at all." Wrapping her arms around his waist, she laid her head on his chest and looked up into the handsome face of the man who no longer seemed a stranger to her. "You *are* awake, Dad, and so am I. We're finally together."

Rendered speechless, tears sprang to Malachi's eyes. He couldn't find any adequate words to express to his daughter how he felt at this very moment. He wasn't going to try. The love shining brightly through his tears should more than express to her his heartfelt emotions. Malachi believed a blind man would be able to see the love brimming over inside of him.

The touching moment ended just as Gregory walked into the marble foyer. "Here you two are. I've been looking all over the place for you. I was just about to leave."

Malachi walked over to Gregory and gave him a warm hug. "We

just finished taking a short walk around the grounds. I plan to give Stephanie a full tour later, including the stables."

Stephanie clapped her hands with excitement. "You have horses, too?"

"Only six, but they are extremely beautiful animals. Arabians. We'll go see them later."

Gregory took Stephanie's hand for a brief moment. "Hello, Stephanie. How are you feeling after the long trip?"

Mindful of the butterflies flitting about in her stomach, Stephanie smiled gently at Gregory. "Still a bit fatigued, but my energy level is starting to rise. And I'm having a great time so far. Dad took me on an inside tour of the house, and then we took a short jaunt outdoors. I'm really excited about exploring all that I haven't seen. This place is incredible, indescribable."

Gregory raised an eyebrow at the way Stephanie had lovingly referred to Malachi. It seemed to him that father and daughter had accomplished a lot in such a short span of time. They certainly looked radiant enough. He was truly pleased to see his godfather looking so happy. Gregory prayed that everything would come together nicely for Malachi and both of his children.

"Let's go into the family room and have a sit down," Malachi suggested.

Gregory looked regretful. "I'm afraid I can't stay, Uncle Mal. I have a couple of things on the court docket for later this afternoon. I dropped by to see how you two were doing." Gregory then turned to Stephanie. "I also wanted to know if you'd made a decision about my offer of dinner and a city tour? Are we on for either one or both?"

"Dinner sounds nice. Let's start with that, and then see where we go from there. Since you've already gotten a taste of how much food I'm capable of consuming, you might want to spring for an all-you-can-eat buffet. It might be easier on your wallet."

Everyone had a good laugh at that.

Gregory gave one last chuckle. "I have a little more in mind than a cheap buffet. Don't worry about my wallet. I think I can afford a couple of dinners in one of the finer restaurants. Is this evening okay for you, Stephanie? Say, seven o'clock?"

Stephanie looked at Malachi, as though she thought she needed to seek his approval. After all, she was his houseguest.

Malachi easily guessed at Stephanie's dilemma by the questioning look she'd given him. "I hope you two youngsters have a grand evening. Perhaps we can all have a cup of coffee or tea together when you return, if it's not too late. If we don't get together later, Stephanie, I'll see you at breakfast in the morning." Malachi placed his hand firmly on his godson's shoulder. "Gregory, I have no doubt that you'll take extreme care with my daughter. She's very precious to me."

Gregory nodded. "I'm sure you already know she'll be in good hands. I promise to take very good care of her, Uncle Mal. I've got to run now, but I'll be back to pick you up at seven, Stephanie. You two have a great time today."

Stephanie waved her farewell. "Thanks, Gregory. I'll be ready by the time you arrive. By the way, is there a certain dress code for me to follow?"

Gregory grinned broadly. "I'm sure you'll look beautiful no matter what you wear. However, the restaurant I have in mind is rather classy. So you can take your clue from that."

"Thanks for the heads up. I'm glad I brought something appropriate with me. I have one more thing to say before you go. If you can arrange for me to fly back to Houston in a couple of days, I'd be so grateful. Don't think I want to take the long drive again. Too tiring."

Gregory looked rather disappointed, since he'd been looking forward to driving her back home. He'd thought of it as a great way for them to become better acquainted with each other.

Gregory reluctantly nodded his agreement. "I'll take care of it. We can get more into the details over dinner. But you should be warned that I'm going to do everything in my power to try and change your mind. Driving you back home would be my pleasure."

Stephanie blushed, laughing. "Good luck! Once this girl makes up her mind about something it's not an easy task to change it. Yet I will allow you to argue your case. Since I hear that you're a brilliant lawyer, I'm sure you'll love the opportunity to showcase your skills."

5

Stephanie was quite impressed with Gregory's choice in restaurants. Brennan's was one of the finest dining establishments located in the heart of the French Quarter. Everything associated with elegance and exquisite ambiance could be found within these seemingly endless walls. Brennan's *was* classy, just as Gregory had said. That he had made reservations for them to dine in one of the private dining rooms was even more remarkable to Stephanie.

Seated at the candlelit, beautifully dressed table for two, waiting for their meals to be served, Stephanie kept stealing glances at her handsome companion. His style of dress was nothing less than dashing sophistication. Stephanie had never seen a dark blue pinstriped suit look so darn good on a man. The stark white shirt and red dotted tie were very complementary. His suit of clothes looked as if they'd been tailored exclusively for him.

Gregory had been completely bowled over by Stephanie's stunning appearance. Her cream-colored silk suit was stylish and elegant, fitting her shapely figure to a tee. The double strand of pearls she wore around her neck and matching pearl-drop earrings lent her an extra touch of simple elegance.

When Gregory had seen her coming down the staircase in Malachi's home, it was as if he was seeing her for the very first time. The memory of that telltale expression on his face made Stephanie smile. That magical episode had also made her happy that she'd brought along a dressy outfit. She still didn't know what had made her pack the evening attire—and she wasn't going to waste a moment trying to figure it out, since she felt more alive than ever before. Everything about Gregory made her hopeful, yet Stephanie didn't have a clue what to hope for.

Gregory reached over and put his forefinger under Stephanie's chin, tilting her head slightly. He then carefully studied her features for a brief moment. "Since you have such a dreamy look in your eyes, I hope you're thinking about me."

Stephanie fought the urge to blush, but she lost the battle. "As a matter of fact, I was thinking about you. I just wish it weren't so obvious."

Gregory was astounded by Stephanie's statement. He'd only been kidding, but her response thrilled him. "Why's that?"

Stephanie shrugged nonchalantly. "I like to keep people guessing. At least until I have things summed up. Don't like to be thought of as an open book."

Gregory chuckled. "Oh, my lady, you're far from an open book. Everything I've learned about you I've practically had to pry out of you. To be perfectly honest with you I'm eager to learn more. Are you open to the idea of us exploring the possibilities?"

Stephanie's heart pounded heavily inside her chest. "Possibilities for what?"

Gregory smiled lazily. "I was hoping we could see if we have something special going for us. I already feel like we do. I'm definitely intrigued with you. I already know you're not romantically involved with anyone, so how about giving us a chance?"

Stephanie's ability to process a rapid-fire comeback wasn't fast enough to catch up with her racing heart. *This fine man doesn't pull any punches,* she mused. He sure knew how to get right down to the real nitty-gritty. Stephanie frowned slightly. "Long distance relationships rarely work, Gregory. We live too far apart to be anything but friends. I'm sorry, but that's how I feel. Nothing personal."

Gregory pursed his lips, looking thoughtful. He hoped his deep disappointment wasn't showing. That wouldn't be good. "I can understand what you're saying, but that doesn't mean I have to agree with it. And you should never apologize for how you feel. It is what it is. By the way, Stephanie, how many long distance relationships have you been in?"

A perplexed look stole across Stephanie's lovely face. "None."

"Then how do you know they rarely work? What are you basing your theory on?"

That she was dealing with a very clever lawyer instantly came to Stephanie's mind. She felt as if he'd already set her up. "I see where this is going, Gregory, and I guess I asked for it. I concede that I don't have firsthand knowledge of a failed long distance relationship, but I really can't see how that kind of affair can be successful."

Gregory lifted his glass of water in a toast. "Here's to us having a long distance friendship, Stephanie. To lasting friendship."

Stephanie picked up her glass and clinked it to his, but she couldn't believe how easily he'd given up on his desires. "I second that. To friendship, a lasting one." Admitting that she was terribly disappointed he'd dropped the matter was hard for her to do, but it was very true.

The waiter couldn't have appeared at a more opportune time and Stephanie was relieved by his presence. Her deep sigh came from within. She hoped the rest of the evening wasn't going to be awkward for them. She also hoped that Gregory wasn't going to take her remarks as a personal rejection. Having him for a friend would really be nice, though she wished she hadn't opted out on the possibility of something more than that. Making hasty decisions wasn't the norm with her . . . and she recognized that she'd been a little too quick in voicing this one. Long distance or not, he had appeared more than willing to see if they could work something out.

Respecting women and their wishes was a must with Gregory. He lived by that code of honor. This thing he had for Stephanie wasn't all about him. A relationship was between two people—and he was of the mind that both parties involved should decide what they wanted to become to each other. He wasn't about to press the issue or try and bully his way into her life.

Friendship always worked for him. It was the strongest kind of foundation to build upon in the beginning of any type of relationship. They may never have a romantic liaison, but he was confident they'd become good friends. If that was the case, he'd have to tamp down his deep desire to become so much more than a friend to her. The last thing he wanted to do was scare Stephanie completely away. He felt a spiritual kinship with her and he wanted them to make the connection in an unworldly way. Being evenly yoked with a woman was also important to him.

Gregory had seen all too often how some men totally disrespected women. His brother was one of those men. Grant was smooth as silk and as sweet as maple syrup during the chase. A woman's wish was his every command at the onset of each of his relationships. He couldn't seem to do enough for them. Once he'd hunted down his prey, and was confident that they were hopelessly caught up in his trap, Grant would then become an altogether different person.

The fact that Grant always seemed to pick women who didn't know how to love themselves was what helped to make him so successful at his game. Although he was never physically abusive to the women he got involved with, the emotional and mental degradation was just as hurtful as any mean-spirited jab. Grant's ill treatment of women sickened Gregory.

Even though they'd grown up in the same household, Gregory didn't know what Grant's rage was really all about. Jealousy was a strong suspect. He had yearned for so long to have a healthy, loving relationship with his older sibling, but Grant had made that impossible. Gregory had recently given up on them ever becoming anything more than blood relatives.

The rest of the evening passed by without the slightest bit of tension between Stephanie and Gregory. He was his usual charming self as he continued to enthusiastically entertain his date. Keeping her talking and laughing came easy for him. His fun-loving personality was one of his greatest assets. By the time dessert was served Stephanie was deeply regretting her remarks about long distance relationships. How to turn things back in her favor would occupy her thoughts throughout the rest of what she expected to be a sleepless night.

Stephanie could only wonder if she'd missed out on an opportunity of lifetime. . . .

Malachi wasn't anywhere to be seen when Stephanie entered the house. He had given her a key to gain access so she hadn't had to ring the doorbell. Gregory had begged off at her reminder of Malachi's suggestion of coffee, citing an extremely early start the next day.

Feeling kind of disappointed that she wouldn't see Malachi before going to bed, Stephanie started up the stairs. She had gotten only halfway up the steps when her father called out to her from below. At the sound of his cheerful voice, she turned around and smiled. "Hi, Dad. I wondered where you were. I had hoped I'd get to see you before turning in."

The warmth in his daughter's sweet tone soared right through

Malachi. That she continued to refer to him as Dad pleased him greatly. He silently thanked God for blessing him with her presence. Having her there with him had become his greatest joy. "I was out in the kitchen fixing something hot to drink. Too tired to join me? I know it's late."

Stephanie started back down the stairs, dismissing his concern with a wave of her hand. "Don't worry about the hour. Every second of this visit counts, especially since we don't have a heck of a lot of time to get better acquainted. I'm kind of thirsty. I'd also like to see the rest of those family pictures if you don't mind."

As soon as Stephanie reached the bottom landing, Malachi took her hand. "I can do you one better than that. Your Uncle Max made it in a short time ago. He told me to call up to his room when you got home. He can hardly wait to meet you, my dear."

Stephanie looked astonished. "He's here in the same house with us?"

Malachi nodded. "Right upstairs. If he'd gone on home, he feared that he wouldn't make it back over here in a timely manner. He's one busy man, Stephanie. Max stays on the go."

Stephanie felt extremely nervous and giddy with excitement, both at the same time. "Let's make that phone call. I can't wait to meet Uncle Max. This is so exciting."

Stephanie had just taken the first sip of her hot tea when she saw the robust figure filling the doorway. The big man, dark as he was handsome, wore a huge smile on his face. Stephanie instantly felt a special kinship with this kind-looking soul. As he rushed toward her, she stood up to receive what she imagined would come next, a great big bear hug from her Uncle Max.

Maxwell hugged Stephanie so hard she thought he might break her in two. "Well ain't this little beauty something else, Mal," Maxwell boomed. "You sure remind me of that gorgeous mother of yours. Come here and give your old uncle another hug. I can't believe this is finally happening. God answers prayers, no matter how long we think He takes. Thank you, Jesus."

Stephanie once again went into her uncle's powerful embrace, hoping Maxwell didn't squeeze her quite as hard as he'd done the last go-round. Seeing tears in his ebony eyes caused her own emotions to give rise. It was then that she began to realize that she and

Stephen weren't the only people adversely affected by their parents' split. Maxwell had been distressed by it too.

If couples only realized that breakups and nasty divorces had a negative impact on everyone involved, especially the children, Stephanie mused, maybe they'd try harder to work things out. She didn't in any way think people should stay in a loveless or abusive marriage, but in an institution mandated by God there shouldn't be so much hurt and dissention, either.

The second that Maxwell released Stephanie he pulled out her chair for her to reclaim. He then plopped his huge frame down on to the seat opposite Malachi's. "What about a cup of that tea for your dear old brother, Mal? If I hadn't given up drinking five years ago, I'd have you lace it with a double splash of brandy. I'm a little uptight after that long haul. Man, I thought that doggone road would never end. I guess I'm getting too old for driving these kinds of distances. I might need to go on and retire my shiny hot wheels."

Malachi chuckled. "Who do you think you're kidding, Max? You're probably going to take your last breath parked at some truck stop or highway rest area, sleeping inside that big old rig of yours, brother of mine. Any choice in teas?"

Maxwell shook his head in the negative. "Anything you put in front of me is okay. My beautiful niece and I are going to start catching up on things while you're away from the table."

Maxwell reached across the table and patted Stephanie's hand. "Tell me all about yourself. But first let me begin by saying that I'm sorry I haven't been in your life. There is no excuse for it, none whatsoever. Just because Doreen and Malachi couldn't keep it to-gether is no reason why I shouldn't have stepped in and done my part for you and your brother, regardless of that silly agreement be-tween your parents. I hope you can find it in your heart to forgive this old man. That would make me real happy. When we're young, some of us are also stupid."

Stephanie appreciated the sincerely voiced apology, but she didn't hold Maxwell accountable for what her parents had seen fit to agree upon. The twins' well-being had been Malachi's responsibility, not their uncle's. The agreement had kept two children from their very own father, silly or not. It almost seemed like a criminal offense to Stephanie.

"There's nothing to forgive, Uncle Maxwell. The sad thing is that I didn't even know you existed until this afternoon. Mama never spoke of anyone on Dad's side of the family. But we can shelve all that old stuff. What's important now is that we've met. I hope all of us will make every effort to stay in touch. We should never let distance or anything else come between us again. As for talking about myself, I'm not very good at that. But I'll try to give you a little sneak preview." Stephanie went on to tell Maxwell a few of the important details of her life.

Maxwell listened intently to what his niece had to say about herself. Malachi joined them after a couple of minutes. He too held on to Stephanie's every word. Although he'd heard before some of the particulars of her life, he was very much interested in hearing it again. He was proud of his daughter's every accomplishment. Despite all she'd had to go through while growing up, especially without her father there to guide her, she hadn't let it stop her from getting a good education and living a decent life. Malachi was grateful to God for those special gifts.

Maxwell reared back in his chair. "How's my nephew, Stephanie?"

"Stephen's good, Uncle Max. Being a firefighter, he stays busy a lot. He has a nice girlfriend, Darcy Coleman. Stephen recently bought himself a brand new house, had it built to his specifications. He has thirty-five hundred square feet with four large bedrooms, a formal dining and living room, a family room, and a game room. He uses one bedroom as an office and he keeps one reserved for me. Stephen and I are very close, Uncle Max."

"It sounds like he's also doing quite well for himself. I'm glad to hear that. I'm sorry he didn't come down here with you. Do you think he'll have any objections to meeting his old neglectful uncle if I come to Houston? I'd understand if he did, but I'd like to meet him."

Stephanie shook her head. "I don't know the answer to that, Uncle Max, but I can ask him. Since he doesn't know about you, he may be open to the idea." Stephanie grew silent. "I just thought of something he said recently, when we were talking about the possibility of other relatives on this side. Stephen said he felt like the entire Trudeaux family had abandoned us. I told him we didn't know that for sure, but he wasn't trying to hear me. Stephen's very angry over Dad not being there for us. I'm hoping he'll soon change. We all need each other."

Malachi looked shamefaced, his heart aching something fierce.

"That is so true, Stephanie. If the truth is known, I need you all more than you need me. I don't want to leave this world without getting close to you and Stephen. I know I have my work cut out for me, but I'm very much up to the challenge. Stephen and I *will* meet face to face, and it'll happen very soon. If I have to come to Houston to meet my son, so be it. One way or the other, the wall of silence between us is about to come tumbling down."

Stephanie laughed nervously. "Yeah, but once you hear how loud Stephen can yell, you might find yourself trying to reerect that wall in a hurry. When he gets super mad, he has the tendency to rant and rave rather loudly. Sometimes he acts as if he thinks I'm deaf. When it comes down to controlling his rage, he's his own worst enemy. I understand why he's so angry, but it's past time for him to start channeling it in a more constructive way. Talking to him about taking anger-management classes is like talking to the dead. He simply doesn't hear me."

Maxwell shook his head from side to side. "He has every right to be angry, Stephanie. You don't seem to be all that upset, which goes to show you how men react differently from women. I've only been around you for a very short time, but I imagine you've had some real difficulties with this situation at some point. How *do* you feel about everything, young lady?"

Malachi looked over at his brother with a concerted glance. "Maybe we shouldn't talk about that right now, Max. I don't want to spoil the end of Stephanie's evening. And it is late."

Stephanie held up her hand. "Don't worry about me, Dad. I'm fine. I've already told you how I felt about everything. If you don't mind, I don't mind sharing it with Uncle Max."

Malachi nodded. "It's up to you, my dear. I just don't want you to be uncomfortable."

Stephanie smiled gently, encompassing both men in her warm gaze. "Uncle Max, I have been terribly upset over Dad not being there. I have handled this differently from Stephen by throwing myself into my work and into any other task I take on. I work very hard and hardly play at all. I have very little social life because of my fear of personal relationships."

She stopped for a moment and smiled broadly, blushing in the process.

"Gregory saw proof of my fears earlier, but we'll talk about the date later . . ."

"Uh oh! I recognize that look," Maxwell teased. "Sorry for the interruption. Please go ahead with your story, but we do have to come back to the subject of young Gregory."

Stephanie laughed heartily. "I think I've already revealed too much. At any rate, once Dad explained everything to me and showed me a few things that proved his honesty and what part he played, I had to accept the evidence at face value. I'm not an angry person by nature, so that may have something to do with my ability to deal with this calmly."

Smiling softly, Stephanie reached over and took Malachi's hand. "But the truth is this. I want you in my life, Dad. I've gone too far for too long without you. It serves no purpose for me to stay stuck in the past. It has been so easy for me to reach this conclusion because I desperately need you in my life. I have so much love stored up inside of me and I'd like nothing better than to spill it out all over you. I just pray that Stephen will come to the same conclusion I have. I love you, Dad."

So much for not revealing my neediness, she mused. Stephanie was aware that she'd done a complete one-eighty where Malachi was concerned. She'd been wrong about all the things she had imagined him to be. Her father was just like every other human being. He was terribly flawed. He'd made many mistakes, and many more missteps would likely befall his life, but she couldn't find it in her heart to hold anything against him. He had already been punished enough. And he still had to stand before God to receive His final judgment.

Tears rolled rapidly down Malachi's cheeks as he reached over and pulled Stephanie into his arms. "I love you, too, daughter. Your forgiving nature is so refreshing. I can only pray that I'd be this forgiving under the same set of circumstances. You are indeed something special, Miss Stephanie. God love you."

Maxwell had a hard time containing his own tears. The loving sight before him was working over his emotions. Seeing his brother embracing the daughter he loved like crazy and had never gotten to know did his heart good. Maxwell prayed that Stephen would find it in his heart to become an integral part of the very small Trudeaux family circle. He'd never know what he was missing out on if he didn't come around. Malachi had a lot of pent-up love to share, too.

*   *   *

Stephanie had had every intention of calling Stephen before it got too late. Now that it was nearly two o'clock in the morning, the call would have to wait until later in the day. As she lay in bed, looking up at the ceiling, she rehashed in her mind her entire stay in New Orleans. Everything had gone so well thus far, much better than she'd ever anticipated. Getting to know her father hadn't been as difficult as she'd imagined. That she'd opened up to him so easily and willingly was the biggest surprise of all, next to agreeing to stay as a guest in his home. Her heart had already united with Malachi's.

In Stephanie's mind there was nothing wrong with her accepting her father for who he was and then professing her love for him, though Stephen would see it differently. Everyone had made mistakes in this situation, including her and Stephen. They were twenty-eight years old, yet Malachi had tracked them down, when they could've easily become the trackers. Stephanie believed they could've easily found Malachi had they tried. Their reason for not doing so was probably more out of respect for Doreen than anything else.

Why they hadn't ever made a decision to look for him was puzzling to her now. Had they met him after they'd turned eighteen, when they could've made their own decisions, things might not be as difficult as they were now. The fact remained that she and her brother had never discussed, as adults, a desire to find their father, so they didn't know if Doreen would've objected to the idea or not. Their mother's feelings were something they'd never know about.

On the other hand, when Stephanie and Stephen were in elementary school, the desire to meet their father had always been strong. She fondly recalled the fantasy games they used to play. They'd often pretended about how happy they'd be when their daddy came home from work and what they'd do when he got there.

As kids often do, the twins had conjured up all sorts of fun scenarios that included their father. Stephanie wanted Malachi to read a story to her and Stephen had always expressed his excitement about them playing football or baseball together. Playing at pretending to be a happy family had been their favorite thing to do. Although they'd never known Malachi, he was very much a part of their fantasy world, the male star in all their make-believe productions.

A broad smile came to Stephanie's lips when she thought of what had happened earlier, when Malachi had walked her upstairs to her suite. Ever since she was a small child, every night before going to sleep, Stephanie had imagined her father tucking her into bed and kissing her good night. When Malachi had earlier expressed his desire to do just what she'd always imagined, saying that it was something he'd always dreamed of doing for his children, she'd had a hard time containing herself. Her tears of joy had come without warning.

Malachi had waited in the kitchen of the suite while Stephanie had put on her nightclothes. Once she had situated herself comfortably on the bed, she'd called out to him. In a matter of seconds her father had entered the room, seating himself on the side of the mattress. Their tears had mingled while he'd so lovingly tucked in his precious daughter.

Malachi's sweet good night kiss on her forehead was everything Stephanie had imagined it would be—and then some. Just before leaving the room, he had blown Stephanie a kiss and had softly whispered "I love you" to her. She couldn't think of anything sentimentally comparable with what she'd just experienced with her father, the gentle man who was no longer a figment of her imagination, the loving dad who was no longer lost to her.

The melodious ringer on her cell phone interrupted her thoughts of one of the most beautiful moments she'd shared with Malachi thus far. The caller ID showed Stephen's home number. Why he wasn't fast asleep was an immediate concern for her, since it was so late. Her mother-hen persona immediately kicked in, causing her to pray that her brother wasn't sick. "Stephen, what's going on? Are you okay?"

Stephen chuckled lightly. "I'm fine, but what about you? Do I still exist for you?"

The jealousy in her brother's tone was not lost on Stephanie. *Tread lightly*, she told herself quietly, knowing Stephen was feeling completely left out. "I had thought of calling you earlier, after I came in from the dinner date with Gregory. Then something unexpected happened. Before I knew it, it was too late to call you. I miss you, Stephen." Reassurance that she hadn't deserted him was what Stephen needed most from her right now. She knew that to be a fact.

Stephen sighed hard. "I miss you, too. By the way, when *are* you coming home?"

"Day after tomorrow, Stephen. I think I'll be flying home instead of someone driving me back. Can you arrange to pick me up or should I get a shuttle?"

"Depends on the time your flight gets into Houston. Find out as soon as you can and let me know. Are you looking at coming into Hobby Airport or IAH?"

"I don't know right now. The flight arrangements haven't been made yet. I'll keep you informed. The door-to-door shuttle is always an option for me, so not to worry."

Stephen laughed softly. "I know you can take good care of yourself, darling angel. You mentioned earlier about something unexpected happening. What was that?"

Stephanie sucked in a deep breath, hoping that by mentioning they have an uncle she wouldn't turn over the applecart. "D . . . Malachi has an older brother," Stephanie said, glad she'd stopped herself from referring to Malachi as dad. That very personal reference to their father would've upset Stephen terribly, no doubt. "His name is Maxwell. He came over here to meet me this evening. He seems like a really nice guy. He wants to meet you, too, Stephen."

The tense moments of pregnant silence had Stephanie holding her breath. She could only guess at what was going through Stephen's mind, sure that none of it was very pleasant. The coughing sounds coming through the phone let her know that what she'd said had made her brother nervous. He had the tendency to cough when his nerves were rattled.

"I don't know what to say to that, Stephanie, so I won't say anything. Is he the only other relative you've met?"

Stephen asking questions about the Trudeaux family was a good sign in Stephanie's estimation. That let her know that he was at least curious about the other side of their family. "He's the only relative, period. I've been told that our grandparents have been dead a long time."

"No cousins or anything? Doesn't Malachi's brother have any children?"

"No first cousins, not a one. Not only does he not have any kids, Maxwell Trudeaux hasn't ever been married. He stays on the open road." Stephanie went on to tell Stephen all she'd learned so far about their Uncle Maxwell, the long distance trucker.

"Does Malachi have other children?"

Stephanie knew how hard it was for Stephen to ask that question. His curiosity had gotten the best of him on that one. "We're it, Stephen. You and I are his only kids."

"That's a huge relief. At least we know there aren't some other poor rascals out there going through what we were put through. Since he and Mama never got a divorce, other kids would've had to happen outside of marriage. Illegitimate is the word I was looking for."

"No, that never happened, Stephen. When I get home, we have a lot to talk about. There are so many things that have happened, so many serious issues for us to clear up. I want us to be face to face when I tell you everything. I can't wait to see you, big brother." Stephanie giggled. "I have a request before I say good night. Think you can do something nice for me?"

"Girl, I know that silly giggle. It means you want something from me. And you know I'm not signing any blank checks. So go ahead and tell me what it is."

"Buttermilk pie, Stephen. Will you have your sweet neighbor, Ms. Mattie Meeks, make one or two for me? No one makes buttermilk pies like she does. Can you hook a sister up with a delicious homecoming dinner?"

Stephen laughed heartily. "Since I have you spoiled rotten, I got no one to blame but myself. Later this morning I'll run next door and see what she can do for me. As for the dinner, I can hook you right on up with one of your favorites, liver and onions. I'll have everything ready for you so don't forget to call me with your arrival time. I'm gonna let you get some sleep now. Talk to you tomorrow. Love you, darling angel."

"Okay, Stephen. Before you go to sleep, just pray that I don't have dreams about all the delicacies we've mentioned. With that combination of heavy foods, I guess I should change dreams to nightmares. Sleep tight. Love you, too, Stevie pooh," Stephanie joked, laughing.

Pleased by how well their conversation had gone, delighted that Stephen hadn't gotten angry over the mention of their uncle, Stephanie turned off the bedside lamp. She then snuggled herself under the lightweight down comforter, looking forward to spending another wonderful day with her New Orleans connections.

Although the early-morning air was cool and crisp, the sun shone brightly overhead. As Stephanie walked down to the stables with Malachi and Maxwell, her eyes darted everywhere. She was eager to see the Arabian horses, but there was plenty of beauty to behold on the way to where the animals were housed. She no longer had to wonder where she'd gotten her love for horses from, especially thoroughbreds. Stephanie had an amazing fascination with the large, sleek, speedy steeds.

Thinking back on the special breakfast she'd shared with her family caused Stephanie to laugh inwardly. Seeing her Uncle Maxwell downing his meal like a starving man had both astounded and amused her. He'd eaten well over a dozen hefty pancakes and a half dozen over-medium eggs, just the way she liked hers cooked. She'd eventually lost count of the sausage links he'd consumed, but he had gobbled down quite a few of them before then. Maxwell was a big man, but he wasn't the least bit obese.

Seated at the head of his table, Malachi had eaten a modest amount of the delicious food. He seemed to be very careful with his diet, Stephanie had noted, which was evident in his great-looking physique. His taste buds appeared to favor fresh fruits and whole-grain cereals. Stephanie had also noticed that he never drank more than one cup of coffee with his meal. Just like her, he drank plenty of milk. It seemed Malachi wasn't a big meat eater—at least, she hadn't noticed him eating an overabundance of animal flesh during the couple of meals she'd taken with him.

This was really a beautiful fall day, she mused, loving the array of seasonal colors all about her. Autumn had been Doreen's favorite season. Stephanie loved all the seasons, but the holidays were her favorite time of the year. She couldn't help wondering if she and Stephen would ever spend a Thanksgiving or Christmas holiday with their father. She sure hoped so.

As the threesome came upon the stables area, Stephanie gasped in amazement. It appeared to her as if Malachi's Arabians lived nearly as well as Malachi did. The building housing the horses was enormous. Calling this place a stable or a barn was a grossly inaccurate description. The outside of the structure looked more like a large auditorium of some sort.

Stephanie's eyes then drank in the beauty of the rolling pastures surrounding the building. The grass was long and green, a paradise for grazing animals. The grounds of the entire estate were kept up beautifully. Stephanie couldn't even guess at the property's market value, but she didn't need to be in real estate to know that Malachi had positioned himself on top of a gold mine.

Malachi reached for Stephanie's hand. "Come on, my dear. It's time for you to meet my beautiful crew. I know you're gonna love these amazing animals as much as I do."

Stephanie gasped with pleasure over and over again. The six Arabians were nothing short of magnificent. Thunder, Lightning, Cloud, Sky, Comet, and Star were Malachi's pride and joy. Sky and Star were the only females. Malachi mentioned to Stephanie that he wasn't in the business of breeding his animals himself, but that he charged hefty stud fees to breeders residing on neighboring horse farms. Malachi was an extremely smart businessman.

"So, what do you think of the horses, kid?" Maxwell asked Stephanie.

"It's hard for me to believe that you can't look at my face and tell, Uncle Max. They're magnificent! I love them."

Maxwell grinned. "Want to take a ride on one of these beauties, niece?"

Stephanie backed up a couple of steps. "No way. I'd be terrified. Just seeing how big they are is enough to scare me senseless. I love horses, but I've never had a desire to ride one."

Malachi reached for his daughter, hugging her briefly. "Nothing to be ashamed of, my dear. As beautiful as they are, they can also be dangerous, especially to someone who doesn't know how to handle them. If you ever want to learn to ride, just let me know. There's a great riding instructor who lives a few miles down the road. Manny Diego is also an accomplished horse trainer. He has quite a reputation around here. He's one of the best horsemen I know."

Stephanie chuckled nervously. "That's one offer I don't think I'll be taking you up on, Dad, but thanks anyway." Stephanie giggled. "However, I'd like to own a pair of those fancy cowboy boots you and Uncle Max are wearing. I've lived in Texas all my life and have never bought any western gear, other than blue jeans. There are stores in Houston that sell nothing but boots and western outfits."

Maxwell laughed heartily. "The boots will be on me, Stephanie. Handmade, of course, cut from any leather of your choice."

Malachi gave a hearty harrumph. "She'll have two pairs, then. Yours will be the second pair. No one but a father should buy his daughter her first genuine cowboy boots."

Stephanie cracked up. "Do I sense a little sibling rivalry going on here? If so, I'll settle it by buying my own boots. Since this girl runs her own lucrative business, she *can* afford them."

Everyone laughed at that.

Stephanie stepped away and leaned against the fence surrounding the stables so that she could drink in the natural beauty of the land. She recalled seeing the picnic tables and benches sprinkled throughout the property, especially the lake, which was stocked with a variety of fish. She had learned during breakfast that fishing was one of her father's favorite pastimes.

As Stephanie continued to look across the property, as far as her eyes could see, she spotted Gregory coming toward the stables. Since he was dressed in his usual designer attire, she assumed he was dropping by before going into his office. The sweet thought that he might be coming to see her made her giggle inwardly. Regardless of whom he'd come to visit, she was very happy to see him. She liked being in his company. As he drew closer, he waved, and she waved back, smiling all over herself.

Stephanie turned around and looked at Malachi. "Dad, Gregory's here. He's coming across the field."

Malachi turned toward the fast-approaching figure. A slight frown crept onto his face. "That's not Gregory, my dear. It's his brother, Grant. I can't imagine what he's doing here this time of day."

"If nothing else, you can bet your bottom dollar he's bringing trouble with him," Maxwell remarked, scowling hard.

Gregory and Grant weren't twins, but if Stephanie hadn't known that already, she would've thought so. The brothers shared the same height and build, though she could see that Grant wasn't as muscular as Gregory. With the same identical eye and hair coloring, they looked so much alike it was darn near uncanny. Stephanie couldn't help staring hard at Grant.

Soon after Malachi introduced Grant to Stephanie, Grant began with the wild flirting, openly, unashamedly. Grant started chatting Stephanie up like she was the only one present. Much to Malachi and Maxwell's dismay, Grant completely ignored the older men's presence.

Malachi saw the trouble brewing, but until he felt that Stephanie needed rescuing, he planned on remaining watchful. He was sure that Grant already knew that Gregory had a personal interest in Stephanie . . . and that he'd taken her out to dinner. Grant made it his business to know his younger brother's every move, always looking for an opportunity to best him. This wasn't the first time

Grant had tried to sell himself to one of Gregory's female friends. But this was the first time Grant would have Malachi to contend with. Malachi would never allow his daughter to get caught up in Grant's dangerous web of deceit. Not if he could help it.

On the other hand, Maxwell was looking at Grant as if the young man had lost his mind somewhere on the way to Malachi's residence. Grant didn't appear to Maxwell as if he was high on something, but that didn't mean he wasn't. In Maxwell's estimation, Grant was a perfect example that sibling rivalry was very much alive and well.

Stephanie was terribly embarrassed by the whole situation, but she continued to let Grant go on and on about himself. That he didn't even know her didn't seem to matter to him. His constant chatting about his amazing accomplishments gave Stephanie a real sense of who he was. He had instantly created a center stage for himself and Stephanie was his captive audience. Malachi and Maxwell didn't exist for him. It didn't take her long to recognize that Grant wasn't at all the person he wanted her to believe he was.

If Grant's outer shell was suddenly stripped away, a lost child would be revealed. His animated body language was that of a small kid begging for attention. Beneath the tailored suit of clothing Grant suffered from a bleeding heart. Indelible crimson stains were highly visible through his expensive silk shirt. Embedded in his Italian loafers, she imagined winged feet dying to fly free of their restraints. He could be free as a bird, only if he let go of self.

Every time Grant opened his mouth, she heard his cry for help. Deep down inside, he wanted to be accepted by all, Stephanie accessed after several very long minutes of listening to his incessant babbling. But she didn't think he knew that about himself. It seemed to her that he didn't know he could be accepted for who he was, even if he didn't know who he was. Grant reminded her of all the people who tried so hard to get everyone to like them. She couldn't help wondering if he was the kind of person who would shove people aside once they began to like him, and move on. Out of fear, no doubt. Don't get too close to me, because you just might figure out who I really am, then you surely won't like me.

That Grant was trying his best to manipulate her was quite evident to Stephanie. It seemed that his manipulation of women was a sick art form of his own creation. Stephanie thought he'd probably keel over and die if he knew how easy it had been for her to figure him out. He'd revealed so much of himself, all in such a short span of time. Instead of getting her to see who he was, who he'd very much like to be, he'd shown her exactly who he wasn't.

Gregory's decision not to mention his older brother to her was now understandable. It suddenly dawned on her that Gregory hadn't spoken of his mother, either, and neither had Malachi. Stephanie's curiosity was instantly heightened in regard to the Saxton family history. She was sure there were many interesting facts for her to learn. Looking over at her Uncle Maxwell, she smiled. If anyone would tell her the Saxton story, she'd be willing to bet her next design contract that her uncle was the one to spill it all.

Although Stephanie felt sorry for Grant, and thought he needed a lot of prayer, she wouldn't think of involving herself with him in any form or fashion. Grant was a time bomb looking for just the right face to explode in. Buried under all that polished veneer was a man who was in desperate need of love. Perhaps love for God and self might just cure what ailed Grant.

6

As Malachi pulled his late-model sedan into the driveway of Stephanie's home, stomach-knotting apprehension hit Stephanie full force. Perhaps this wasn't such a good idea after all, she mused. When Malachi had first approached her about driving her home so that he could try to see Stephen, she had given it a lot of serious thought. The very depths of her soul had been thoroughly searched in order to find the appropriate answer. Her desire to have everything out in the open had weighed heavily upon her during the decision-making process.

Stephanie had later come to the conclusion that the meeting between father and son was going to happen one way or the other, with her or without her. Malachi was determined in that. Now that she wasn't feeling so sure about her decision to be a part of this surprise visit, which Stephen would more than likely see as an outright ambush, Stephanie didn't know what to do about it. Her father had driven the distance . . . and now she had to see this situation through to the end. It was the only fair thing to do.

Malachi turned his body slightly toward the right, and then slid his arm across the back of the car seat. "Having second thoughts about all this, my dear?"

Stephanie moaned softly. "I'm so transparent. The one thing I hate about me is my inability to hide my feelings and thoughts. I'm sorry, but I've been second-guessing my part in this surprise visit. I'm no longer sure I did the right thing by agreeing to your suggestion. I'm also afraid of the bigger rift this might cause between Stephen and me."

Malachi looked concerned. "Do you really expect it to be that bad?"

Stephanie vigorously nodded her head. "He just won't understand our intent, Dad. And he's going to label me a traitor before all is said and done. You're here now, so I'm going to let God handle what comes next. This family showdown is imminent. Let's go inside and face the music. I expect Stephen's dinner celebration will become soured the moment he lays eyes on us. He'll know you because I told him what you look like in one of our phone conversations. Please forgive him if he speaks out from his searing pain. His tongue can be rather sharp."

Malachi dropped his arm around his daughter's shoulder in a comforting way. "This old man has a hide of steel. Letting Stephen get his anger out is my main reason for wanting to get on with this meeting. I believe that until the anger is outside of him he won't be able to deal rationally with any of the issues between us. I don't want you to worry about a thing. I can handle anything he throws my way. In fact, I welcome it. I'm confident in my mission."

Stephanie's hands shook as she inserted the key into the lock. It felt as if she was about to enter the cavern of doom. Her stomach was doing jumping jacks and her heart felt as if it might pound its way right out of her chest. Her best weapon to use in this instance was prayer, lots of it.

If Stephen was somewhere nearby, Stephanie knew he'd hear the front door open and come running to see her. She could imagine his enthusiastic greeting getting stuck in his craw the moment he laid eyes on Malachi. It was easy for her to conjure up the hateful look Stephen would shoot her way. Cringing at what she'd gotten herself too deeply involved with, Stephanie entered the house. Malachi followed right behind her, carrying her baggage.

Nothing but stillness greeted Stephanie and Malachi. She waited for Stephen to come bounding from one of the rooms, but there was no sign of him. The house was downright chilly, causing her to shiver slightly. The furnace hadn't been turned on, which was unusual. Her brother would've warmed the house for her with the weather having turned this cold.

"Where do you want me to put your luggage, Stephanie?"

Seeing Malachi standing there with his hands still wrapped around her baggage snapped her mind to attention. "Oh, how rude of me. Follow me, Dad. You can put them in my bedroom."

Although the house was eerily quiet, Stephanie still expected Stephen to suddenly appear. By the time they reached the back of the house, she realized it wasn't going to happen. He simply wasn't there. His absence was confirmed for her the moment she saw the sheet of paper propped up on one of the pillow shams on her bed. No one but Stephen could've left the note.

Stephanie rushed over to the bed and picked up the note, reading it rather rapidly. A sigh of relief gushed from her lips. She had gotten a reprieve for now. Since she had instructed him not to pick her up at the airport, due to the last-minute changes in plans, Stephen had changed the venue for the welcome-home dinner. Everything would be waiting for her at his place. According to what she'd read, he had also invited Darcy and Farrah. All Stephanie needed to do was phone her brother and let him know she was on the way so the food would be ready when she got there.

Stephanie turned to face Malachi. "Stephen is having the dinner at his place. He's expecting me to come there." She hesitated a moment. "In a way this is good. I know how badly you want to see him, but I'm thinking I should talk to him about everything first. Then I can tell him you're here to see him. The more thought I give to this situation, the more I realize that springing you on Stephen is the wrong approach. Do you understand what I'm saying?"

Malachi dropped down in the comfortable chair situated not too far from the bed. "I was beginning to feel the same as you do. Maybe this is for the best. I was hasty in my decision to come here. If I can lie down and get a couple hours of rest, I can be on my way back home. We'll just have to resolve this matter another time, though I admit my disappointment is great."

Stephanie looked horrified. "No, Dad, it doesn't have to happen like that. You can stay here while I go see Stephen. I don't want you to leave. I just think it's better if I tell Stephen all that I've learned, and then tell him you're here to see him. You can rest while I'm gone. Please don't go back to New Orleans, not until after you find out if Stephen will meet with you."

Malachi looked totally relieved. The last thing he wanted to do was go back home without seeing his son. He could stand to wait a little while longer if it meant meeting Stephen. "That's the best solution to our dilemma. We should've thought things through more carefully. When you want something so badly, you tend to lose your grip on reality. Your suggestion is the more amicable way to do it, my dear."

"I'm glad you agree. Now let me show you into the guestroom and get you settled in so I can be on my way. The sooner we get this over with, the better we'll both feel."

With the celebratory dinner now over, and Darcy and Farrah having left already, Stephanie knew that she had to choose her words carefully. Telling Stephen all the things she learned about their parents while visiting Malachi in New Orleans wouldn't be an easy task. She expected her brother to reject every word she'd say. She'd denounced Malachi's story too, until she'd seen numerous articles of proof to back up Malachi's woeful tale.

Before Stephanie took a seat on the sofa, where Stephen had already made himself comfortable, she turned down the thermostat. The living room in Stephen's home was a tad warmer than she liked it. The last thing they needed to feel was stuffy and overheated. The red-hot topic of discussion was going to be enough prickly heat for them to contend with without adding more warmth to the mix.

As Stephanie launched into the less important details of her visit with Malachi, she noticed right away that Stephen's restlessness had grown tenfold from when she'd first come through his front door. His body language spoke volumes. With them having been at odds over the trip in the first place, Stephanie knew firsthand how Stephen had a tendency to sit around and stew in his own juices, often allowing them to rise to the boiling point. Their long distance phone calls to each other hadn't gone over very well—with the exception of the last couple—which wasn't in her favor, either. Stephen wanted her to see everything that had to do with Malachi his way, or he'd clam up and refuse to discuss it any further.

Despite the evil looks her brother continually shot her way, Stephanie went on to tell him the unpleasant things she thought he needed to be aware of. The disbelief in his eyes was easy for Stephanie to discern. However, she was glad that he hadn't yet interrupted her with one of his angry tirades. Not for one second did she believe his anger wouldn't make an appearance.

Finished with what she had to say, Stephanie rested her head against the sofa back. "That's all I have to tell you, Stephen. I know I've said a mouthful, but it had to be said."

Stephen eyed his sister with open curiosity. "You really believe all that crap, Stephanie?"

Stephanie nodded, hoping her brother didn't go off the deep end like he normally did. "I'm afraid so, Stephen. There's nothing to indicate I've been lied to."

Stephen looked ready to burst from his anger. "Let me get this straight." Scowling hard, he put a finger up to his right temple. "Malachi cheated on Mom while she was pregnant with you and me. She found out about his awful indiscretion and kicked him out of the house, forbidding him to be involved in our lives once we were born. She later softens towards him and allows him to be involved in our lives, but only in a covert manner. How am I doing so far?"

"You haven't missed a beat yet, Stephen."

Stephen sighed hard. "What I don't get is that you believe all the stuff Malachi filled your head with. What happened to you while you were in New Orleans, Stephanie? It seems to me that you've been brainwashed. I should've never let you go."

Her eyes widened in disbelief. "*Let* me, Stephen? Boy, you'd better come again. You had no choice in the matter. And you need to stop trying to make me feel foolish. I was there with Malachi. I saw his naked emotions. He loved Mama, still loves her. I don't doubt that any longer. After seeing proof of some of the things he was saying, I didn't need anything more to convince me of his sincerity. Dad made a big mistake and Mama made him pay for it, big time. You need to see him and talk to him yourself. Maybe you also need to see some of the proof he has."

Stephen did a double take. "Dad! You mean to tell me you're calling him Dad now? Stephanie, how could you dare do that? This is such a devastating betrayal on your part. I always thought you had my back."

In a show of frustration, Stephanie slapped her palms against the side of her face. "Having your back doesn't mean I have to agree with you about everything. I don't have to hate or dislike someone just because you do. We were wrong about Dad. Face the facts, Stephen."

"Whose facts, Stephanie? Malachi's?"

"The facts, period. Here are more of the specifics, as I see them. Mama crammed the importance of forgiveness down our throats on a daily basis, but it's obvious that she didn't practice what she preached. No one can tell me that she wouldn't want us to forgive him. Don't you get it? They never stopped loving each other. Theirs was a sick game of cat and mouse."

"You don't know that for a fact, Stephanie, so don't try to sell me on that idea."

"It is a fact, since I saw letters that indicated it. Mama deliberately kept Dad believing that he still had a chance with her, just so she could keep on punishing him. This sort of thing happens more than you think. Children are often used as pawns in grown-ups' disputes. Pride and the inability to forgive is what kept her from allowing him to make atonement for his wrongdoings. Mama died loving our father. He loves her still. With all that said, will you please change your mind about meeting our father? You have to end your silence in this matter."

Stephen punched his left palm with his right fist. "You're crazy if you think I'm going to meet him. No way am I doing that. You may've lost your mind, but I'm not losing mine."

"I may be crazy, but I think you're scared of the truth, afraid to find out that Mama was in part responsible for us growing up without our father. We can't change the past, but we can live in the moment. Our father is not getting any younger. Do you want your anger to keep you stuck in the past until he eventually dies? What will you do with all your rage then? You won't have Malachi to hold accountable for your wrath once he's dead and gone."

"As far as I'm concerned, Malachi Trudeaux is already dead. I won't meet him. I don't want anything to do with him, nor do I want anything from him, money or otherwise."

Stephanie threw her hands up in a show of defeat. "In that case, you'd better give him back what's left of your inheritance. While you're at it, you'll also need to hand over to him a quit deed to this fancy new house of yours."

Stephen's brows furrowed, his forehead creasing with wrinkles. He appeared totally perplexed. "What are you talking about? We haven't inherited a single dime from that old man."

Stephanie's eyes softened as they soulfully connected with her brother's. "Sorry to inform you of this, but we have. Where do you think Mama got all that money she left us? We've both wondered about it time and time again. There was no large sum of insurance money, only the one policy that didn't amount to much. It wasn't even enough to pay for her burial, but she'd already taken care of that through the preneed program at the mortuary."

Stephanie wished she hadn't been as boisterous with her initial outburst. Stephen didn't look as if he could take much more. But she thought it was better to get everything out in the open so that he could start to deal with the truth. Stephanie would always believe that Stephen suffered through Malachi's absence far more than she did. Every son wanted to have his father around to do guy things with. Stephen was very athletic and he loved all kinds of sports.

Stephen appeared downright distressed. None of what his sister had said made any sense to him. "You've lost me. Completely."

"Malachi did pay child support, Stephen. Mama obviously stockpiled all that money he'd sent her on a regular basis. She then willed it to us to receive after she died."

Stephen couldn't begin to imagine that something like that had occurred, not when they'd had to do without so much. If Doreen had had mad money like that, why had she let them live as poorly as they had? He then thought of how he and Stephanie had gone to college on academic scholarships, how they'd worked hard at staying on the honor roll just so they could receive the grants. Doreen had told them she'd never be able to afford college on her meager earnings. Wanting to make their mother proud of them was just as important to the twins as attending college. Stephen and Stephanie had desperately wanted to show Doreen that all her hard work would never be in vain. Giving something back to their mother had been important to them also.

If all along Doreen had had the kind of money she'd left them in her will, then that meant she'd lied to her own kids. Not only did these allegations mean that she'd lied to them, she'd also made them live the fabrications. Stephanie and Stephen had eventually made themselves believe that one of Doreen's rich employers had been responsible for the money she'd left to them.

Then Stephen began trying to reason things out, his mind coming up with numerous excuses for why their mother would do something terrible like that, if it was true. All sorts of scenarios passed through his head, but none of them made him feel any better. "Mama probably thought she was doing the right thing by us. Maybe she thought if we grew up with too much that we'd become spoiled and not become hungry enough for more than what we had . . ."

"Stephen," Stephanie yelled, getting up from the sofa, "we wore shoes with holes in them. Out in the rain and the cold. How can you dare to try and justify that? It just can't be justified, ever. It seems to me that Mama's issues with Dad were taken out on us. She taught us a lot of values, taught us to be self-sufficient, but it looks to me like she wasn't the saint we thought of her as. I don't love her any less, but I am rather upset with her poor choices."

Stephanie knew that it was bothering Stephen to no end to hear her speak of their mother in that light. The expression of sadness on his face told her that much. But she'd seen the hard, cold evidence of Doreen's numerous deceptions. Knowing what their mother had done had nearly killed Stephanie's spirit, too, but once she'd put it all together she'd had no choice but to accept the facts of the matter. Malachi hadn't manufactured all the substantiating data he'd shown her.

Stephen had a hard time rejecting and then completely dismissing what he'd heard, but he was having an even tougher time trying to accept it as the truth. What loving mother would allow her children to go without some of the basic necessities of life if she'd had an alternative? And the fact that she'd worked so hard and hadn't spent a dime on herself made it even worse.

"This doesn't make sense, Stephanie. None of it. I just can't fathom it."

"I understand how hard it is for you. It's hard for me, too, but we have to accept it."

"Why do I have to accept it? Exactly what proof do you have that Malachi is not lying, that he's not trying to undermine our mother so that he can lift himself up in our eyes? Mama can't defend herself from the grave . . . and he knows that."

"Of course she can't defend herself and of course he knows that. But think of this, Stephen. If he hasn't tried to contact us in all these years out of his own selfishness, why would it matter to him what we thought of him now? Why would he come to us as soon as Mama died?"

Stephen shook his head from side to side. "I don't know. I may never know why."

"Not to worry. I'll tell you why. Because that's the pact he made with her to keep her from leaving town and taking us with her. She'd threatened to never let him know where she was, which meant he might never see his kids again. He did it because he loved her and he didn't want to cause her any more pain than he'd already caused her. He never stopped believing they'd get back together, because she kept him hanging on. I know it sounds crazy, but life is crazy, just one big ball of confusion. Mama played poker with Malachi's life, bluffing him at every turn, using us as the bargaining chips. Unfortunately for all of us, he never received the big payoff. He was only in that insane poker game with Mama to win his family back."

Stephen shoved his hands haphazardly through his hair, looking as if he was about to break down and cry. His emotions were hitting him hard, attacking him from all sides. He felt surrounded by an evil enemy he couldn't even see. It seemed that the one person who'd always been on his side was now fighting for the opposition. The thought of losing his twin sister to the likes of Malachi Trudeaux was absolutely devastating to Stephen.

Stephanie was acting like Malachi's mouth was a prayer book. Since she knew without a doubt that the man was a cheater, how could she believe that he was anything but a liar? How their father had managed to turn Stephanie completely around to his way of thinking in just a few days was puzzling to Stephen. "This all seems so far-fetched, especially when he could've gone to court and won visitation rights. That's what family courts are for."

Stephanie pursed her lips. "I don't think you've been listening to everything I've said. He had hurt her enough with the one-night stand. For God's sake, Stephen, she was pregnant when that happened. He wasn't going to add insult to injury by dragging her into a court of law and having a judge force her to do anything she didn't want to. Love, Stephen. Dad was in love with Mama. He would've done anything she asked him to . . . and she knew that. He is still paying the ultimate price for cheating on the woman he loved more than life itself."

Stephen sucked his teeth. "If he loved her so much, why did he cheat on her?"

"Well, we did discuss that, as awkward as it was for us to do so. He wasn't trying to condone what he'd done by telling me what had occurred, but he wanted to be completely honest with me about everything. His explanation was a simple one. His physical needs weren't being met. According to him, Mama was afraid of hurting her babies by making love to him. The physical withholdings started right after the first trimester. You figure out the rest."

"What kind of man is he to tell his own daughter something like that about her mother?"

"A very honest man, Stephen. He said it only happened that one time. From what I read in one of the letters Mama wrote to him she believed him. He's still mortified by what he did."

"Why are you defending him like this? He cheated on Mama and then he walked out and left his family behind. I don't hear you defending Mama—and she was the one he hurt the most."

"I'm not defending either one. Both of them were dead wrong. Mama was just as guilty of duplicity as Dad was, but only in a different manner. And he didn't leave; he was put out. Let's put the past issues aside for now and give some serious thought to the present."

Stephanie sat back down next to her brother, taking his hand in hers. She looked into his eyes, hoping he could see how much she loved him in the reflection of hers. "What's happening with me is all about forgiveness, Stephen Trudeaux. For me, this is not about who did what or why they did it. In my heart I have forgiven Dad and I've forgiven Mama." She playfully bumped him with her shoulder. "You should try a little mercy on for size. It fits and feels real good, big brother. Forgiveness cleanses the soul. When Jesus died, He wiped the slate clean for all of us, including the liars and the cheaters. Absolution was only made possible at the cross."

Stephen kissed Stephanie on the forehead, wishing they weren't at odds like this. They'd had their share of disagreements, but none as serious as this one. She wanted him to just get up and go to New Orleans and take up with a man he'd spent his entire life loathing. How was that possible for him to do? With all the anger he had pent up inside of him, Stephen feared what he might try to do to his father when face to face with him. Unleashing his rage against Malachi wasn't something he'd want to happen. Disrespecting his father went against everything he was taught to believe, yet he didn't have any respect for him whatsoever. Would he be able to stop himself from verbally abusing or even physically attacking him? That was the big question. His biggest fear in confronting Malachi was that he might not be able to hold back his rage.

Stephen turned his body slightly to the side so that he could look right into Stephanie's eyes. He instantly realized that his idea of direct eye contact wasn't a good one. The pain in his sister's eyes made him feel awful. If only they both could've been spared all this melodrama.

To lessen his anguish Stephen wrung his hands together. "I'm going to recap what I think you've been saying to me, what I think you want me to believe. Mama was a woman scorned and she never let her husband forget his betrayal of her. She then cleverly kept him on the hook. I don't want you, but no one else will have you, either. You can't have an up-close and personal relationship with your kids, but you can be involved in their lives undercover. Don't speak to them and make sure you don't let them see you." He shook his head. "How in the world, girl, do you expect me to believe that load of crap?"

"It's not about what I want you to believe. It's the truth. People do things like that, you know. Go and talk to Malachi. He's at my place, Stephen, hoping against hope to meet you. Later on you can see the proof of his honesty for yourself. I can only conclude that you don't want to deal with the truth if you don't go, and that you want your life to stay stuck on rage."

Stephen's facial expression quickly changed. He looked like a dark thundercloud. That she had invited Malachi into her home had enraged him. This was so unlike Stephanie. She'd always been considerate of his feelings. What was making her behave so out of character?

His sister was right about one thing. He didn't want to deal with the truth, Malachi's so-called truth. Believing an ungodly man like that was out of the question for Stephen. He hated to be the one to take such a hard line in this instance, but someone had to. Stephanie's marshmallow heart had already warmed up toward Malachi. In fact, it was completely roasted.

Feeling that it was time for him to get away from his sister, before things got any further out of hand, Stephen jumped up from the couch. "You do what you want, Stephanie, but don't expect me to be a part of your life if you continue to have a relationship with the devil. Call me when you've made your choice. The father you've never known or the brother who's always been there for you is what you have to consider. You can let yourself out."

Feeling as if she was rooted to the sofa by some alien force, Stephanie watched as Stephen stormed out of the room. The pain she felt from his remarks was unbearable. Her twin brother had just given her an unreasonable ultimatum, a relationship with him or their father. How was she supposed to make a choice between them? She couldn't, shouldn't have to . . . and wouldn't do so. Upon closing her eyes, she prayed that Stephen would eventually come to his senses. Putting her problems in God's hands was the only thing left for her to do. God was the only one who could make beautiful dreams out of this ugly nightmare.

"God," she prayed, "please make this pain go away. Please make this family whole."

Not only was Malachi not going to meet Stephen on this trip, it appeared that spending Thanksgiving in New Orleans with him was a complete bust. She couldn't go to New Orleans without her brother, not on a special holiday, not when they'd spent all their holidays together for the past twenty-eight years. Holidays should always be special for families, even broken ones.

As Stephanie began to gather her belongings to leave for home, Stephen reappeared, looking as if he could annihilate the world. When he got in her face, she backed up a few steps.

"So you want me to meet *your* father," he ground out. "Okay, I can do that. But you may be terribly sorry that you forced this meeting between us. You're as deceptive as you've accused Mama of being. I'm going over to your place to see that old man, but you might not like the outcome. If I end up tearing him from limb to limb, you'll only have yourself to blame. If it's a meeting Malachi wants with me, he's going to get it. Up real close and down-and-dirty personal. And I only hope he lives long enough to regret the day he ever came face to face with his son."

Before Stephanie could take her next breath, let alone respond to Stephen, he was headed for the door leading out to the garage. Because of the other cars parked in the driveway when she'd arrived at her brother's house, she'd parked on the street. Seeing how reckless Stephen was acting, she was glad for that. In the rage he was in, she'd hate for him to back out of the garage, forgetting that her car was there in the driveway. Stephen was out of control.

It was apparent to Stephanie that she'd bitten off more than she could chew, but her deepest concern was for Malachi. There was no way she could get to him before Stephen did. She was positive that her brother would break the speed laws in getting to her house. Calling Malachi to warn him wasn't going to help. She couldn't imagine her father answering her phone; this was only his first visit to her home.

Making a beeline for the front door, Stephanie realized she couldn't get home before Stephen made it there, but hopefully she'd make it before the fireworks went off. A vision of her father and brother engaged in a physical altercation had her quickly securing the locks on the front door. In getting to her car, she ran as fast as her legs would carry her, praying all the while. This outcome wasn't at all what she'd hoped for. *Poor Malachi,* she mused, worried sick for her father. If he knew what was about to go down, he'd probably hightail it back to New Orleans.

In his valiant attempt to keep his temper under control, Stephen continuously balled and unballed his fists. Hitting Malachi wasn't something he wanted to resort to, regardless of how much he felt like pummeling him into the ground. This man may've pulled the wool over his sister's eyes, but there wasn't enough yarn in the world to cover up how Stephen envisioned him. Malachi had manipulated Stephanie into believing his pack of lies, but Stephen wasn't about to fall into the same cleverly laid trap.

Clenching and unclenching his teeth, Stephen wrung his hands together, trying to keep them under tight control. "It's 2005, man. Up until the very day Mama died she was still scrubbing floors and washing and ironing folk's laundry. I lost count of the times she'd come home with broken nails and bruised blood underneath them. Where the heck were you when she was working her fingers to the bone? Try to explain that one away."

Malachi lowered his head into his hands. "You haven't heard a word I've said, son. Your anger won't let you hear me. No one can reason with you in your current state of mind. You're stubborn and bullheaded just like your Mama was."

Those were fighting words to Stephen. Ready to pounce, yet holding himself back with every ounce of his strength, Stephen glared at Malachi, prepared to take him down to the carpet if necessary. Starting a physical fight with his father went against everything he'd been taught by his mother, but he wasn't going to stand by and let his father disrespect him or Doreen. She had worked too hard and had endured too much physical and emotional stress for Malachi to refer to her in such a contemptible way. Doreen had given her all to her children while Malachi hadn't given them a single thing. Despite the proof he'd shown Stephanie, Stephen just didn't care.

Stephen stood up and advanced on his father in a menacing way. "Man," Stephen ground out, shaking his forefinger with fury, "don't you dare to ever talk to me about what my mama was or wasn't. You have no clue as to who Mama was. You don't have the right to speak her name, let alone try to undermine her goodness and her unending love for her kids. She was always there for Stephanie and me. Again I ask, where the Sam Hill were you?"

Malachi got up from his chair and moved behind the breakfast bar, as though to shield himself from Stephen's fury. He had no desire to get into a physical altercation with his son, but he was quite capable of defending himself if he had to. His boy's anger was understandable, but it would do no good to tell him he was directing it at the wrong person. He had already tried to tell Stephen where he was and why he hadn't been visible in his life. Either Stephen didn't believe him or he couldn't handle the truth of the matter, which in reality was a no-win situation for everyone in the family.

If Stephen couldn't believe his sister, whom he adored, Malachi didn't know whom Stephen could trust. During Stephen's tirade, Stephanie had made numerous attempts to try and get through to her brother. In order for Stephen to accept Malachi's truth, it meant that he had to question his own mother's integrity, making Malachi realize it was much easier for his son to disbelieve him. After all, he had been the absent parent. The hatred Malachi saw in Stephen's eyes had him trembling within. How was he ever going to turn this grave situation around? Only God had the answer to that one. Malachi wasted no time in calling on the Lord for help.

Stephanie stood up, too. "I think we all need to calm down. This mess has gone too far. Nothing good can come of this situation if you keep yelling at everyone, Stephen. Can you please sit back down so we can discuss this in a less volatile way? Exploding all over the place isn't doing you any good. Please come back to the table. Both of you."

Stephen looked at Stephanie like she was crazy. "You can't possibly think we can continue this discussion in a calm manner. It's over for me. I don't need to hear another thing. I gave you an ultimatum earlier, Stephanie. It still stands. Him or me. It's all up to you."

Stephanie came to within an inch of where Stephen stood, fuming uncontrollably. "No, dear brother, you're the one who has to make the choice. I love both of you and I'm not choosing between the two of you. If you don't want me in your life, Stephen, you take possession of your unjust decision. Then you need to claim exclusive ownership of it. I won't allow you to put this burden off on me. Your ultimatum sucks . . . and you darn well know it. I knew you'd have difficulties with all this, Stephen, but I never dreamed you'd be this unreasonable."

Unable to believe the stance Stephanie had taken, Stephen looked between his sister and their father. It seemed to him that Stephanie had already chosen, regardless of what she'd just said. It was clear to him that Malachi was the victor. "Whatever, Stephanie." He looked back at his father. "I hope you're happy with all the dissention you've caused between your kids. You may've won Stephanie over, but you'll never win me. I don't hang out with cheating liars. You are the devil and everyone in your camp is an advocate for evil."

With that said, Stephen stomped out of the room, leaving both Stephanie and Malachi utterly bewildered. It appeared to Malachi that things had gone from bad to worse. From Stephanie's point of view, there didn't seem to be a harmonious end in sight.

What the future held for the Trudeaux family was anyone's guess, Stephanie mused. Right after that very defeatist thought Stephanie's faith was instantly revived. This entire situation was in God's hands— and that's exactly where she planned to leave it.

7

Stephanie stopped dead in her tracks when the phone rang. Hoping it was a very contrite Stephen, she rushed across the room and sat down on the side of the bed. She'd like nothing better than for him to take back his ultimatum. She then took a deep breath before answering the call. She'd made the decision not to look at the caller ID in hopes of being pleasantly surprised.

Upon hearing Gregory's voice, she smiled softly. As pleasant as it was for her to hear from her new friend, she was disappointed that it wasn't her brother. Only two days had passed by since Stephen had stormed out of her house, but to her it seemed like an eternity.

Stephanie closed her eyes for a brief moment, just to regain her composure. She certainly didn't want her voice to tremble. "Hey, guy, how's it going?"

"Things couldn't be better down here. What's happening in your neck of the woods?"

"Lots of turmoil, Gregory. Dad is still here, but he'll be leaving right after we get out of church this morning. The meeting between him and Stephen was a complete failure."

"I hate to hear that. Do you think there's still a chance for them to come together?"

"Yeah, I do. If it's God's will for them to be involved in each other's life, it'll happen. I'm holding on to that belief with all my might. When you have faith, hope has every chance of surviving the worst possible situations."

"Faith is everything, Stephanie. Although we never really talked about it in depth, I'm glad to know that you believe in God and rely on Him to take care of your needs. If you leave it with Him, your prayers will be answered. Just don't make the mistake of taking it out of His hands. He can't work out your issues for you if you're still holding on to them."

"Do you leave everything in His hands, Gregory?"

"I try to. But there are those times when I take things back from God and try to solve them myself, like the bad blood between my older brother and me. I know I haven't mentioned him to you . . . and I'm sorry about that. Grant and I have been feuding for years over nothing I can make any sense of. I suspect that I haven't turned it over to God completely, 'cause I still find myself trying to figure out why our relationship is so darn bad."

"I know what you mean. It's one thing to pray for something, but it's another matter entirely to wait on God to supply the answer. I like everything to be quick and easy."

Smiling devilishly, he raised an eyebrow. "Did you really mean to say *everything*?"

Blushing uncontrollably, Stephanie busted up laughing. "Well, not everything."

"Whew!" He wiped his brow. "That's good to know, because I like everything slow and easy, my lady. Fewer mistakes are made that way."

"Slow and easy, huh?" Stephanie raised an eyebrow. "Hmmm. I like the sound of that. Maybe I'll have to change my approach to some of the things I normally do in haste."

"Taking my time always works for me, so I'm sure you'll see the benefit in it too." Gregory turned sideways in his chair and then crossed his left leg over his right thigh. "Since Uncle Mal is still there in Houston, I'm assuming things are going very well for you two."

Stephanie sighed. "I'd be lying if I told you things couldn't be any better, but everything hasn't come together for all of us yet. Dad and I are doing great with our relationship. We really understand each other, much better than I ever dreamed we would."

"I wish that it was all settled for your sake, Stephanie. I'd hoped Stephen and Uncle Mal would've made more headway by now. The last time we talked you said they'd already met, but that the first meeting hadn't gone over very well."

Stephanie shrugged. "Nothing has changed since then. All that has happened so far is what I've already told you. I'd hoped for more. I guess I need to be more patient."

"Patience is the key, Stephanie. Give God more time to work another miracle in all your lives," Gregory remarked. "No one can bring you all together if He can't. Despite the rest of what's happening, are you happy about how well everything seems to be going for you and your dad, Stephanie?"

Stephanie put her hand over her heart. "If only I could adequately express my joy. I can't. If only Stephen would have a sudden change of heart. That'd make all of us so happy."

"I'm happy for you and Uncle Mal." Gregory grew silent for a moment. "Now that you've shared so much of your private life with me, I want to get a few personal things out in the open. My brother is the first one. Again, I'm sorry for not telling you about him before, even sorrier that you had to put up with him without any prior warning. Grant can be a real challenge at times."

"Is that why you never mentioned Grant to me? Before you answer that, I did know of your brother. Dad had mentioned him to me a time or two."

"Nothing favorable, I'm sure. Grant is a hard explanation, so I find it easier just not to mention him at all. People often don't understand it when siblings aren't very close. I wish our relationship was different, but we're not typical brothers. Being around Grant is always emotionally draining. Once he locates your vulnerable buttons, he jabs at them at every turn."

"Why do you think it's like that between you two?"

Gregory hunched his shoulders. "Sibling rivalry, I guess. But I don't even try to compete with Grant. On the other hand, he always thinks he has to be one up on me, for whatever reason."

Stephanie saw this as a good opportunity to ask Gregory the question she'd been dying to know the answer to. "What about your mother? You haven't mentioned her, either."

Gregory's eyes fluttered wildly, as though he was fighting off tears. He was glad that this conversation was taking place over the phone, since he wasn't so sure he could face Stephanie otherwise. "She's a hard explanation, too. That was another of the things I wanted to discuss with you. She left my father a couple of years ago for a much younger man."

Stephanie squirmed about uncomfortably on her bed, relieved that Gregory couldn't see her discomfort. "I'm sorry. And really, you don't have to explain a thing to me. It was probably insensitive of me to ask about your mother since you've never brought her up."

"I know that I don't have to explain. But it just might make our family issues a little clearer for you. No one has been the same since Aretha Saxton left Dad for someone else. It seems to me that Grant has paid a higher price than Dad and me."

"How's that, Gregory?"

"Mom doted on Grant, had spoiled him rotten. I think she's the reason he treats women the way he does, though I don't believe there's any excuse for that sort of bad behavior. She never made Grant respect her. He may transfer his feelings about Mom on to other women."

Stephanie thought Gregory might be right. "Could be exactly that. Grant seems to think he can have any woman he wants."

"That defect in his character always shows up rather quickly. I heard he also came on to you. Knowing how much you respect yourself, I'm sure you were offended by his tactics."

Stephanie took a moment to think about Grant's totally off-the-wall comments to her that day. He had indeed come on to her, but he wasn't someone she could even begin to take seriously. Grant had commanded her attention by his bizarre behavior, but he'd never gain her personal or romantic interest. In fact, Gregory's brother was the kind of man she'd immediately run fast and far away from. Among the numerous other things that weren't in his favor, Grant Saxton simply wasn't Stephanie's type.

Stephanie pursed her lips. "I didn't find Grant as offensive as much as I felt sorry for him. He was rather pitiful that day. He seemed to have no clue he was making a silly spectacle of himself, not to mention him being a downright nuisance. But I can't judge him. I don't know the facts of his life, or all the things that make him seem so unstable. I just believe there's a root cause for every kind of behavior, good or bad."

"That's fair enough. In view of some of the facts that I've told you about my family, do you think those things might interfere in our friendship?"

Stephanie was surprised by the rather strange question. "I can't see a reason why they would. Our friendship is independent of anything to do with your family, isn't it?"

Grant sighed hard. "I love my family, Stephanie. Like you've done with Stephen and Malachi, I hold on to the belief that one day Grant and I'll work out our differences, whatever they are. In the meantime, I have to leave it in God's hands. I know you already know that I'm interested in far more than a friendship with you, because I've told you so. From the very beginning you expressed your doubts about long distance relationships. I need to know if you still feel that way. I'd also like to know if you'd consider us taking our relationship to another level, that is, if you can now deal with the distance issue?"

Stephanie wished she could reach for Gregory's hand. "I'm going to get straight to the point here. I don't want to miss out on another golden opportunity. I'm very interested in taking our relationship to another level. I jumped the gun earlier with the long distance speech and I've regretted it ever since. I believe I can deal with the distance issue, but can you deal with the things I'd expect from you if we became romantically involved?"

Gregory shrugged. "I probably can, but I first need to know what they are."

"Here goes. A spiritual, God-loving man is what I'm looking for, Gregory. Honesty with each other and trusting in one another are absolutely a must in any relationship I get involved in. I demand and will give nothing less than the utmost respect. If things should progress to the desire for marriage, God has to be the head of the household I reside in. I know that might sound like a lot to ask of someone, but it is what it is. I refuse to settle for anything else."

"Remember what I said about liking to take things slow and easy?"

Stephanie nodded. "I do, but what does that have to do with what we're talking about?"

"Everything. If we take things slow and easy, we'll make fewer mistakes in building a solid relationship. I believe we're on the same page, Stephanie, that we both want a meaningful relationship, one that'll withstand the test of time. I *am* a God-loving man and I'm very spiritual. I rarely take a step without consulting God first. He's already the head of my household. All of the things you've mentioned I agree wholeheartedly with. I *can* deal with your expectations, especially since they're not at all any different from mine. I only ask that you don't expect anything from me that you don't expect from yourself. Don't demand anything of me that you're not willing to also give in return."

"Gregory, I don't expect anything from anyone without expecting the same of myself. You can rest assured of that." Stephanie glanced at the bedside clock. "I'd like to get more into this conversation, but I've got to finish getting ready for church. Can we talk later on?"

"We can actually finish our conversation in person. I called to let you know I'll be in Houston on business this entire week. I should arrive late tomorrow afternoon. Think we can get together again? Dinner or something?"

"I'll look forward to seeing you." She laughed softly. "Dinner or something works for me. We can get deeper into this discussion then, but I think we understand all the issues at stake. Can I consider our next outing a real date, romantically speaking?"

"Yeah, something like that," he said, chuckling at her question. "I look forward to staring into your beautiful eyes again. I can guarantee you our time together will be romantic."

Seated on a pew near the back of the church, the area she always sat in, Stephanie had kept a watchful eye out for Stephen. When Stephen finally showed up for the early-morning worship service, the song service was just about over. She wasn't a bit surprised that her brother had chosen not to sit with her and Malachi. Not to have him share the bench seat with her as he normally did hurt more than it angered her. Although he occupied a seat across the aisle from her, and he was in plain sight, Stephanie wished he'd had a serious change of heart by now. It wasn't often that Stephen made it to church, because of his unpredictable work schedule, but he came whenever he could. She was happy that their disagreements hadn't kept him away.

As the pastor led his congregation in one last song, "What a Friend We Have in Jesus," one of Stephanie's favorites, she was grateful to God that Stephen hadn't forsaken church altogether. Jesus was indeed a friend to her and her brother and that's why she was so confident that everything would eventually work out between them. She'd never demand that her brother make a choice between her and another human being. Although he had been unfair to her with his unsavory ultimatum, she believed that she and Stephen would also carry on with their closeness regardless of what their independent relationships to Malachi turned out to be.

Yes, Stephanie desperately wanted the two men in her life to come together in peace and love, but she wouldn't stop loving either one if it didn't happen.

Upon hearing the booming voice of Pastor Aaron Ellsworth

beckoning the morning worshipers to come down front to kneel and pray at the altar, Stephanie turned her gaze toward the pulpit. Without looking over at Malachi, she extended her hand to him, which he readily took a hold of, squeezing her fingers gently.

In allowing the Holy Spirit to take over her mind and soul, Stephanie quietly thanked God for the outcome she knew was to come. Her faith in God was so strong that she could thank Him for what He was about to do in her life. If one of her prayers went unanswered, it was only because whatever she'd asked God for just wasn't good for her. No one could make her believe that God wanted her and Stephen separated. Therefore, Stephanie believed that what she'd asked God for was pure and good in His eyes. His will be done in her life was her humble prayer.

"My sermon today is entitled 'Deceptive Women of the Bible.' On this fine Lord's Day, we're going to explore the stories of a few women who chose to practice the worse deceptions modern man can imagine. Please turn your Bibles to Genesis 19:27–28 and read along with me."

Stephanie didn't need to turn and look at Stephen to know that his eyes were on her. The title of the sermon had gripped her attention, too. God's will was fast at work, she suspected. Knowing that God may be ready to supply the answers to her prayers, her heart leapt for joy. She silently prayed that Stephen would stay and listen to the sermon, that he'd benefit greatly from it.

"From the previous verses we know that Lot's daughters' fiancé thought Lot was crazy when he told them to flee the city, that it was about to be destroyed by God's angels. We know that Lot's wife was turned into a pillar of salt because she dared to look back after being instructed not to do so. What came next is the unimaginable for all of us.

"Lot's own daughters, believing there wasn't a man anywhere in the entire area that their father would allow them to marry, decided to fill their father with wine so they could become impregnated by him. It was the daughters' desire that their clan not come to an end."

The pastor took a brief pause. Looking out over the pews in his church, it appeared that he was waiting for the congregation's loud gasps and moans to die down before he continued.

"And so it was that both girls became pregnant from their father. The older girl's baby was named Moab; he became the ancestor of the nation of the Moabites. The name of the younger girl's baby was Benammi; he became the ancestor of the nation of the Ammonites."

"Let us now turn to Genesis 25:19–34, the story of Rebekah and Isaac, and their twin boys, Esau and Jacob. Esau was born first, making him the eldest of the twins. Esau was Isaac's favorite son and Jacob was Rebekah's. One day Esau traded his birthright to Jacob for a bowl of stew and a few other items of food. The trade had come at Jacob's request. Imagine that, a meal for your birthright entitlements. Esau said the following to Jacob in response to his request:

'When a man is dying from starvation, what good is his birthright?'—Genesis 26:32.

"Jacob's response went like this: 'Well then, vow to God that it is mine!'—Genesis 26:33.

'And Esau vowed, therefore selling all his eldest-son rights to his younger brother.

'Then Jacob gave Esau bread, peas, and stew; so he ate and drank and went on about his business, indifferent to the loss of the rights he had thrown away.'—Genesis 26:34.

"Later in the story, when a half-blind Isaac was about to die, he called for Esau. It was time for Isaac to give Esau the blessings belonging to the first-born son. As the story goes, Rebekah overheard the conversation between father and son. Willfully practicing deception, Rebekah instructed Jacob to do the very same things Isaac had instructed Esau to do. She then had Jacob take his brother's place in order to receive the blessings intended for Esau.

"Please read this story thoroughly for yourself. It just goes to show us what lengths people will go to in practicing deception, just to have their way. These types of deceptions still go on today and are practiced in many different forms. Don't forget the story of Samson and Delilah and how she deceived him into telling her his secrets so that he might be defeated."

At that very moment Stephanie and Stephen's eyes met, connecting in truth and compassion. Stephanie could see the regret in her brother's concentrated gaze. Although the Bible stories had happened eons ago, the same sort of deceptive practices continue to go on to this very day with parents and their children, fathers and mothers alike. Doreen had also been deceiving.

Stephanie blinked back her tears when Stephen got up from his pew. Expecting him to walk out of the service, her heart palpitated painfully. When her brother suddenly crossed the aisle, and then slid in next to her, reaching for her free hand, she let go of her tears. Beside herself with joy, relieved beyond description, Stephanie laid her head on Stephen's shoulder. Her humble thanks to God came simultaneously.

Malachi tearfully looked upon his children as his heartfelt emotions rocked his soul right down to the core of his being. Although his expectations for him and Stephen to work everything out between them weren't soaring through the roof, seeing his kids attempting to patch their torn hearts was a beautiful sight for him to behold. Malachi prayed that Stephen and Stephanie's broken relationship was truly on the mend. He'd like nothing better than to see them quickly resolve all their issues. He didn't know where he'd fit into the family portrait, if at all, but he also prayed for a favorable outcome for him and his son.

Stephanie and Stephen continued to hold hands during the rest of the service. Pastor Ellsworth couldn't have painted a clearer picture for the twins to closely examine. Stephanie was sure that his profound message was for other members in the church as well, but this sermon was definitely meant for her and her brother. She figured that Malachi had benefited from it also. When she'd periodically glanced over at her father, he'd seemed quite intent on what was being said. She felt at peace for the first time in a long while. Although she didn't know what might happen next, Stephanie felt even more strengthened by the miracles that had already occurred.

The moment the church ushers appeared to direct the members toward the exit doors, Stephen stood up. He then switched places with Stephanie. Looking directly into Malachi's eyes, Stephen extended his hand to his father. When Malachi returned the gesture, Stephen firmly shook the older man's hand. "I'd like to sit down with you over a cup of hot coffee."

Malachi had had every intention of hitting the highway back to Louisiana as soon as he'd dropped off Stephanie back at her home, but this was one incredible offer he wasn't about to turn down. New Orleans wasn't going anywhere, but he was. He was going to have coffee with his son. "I can't think of anything I'd like better, Stephen. Do you have a nearby place in mind?"

Stephen nodded. "How about my place? We'll have complete privacy there."

Malachi shrugged. "Fine with me. Do you want me to follow you in my car?"

"That'll work." Stephen turned to Stephanie. "Maybe you should ride with Malachi so he'll feel more comfortable with everything. If we get separated in traffic, you'll be with him."

The female usher stopping right in front of their pew, instructing the Trudeaux family to move on down the aisle toward the exit, kept Stephanie from responding to Stephen's suggestion. As the threesome moved right along with the crowd, Stephanie's emotions were going berserk. She was glad that she hadn't had to respond to Stephen right away, since she probably would've come off as a babbling idiot. All she could do was silently thank God for what had just occurred. He had worked another of His miracles. He had come through yet again.

Once outside in the fresh air Stephanie took in a few deep breaths. The pit of her stomach felt like a bundle of badly frayed nerves. She was excited and fearful at the same time. She prayed that this was a new beginning for all of them. Life would be much less complicated if they all just openly admitted their need for each other. Despite the past, they were a family.

Stephen took hold of Stephanie's hand. "What do you think of my suggestion?"

Stephanie reached for Malachi's hand, bringing him into the circle. "I think I should go on home and let you two have some time alone. Stephen, I can drive your car and you can ride with Dad. I can bring your SUV home later. How does that sound to the two of you?"

Stephen looked from Stephanie to Malachi. "I think we should all sit down together and talk about where we want things to go from here. We've already been separated long enough," Stephen commented. "Since whatever happens from here on in will affect all of us, you should be included, Stephanie."

"We'll do it your way, Stephen," Stephanie said. She was too eager to have her father and brother establish some common ground to care how it was to be achieved. With her or without her, she was ready for the war of the Trudeauxs to be over. "I'll go ahead and ride with Dad."

Stephen smiled at his sister. "Thanks, Stephanie. Just before I started to get ready for church this morning, I read a very deep e-mail that was sent to me by a friend of mine. It was simply entitled 'Let Go.' I actually broke down and cried after I read it. I now feel as if I'm ready to let go of the hate and anger I've been living with all my adult life. Although I still have a few questions I need answered, I don't think it's a good idea for us to get too heavily into rehashing the past. We can't change it. It is what it is."

Stephanie remembered Gregory saying that very thing to her, when he'd told her she should never apologize for her feelings. "It is what it is" was his exact quote. Stephen had no knowledge of that conversation with Gregory, which made her take special note of it.

"With everything all settled, we need to be on our way, guys," Stephanie remarked.

Within thirty minutes of entering Stephen's beautiful suburban home, the Trudeaux family had comfortably seated themselves at the kitchen table. Working together harmoniously, the threesome had made quick work of preparing a light breakfast consisting of microwaved beef bacon, eggs scrambled soft, toast, freshly brewed coffee, and fresh orange juice.

When Stephen asked Malachi to pass the blessing on the food, Malachi felt honored. Stephen was doing his level best to try and make his father feel welcome in his home and Malachi was very much aware of it. Tension was definitely present, yet Malachi didn't feel as though it was so thick that it couldn't be carefully cut through. Patience was the operative word. Malachi felt that he had no choice but to be patient with his son.

Stephen took a sip of his coffee and sat the mug down on the placemat. He then made direct eye contact with his father. "There's something I want to get resolved right away. All the way home, I struggled to figure out what name I should call you by. Just a short time ago calling you dad seemed so improper, an impossibility. However, I couldn't think of anything else suitable to call you by. So, if you don't mind, I'm going to follow Stephanie's lead and just call you dad. I don't want to make things anymore complicated for us than they already are."

Malachi took a deep breath to calm his emotions. Stephen had no idea how good he'd made his father feel. His son had certainly changed gears rather quickly, but Malachi couldn't have been happier with the sudden change in Stephen's attitude. "I'll do everything in my power to earn the honorable title, Stephen. Everything possible."

Stephen nodded. "I believe you will, Dad. Since you'll be leaving

Houston soon, I don't want to spend a lot of time rehashing the past, as I mentioned earlier. I want us to get to know each other without feeling a lot of stress and strain. Talking sports is always a good way for men to break the ice. So with that in mind, what's your favorite sport?"

Malachi chuckled, relaxing back in his chair. "Football is my all-time favorite. Baseball is my least favorite, though I do watch it intently during the pennant races. What about you?"

"Straight-up basketball fanatic! Football comes in second place. Tennis and golf run neck and neck. Tiger Woods and the Williams sisters have brought a whole new meaning to those games for me. I don't know that I'd be watching either sport if it wasn't for them. They sure make it pretty exciting."

"I'm with you on that," Malachi said, grinning. "In my heyday Arthur Ashe was the man who made tennis an exciting sport to watch. I even took tennis lessons while he was still on the circuit. Your old man is not too bad at the game, either. I play a game or two of tennis a couple of times a week."

Stephen dropped his fork onto his plate, sighing heavily. He then pushed his hand frantically through his hair. "I guess this small talk just isn't working for me. I've heard it from Stephanie, but now I need to hear it from you, Dad. How do you justify cheating on Mama and then leaving us behind, as if we never existed for you? I promise to listen to you this time."

Malachi looked relieved by Stephen's pointed question rather than worried by it. He had clearly recognized how anxious his son was, had known from the start that Stephen was just being polite to keep from showing his true feelings. Malachi sensed that Stephen didn't want a war with him, either. He simply wanted answers to a lifetime's worth of questions.

Malachi stroked his chin. Happy thoughts of him and Doreen sped through his mind. It was like seeing a small film of their life together. They'd been so in love with each other. He'd fallen for her the first moment he'd laid his eyes on her in the high school cafeteria.

Doreen had had total respect for herself, setting her far apart from many of the girls Malachi had known. He suspected that her self-respect was what had kept her from taking him back. He recalled her clearly telling him that if a woman didn't respect herself, then she couldn't demand it from anyone else. Doreen had kept him hanging on, something Malachi was only too willing to do. She was worth it all, but he had made the mistake of taking her love for granted.

"Stephen, I loved your mother and she loved me. Up until the day she died, I still believed there was a chance for us to get back together. I made a colossal mistake, son, but I'm not going to make an even bigger one by trying to justify what I did. There is no acceptable excuse for cheating on my wife. I was wrong. No two ways about it."

"I'm glad that you see it that way," Stephen said dryly. "There isn't any excuse for lying to and cheating on someone we profess to love."

Malachi nodded his agreement with Stephen's statement. "There were times when I felt that the punishment Doreen had doled out to me fit the crime, but it was also very harsh. I tried again and again to get parole with her. I don't ever want to insult her memory. She obviously did what she felt she had to do in order to live with herself. She was a proud woman, had a lot of respect for herself. I did everything I could to make it right, to make it up to her, but infidelity is just one of those wrongs that a man can't ever seem to make right. I'm still working on making it right with God, kids. He has the final say in the punishment phase. I'm sure you know that."

Malachi went on to explain to Stephen the same things he'd told Stephanie. The story was exactly the same as he'd told it before. A liar often got the issues confused, but the honest-to-goodness truth would always remain the same. Honesty was hard to find fault with.

Malachi was a human being who had made human errors, deeply regrettable ones. No one but Malachi knew the high price he'd paid for cheating, a costly mistake that he'd continue to pay for for the rest of his life. He'd lost his entire family because of a serious mistake. He'd lost the woman who had meant the world to him because he'd put his physical needs before all else.

Battling his emotions, Stephen wrung his hands together. "Why didn't you fight for us?"

Deep in thought, Malachi twisted his bottom lip. "In a way, I did. There wasn't a day that went by that I didn't try to get Doreen to change her mind about the agreement we'd made. We had several verbal fights over it. When she decided to let me know what was happening in your life, and for me to be a part of it without your knowledge, I felt that that was better than nothing at all. You might see my acts as cowardly, but I didn't want to drag Doreen through the courts. I'd already damaged her beyond repair. I know how deeply I hurt your mother—and I've had to live with the knowledge of her pain every day of my life. No one can punish me any more than I've punished myself. But I'm finally starting to forgive myself. I hope you'll forgive me, too."

Aware that it might turn out to be a costly error in judgment, Malachi dared to tell Stephanie and Stephen that he and Doreen had carried on somewhat of a covert love affair over all the years of their separation. He then spoke of their almost nightly conversations and how they'd gotten together for dinner at least once a month. Although he didn't mention to his kids whether he and Doreen had made love or not during the times they'd spent together, the deep sparkle of satisfaction in Malachi's eyes revealed more about those undercover dates than he realized. His expression of awesome wonder carried all the telltale signs of a man deeply in love.

The relief on Stephen's face was quite obvious. The tears in his eyes were one blink away from release. No matter how much he wanted to deny Malachi's truth, he'd believed every word his father had said, believed that he had deeply loved his wife and his kids. It was the part his mother had played in this crazy game of charades that Stephen had yet to fully accept. Taking Doreen down from her lofty pedestal would be hard for him to do.

Malachi's story had also made Stephen think of sweet Darcy, the only woman other than his sister who'd ever helped him to make sense of his life. He hadn't exactly cheated on her, but he'd come close to it quite a few times. The thought of what he'd already done wrong in his relationship with Darcy made Stephen think of the pot calling the skillet black.

Up until this very moment Stephen hadn't seen anything wrong with flirting with other women. He thought it was A-OK to look at the tasty menu just as long as he didn't order from it. He had even accepted a few phone numbers, and had later called them up, only to chicken out once getting together was mentioned. Although he hadn't ever set up a date with these women, he hadn't acted too differently from Malachi. The desire and the potential for him to cheat on Darcy had been there—and those were the undeniable facts he needed to face.

Stephen now realized that he'd been dead wrong in his illicit behavior. Darcy deserved one hundred percent loyalty from him, which was exactly what she'd always given to him. From this moment on she'd get the same allegiance from him in return, he silently vowed. It wasn't going to upset him one iota to burn his little black book. After all, Stephen was madly in love with Darcella Coleman. The powerful revelation of his love for her had just hit him right in the dead center of his heart. Now all he had to do was act responsibly on his love for her.

Stephen got to his feet and walked behind his father's chair. Leaning forward, he placed his arms around Malachi's neck, resting his chin atop his father's head. "Hearing the story straight from your lips has been cleansing for me. I feel free because of what you've said. I can clearly see how this all happened, but I'll never be able to blame Mama for any of it. She was only responding to the worst kind of pain a woman can endure."

Stephen tightened his hold on Malachi. "My eyes have been opened more than you can imagine. I desperately want to forgive you, Dad. I need to forgive you, as much for me as anything—and I know now that I can. I do forgive you, Dad. With all my heart and soul, I want us to have a meaningful relationship, a father-and-son camaraderie. I want us all to be a family."

Stephen's tears spilled into Malachi's hair. His sobs came next, hard and broken.

As she'd always done, Stephanie immediately came to her brother's rescue. After putting an arm around Stephen's shoulders, she reached down and gripped Malachi's hand, squeezing it tightly. This was a very emotional time for her, too. There was no shame in letting her tears flow. Wearing her heart on her sleeve wasn't a problem for Stephanie, not when all of her prayers for her family had been answered. *Thank you, God,* she whispered from within. Optimistic about starting a spiritually inspiring relationship with Gregory, Stephanie thanked God for that also.

With his tears flowing like the River Jordan, Malachi couldn't get to his feet fast enough. Gathering his children into his arms, he hugged and kissed each of them, telling Stephanie and Stephen how much he loved them, how happy he was to finally be a part of their lives.

Malachi swiped at his tears with the back of his hand. "You two kids don't know how happy you've made this old man. If I die tomorrow, I'll close my eyes in peace. I truly feel that Doreen is at peace also. Despite how things played out with us, I believe she'd want us to be together. I thank God for performing yet another miracle in my life."

Malachi, smiling all over the place, held his children at arm's length. "I don't want to push the envelope here, but I can't help asking if we can have that big holiday celebration I've constantly dreamed of. What about us revisiting the idea of Thanksgiving in New Orleans? If you both can't make it there, I'll come here if you'll have me."

Stephanie reached up and kissed Malachi on the cheek. "I'm there, Dad. I can hardly wait for the celebration to begin. Hopefully the Trudeaux family celebrations will be nonstop. Uncle Maxwell is absolutely going to be delighted. We all have so much to be thankful for. I know that God is smiling down upon us. And so is Mama."

Stephen playfully punched at his father's chest. "You can count me in, too, Dad. Of course my unpredictable work schedule may wreak havoc on our holiday plans. But I'll be there if at all possible. In fact, I'm looking forward to us all being together, one way or another. Though only in spirit, Mama will be there with us too, just as she's always been."

God in all his wisdom and love had made a way out of a no-way situation. Prayer had worked for the Trudeaux family. God never responds to just the requests of his people. He responds to the faith of His children. The Heavenly Father is ever listening for the prayerful cries of his loved ones. No matter how many advocates the devil has working for him, God has far more guardian angels on His side. Jesus had already won the battle at Calvary.

As is the distance between a pair of knees and the floor, God is only a prayer away.

Epilogue

To Stephanie this was the most extraordinary Thanksgiving Day celebration she'd ever had. Practically every one of her dreams for the Trudeaux family had come true. She was at long last experiencing the love of the family she'd longed for. She fiercely felt Doreen's absence, but, as always, Stephanie felt her mother's spirit, felt her smiling down on them with much pleasure.

Stephanie, Stephen, and Darcella had arrived in New Orleans on Tuesday and were scheduled to depart on Sunday afternoon. Seeing Stephen laughing and talking up a storm with Malachi and their Uncle Maxwell was a treasured sight for Stephanie. Her brother and Malachi had come a long way. The three men had several heart-to-heart conversations, which had brought them all closer and closer together. Now it was as if they'd known each other forever. Stephen had taken to Maxwell in the same quick way Stephanie had. Their uncle was a delightful riot.

The lively celebrating had begun the very moment they'd entered Malachi's front door. After a couple of hours of animated chitchat, Malachi had driven his children down to his corporate offices, where Stephanie and Stephen got an up-close and personal look at the operation Malachi wanted them to run one day. The cheerful welcoming committee that had shown up at the house later that evening had included many of Malachi's personal friends, quite a few of his employees, and several of his close neighbors. The big old house had seemed to grow warmer and warmer with each arriving guest. A lot of love had attended.

Stephanie stole a glance at Gregory, who was seated directly across from her. The desire to be seated right next to him was strong. Then the memory of their first passionate kiss instantly sailed into her mind, warming her up all over. The chemistry between them was incredible, yet it was their spiritual connection that had her on cloud nine. That they'd decided to explore all the possibilities for a meaningful relationship had each of them eager to know how far they could go. If Stephanie and Gregory were a match made in heaven, a perfect match ordained by God, they were both aware that only time would tell.

Gregory and his father had been over to the house every evening since the Trudeaux twins had arrived. Stephanie had gotten well acquainted with Gregory II, and she couldn't help noticing how sad he had appeared. It was her best guess that he suffered from the same family problems the Trudeauxs had experienced.

The Saxtons had been invited to Malachi's for the holiday dinner, but Gregory had told Stephanie sometime during the previous evening that he didn't expect Grant to make a showing. That Gregory had been wrong about his brother was a pleasant surprise for everyone. Although Grant had hardly spoken a word since he'd first arrived, he was present and accounted for.

Smiling broadly, Stephanie looked over at her beloved father, who was dressed to the nines. It was as if a permanent smile had been painted on his handsome face. He seemed happier than everyone present. He looked almost as elegant as the exquisitely set dining tables and all the delicious-looking holiday food laid out on the mahogany serving station. The brilliant shards of light shining down from the crystal chandelier illuminated his angelic expression even more.

Seated at the head of his table, Malachi gently clanged his fork against the rim of his crystal goblet, drawing the immediate attention of all his guests. He then stood. "I first want to welcome each and every one of you to my home. It's a pleasure to host you on this beautiful Thanksgiving Day. These last few weeks have been some of the best days of my life."

Malachi looked at his children, beaming brightly. "Having my son and daughter, Stephen and Stephanie, joining me for this holiday celebration is a true blessing from God. So I also want to give thanks and all the glory to our Father in heaven. Without Him, having my family together like this wouldn't have been possible. For those of you who'd like to participate, no pressure to bear, I'd like to hear what you're thankful for. Then we can polish off the divine holiday meal."

Maxwell pushed back his chair and got to his feet. "I thank God for the gift of this very moment. Being in the presence of God and my family is what I'm most grateful for although there are numerous other things I'm thankful for. The glory is all His."

Before standing, Gregory looked over at Stephanie and smiled. "Well, for me, the list is too long for me to cover everything I'm thankful for. Like those who've already spoken, I've been so blessed by God. One of the things that stands out in my mind is the conversation I had with my brother, Grant, early this morning. The words spoken between us were of the healing kind. I thank God for what we shared from our hearts. I'm also thankful for the beautiful lady seated across the table from me. I thank Jesus for bringing Stephanie Trudeaux into my life."

Stephen got up from his chair and walked around to where Stephanie was seated. He then reached out for her hand, waiting patiently until she got to her feet. He then went over to Malachi and extended his other hand to him. Maxwell was the next person Stephen reached out to. Stephen warmly hugged each of his family members, opening himself wide to receive their return affection. He then turned his attention to the guests. "As you all know, we are the Trudeaux clan. I'm more than grateful to God for bringing us together as a family. I'm particularly thankful for the twin sister God saw fit to give me. I'm genuinely grateful for my father and uncle, the two strong male figures that I can be proud to pattern myself after. Will everyone please take up your glass and lift it in a toast to the Almighty, our loving heavenly Father who makes all things possible."

Stephen summoned Darcella to his side, kissing her gently on the mouth as she reached him. Taking his cue from Stephen, Gregory came up and stood behind Stephanie, placing each of his hands on her shoulders.

Stephen looked around to make sure everyone had a glass in hand as he lifted up his. "To our Lord and Savior, our strength, our redeemer. To Him be the glory, both now and to the day of eternity."

"Hear, hear!" everyone said in unison. "Happy Thanksgiving!"

Dear Readers:

I sincerely hope that you enjoyed reading *The Devil's Advocate* from cover to cover. I'm very interested in hearing your comments and thoughts on the entire Trudeaux family. I love hearing from my readers and I do appreciate the time you take out of your busy schedule to respond. Please enclose a self-addressed, stamped envelope with all your correspondence and mail to: Linda Hudson-Smith, 16516 El Camino Real, Box #174, Houston, TX 77062. Or you can e-mail your comments to *LHS4romance@yahoo.com*. Please also visit my website and sign my guest book at *www.lindahudson smith.com*.